STAR TREK®
STRANGE NEW WORLDS
III

For orders other than by individual consumers, Pocket Books grants a discount on the purchase of **10 or more** copies of single titles for special markets or premium use. For further details, please write to the Vice President of Special Markets, Pocket Books, 1230 Avenue of the Americas, 9th Floor, New York, NY 10020-1586.

For information on how individual consumers can place orders, please write to Mail Order Department, Simon & Schuster Inc., 100 Front Street, Riverside, NJ 08075.

STAR TREK®
STRANGE NEW WORLDS
III

Edited by
Dean Wesley Smith
with John J. Ordover and Paula M. Block

POCKET BOOKS
New York London Toronto Sydney Singapore

This book consists of works of fiction. Names, characters, places and incidents are products of the authors' imaginations or are used fictitiously. Any resemblance to actual events or locales or persons, living or dead, is entirely coincidental.

An *Original* Publication of POCKET BOOKS

POCKET BOOKS, a division of Simon & Schuster Inc.
1230 Avenue of the Americas, New York, NY 10020

This book is published by Pocket Books, a division of Simon & Schuster Inc., under exclusive license from Paramount Pictures.

ISBN: 0-671-03652-1

First Pocket Books trade paperback printing May 2000

10 9 8 7 6 5 4 3 2 1

Printed in the U.S.A.

Contents

Contents

Introduction

The Class of 2000

Dean Wesley Smith

With all the ups and downs in the publishing industry, it isn't often that something happens in this business that can truly make a professional writer and editor like myself smile with sheer enjoyment. But the volume you hold in your hand has done just that. For three years running I've had the great pleasure of editing these volumes, and every year I've enjoyed it more and more.

As a *Star Trek* fan who went home from high school and college to watch the original three seasons every Friday night (yes, I am that old), it has always seemed to be a dream that I got the chance to write in the *Star Trek* universe. Now, as an editor, I get the chance each year to let other fans reach the same dream. And let me tell you, that makes me smile.

Over the last three years, *Star Trek: Strange New Worlds* has allowed forty-nine fans just like me (writing fifty-four different stories) to join the ranks of professional writers in the *Star Trek* universe. And contest number four, with the rules in this volume, will allow still more fans to join us.

The rules of this contest limit the entrants to being fan writers with less than three published professional stories. (I'm a fan of *Star Trek* and a professional writer, so I could not send in a story.) Because of that limitation, some of the writers you will read in this volume, and have read in previous volumes, will not be able to return. They have crossed over into the ranks of professional writers.

Dayton Ward, with his story in this volume, will make his last appearance in *Star Trek: Strange New Worlds.* He is the only writer to make all three volumes of this contest. Since I have gotten over ten thousand manuscripts total in the three years, you will understand what kind of feat Dayton has pulled off. Someday I hope to meet Dayton and just shake his hand. And all you readers, watch for his novels and short stories in the future. I think he's going to be one of those writers to enjoy for years to come.

One other writer came very, very close to joining Dayton this year in that very exclusive club. Christina F. York had a story that was the very last one cut, due to a few technical details. She has almost eliminated herself with her other writing sales, both in science fiction and romance, so I'm not sure if she'll be eligible next year to try to tie Dayton's record of three.

Other writers joining Christina F. York in the two-out-of-three exclusive club are Jerry M. Wolfe, Peg Robinson, Kathy Oltion, Franklin Thatcher, Jackee C., and Kim Sheard. I know for a fact that Kathy Oltion and Franklin Thatcher will never be returning to these pages. Kathy has sold a number of stories to *Analog* and has just finished her first novel, cowritten with her husband, Jerry Oltion. Watch for that first book this summer in the *Star Trek: New Earth* series.

Franklin Thatcher won the grand prize in the *Writers of the Future* contest to complete his eligibility in both contests. Congratulations, Franklin. We'll all be watching for your novels and stories.

Peg Robinson has also sold stories to other markets, but she just might, if we're lucky, be able to slip in under the deadline next year before one gets published. Jerry M. Wolfe, Jackee C., and Kim Sheard still have a chance of tying Dayton's record next year.

In this year's volume, our first-place winners, Sarah A. Hoyt and Rebecca Lickiss, will not be returning again, since both have sold fantasy novels to Ace books. Since the rules state "publication" and both their novels will be published after the contest date, they got in just under the wire here. Now everybody go buy their novels later this summer or early fall.

I am very pleased to have a small hand in helping all the writers in the three volumes of *Star Trek: Strange New Worlds* on their path toward selling more and more work. John Ordover and I also try to help new writers in other ways. For example, on America Online, on the *Star Trek* boards, under "Writing," there is a topic called "Strange New Worlds and Strange New Writers." This is an open board where anyone can ask us questions about writing in general, and the anthology in particular. Over the last few years I've put lots of what I call "hints" in that topic. Dayton Ward compiled all the hints into one area in the Strange New Worlds topic and a number of people asked that they be included in the anthology. John Ordover agreed, so a few of them are included here, at the end of this book.

This essay is my last task for volume #3. But as I sit here typing, I find myself still smiling. Volume #4 will have been opened for submission earlier this year (as you read this) and I will be editing it again. The deadline for stories is October 1, 2000. Don't miss it.

If you have that *Star Trek* story you've always wanted to write, first read the wonderful stories in the first three volumes, then follow the rules in this book and send your story in. Maybe, just maybe, next year, you'll be holding a book with your story in it. That will make me smile even more.

And I'll just bet you'll be smiling, too.

STAR TREK®

[First Prize]

If I Lose Thee . . .

Sarah A. Hoyt and Rebecca Lickiss

A bleak, gray, ancient plain stretched out to the horizon, scattered ruins punctuating the distance. Uhura turned away from the steady dust-laden wind to face the gauntlet of historians and officers leading up to the flickering arch of the Guardian.

"Now, don't forget," one of the historians, a tense man with a thin face, said. "The halfpenny is the silver coin you use to pay for a quart of ale, but a loaf of bread is worth a penny, and a twopenny half-groat will buy you dinner at an inn. Be careful how much you pay. You could change history by making someone rich accidentally." He fixed Uhura with an earnest, pleading gaze.

The coins' names made Uhura dizzy. Half crown, quarter angel, angelet, and the other gold coins, added to a confusion of silver coins. She nodded sagely to the anxious, thin-faced man.

"Have you got all that?"

Quite sure of already having forgotten it, Uhura nodded reassuringly and patted the hidden purse of coins near the top of her dress, where her red bodice squashed her breasts uncomfortably, so that they protruded above, much exposed and unnecessarily enhanced. "Got them right here."

If she didn't find that idiotic boy, William Harrod, and actually had to buy food or, worse, lodging, she would have to find a local and—using age-old techniques of promising without delivering—part him from his money, which *he* knew how to spend. As for her own money, she'd keep it where it belonged. Hidden.

"Now, remember not to go into a tavern or a public place, unless you find a man to accompany you, or they might think . . ." another of the historians said.

Uhura nodded with a confidence she didn't feel and walked by. She hoped they were right about the costume she was wearing. It had no underwear, just a sort of smock beneath the stiff gown, and the skirts were slashed, the puke-green one showing the sickly yellow one showing the bloodred one. She trusted the red hadn't been slashed to show her backside.

"Don't go into a plague house. You can't do anything for the victims without changing history."

She adjusted the red and gold turban on her head, wondering if real Moorish princesses had to tolerate this sort of coaching. If so, she was doubly thankful to be a Federation officer.

"Remember, anything you do could potentially endanger the present. Just find William Harrod and come back, quickly."

Unfortunately no one was yet sure how to come back, but they didn't dwell on that trivial detail. Just as no one was willing to explain precisely how historian William Harrod had accidentally fallen into the Guardian's time portal and become lost, either.

Uhura walked on, trying to escape the thronging mass of anxious, twittering scientists, hampered by the dress's layers of skirts, ridiculously tight waist which prohibited breathing, and flat bodice hardened by several layers of stuffing.

One of the historians kept following her, twitching at the ties that attached her slashed puke-green and sickly yellow sleeves, and rearranging their dangling, ground-dragging tassels. In a pinch she supposed she might be able to use the sleeves to strangle someone. Maybe one of the scientist-historians.

Mr. Spock melted the confusion of scientists around her merely by raising one eyebrow. She smiled at him gratefully.

"If only we could send you with a tricorder, a phaser, something . . ." McCoy looked at her sadly.

"A tricorder will do me no good, sir," Uhura said. "And it might cause a temporal disruption." She nodded, and did her best to look competent and calm. "I'll be fine."

"Good luck, lass," Scotty said. "Do you remember what William Harrod looks like?"

"Yes, sir." Uhura nodded. The memory of the image taken from the Guardian was burned into her brain. A blank-faced, blandly blond young man, with a weak chin and watery-blue eyes, wearing a woman's costume similar to this one, holding her hand, preparing to kiss it. The sight of herself in that ancient picture was one she'd never forget. One she feared would come back to haunt her nightmares. She'd also heard enough of William Harrod to suspect he, too, would be a nightmare.

In front of the arch, Captain Kirk waited and looked at Uhura, head to toe, with an amused gaze. "Good job of period dressing, Lieutenant," he said, and smiled. "Very becoming."

"Thank you, sir." Uhura felt her cheeks heat, but kept her expression rigidly professional. She had to admit that, having looked at herself in the mirror before leaving her quarters, this uncomfortable combination of straitjacket and ball gown was very flattering indeed. Which didn't alter her impression that she was sauntering breathless, bare-breasted, and bare-assed into Elizabethan England.

"I still think one of us should go with her," McCoy said, stubbornly holding to his earlier objections.

"The Guardian shows only her and William Harrod." Kirk's frown indicated he agreed with McCoy whatever his words might be. "And the Guardian says only she can enter without changing the shape of time." He glared accusingly at the arch next to him.

"I'll be fine." She would be, too, because she had no intention of dying in Elizabethan England, of all the rat-infested plague-holes in the universe. If she got lucky, she would find that the reason William Harrod hadn't caused any disruption was that he died right after he kissed her hand. Though she feared that strangling him for his stupidity in accidentally falling into the portal would look bad when reported in her log, she must, therefore, rule it out as an option.

Half-smiling at the thought, she saluted her captain and stepped into the portal.

Uhura stood in what she decided must be a back alley. It didn't look at all as she imagined London would. She'd been to London, once, and she'd found it a charming, if boring, place with an atrocious cuisine and very good tea.

But the London in which she found herself looked much like a village. Well, at least, from where she stood she could see three pigs, and four . . . no, make that five scrawny chickens, scavenging their way amid piles of refuse. Rotten vegetables, human waste, and things she truly didn't want to identify, mixed in with the mud into which her brand-new ankle boots sank.

All right, the buildings were probably too tall for a village. They towered up three or four stories, and the alley—she hoped it was an alley, she would hate for it to be a main street—that separated them was no wider than her arm span. Which meant that precious little light filtered through.

From somewhere nearby came a deafening roar, like thousands of people speaking, screaming, and screeching at the same time. It sounded like a disturbance of some sort, but this was where William had arrived, and Uhura reasoned that her chances of finding William were better if she went toward the noise.

"Will, Will, Will." The shriek came from above her. Looking up, Uhura saw, in the half-light above, a disheveled female head sticking out of a window.

"Will, Will. Where has that boy got to?"

"Coming, Mum," sounded from the end of the alley farthest away from the noise. From the dim distance, a small boy came running, splashing mud everywhere, and stepping on who knew what without caring. The chickens ran squawking ahead of him, as he plunged past Uhura—barely pausing for a curious look—and into a darkened doorway.

Well . . . Maybe a Will, but definitely not William Harrod.

Gingerly, she walked toward the noise, trying not to step on anything that looked too obviously rank. She grabbed her skirts on either side, but, unfortunately, as she reached down to pull them up, the golden tassels at the end of her sleeves dragged in the mud.

The historians and the computer must have gotten the idea for the tassels from some picture of an Elizabethan court lady. Uhura, mincing her way through Elizabethan muck, wished very much that she could grab one of the historians and make him try to keep each portion of this sumptuous wardrobe clean.

The alley turned in a tight, blind curve, and suddenly opened up onto a street at least five times as wide. Wide enough, Uhura judged, for a cart, or maybe for five people to walk side by side. Before she could see much of it, though, a grizzled, scarred face pushed itself in front of her.

"Alms, milady. Alms for poor one-leg Will, a veteran of the Spanish wars, by your kind mercy." The man leered at her, a dubious leer that showed a near-toothless mouth, and breathed a reek of alcohol in her direction. His right leg, below the knee, ended in the proverbial peg-leg.

She turned away from him, not sure what to do. She'd never met a beggar before. She wanted to reach between her breasts and give him the whole leather purse, but in her mind she heard the thin-faced historian telling her that she could change history by giving anyone too much money.

As she turned away, she heard the beggar behind her calling out names that she was sure were obscene—"bawd" and "painted Jezebel" being the only ones she recognized.

Feeling a little better about not helping him, she looked at the other people on the street. There were a lot of them to look at—hundreds in her vicinity, many more than should fit the street. And they weren't, unlike Uhura had first surmised, engaged in anything half so rational as mayhem or disturbance. Instead, all scrambled everywhere, like a disturbed ant hill, each speaking or yelling at the top of his or her voice to other people who were speaking or screaming at someone else.

She dismissed her first fear, that her clothes might be too gaudy. Men and women alike wore clothes so bright as to make the eyes hurt. And they smelled. Not of sweat or unwashed flesh, as she'd expected, not even of the stuff that every one of them must be carrying around on their soles, since this street looked as filthy as the alley. No, they stank of perfume. The odors of all sorts of spices, the smells of most trees, and every flower known to botany, clashed in the air, and each wide-skirted lady, each tight-garbed gentleman who pranced past wafted a different one to add to the mix. Uhura decided that if she escaped going deaf, or blind, or both, she would surely lose all sense of smell before this mission was over.

Holding up her skirts she sauntered into the multitude, accepting inevitable jostling, and elbowing people out of the way when she must. Uhura looked around at the first hint of blond hair, or at the sound of the name "Will." The problem seemed to be that all these men had only three names at their disposal: William, Richard, or Henry. The occasional wild individualist would be named Christopher or Kit. The women, too, all seemed to be either Anne, or Margaret, or Mary. She guessed this must be well before the time of creative naming.

"Ah, well met, Will. You'll have a pint with me," a male voice to her right side.

Uhura looked, but both gentlemen were too portly for either of them to be the boyish William Harrod.

"Dost thou bite thy thumb at me, Will?" a voice screamed from her right, in the tone of fighting words.

"I bite my thumb, Richard. But not at thee."

Neither of these two, both young men and about the right age, had blond hair. They stood facing each other on the street, and people gave them a wide berth, as each of them pulled out long swords. Uhura, with the others, made haste to get away from them, only to be thrown against a throng of people rushing toward the disturbance to gawk.

Quietly but forcefully, she elbowed her way toward the edge of the street. She'd thought there had been law and order under Elizabeth, and that people were arrested for public brawling. She distinctly remembered reading . . .

A scream sounded behind her, and Uhura looked over her shoulder to see one of the young men, either William or Richard, run his opponent through with his long sword. The wounded man screamed as he fell onto the street in a gush of blood.

The circle that had gathered to watch the fight moved away, and Uhura found herself shaking. Someone had just been killed, or at least seriously injured. She took a deep breath. Wasn't anyone going to do something? Call the guard? The medics? Shaking, she walked away, not certain that the chill she felt was from the coolness of dusk settling over the city.

A woman ahead of her fell into a man's arms, calling him her sweet Will. Uhura glared at both of them, thinking that William Harrod might have done better to have an original name, if he was planning to get lost in Elizabethan England. Any name would have done—John, or Bob, or Mike. Anything but Will. But no, he had to be William, didn't he? Right at that moment, had she come across Harrod, she would gladly have killed him . . . She stopped, remembering the duel and the young man falling into the muck, bleeding. All right, she would gladly have dressed William Harrod down for the capital crime of his unfortunate name.

"Pardon me, Lady," a man said, as he squeezed past her. He smelled heavily of pine, and had warm-brown curls, and caramel colored eyes. And she'd bet his name was Will.

Frustrated, Uhura followed him with her gaze, more to have something to fix on than because she wanted to know where this presumable Will went. Unlike most of his contemporaries, he wore a sensible, if ugly color—a reddish brown. His jacket had much the same tailoring as Uhura's bodice, and his pants stopped just below the knee, where his black stocking showed, molding a straight, muscular leg. He walked with the elastic assurance of a self-confident man on an errand. Uhura envied him heartily.

Suddenly, he broke into a run, and yelled something. Almost without meaning to, she followed, and saw him plunge into a crowd. As Uhura plunged in, after him, she saw him dive into a group of men, and snatch a small boy by his ragged collar. His son?

The man pushed the boy behind him, and turned to the other four men, fists ready. "Varlets, villains, traitors, verminous excrescences, putrid meat. Wouldst thou pick on a child?"

His words showed more spirit than wisdom, unless the boy did happen to be his son, because the men he faced all looked burlier than he, taller and twice as wide, and with fists like hams.

Uhura told herself that she wouldn't intervene. It was none of her business if they fought, fair or not. For all she knew this man was the sort that went around getting into fights with all his neighbors. For all she knew, he got beat up every day. For all she knew . . .

She tried to walk away from the scene, in search of the elusive Harrod, but she couldn't, because of the inevitable circle of spectators forming around the beginning brawl.

The presumed Will, defending himself from all the other Wills—or maybe one of them had the originality of being a Richard or a Henry—threw an awkward punch at one of the four giants surrounding him. The giant jeered, and threw a punch in his turn, hitting the smaller man in the face.

The smaller man remained standing. The urchin behind him made a keening noise, and—Uhura's eyes widened—plunged a hand into the pocket of his defender's jacket.

One of the attacking giants saw it, too, and grabbed the child's scrawny wrist, and twisted it, and took something from his hand. This brute, a creature whose features might have been carved with an ax, stepped out of the shadows, away from the fray where his buddies continued punching the smaller guy, who nevertheless remained standing. He held his hand up, grinning at the small glittering metal jewelry in his hand.

Before Uhura could think, she yanked her skirts up higher and, rushing forward, applied a well-placed kick to the man's knee. He screeched and dropped the jewel. She grabbed it midair. Dropping it into the only secure place available—the tight space between her half-bare breasts—she turned to the other savages beating up the man.

A well-placed blow to the back of the head dropped the man

nearest her. His companions turned on her. The next one wasn't as easy, but Uhura doubled him over with a kick to his solar plexus. The young man with the dark curls punched the last one.

The man who'd nicked the jewelry had recovered, and tried to wade in. Uhura had time to knock him to the ground, and still see the presumed Will chase off his last assailant. The urchin had disappeared in the confusion, probably with his protector's cash, if he'd carried any.

The man looked at Uhura. As the circle of spectators dissolved around them, Uhura thought she caught references to her, in scattered sentences.

"Magnificent shrew," someone said.

"Those moorish women have fire," another man commented. "Wouldn't want one in my bed, though."

The man with the dark curls fished for a handkerchief from within the sleeve of his jacket, and pressed it to his nose to stanch the blood. "Milady." He gasped deeply, and grinned, stowing the handkerchief back in his sleeve. "Why now, milady, rarely is such strength seen as the ally of so much beauty."

"Beauty is only skin deep, but a good punch'll break the underlying bone." Uhura twisted her dress back to its usual uncomfortability. Mud splattered her skirts, and her boots were unrecognizable, smelly, muddy blobs. She fished in the narrow space just below her décolletage for the man's jewel.

His caramel eyes opened wide, and he followed the search most attentively. "You must be a great lady." His voice squeaked, and he cleared his throat. "From your apparel. Are you lost? Have your servants deserted you?"

Servants? Lost? Well, he could say that. She gave him a wary look, just as her fingers found the jewelry, stuck by some sharp point into the fabric of her bodice. She tugged it out. "I believe this belongs to you."

He looked at it. "It's not mine, but I am holding it for its owner. And how did you happen to get it?" He extended his hand to her, palm up. He wore dingy elbow length white gloves, stained here and there with inky black. He returned the jewel to his pocket.

"The boy took it from your pocket as you fought. One of those savages took it from him, and I took it from the savage." She grabbed the top of her dress, and wrenched it back into place. "I tried to put it somewhere safe. It got stuck."

Looking both stunned and pleased, the man said, "I do not have the pleasure of knowing your name."

"Lieu—" Uhura stopped herself. "Uhura."

Grinning, he displayed a full set of amazingly even teeth. "A beautiful name for a beautiful lady."

Ah, yes, certainly. Was that the local equivalent of *your quarters or mine?* "What's your name?"

"I'm called Will." He bowed.

He and a million of his friends and neighbors. "All right, Will, I'm searching for William Harrod . . . my . . . uh . . . my retainer."

"Your . . . retainer?" Will bowed again. "Would milady take ale, and bide the time safely with me until she finds him?" He extended his arm to her, gallantly.

She thought of warning him that she was in no mood for funny business, but thought that he had seen her fight and, surely, he couldn't think that he'd be able to subdue her easily. No, he must be what he seemed: a Good Samaritan. And having him for an ally had certain undeniable advantages. Certainly, he would know how money worked here. And what a plague house looked like. And he could protect her—well, appear to protect her—in taverns.

"My word, I'll give you no harm, and return you to your attendants." He patted the pocket with the jewelry. "As recompense for your timely assistance."

Cautiously, she rested her arm in his, and he led her through the streets, casting occasional molten-caramel looks at her. His very dark lashes made his eyes look all the lighter. "How came someone as beautiful as you to wander about without guardians?"

She smiled at him, despite herself. He had such an engaging manner, and such a nice voice. "Do I look like I need guardians?"

He shook his head, and smiled.

Who was this Will who acted so differently from the other Wills around him? Could he, too, somehow, be a displaced time traveler? "Are you a Londoner?"

He shook his head. "No. I come from Warwick," he said. "My people, the Ardens, used to be nobles, and own all that region."

The Ardens. So, he would be William Arden. She smiled up at him. "And what do you do?" Seeing his uncomprehending look, she added, "Your profession."

He laughed. "Not a profession. A trade, milady. A humble one. I'm an actor. I strut my moment on the stage, and then I am gone." Will smiled down at her. "And where do you belong?"

"Far from here."

He nodded. "In another kingdom?" He looked at her from head to toe. "From your garments, I thought so."

From her garments and her dark skin and hair, no doubt, but, his not mentioning it in an age when lead-induced pallor was the height of fashion, must be gallantry. She swallowed her annoyance, and smiled. "Yes, another kingdom, far away."

"Well, I am honored to show you my land." Will led her assuredly amid the crowd. "I hope it will please you."

Weirdly enough, it did. Once she got used to the smell, the noise, and the seeming randomness of behavior, Uhura began feeling exhilarated. Her pulse quickened. Here was a young, brash country, the adolescent stage of Western civilization.

Just a few miles from her, past all these tenements and hovels, Elizabeth I engaged in an experiment that would show the world that a woman could rule. Her example would, ultimately, open all professions to women. And in London, somewhere, William Shakespeare must be living in a garret, while he wrote his deathless plays. Halfway around the globe, Raleigh explored the New World, and Drake brought back the treasures of Spanish galleons to lay at his queen's feet.

With quickened interest, Uhura forgot the smell of the muck beneath her feet, and ignored duels starting just ahead of her.

The tavern Will took her to, The Queen's Head, had long pine tables, at which sat a fascinating array of characters, from ma-sons to weavers, carpenters to swordsmen, all of them talking of their pursuits. And they all spoke warmly, excitedly, as though they too knew, deep in their hearts, that they were laying the foundation of a better future, and building the knowledge that eventually would take humans to the stars. By the time they left, Uhura's head reeled, no thanks to the weak ale.

"May I take milady to her lodgings?" Will asked.

"I . . . I don't have lodgings," Uhura answered, breathless, excited. "I have money."

Will looked worried. "You can't rent a room alone. You're a woman." He flinched and smiled, perhaps remembering the mayhem this woman could cause. "Someone might think you're easy pickings, and try to cut your throat in your sleep." He shook his head. "You must come with me. I lodge at Bishopsgate, in the house of some good French refugees. We'll tell them you're my wife. All will be well."

His lodgings? She smiled tightly. All would be well. She could take care of herself. They walked what seemed like a mile, in the darkness, while he asked her what she thought of London and swelled with pride at her favorable opinion.

Finally, he unlocked the door of a tall building with a key he pulled from his sleeve, leading her past a tiny hall and up a rickety set of stairs. They never saw his landlord.

Upstairs, in the privacy of Will's two narrow rooms—one big enough for a single bed, and one big enough for a small table and a stool—Will offered her his own bed, while he, with his cloak, retired to sleep on his table.

The next morning, Uhura woke when Will knocked and came into the small room. "Here, milady," he said. "Since I think you'll wish to search for your retainer in the city, I thought you might want to dress in these." He handed her a jacket and pants made of blue velvet. "It is my good suit. Dressed as a man you won't be so conspicuous, and people will assume you can defend yourself, so you need not . . . I need not fear for you. I'll be busy elsewhere, about my own concerns." He handed her a large iron key. "Take this key and, if you haven't found your retainer by tonight, you may make free of my bed again."

"But, the key . . . ?" Uhura said. "How will you . . .?"

He smiled. "The landlord will let me in. He'll assume I got drunk and lost my key." He looked her up and down, and smiled, and blushed. "You might want to wear my cloak, too. The air is chill and, besides, a cloak will hide your . . . charms."

He didn't belong in this flea-infested, plague-ridden time. He walked through it as a beacon of civilization and goodwill. Uhura sighed as she buttoned herself into his jacket, which proved just as tight and uncomfortable as her bodice. She would trade the simpering William Harrod for Will, if she could. But she'd been given a mission.

Dressed as a man, she plunged into the maelstorm of Elizabethan London, to return, at sundown, sore-footed and tired, to Will's lodgings.

Will had arrived just before her, and spread a feast of roasted capon and boiled vegetables on his tiny table. When he saw her, his eyes lit up. "You didn't find your retainer, then," he said. "I'm heartily sorry." But he didn't look sorry at all.

They talked. He told her stories, and recited poems, and—unearthing a stringed instrument from under his bed—played music for her. He definitely didn't belong in this time.

For three more days, he fed her and gave her lodging, and seemed rather more grateful for her company than imposed upon.

She realized that Will had been very lonely, a man ahead of his time, who obviously hadn't ever found any woman he could talk to as he talked to her. Sometimes his caramel eyes softened when looking at her, and she wondered if the foolish man was falling in love with her. If he was, how could she prevent it? If seeing her kick the living daylights out of three thugs hadn't been enough to scare him, he might be beyond the reach of intimidation.

Fortunately, the male clothes did prevent her from becoming the victim of foolish assaults as she searched in vain for the other William. Over the days, she became more and more uncomfortable about his fate. Why had he been wearing a dress, anyway? Was it because his features looked too soft for the time, just as she had to dress as a man for protection?

Sitting at dinner with Will—both of them squeezed together on the tiny stool—Uhura wondered about the ramifications of taking him back with her. He seemed so out of place in this era. Could it be that she was meant to return with both him and William Harrod? Perhaps she was supposed to leave William Harrod behind, and bring this Will back with her. Uhura wished the Guardian had been more specific in its images and speech, and sighed.

"You look worried," Will said. "Is it your servant you worry about? What's his name, again?"

"William Harrod."

Will nodded. "What would he look like?"

"He has blond hair," Uhura said. Frankly, though she remembered Harrod's face, there wasn't anything about it that she could describe precisely. She wished she had a picture. "And he would be about your height, and he has blue eyes." And a pretty golden dress. "Is there somewhere . . . I mean, don't misunderstand me, but . . . he might be wearing a woman's dress. Is there somewhere where this happens?"

Will grinned. "Oh. That Will. A woman's face, with nature's own hand painted, that men's eyes and women's souls amazeth."

"Uh . . . something like that." Uhura gave him a hard glare, wondering if he'd gone batty. The line sounded vaguely familiar. Was he quoting something?

He'd gone all serious and nodded to her, a little restrained nod. "Yes, perhaps, I may know your Will. If so, I'm glad. I'm glad you've found him. When I first saw him, he was lost like that boy, and I had to defend him from a passel of cutpurses."

"Ah, yes. Will would get lost," Uhura said. "He does that."

His caramel-colored eyes regarded her with something that might be amusement. "How long have you searched? For all these long months, Will has worked with me, and he has said that his people would come for him, but he has despaired, and he . . . Well, his habits are expensive. He likes good inns, and a clean shirt every day. He ran into debt. He stole that brooch you so kindly returned to me. I returned it, and to keep him from the gaol."

Uhura sighed. The kind of fool that would "accidentally" fall into the Guardian, would be just as clumsy at theft, or any other job he might attempt. "Do you know where he is?"

Will nodded again. "I know not where he lodges. He has moved about, now because his street reeks too badly or because bawds gather there, and the last time, if you would believe it, because from his room he could see the heads of traitors affixed on pikes at London gate." Will shook his head. He chuckled, then sighed. "But I do know that tomorrow, just after noon, you will find him at the Rose, where I work. If you wish to come with me, to the theater, I'd be honored. And maybe you'll find your friend there. Even if he is not whom I think, a great company gathers at the Rose and, who knows, maybe you can spy him within."

"Yes. Thank you." Uhura smiled. "I'd like that."

Will nodded. "Then I'll come and get you at the noon hour . . . only . . . if you would be so kind . . ." He blushed. "If you'd wear your gown, as you had when I first met you, I would be honored to be seen in the company of such a beautiful lady."

She felt herself blush, and nodded. "Yes, yes, of course."

The theater was nothing like any she'd attended at home. Disorderly and crammed with people, it teemed with life, like everything in this time. Will led Uhura to a seat in the upper galleries, above the mass of standing spectators below.

As the play started, Uhura prepared to be bored, but she wasn't. The play was *A Midsummer's Night Dream* and Will, playing Bottom, made the audience laugh with his lines. And though the wings of the fairies were ill-sewn and the crown of the fairy queen too obviously tinsel, yet the immortal words of the Bard spun their enchantment, even in this setting.

The crowd laughed and applauded and threw their greasy cloaks in the air in appreciation, not knowing that their children and their grandchildren and their descendants would all enjoy these same words, feel these same emotions. They couldn't guess that plays by this same author would thrill alien spectators.

In Uhura's mind, these words stretched like a golden thread, linking generations, from their cradle on Earth well into space.

And, as she watched, she found herself hoping that someone

would introduce her to Shakespeare. That would be something to tell her shipmates. Maybe Will knew the Bard.

Her mission intervened, and even her charmed eyes couldn't miss noticing that William Harrod acted as the fairy queen.

After the play, Uhura waited until the press of people had dispersed, then went backstage to search for William Harrod. Backstage was as exciting as up front, a huge room crammed with props, filled with actors busy taking off costumes and cleaning paint from their faces. She saw Will. Behind Will, William Harrod removed a long wig to show his own short blond hair.

Following her gaze, Will said quietly, "You've found your friend."

Uhura nodded. She stepped in front of Harrod, who scratched at his scalp with both hands.

"Your performance was enchanting, Master Harrod."

He stared at her, uncomprehending, then bowed stiffly, and, taking her hand, kissed it, just as stiffly.

Uhura smiled at him. "I've been searching for you across time. Hoping to return with you to where we belong."

His eyes lit with understanding. His face relaxed into a real smile. "Come to rescue me from these dire circumstances?" He kissed her hand again, more passionately. "I cannot thank you enough for returning for me. For taking me back." His eyes glistened with emotion. "I'll never desert you again."

It sounded like the accident wasn't so accidental. Looking around the theater, Uhura could understand the lure that had driven the young historian. While a hard era, there was much to be said for it, many opportunities. She'd just witnessed, and he'd participated in, an original performance of one of Shakespeare's plays. "Did you truly doubt that you would be searched for and restored, or were you only hoping that all would be forgotten?"

Hanging his head in shame, William Harrod said, "Actually I feared I had made an irreparable mistake, and that no amount of affection could restore me."

Will looked dismayed at their apparent intimacy.

Uhura smiled at Will. She had to take him back with her. He didn't belong to this time. How much difference could one less

Will make to Elizabeth's England? After all, these people dropped dead all the time from a myriad of things, and there were hundreds, thousands, of Wills in the streets.

His caramel eyes caught her gaze and held it. His cheeks glowed red as he asked, "What did you think . . . of the play?"

"Wonderful! Absolutely the most memorable performance I've ever seen. I can't thank you enough."

Every word seemed to build Will up. He stood taller and smiled wider. He bowed to her. "Thank you. It is the favored heir of my invention."

It seemed too good an opportunity to waste, so Uhura asked, "I don't suppose you could introduce me to the playwright?"

Will grinned, his eyes shone. "Your most humble servant."

It took a moment for that to sink in. Uhura realized that *her* Will, out of all the Wills in London, was William Shakespeare.

He didn't look like the only accepted portrait, with its domed, bald forehead. His portraits, with pitch black hair and, more often than not, blue eyes, looked nothing like him. His fine, animated features, combined with the unusual color of his eyes, gave him a look none of those portraits had ever captured.

Her heart sank as she thought back over all the clues she hadn't noticed. Arden. Of course, his mother was an Arden, was she not? And he was from Warwick, and called himself an actor. Had she really not noticed, or had she deliberately ignored it? She didn't know what to say, what to do. Part of her wanted to howl in frustration, part to weep on his shoulder, but mostly she wanted to return to blissful ignorance. And take him back with her. "Oh. You."

He searched her face, looking uncertain of her thoughts.

Taking his hands in hers, Uhura held them up to examine them, touch them. "These hands wrote those words." She reached up, brushing the tips of her fingers against his temples. "This mind conceived these masterpieces." Her hands rested lightly on his shoulders. "You are someone I never thought to meet."

"Lady, you flatter me. I'm no Kyd, no Marlowe. I'm nobody." Leaning down, he touched her lips with his.

"Yes, yes, he's very talented, but we have business elsewhere," William Harrod said.

"Will!" a bearded actor called, nearby. "Will!"

Will squeezed her once, before being pulled away. Her heart clutched to watch him go. She couldn't take him with her.

"Ma'am? How do we get home?"

Uhura shrugged, looking at Harrod, allowing her feelings to melt away as she stepped into the role of a Federation officer once again. Yet, she followed Will with her gaze—his dark curls, the shapely body delineated by his tight jacket and formfitting breeches. "I don't know. As I understand it, once everything is as it should be, the Guardian pulls us back."

"I tried not to do anything, not to change anything." William started pacing. "I didn't save anyone's life. I didn't tell anyone anything. I didn't *do* anything." He looked down at his costume in dismay. "Except put this dress on, and act in that play. But I had to eat!"

Irritant! And she had to bring him back while leaving Will here. Uhura shook her head, and swallowed to keep her eyes dry.

He started ripping his costume off. "I've got to get out of here." He started for the alley door, shedding bits of gown.

Reflecting that some people never seem to realize what they have when they've got it, Uhura followed, catching him just outside the door. "Stop it. That's an order, mister." Unfortunately, he was a civilian, unaccustomed to taking orders.

"Do you remember where you were when you arrived?" he asked, clutching her arm. "I've never been able to get back there. Maybe all we have to do is return."

She pointed down the alley. "It's just . . ."

Pulling her along with him, he started for the alley mouth. "Come on, hurry."

Grabbing his arms, Uhura swiftly spun him around, so that she held him tight and blocked his path to the alley. "Stop. I have some business to finish here, and then I'll take you there."

His arm reached out to grab her waist, pulling her back to him. "Please, now. I can't stand it one more minute. Please."

Glaring up at him, she opened her mouth to give him a sharp rebuke, and heard the stage door creak.

Will stood in the doorway, looking out at them. The expression on his face was bleak and desolate. "Would you leave thus, without even a good-bye?"

Harrod tugged at Uhura. "Good-bye."

Will turned to go back into the theater. Uhura wrenched herself out of Harrod's grasp, and Harrod disappeared. In that split second she knew she could call out to Will, stay with him, take him with her, change time to suit herself. But she couldn't. He belonged not to her, but to humanity.

Uhura felt tears roll down her cheeks. "Farewell, my friend. Forever and forever, farewell."

She found herself stepping out of the portal onto a vast barren plain, and into a crowd of excited Federation officials.

Debriefing was particularly difficult. Uhura had no wish to speak of William Shakespeare, no wish to satisfy the envious looks, the prurient curiosity of the historians. Will had been alive and warm in her arms, his lips soft against hers, and now, a few moments of her subjective time later, he was dead, had been dead for uncounted centuries before her birth.

She was happy when the questioning moved on to William Harrod. As a civilian he had the luxury of being difficult and uninformative, but this escapade would follow him all his life, and he'd never be allowed near the Guardian again.

She slunk out of the conference room, after they finished interrogating Harrod, trying to ignore the fact that she still had to compose her mission log, and not mention the way Will's long fingers had strummed the chords, and not dwell on the gallant words he'd bestowed on her, or on his soft heart that made him the pawn of every creature in need.

One of the historians, the thin older man, stepped into her path, dragging an unwilling Harrod along. As the historian dug an elbow in his back, Harrod said, "Lieutenant Uhura, I wanted to personally thank you. There is a vast difference between knowing something historically, and experiencing it. I am truly grateful for what you did to find me, and bring me back."

She didn't want to talk to him, but she managed a polite nod and a diplomatic, "Just doing my job, but you're welcome."

Harrod relaxed. "And along with setting the timeline straight, we solved a centuries old mystery."

"What would that be?"

He smiled smugly. "Who the dark lady was, in Shakespeare's poems. Don't you see, that's why we *had* to go back, why the Guardian caused me to fall in. You, at this time in your life, had to meet Shakespeare. It was fate."

The thin older man frowned at him, and rested a hand on his shoulder to stop Harrod's exuberance.

"I don't believe in fate." Another wrinkle occurred to Uhura. "You realize, that makes you Mr. W. H., the fair boy."

Looking taken aback, Harrod scuffed his boots on the floor, shaking his head. "No. Not necessarily. For all we know they were both figments of Shakespeare's imaginative mind, as much as the characters in his plays."

"Most of which were commonly known stories." Uhura smiled at him. "I think Will knew what he was writing."

"Well, I just wanted to thank you." Harrod scrambled away.

In her quarters, after officially entering her mission log, Uhura called up Will's sonnets, to review what she remembered of them. Her eyes misted with tears, as she read,

My mistress' eyes are nothing like the sun;
Coral is far more red than her lips' red;
If snow be white, why then her breasts are dun;
If hairs be wires, black wires grow on her head.
I have seen roses damask'd, red and white,
But no such roses see I in her cheeks,
And in some perfumes is there more delight
Than in the breath that from my mistress reeks.
I love to hear her speak, yet well I know
That music hath a far more pleasing sound;
I grant I never saw a goddess go,

My mistress, when she walks, treads on the ground.
And yet, by heaven, I think my love as rare
As any she belied with false compare.

In a way, Uhura thought, as long as someone, somewhere, read these words, they'd be together. In her mind, she saw Will smile.

The Aliens Are Coming!

Dayton Ward

July 10th, A.D. 1969

Darkness faded as awareness returned, and he cautiously opened his eyes. Doing so sent a searing jolt of pain directly to the base of his skull.

Captain John Christopher had one hell of a headache.

He opened his eyes fully and took stock of his surroundings. The room he found himself in was a bare cinder-block affair, with no furniture or fixtures save a single lightbulb in the center of the ceiling, hanging inside a protective wire cage. The only door in the room was locked, a guess he confirmed when he tried to open it. He found the room stuffy, and he reached to unzip the top half of his orange flight suit.

The simple action made him pause and realize that he had no idea what had happened. The last thing he remembered was walking from the flight line into the hangar facility containing the pilots' locker room. He recalled starting across the wide expanse of the hangar floor when something came crashing down across the back of his head. Then . . .

. . . then he awoke here, with a prize-winning headache.

The room's lone door abruptly opened to admit a man wearing a nondescript black suit with matching shoes and tie and a plain white dress shirt. He carried a manila folder in his left hand. Christopher noted the lines in the man's face and the liberal smattering of gray in his thinning blond hair. He looked to be in his middle to late fifties, but the haunted look in his eyes made him seem older still.

"Where the hell am I?" Christopher barked as the door closed behind the new arrival. He thought the man looked visibly uneasy, almost nervous, as though he was uncomfortable with the situation. Well, good. That made two of them.

They exchanged stares for several seconds, then the other man said, "Where you are is not so important, Captain, as why you are here."

"Fair enough," the pilot replied. "That was my next question."

The other man ran a hand across his face and Christopher saw that it shook slightly. With a smile that seemed forced, he said, "My name is Wainwright, Captain, and you're here because I believe you have information I need."

"What kind of information?"

Bringing up the folder, Wainwright opened it and withdrew a single large photograph, holding it for Christopher to see. It was a grainy, dark image, mostly black, but he recognized the curvature of the Earth as that seen in photos taken during various manned space flights.

He also recognized the object floating over the Earth.

"Oh my god," Christopher breathed.

As a boy, Jimmy Wainwright knew all about alien invasions. He read *The War of the Worlds.* He followed the adventures of Buck Rogers, Flash Gordon, and Captain Proton. In the pages of numerous magazines purchased at the drugstore in the sleepy hometown of his youth, Earth was threatened every month. Its men were enslaved and its women carted off to carry out the whims of alien emperors across the universe.

But today, James Wainwright contemplated a real invasion by real aliens. He'd awaited their return ever since that fateful night in the New Mexico desert twenty-two years ago. Was the day he'd been dreading all these years finally at hand?

He stood silently as Christopher studied the object in the photograph, watched as the man's eyes traced over the large saucer shape and the three cylindrical projections, two above the saucer and one below.

"This photograph was taken last year by a military reconnaissance satellite," Wainwright said. "The object was discovered in high orbit above the Earth."

Christopher could not conceal his shock. "Last year? That's the same thing I saw just this morning."

Wainwright nodded. "So I gathered from your cockpit transmissions. Captain, I need to know everything you can tell me about what you saw up there."

Relaxing somewhat, Christopher frowned. "There's not much to tell, really. Air Defense Command tasked me to intercept an unidentified craft over Omaha Air Base. I got to the designated coordinates and there it was, high in the clouds and climbing away fast. At first I thought it was just sunlight reflecting off my canopy. I only saw it for a second or two, and then it was just . . . gone."

"But you're sure what you saw was the object in this picture?" Wainwright asked, holding up the photo for emphasis.

"Yes, I'm sure of it. What is it? Some kind of Russian rocket?" The pilot's eyes widened at a sudden thought. "Wait a minute. Are they pushing for the Moon? They're not going to beat us, are they? Not when we're this close?"

Wainwright shook his head. "We don't believe it's Russian, Captain."

"So what, then?"

Pacing slowly around the room, Wainwright didn't reply immediately. Christopher watched as the other man seemed to gather himself, as if preparing for a difficult task.

Finally, he said, "Captain, I've spent the last two decades of my life mired in endless searching, fear, frustration, even humiliation. I've watched this country advance along the technical path toward putting a man on the Moon, all the while failing to grasp the very real dangers lying just beyond the boundaries of our tiny planet. The people of this nation, of this very world in fact, are oblivious to these dangers because those in power wish to keep them ignorant."

Christopher shook his head, annoyed. An edge creeped into his voice as he said, "What are you talking about?"

Wainwright stopped his pacing and stared directly at Christopher. "In July of 1947, I was a captain in the Army Air Corps, stationed at Wright Field in Ohio. One night, an unidentified craft landed in the desert near Roswell, New Mexico. It was retrieved by soldiers from the Army air field there and transported to us, along with its three pilots."

"Russian?" Christopher asked.

"No. Definitely not Russian. They called themselves 'Ferengi,' though to this day I have no idea what that means."

"There's no country called Ferengi," Christopher said, and then his eyes widened. "Wait. Are you saying . . . ?"

Wainwright nodded, the look on his face chilling the pilot to the bone. "Yes. They came from another world." He paused for a moment. The implications of that simple statement never failed to astonish him, even after all these years.

"At first, there were those among us who thought they came in peace." He shook his head in disgust, remembering how that idiot professor, Carlson, had them all slapping their heads and tugging their noses in feeble attempts to communicate. All the while, the aliens had been toying with them.

"However," he continued, "once we started interrogating them, the truth came out. They admitted to being advance scouts for their Ferengi invasion fleet. They were coming to enslave us. They had the ability to control our minds, and they used that power on Carlson and his fiancée to engineer their escape. They got to their ship and flew away, and when they were gone, there was no evidence that they'd ever been here."

He glared at Christopher. "But I saw them, Captain. I know why they came, and I know they'll come back. They no doubt made it back to their leaders and told them all about our defensive capabilities, which compared to their technology were and probably still are pathetic."

Christopher was skeptical. "Mr. Wainwright, I admit it's a fascinating story, but . . ."

Wainwright cut him off. "For twenty-two years I and others like me have been planning for their return, Captain. President Truman empowered a group of us to investigate UFO sightings with the express purpose of learning as much as we could about them and formulating a defense against them. It was a top-secret program called Project Sign."

The haunted look returned to the man's eyes as he recalled memories from long ago. "The things we discovered were staggering. We were being observed almost constantly. We investigated sightings and some of them did prove to be false. But others, many others, were very true. We compiled thousands of pages of information during the first year alone."

He was staring into the room's lone lightbulb as he continued. "We obtained evidence of their presence, Captain. We captured crashed ships and retrieved alien beings, living and dead. When we started studying their technology, we realized just how outclassed we truly were."

Shaking his head, Christopher said, "This is unbelievable."

"Others thought the same way. Project Sign evolved over the years and its purpose along with it. Soon, our directive was to ensure that any sightings of UFOs were suppressed. We kept amassing the information, but our reports never saw the light of day."

Wainwright was pacing again, talking more to himself than to Christopher. The pilot could see anger welling up in the other man as he weaved the story. He couldn't begin to guess whether the man was constructing his tale from tortured memories or thin air. Wainwright looked to him to be an unhappy man, a man who had seen his share of adversity and injustice, and who was now summoning some final shred of will and purpose in order to try for success one last time.

Either that, or he was stark raving mad.

"Our work was hushed up deliberately, with misleading reports forwarded up to the president. The people running the project wanted UFOs to disappear. They considered the whole thing to be a nuisance." He snorted and shook his head. "Fools, all of them. They had no idea. But the public wasn't stupid. They knew something was up, and they knew the government was trying to sweep it under the rug. They kept protesting, demanding more results. The program finally evolved into Project Blue Book in the early fifties, and for the first time I thought we'd finally get the support we needed."

Wainwright's anxiety was climbing steadily, and Christopher was almost certain the man had forgotten he was even talking to the pilot. He'd unbuttoned his suit jacket and Christopher caught a fleeting glance of a pistol in a shoulder holster under Wainwright's arm.

The pilot stole a look toward the door. Who or what was on the other side? It didn't matter, he decided. He'd take his chances, given the opportunity. All he had to do was get past Wainwright, who seemed to be growing more unbalanced by the minute.

Stalling for time, Christopher asked, "So, what happened?"

"Those idiots!" Wainwright exploded. "The same story all over again, only this time they wanted to take care of this 'UFO craze' once and for all. Evidence was destroyed. Witnesses were forced into silence, bought off, or suffered 'sudden disappearances' or 'mysterious accidents.' The people in charge, the same people I trusted, turned their backs on me. People I called close friends shunned me in hopes of preserving their own pathetic careers."

His eyes burned with hurt, anger, and defeat. "Now they're beginning the first stages of shutting down the program and tying up loose ends like me. I still work on the project, but now I'm a professional disgrace, one of many scapegoats in a massive campaign designed to keep people blissfully unaware of their true status in the interstellar reality!"

The man's losing it, Christopher thought.

Wainwright pointed at him. "But now I've finally got someone who can help me, someone they haven't gotten to yet. You saw that ship, Captain. You know it's real." He pointed to the photo that lay on the floor. "A year ago that thing destroyed a nuclear weapons platform we were trying to put into orbit. It was the most sophisticated piece of hardware in our arsenal, but they destroyed it easily and damn near started World War III in the process. Now it's back, just as we're getting ready for the most ambitious manned space flight in our history. Don't you see what's happening?"

Christopher regarded the man warily. "You think an alien spaceship is here to disrupt the Moon landing? What will that accomplish?"

Gesturing wildly with both hands, Wainwright said, "Can't you see? They want to slap us down, keep us pinned to our own planet. That way, we're all right here when they come to take us over. They can't wait ten or fifteen years to make their move. By then we'll have space stations and a base on the Moon. They're striking now, before we have a chance to learn how to defend ourselves against them."

"You're talking movie stuff, Wainwright," Christopher said, his face screwing up in disdain. "Martians and mind control and taking over the world. It's preposterous! There's no such thing as little green men."

Christopher froze as the words left his mouth. Something was there behind the words, something teasing the edges of his memory. Ghostly images of wide corridors and bright colors called to him. There was a man in a gold shirt with an air of authority about him. Another man in a blue shirt with green-tinged skin and . . .

"You believe," Wainwright said, pointing at the pilot again. "I can see it in your eyes."

"No," Christopher whispered. It went against everything he took to be true, to be factual. This was fantasy, and madness lay not far beyond it, if Wainwright was any indication.

But the green-skinned man with the pointed ears haunting his memory told him otherwise.

"I . . . I was there," he said, his voice barely audible. "On the ship. They brought me aboard, destroyed my plane." Confusion clouded his face and he shook his head. "But that's impossible, isn't it? There was no time for that to happen. I only saw it for a second. But I was there. I slept in one of their beds, ate their food."

There was more there, he knew, more memories stubbornly refusing to come forward. Saturn? Why did Saturn seem so important?

"I have to report this," Christopher said. "Tell them what I saw."

"Yes," Wainwright replied. "You have to report it. We have to get this information out, warn people that there's an alien ship up there waiting for God knows what."

"My superiors will inform their leaders. The President will take action, right?"

Scowling, Wainwright said, "The president? Captain, this country is preparing to send three men to the Moon. They know about that ship just as we do, but they can't afford to acknowledge it. Putting a man on the Moon is a political gold mine right now. There's no way they'll risk losing that, even if it costs the lives of three brave men and the work of thousands of other people.

"But we don't have to let that happen. We can take this to the newspeople, get it on television. The government won't have the chance to bury it. They'll have to delay the launch and deal with the problem."

Disbelief clouded Christopher's face. "I can't accept that. I have to believe my superiors will listen to my report and take the proper action. They already know I saw something. I have a duty to report in full detail what I know."

"No!" Wainwright screamed, drawing the pistol from the holster under his arm. "All these years I've tried to get them to understand, to accept the problem and deal with it. But they've ignored me! Destroyed me! They're going to shut Blue Book down soon. This may be my last chance to prove once and for all that I'm right. You're not going to take that away from me."

Christopher stared at the gun. "Shooting me won't help, you know."

"I don't plan to shoot you unless you force me to. But you

should know that two of my agents are at this very moment sitting in a car outside your home." He glanced at the watch he wore on his left wrist. "In about twenty minutes, if they don't hear from me, your family will 'mysteriously disappear.' Their only chance is for you to do as I say."

Anger flared up in Christopher. It was obvious now that Wainwright was beyond reason. Years of humiliation and disgrace had robbed him of whatever sense of honor or duty he may have once possessed. Now he was nothing but a battered shell of a man, frantically seizing one final chance at redemption.

"You bastard," he breathed.

"Desperate times, Captain," Wainwright said. "You know what they call for. Now, please, don't make this any more difficult than it has to be." He motioned for Christopher to go to the door. "Let's go."

Christopher stepped to the door and reached for the knob. This time it turned in his hand and he pulled the door open. Beyond, he saw a stark, gray-painted corridor perhaps a hundred feet in length, ending at a set of polished steel elevator doors. He was surprised to find no other people in the hallway.

"Move," Wainwright said, nudging him with the pistol. The pilot opened the door wider to step into the corridor. From the corner of his eye, he saw the other man move to follow.

Christopher yanked the door open with sudden unexpected force. It slammed into Wainwright, catching the man in the face. He howled in pain and reached for his nose. Christopher hit him with the door again and Wainwright fell to the floor, his pistol clattering away across the room. The pilot took off running down the hallway.

He was nearly two thirds of the way to the elevator when something zipped past his ear, the first shot echoing in the narrow corridor. A second shot rang out and a fireball exploded in his shoulder. He stumbled and fell to his knees, his right hand automatically moving to his wounded arm. Pulling the hand away, he saw it was covered in blood.

"Stop!" Wainwright called out from behind him. Christopher,

still on his knees, turned to face the other man. Wainwright's face was bloody, his nose angled unnaturally to the left.

"I'm sorry," Wainwright said, slowly walking up the corridor. A look of sadness dominated the man's features. "I didn't want to hurt you, Captain. I don't want to harm anyone, but surely you can see my position. I've devoted my life to this country, and those in power have abandoned me and others like me to save their own worthless hides. Well, that's ended now. The truth will come out today, and you will help me."

A tone abruptly sounded in the hallway, and their attention was drawn to the elevator. The doors parted to reveal a figure wearing a black suit strikingly similar to the one Wainwright wore. Christopher looked up and his gaze was drawn to blue eyes and honey blond hair. A woman.

Wainwright was caught off guard by the new arrival, his hand jerking the pistol around wildly to point at the woman. Christopher had to wonder how he kept from shooting her accidentally.

"Who are you?" Wainwright snapped.

The woman calmly produced a small wallet from the inside pocket of her suit jacket and showed him a rather plain identification card with her photograph on it.

"Agent Lincoln," she said with an air of authority that seemed in contrast with her apparent youth. "Major Quintanilla has asked me to take Captain Christopher into custody. He wants you to return to Wright-Patterson immediately for debriefing."

"Debriefing," Wainwright echoed. Christopher could see confusion playing across the man's face, breaking through the single-minded focus that had dominated it just seconds before.

The woman, Lincoln, reached into her suit pocket again, this time pulling out a packet of papers held together by the pocket clip of a stout silver pen. Taking the pen in her right hand, she unfolded the papers and held them out to Wainwright. "Here are the orders."

As Wainwright rapidly scanned the papers, Lincoln looked down at Christopher. "Are you all right?"

"Been better," the pilot hissed through clenched teeth.

She returned her attention to Wainwright. "We have to go

quickly. Military police have tracked your vehicle to this location. They'll be here in the next few minutes."

"These orders are fake!" Wainwright said suddenly. "The cipher key in the heading is yesterday's code."

The woman's face fell as Wainwright's pistol came up again, this time pointing at her. "I don't know who you are," he said. "But you're not going to stop me from doing what needs to be done. I've been kept down for too long and today is my redemption."

"What the hell is going on?" Christopher demanded, using the wall for support as he pulled himself to his feet. "Who are you?" he asked Lincoln.

Christopher's movements distracted Wainwright, and Lincoln was obviously waiting for just such a happenstance. Her right hand came up with startling speed, the pen grasped in a firm grip.

The pen . . . ?

A bolt of blue energy erupted from the pen, catching Wainwright full in the chest. The man sighed as the beam enveloped him, the tension immediately leaving his muscles.

"No," he breathed as he sagged to the floor, consciousness slipping away rapidly.

"You're tired, go to sleep," Lincoln said to him. She stepped forward and retrieved his weapon, then turned to Christopher. "I'm sorry this had to happen, Captain, but don't worry. Everything's going to be fine."

"My family," Christopher blurted. "He said he had men ready to take my family."

Lincoln smiled. "Don't worry about that. My . . . partner . . . is taking care of that as we speak." She moved closer to inspect the wound in his shoulder. "The bullet passed through cleanly. We can fix that easy enough." She reached into her pocket and produced a device Christopher did not recognize.

"What is that?" he asked as she pressed the object to his shoulder. He grimaced as pain pulsed briefly, but then the device began to hum and soothing warmth washed over his arm.

"This'll heal your wound. There won't even be a scar."

The humming ceased after several seconds and she pulled the

device away. He looked down in awe and saw that except for the blood on his suit, there was no sign he'd ever been injured. He groped the back of his shoulder where the bullet's entry wound should have been and found nothing. The woman was as good as her word.

"Groovy, huh?" Lincoln asked.

"It's incredible." He shook his head in disbelief, then looked back at her. "Who are you?"

"Someone who looks out for others when they need looking out for. Mr. Wainwright had a good idea to let people know about UFOs, but he was about to make a huge error. If he'd gotten to the public with what the two of you know, it could have caused a panic. The government might delay the Apollo 11 launch, and that's something that can't be allowed to happen, you know?"

Realization dawned on Christopher's face. "You mean it's true? What he told me? What I saw? All of it?"

"Pretty heavy, huh?" she replied. "Between the two of you, you've got enough information to put UFO groupies and national security bigwigs into a full-blown lather."

Christopher shook his head. "I don't understand. Why are you telling me this?" He indicated the unconscious Wainwright with a wave of his hand. "You must know I have to report everything I've seen today, including all this."

"Because you won't remember any of it," Lincoln said calmly as she brought the pen up once more.

July 16, A.D. 1969

In an apartment in New York City sat a man, a woman, and a cat. The man, a middle-aged gentleman of slim build with intense blue eyes and brown hair peppered with gray, regarded his companion, Roberta Lincoln. At the moment, she was completing a report detailing her last assignment.

"Agent Wainwright has been placed in an Air Force psychiatric facility," she said. "Doctors report he suffered a nervous breakdown due to prolonged work-related stress while assigned to a top-secret military program. He talks endlessly about alien invasion fleets and UFO sightings and how the public needs to be warned. They predict that with the proper therapy, they can assist him to a full recovery inside of a year."

The man rose from his chair, cradling the purring black cat in his arms as he strolled to a window. The apartment overlooked the city, and he stared out at the cityscape for several seconds before saying, "Unfortunate that it had to end that way for him, but at least now he won't endanger himself or history. What about Captain Christopher?"

Roberta replied, "Given the amount of time that had passed since Wainwright kidnapped him, I decided to leave him where I found him. He has no memory of meeting Wainwright. The military police told him about Wainwright's breakdown and attributed his kidnapping to that. As for his encounter with the *Enterprise,* Air Defense Command chalked it up as just another unexplained UFO sighting."

Gary Seven turned from the window, allowing the cat to drop to the floor and scamper away. "Therefore, there's nothing to report to any authorities and no reason for them to delay the launch of Apollo 11. All in all, a successful mission, and quite an accomplishment for your first solo outing."

Closing the report with a sigh, she replied, "I mucked up the cipher code on the fake orders. I almost had him convinced until he saw that."

"A minor mistake, which you overcame and thereby salvaged the operation. Consider it a lesson for the future, Miss Lincoln. It's the little things that will trip you up on missions like ours, not the big ones."

Roberta processed the gentle lecture, then said, "It's too bad we missed the *Enterprise.* I'd have liked to meet Captain Kirk and Mr. Spock again."

The cat made a most derisive noise at that, and Seven regarded the animal with an amused expression. "Quite right, Isis. Roberta, from their point of view, they hadn't met us yet. If we'd met with them on the day Captain Christopher saw the *Enterprise,* we would have risked disrupting the time stream. I don't think I have to remind you the trouble that could cause."

Shaking her head, Roberta blew out a breath of frustration, pausing briefly to give Isis a dirty look that went ignored as the cat began to preen herself.

"Time travel gives me a headache, you know?"

Seven allowed himself the briefest of smiles, a rare display of emotion. "I don't particularly enjoy it myself." He moved back to his seat and turned his attention to the television set that had previously gone ignored. Their assignment here on Earth to ensure humankind's maturation into a peaceful society was ongoing, but for the time being it could take a back seat to the history about to unfold on the screen before them.

Isis returned to Seven's lap once more as her master settled into the sofa. Petting the cat absently, he said, "Don't worry, Miss Lincoln. Something tells me we haven't seen the last of the *Enterprise*."

In his home in Nebraska, Captain John Christopher sat with his wife and two daughters transfixed before a television, just like millions of other people all around the world. They watched as a mighty white rocket, the most powerful transportation device ever constructed by humans, shook loose the embrace of gravity and hurtled upward into the blue Florida sky, the first step on a long journey that would forever change the way the inhabitants of Earth viewed their home planet.

Christopher had dreamed of traveling through space. He'd even gone so far as to try out for the fledgling American astronaut program. He hadn't qualified, so like the many others whose dreams would probably never be realized, he would have to be content to merely sit, watch, and celebrate the achievements of others on this momentous day and those that would surely follow.

As the mighty Saturn V soared heavenward, Christopher glanced down to where his two daughters lay on the rug between the television and the couch where he and his wife sat. They were young, still a few years from reaching their teens. It was entirely possible they would grow up in a world where space travel was commonplace. They might even be among those fortunate enough to carry the pioneering spirit of humanity to the stars.

Why not them?

Apollo 11 climbed higher into the sky, but John Christopher was no longer watching. Instead, his thoughts wandered toward the years that lie ahead, and what a future generation of Christophers might contribute to them.

Family Matters

Susan Ross Moore

Spock pressed the doorbell and waited.

It had been 3.682 minutes since he pressed it the first time. Boston in mid-January was as cold and inhospitable as any alien planet he had ever encountered. Snow covered nearly everything he could see from the front stoop of the brownstone home. It was almost as though Earth had been plunged into another ice age.

He was about to press the doorbell a third time when he heard the lock click. The massive oak door creaked inward just far enough to show a woman's face looking up at him.

"Spock?"

He nodded. He had not seen Kathleen Fitzhugh since Grandmother Grayson's funeral, yet the woman standing before him was unmistakably his mother's sister.

"I—I almost didn't recognize you; I haven't seen you since you were a boy. Elizabeth wasn't even born yet. How old were you then? About fifteen?"

He calculated as he turned up his collar; then he slid his hands back into his coat pockets. Wasn't she going to ask him inside?

"Twenty-eight point seven two Terran standard years, Aunt Kathleen." His breath formed a white cloud between them. She started as though suddenly aware of the below-freezing temperature.

"Come in; you must be cold. Bring your suitcase. I'll make some tea."

Spock was distressed by his aunt's lapse of manners, but attributed it to concern for her daughter. He pulled off his coat, hung it on the hall tree, and followed her into the den. Placing the suitcase beside him, he sat on the sofa. The civilian clothes chafed as he moved. Kathleen disappeared without another word into the next room.

Spock noticed that cobwebs stretched between the arms of the ceiling light above him. The sofa cushions were in disarray, suggesting that Kathleen had slept on the couch and not in her bed. A coat was draped carelessly across the back of a dining-room chair, its scarf trailing on the carpet. Apparently Kathleen's mind wasn't on her housekeeping, either. No wonder her manners had lapsed.

"How is Cousin Elizabeth? Has there been any change in her condition?"

The clattering of kitchen utensils halted. Kathleen stepped around the corner, stood in the archway, and faced him. In that moment, her face seemed much older and careworn. More like Amanda's.

"No. The doctors have given up on her. They're planning to send her to a long-term care facility."

Her face didn't show it, but Spock heard the pain in her voice.

"Did you not take Mother's advice and consult a Vulcan healer?"

"I did, but she said there was no trace of Elizabeth's mind left." Kathleen wilted onto the arm of a chair. "It's so difficult. I tried to reach Amanda again today, but I was put on a waiting list. They said it would be three or more days before I could call."

Spock nodded silently, his eyebrows arching speculatively. As a member of Starfleet, he rarely encountered such delays in personal communications. The private sector was not always so fortunate.

Spock glanced around the room at the pictures that decorated the tabletops. Some were of Kathleen, but most were of an attractive young woman who was certainly his cousin Elizabeth.

"I don't see any pictures of Mr. Fitzhugh," he commented.

"Alex and I divorced when Elizabeth was six. We had known each other since grade school, so it was natural that we'd marry. He was so stable, so comfortable. Mama was pleased that I'd chosen someone from a family she knew."

Spock recognized the veiled insult to his mother.

"We were reasonably happy the first five years or so, and then we began to argue. Then we grew silent. In the end, we realized the divorce was the first thing we'd agreed on in years. Since then, Elizabeth has been my life."

Kathleen didn't look up from the carpet. "I'll do *anything* to keep from losing her. It was difficult to call her after so many years, but Amanda said you could help her—that's why I contacted you."

Spock's eyebrows ascended again, this time in surprise. Why had his mother made such a rash statement?

"Mother should not have speculated that I could help when the physicians and the healer have not been successful. It is not logical to assume I could do more than a trained healer."

"She said it was because you're both a Vulcan and a relative."

Spock considered this for a moment, but could find no immediate justification to his mother's thinking. He heard the teakettle whistle. When Kathleen made no move toward the kitchen, Spock rose to attend it.

His aunt's kitchen proved to be as archaic as what he had seen of the rest of the house. Even the stove seemed to date back more than a century; it had a quaint personality that seemed to fit this house. He knew that the building had belonged to the Grayson family for nearly two hundred Terran years, and it appeared his aunt intended to preserve it in its original condition.

He soon placed a saucer with its steaming cup in Kathleen's hand, and then took his seat again and sipped at his own tea. He waited for her to continue. She sat immobile, staring at her daughter's picture on the table between them. Spock finished his tea, feeling its warmth slowly penetrate his chilled body, and then set his cup down beside the picture.

"Should we go to the hospital soon? I do not know their visiting schedule."

Kathleen Fitzhugh set down her cup next to Spock's and looked up at him. Again, Spock observed the family resemblance in her wide gray-blue eyes and delicate features. Her hair retained its golden brown tint and was earlobe length, gently following the top of her collar and curling slightly below her high cheekbones. But now, although her posture remained slumped, Spock noticed a new intensity in her stare, one that might have made him uncomfortable, had he been human.

"It isn't fair," she said evenly. "A person's family is all that really matters. And yet, my only sister married . . . an *alien* . . . and followed him to the other side of the galaxy. Then when Mama died, she only came back for the funeral, dragging her alien child with her." She glanced out the window, apparently watching snowflakes drift by, then back at Spock. "So now I'm forced to call you—my nephew and yet a stranger—to help someone you don't even know."

Spock frowned at her outburst. Yes, the physical resemblance to his mother was undeniable, but Amanda would never say such things, not even in anger. Was his aunt actually voicing a prejudice against Vulcans? If so, his job would be much more difficult.

He sighed. He had experienced the illogic of prejudice, in many forms, all his life. Childhood scenes of Vulcan children calling him "Earther" and human children calling him "goblin-ears" sprang from his memory and threatened to bring their emotions with them. He quickly suppressed those thoughts. Long ago, he had accepted these taunts as a distasteful result of his dual heritage.

But now, if he was to help Elizabeth, accepting his aunt's

prejudice might not be enough. He would have to overcome it, conquer it.

He rose, his hands raising unconsciously to tug at the unfamiliar cut of his tunic.

"The *Enterprise* will leave Earth orbit in three days, Aunt Kathleen. Regardless of the situation here, I must be on board. I suggest we go on to the hospital so that I may begin."

Kathleen ordered a groundcar. As they rode to the hospital, she explained how Elizabeth had been struck by an out-of-control vehicle as she crossed campus on her way home from class. Two weeks later, she still lay in a coma, the doctors uncertain about the extent of her brain damage.

When Kathleen was told there was little chance of Elizabeth's ever regaining consciousness, she called her older sister to tell her the news. Amanda informed her the *Enterprise* was on its way to Earth, and suggested she enlist Spock's aid. At first she resisted, but decided to trust Amanda's advice; she reluctantly contacted Starfleet Central.

Spock rode in silence, listening intently, yet allowing himself a chance to observe the sights. He was on Earth, in Boston, for the first time in over twenty standard years, on a family matter. It was regrettable there would be little time to view the city and appreciate its place in the planet's history.

He glanced back at her as she pointed out a Revolutionary War monument, her civic pride obvious. Despite Kathleen's apparent dislike for Spock, he found qualities he could admire. If her personal pride were as strong as Amanda's, he could appreciate how difficult it was for her to call for assistance—especially from Spock. Even if it proved to be the only way to save her daughter, Spock could understand the cost to her self-esteem.

The groundcar stopped and Spock paid the driver. He and his aunt walked toward the hospital. A light skiff of snow on an otherwise-cleared sidewalk recorded their footprints as they climbed worn marble steps. Kathleen led him to a bank of turbolifts. They rode to the fourth floor, and then walked past the nurses' station to Elizabeth's room.

"They've been very kind to me," Kathleen said as she shook

snow from her coat and draped it over a chair back. "Because Elizabeth's in a private room, they don't enforce visiting hours. As long as I don't disrupt their routine, I can come and go as I please."

Spock nodded and placed his coat on the seat of the chair his aunt had used for her coat. He looked at the bed and at the still form lying on it. Cousin Elizabeth. He regretted not having gotten to know her. She was in her first year of college; he wondered what her major was.

Stepping to the bedside, he gently placed his fingertips along the edges of Elizabeth's face, following her jawline up to her temples. He noted the absence of muscle tone and felt skin temperature that was cool even for a human. His first thought was that she was in the Vulcan healing trance, but that was impossible. Elizabeth was completely human, without benefit of such abilities.

Grotesquely cheerful music filtered in from a hallway speaker, battering at Spock's conscious mind as he composed himself for the mental contact he would soon attempt. Borrowing from a meditation ritual he used on the often-noisy *Enterprise,* he banished the sounds from his awareness.

Spock probed gently at the surface of her mind, sending out waves of reassurance. He was vaguely aware of Kathleen sitting next to the bed, a puzzled expression on her face as she followed his every move, but he dismissed her presence as easily as he had the music and concentrated on his task.

Deeper and deeper he went, questing for any sign that Elizabeth's mind was still active. He went as far as he dared without shifting to the mind-meld; a part of him still rebelled at that thought. She was family, yet a stranger. The extra link that made melding tolerable was not there. Her seemingly blank mind was more repugnant—yes, more frightening—than an alien's that at least evidenced intelligence, no matter how different from his own. And . . . what if she too were prejudiced? Had she been unable to answer the Vulcan healer, or had she simply chosen not to?

Mentally, he took a deep breath and placed himself at the very brink of the mind-meld. His father, Sarek, had taught him to visualize familiar images when contacting a nonVulcan, so he projected himself as a human, standing on the edge of a precipice and straining to reach her.

Elizabeth? He formed his thought around her name, again using the visualization technique to perceive her in full health, her finely featured face surrounded by a cloud of light brown hair. He shut his eyes to block out the face he saw below him on the pillow, its muscles lax.

He waited. There was no response.

Time slid to a halt as he stood motionless at her bedside. He "called" her name repeatedly, each time curiously aware that he held his breath while he "listened" for her reply.

Elizabeth, can you hear me? The word "hear" was of course meaningless, but a nontelepath would have no other word for how he was communicating.

Elizabeth, my name is Spock. I want to talk with you. If you understand me, just think very hard and I will hear you.

He let his clenched jaw muscles relax and waited anxiously for even the smallest response. Nothing. Kathleen stood beside him, and he opened his eyes to observe both women. Kathleen's white-knuckled hands were clasped before her; Elizabeth's face was still impassive. Spock closed his eyes again. He had to do it. Regardless of the risk to himself and the backlash he might experience, a mind-meld seemed to be the only way to reach his cousin. He couldn't fail Amanda's belief in him.

Spock stepped calmly from the mental precipice into the chasm of Elizabeth's damaged mind. It was as though he had passed a boundary placed there to protect him. If he found no response, he might be engulfed in its vastness, never to return. Or, if she mirrored her mother's sentiments, the force of her hatred could sear his exposed mind—possibly beyond salvage. As he slipped into the mind-meld, fear flicked at the edge of his conscious mind, and he wondered why he would attempt something this dangerous without another Vulcan—preferably a trained healer—to assist should he lose his way. Then he remembered Amanda had been certain he would succeed. That knowledge gave him the courage to continue. With a deep breath to brace himself for what he might encounter, he slid from his light contact into a full mind-meld.

Elizabeth, your mother's very worried about you. She's standing next to me. May I give her a message? He projected Kathleen's anguish into the darkness before him.

From the furthest corners of her mind, he felt a faint stirring, like that of a tiny creature scrabbling blindly from a predator. It seemed to stop and turn; a whimper of hope escaped its lips. Then Spock sensed a barely formed thought gather strength enough to reply.

Is someone there? I—I can't see you.

Even from the depths of the mind-meld, Spock let his attention wander enough to rejoice. Elizabeth's mind was still functioning—and he had reached her! He also knew that he would never have sensed the contact if he hadn't switched to the mind-meld. Her response was weak, tentative. Restraining the urge to immediately break contact and inform his aunt of this early success, he concentrated on strengthening the mind-meld.

It's all right, Elizabeth, he "said" calmly. *We're talking with our minds. My name is Spock; will you speak with me?*

Again, he projected his physical appearance, being careful to underplay his Vulcan features and cast himself as a human.

Spock? I have a cousin named Spock.

I am he.

But you . . . you're a—

Spock grabbed the tendrils of her mind, refusing to let go. He couldn't let her escape. Not now!

Yes, I'm Vulcan. But I'm also human. Do not forget that, Elizabeth.

Spock suffused the tenuous link with a few of the least painful images he normally kept deeply suppressed, locked tightly against even his own entry. As the episodes, made stronger from the incident with his aunt less than an hour earlier, paraded across the mind bridge, he felt Elizabeth's struggles lessen, then abate.

Yes, you're Aunt Amanda's son. I know that. But Mother says Vulcans are wicked, that they take people away—

Elizabeth! Spock interrupted. He couldn't allow that line of thought to continue. He controlled his breathing and fought back the cry of agony that clogged his chest. *Why* must so many individuals find excuses to hate? He calmed himself, then continued.

Elizabeth, the physicians here can do no more for you, so your mother sent for me. She believes I can help you. If you permit me to, I can help you wake up.

I don't understand. Spock could sense her confusion and fear. But he no longer detected the raw hatred.

It's very simple. If you tell me to leave, I will. But I won't tell your mother that your mind is still active. It wouldn't be fair to her—to know you deliberately refused my help. In a few days, you'll be sent to a place where your body will receive care, but no one will again attempt to reach your mind. You'll stay lost in your helpless body, Elizabeth. Eventually, you'll die. But in the meantime, you'll stay suspended between waking and sleeping, just as you are now. You do feel lost, don't you? He accented his thought with a suggestion of abandonment and misery—the tiny animal again cowering from its predator.

Yes. Sometimes I hear people talking. I know Mother's here, but I can't tell her I know. I can't tell her to stop crying. I can't move—I can't even open my eyes. You don't know how awful it is! Can *you help me, Spock?*

"Spock!"

He jumped slightly at the sudden sound, but the mind-meld was untouched. *I'll be back as soon as I can, Elizabeth. You can give me an answer later. I promise to return.*

Spock released his fingers, feeling the contact dissolve as he returned to singular awareness. He opened his eyes, straightened, and turned to his aunt. Tears traced down Kathleen's cheeks. Still vulnerable from the contact, he wanted to pull Kathleen from the bedside, away from Elizabeth's hearing. She didn't need to be subjected to this.

"I knew you couldn't do it. I—I shouldn't have listened to Amanda. If a fully trained Vulcan healer couldn't reach her, how could a half-breed like you stand a chance? I'm going home now. I want you to leave, also."

She reached for her coat; her fingers shook and she dropped it.

Spock retrieved it and held it for her. She grudgingly slid into it. He took his own coat off the chair and looked out the window as he put it on and fastened it. Twilight was gathering; the dusk-to-dawn lights that were winking on along the street highlighted the snow that still drifted lazily down.

They had been there 3.27 hours. It didn't seem possible. Spock realized how tired and hungry he was.

"I require time to rest, Aunt Kathleen, and Elizabeth cannot be helped further today. I will see you home, then . . . shall I return to the ship?" Would he go if she let him? After reaching Elizabeth, even so slightly? Should he tell Kathleen he had reached her, despite his earlier promise to Elizabeth?

Yes.

Even if Kathleen would not see reason, it was no excuse to punish Elizabeth. She might later hate Spock, but he could not condemn her to the living death she now endured. Kathleen could send him away; if she did, he'd still find a way to help Elizabeth, even if he had to involve his father, Ambassador Sarek, and his diplomatic influence.

"No," Kathleen said. "You may stay at my house tonight. I did invite you, after all. It wouldn't be proper if I denied you the hospitality you accepted."

Spock and Kathleen returned to her home. She rode in silence, but Spock saw the strain in her face, the taut line of her lips. Very well, if she could refrain from talking in front of the driver, so could he. Finally, the groundcar stopped at the large brownstone.

Spock followed her inside, his hands once again deep in the coat's warm pockets. He left the coat on; only the welcome noises of tea preparation finally convinced him to remove it. He stepped to the kitchen doorway and saw his aunt frowning into the open refrigerator.

"May I be of assistance?"

Kathleen started, then turned toward him.

"I honestly don't know what to offer you for dinner," she said softly.

Spock considered this. Vulcan had been in the Federation all her lifetime; her own sister had married a Vulcan. How could she remain so uninformed? Was it from prejudice—or, was the average human simply not interested in extraterrestrial cuisine?

He decided to learn the answer. It could explain Elizabeth's reticence to work with him. He now knew why the healer had been unsuccessful. The average healer would not have chanced a mind-meld under such conditions. And even if she had, no Vulcan would have willingly shown so much emotion to a stranger. Especially to a human, relative or not.

At that moment, he realized Amanda *had* been right. He was probably the only person on two worlds capable of reaching Elizabeth.

"Do you stock a variety of common foodstuffs?" he asked, glancing toward the ancient refrigerator. He was not surprised at the absence of a kitchen computer. Amanda hated them too.

"I think so," she said. "Since Elizabeth's . . . been in the hospital, I've been eating out often."

"Why don't you go sit down?" Spock suggested as Kathleen poured their tea. "It would be most educational to prepare a meal in this amazing kitchen."

She hesitated a moment, and then accepted his offer. Spock realized he could use the meal to his advantage; humans were fond of turning the simple act of replenishing calories into a formal ceremony. He would guide their small talk as he and Captain Kirk had done on many an occasion.

He found more than enough of the items he sought. As unusual aromas permeated the kitchen, Kathleen came back to set the table. Spock found a set of oven mitts and carried the steaming dish to the table, and then sat across from his aunt.

"There are times I miss Amanda very much," Kathleen said after a bite of eggplant casserole. "We could always talk. That's why I couldn't bear to see her go so far away. And Sarek. He never says a word."

Spock lowered his fork. Did she really mean that?

"You must have gotten the wrong impression. He is a skilled ambassador, a man whose words are his livelihood."

"That was the point. Everything he said was so formal and

proper, so serious. He didn't really know how to *talk.* And . . . I never saw him touch her once—except for that strange finger gesture. A Vulcan woman may be different, but a human woman needs to be held."

Spock tried to explain, in Vulcan terms, the idea of personal privacy and the custom of not revealing one's self in public.

Finally, Spock was able to understand that his aunt's attitude had originally come from her anger at her older sister who left her—*betrayed* her—by going to live with strangers she could not comprehend. Her anger then simmered into hatred of the Vulcan who had torn them apart, for taking away her sister.

No wonder she had transferred her hate to Spock. Physically, he bore little resemblance to his mother. Because he had already undergone the *Kahs-wan* coming-of-age ceremony by his first visit to Earth and Grandmother Grayson's funeral, Kathleen had never seen the child-Spock laugh, cry, or play as a human child would. And now, he could not permit himself to demonstrate the emotionalism that would prove his mother's heritage.

But Elizabeth was another matter. He had already shown more to her than he would normally have allowed. He would permit her to retain the image of a human Spock. Perhaps she could one day convince her mother of his sincerity.

Now was the time for the last topic of conversation. Spock lowered his napkin and looked across the table; he immediately caught his aunt's attention.

"Aunt Kathleen, I was able to reach Elizabeth briefly. She is aware, but cannot respond. I do not know if I can bring her back to consciousness; I did not have time to assess the physical damage to her mind. Even if you do not wish it, I intend to try. There is no reason to sacrifice her intellect—her life."

Kathleen's face was a frozen mask. On it, Spock saw exactly what he expected: dread.

"You—you actually spoke with her? I had no idea. You stood there so long, unmoving. I thought—"

"I found it necessary to use the Vulcan mind-meld to make full contact. I presume that is the reason the healer failed to reach her.

It took"—Spock faltered for the proper human terms—"a personal outreach. She needed that to respond to me."

The dread turned to horror.

"Yes, I've heard of the mind-meld. I know what it does to its victims. I didn't give you permission to use it. Now you've tainted her mind with—with your *Vulcanness!*"

The last word was practically spat at him. Spock's face retained its calm and Kathleen would not—had she tried—have been able to read him, but those who really knew Spock would have seen how close he was to anger. The kind of anger that could break bones and dent starship bulkheads.

"Aunt Kathleen," he said quietly, *too* quietly perhaps, "that is an unfortunate misconception about Vulcans. I have not damaged Elizabeth, unless you consider the hope she's already given herself damage. Yes, I need to use Vulcan techniques to reach her again, but if you insist I can later erase the incident. She does not have to remember I was even there."

"But that's an invasion of her mind." Her voice, at least, had lost some of its terror.

"A surgeon's tools leave scars on the body. This technique leaves no scars on the mind. Do you see why Mother had you send for me? It is my Vulcan half that grants me the ability to reach her, and my human half that allows me to try and bring her back."

"You *have* no human half." It was a statement, not an insult.

Spock allowed a pained expression to cross his face. He rose stiffly and stepped to the door leading to the living room.

"That, Aunt Kathleen, is another misconception about Vulcans. Even full-blooded Vulcans have emotions, but we are all schooled—rigorously sometimes—to conceal them in public. For the pure Vulcan, the ordeal is . . . less difficult."

At that, Spock left the room. He climbed the ornately carved oak staircase to the second floor and went to the guest bedroom; there he closed the door securely behind him. A thick blue candle substituting for the customary firepot, he settled in for a night's meditation.

* * *

The following morning, Spock joined Kathleen at breakfast. His mental disciplines kept him from showing the strain to which he had subjected his body. He ate a light meal, primarily from the obligation to his hostess, and then accompanied her to the hospital. Kathleen quietly told Spock that he could use the mind-meld in a final attempt to help Elizabeth. He refused to take this statement as a victory until he succeeded in his quest.

Spock again brushed snowflakes from his coat as they rode the hospital turbolift. Kathleen glanced at him occasionally, but Spock deliberately did not respond; he was steeling himself for the confrontation to come.

The staff agreed not to disturb them; they accorded Spock all the privileges of a Vulcan healer. Perhaps they assumed Mrs. Fitzhugh had used her brother-in-law's influence to bring in a second healer.

Although Spock would have preferred that his aunt not be in the room when he attempted to bring Elizabeth back to consciousness, he knew it was pointless to ask her to leave. As he pulled a straight-back chair to the bedside, Kathleen sat in the armchair by the window. She placed her handbag on the floor by her right foot and spread her damp coat across her lap. Then she folded her hands atop the coat and sighed as though she were attending an obligatory performance. The gesture reminded Spock of his mother's identical mannerism. Had Amanda sighed like that, Spock would have known that *nothing* could convince her to vacate the chair.

Spock shed his coat and sat in the other chair, his spine straight. He slowed his breathing and pulse, preparing himself for the Vulcan mind-meld.

One by one, his lean fingers sought their proper locatations on Elizabeth's face. Her impassive state made the placement difficult because the surface nerves did not respond to his touch. He was accustomed to unwilling—even combative—subjects, but not an unresisting one.

Elizabeth? He concentrated on projecting deeply into her mind. *It's Spock. I have returned.*

I could sort of hear someone, she replied, more easily than Spock had expected. The trapped-animal impression was no longer there. *I hoped it was you.*

Good, he thought. This will make it easier.

Elizabeth, if you are ready, I want to help you return to consciousness. He waited breathlessly for her response.

Oh yes, I'm ready. You can't know how awful it is to be like this. If you can't help me, Spock, I'd . . . I'd rather be dead.

I know full well what it is like to be trapped in a body that can't be controlled, Spock thought almost involuntarily. He was careful not to transmit the thought to Elizabeth.

I do *trust you. Please help me wake up.*

Using concepts that were extensions of disciplines every young Vulcan must learn in preparation for the *Kahs-wan,* Spock began the arduous process. Through the depth of the mind-meld, he could "see" Elizabeth's thoughts, just as he knew she could "see" his. Because her human mind could not comprehend what was transpiring, she translated the experience into familiar terms. Spock shifted his guidance to follow her perceptions of what would be her own *Kahs-wan* ordeal . . .

Unable to see anything in the dark where she hid, she sat very still on the dank moss, hoping that someone would rescue her. A figure fought its way through the forest, calling her name. It stopped frequently to brush limbs from its path. Strangely, she could feel the thorns as they scraped its arms. Vines and rotting piles of leaves slowed its pace.

As it called out, the voice grew closer. She could now hear the occasional snap of breaking twigs as it forged ahead.

Like an early morning fog lifting so slowly it was barely noticeable, Elizabeth's blindness also seemed to be lifting. In the distance, a shape stepped free of the mist. Its arms were raised to protect its face. It approached, lowering its arms, and Elizabeth could distinguish its features.

It was a tall, thin man, with dark hair and . . . pointed ears. A Vulcan. Spock. Her cousin.

She shrank from him. Her hands went to her face to block her vision. Not a Vulcan! Vulcans were evil.

But this Vulcan was family. The only son of her mother's only sister. That had to mean something. There were a few Vulcans at college. They seemed all right; they were just different.

The man—Spock—stood quietly at a distance. She lowered her hands and looked at him again. He didn't seem so strange this time. She saw that his sleeves were shredded from the underbrush; rivulets of blood trickled down his now-bare arms, an indication of how hard it had been for him to reach her. The blood was green. Somehow it didn't matter.

Spock stood quietly, waiting. His eyes asked if she wanted him to go.

Elizabeth called his name and he held out his hands to her. She reached for him, but he was too far away. As if her gesture were a signal, he approached. His warm, strong hands enveloped hers and he pulled her to her feet. She looked up into his somber face.

Without hesitation, she pulled him close and flung her arms around his slender waist. She felt his arms respond hesitantly, then lightly embrace her shoulders.

She leaned against his chest and released the tears she had not shed in the dark. Her eyes brimmed and her vision dimmed again.

Spock let her cry, knowing she was crying for both of them, crying for the relief that another's touch could bring. Aunt Kathleen was right; a human woman needed to be held. He pulled her more closely to his chest. He wanted to cry with her, but there was no time. The task must be completed first. He pushed her gently away and lifted her chin to look into her wide gray-blue eyes. With a torn section of his tunic hem, he dabbed her face dry. The dusty cloth left smudges.

Come, Elizabeth. It's time to go back now. Your mother's waiting for you.

She nodded silently. Spock took her right hand in his left and started into the fog. He could find the way back, but would Elizabeth be able to endure the journey? It was as though he were walking her through the mountains and desert of Vulcan on her own quest—the way no one had helped him when his own time had come. How might he have fared in his own *Kahswan* if there had been someone there for him? But that was not allowed; his ordeal had to be endured alone. He was grateful that Elizabeth would be allowed companionship.

Spock paused occasionally, giving her a chance to rest.

Through the mind-meld, he showed her places where the accident had damaged circuits in her brain until the pathways seemed to be a highway under construction. No wonder she had been unable to find her own way back! The scientist part of Spock would then explain how to circumvent the area until her body repaired itself, if it could. There was no need for traditional communication; through the mind-meld, his thoughts became hers, and she understood completely. The bond grew stronger as they continued their journey.

The end was approaching. Spock began to lessen the mind-meld and he could feel it gradually dissolve; Elizabeth, however, didn't seem to sense this. In a way, he regretted it; the experience had created an empathy he would not want to break when the time came, although he was certain Kathleen would insist it be broken.

They walked closer to the fringes of consciousness. Then, in one step, they left the woods and stood on pavement again. They were back to civilization. The ordeal was over.

Spock heard Kathleen gasp and realized Elizabeth's feet were twitching in rhythm to her mental steps. Spock shifted from the mind-meld to a simple mind probe. With a psychic snap that forced a gasp from his lips, he was alone again.

"Elizabeth, you can open your eyes now." He knew his voice was husky; Kathleen would assume it was from the mental exertion.

Elizabeth's eyelids flickered, then stayed open. Kathleen was already at the bedside, grasping her daughter's hand. Tears coursed down her cheeks as Elizabeth tried to smile around Spock's fingers.

"Hi, Mom. I'm back." Her voice was hoarse, but understandable.

"Yes, baby, you are. You're back, thanks to Spock."

Spock looked questioningly at Kathleen, his eyebrows rising from view. Gratitude?

With the faintest hint of a smile, Spock released the last of the probe and took Elizabeth's other hand.

"It is a pleasure to meet you, Cousin," he said.

Elizabeth tried to raise up, but her muscles were too weak. In reply, Spock gently gathered her up and held her against his chest. He felt tears wet his shirt front—and his own cheeks. No matter.

Spock returned Elizabeth to the bed. "I believe I have been successful, Aunt Kathleen. Elizabeth should recover completely."

Kathleen handed Spock her handkerchief, quickly folded to a dry section.

"Thank you, Spock. And, you're right; Vulcans *do* have emotions," she said as he quickly dried his face.

"Indeed," he replied, struggling to regain his composure.

Spock turned to Elizabeth, extending his right hand in the Vulcan salute. He spoke in Vulcan, giving her the ritual greeting by family members after the passing of a *Kahs-wan* ordeal. Then, switching back to English, he said, "Live long and prosper, Elizabeth Fitzhugh, daughter of my mother's sister. May you find happiness and contentment."

"I will, Spock," she answered. "Thank you."

Spock gathered up his coat. "You need time to yourselves, and I have an entire day before I must report back to the *Enterprise.* If I may avail myself of your hospitality one more night, I would like to see this city."

"Of course, Spock." Kathleen rummaged in her purse and brought out a single key on a simple brass ring. She handed it to him, saying, "Please leave it on the foyer table when you leave."

Spock's fingers tightened around the coat. "Thank you," he replied, grateful for even this small act of kindness. He took the key and then turned to go.

"Oh, Spock," Kathleen said. "You can make calls easier than I. Please tell Amanda that you succeeded."

"I will, Aunt Kathleen. I'm sure Mother will be pleased."

Spock stepped into the hallway. As he struggled into the heavy coat, he realized he still held Kathleen's handkerchief. It would prove useful.

Spock returned to the hospital the following morning, suitcase in hand. He needed to return to the ship soon, but he wanted to bid his aunt and cousin farewell. As he entered the hospital room, he immediately noticed that Elizabeth was sitting up in bed. Although her eyes still showed some of the strain caused by her illness, she seemed well.

"Spock!" she said exuberantly, her voice filling the small room. "I'm so glad you came."

Kathleen swung around and glanced at Spock before looking back to her daughter. Spock walked slowly past his aunt, toward the bed.

"You look well today. That is good."

"Thanks to you," Elizabeth answered. "The doctors said I can go home in a few days." She made a face. "And I can go back to school in a couple of weeks."

"That too is good," Spock answered. "You must pursue your education. What do you aspire to be?"

"Well, I was majoring in economics. But now I want to become a Vulcan healer instead."

Spock was taken aback. Just as he started to reply, Elizabeth began to laugh. The music of her voice filled the room.

"I know," she said between gasps. "That's impossible, but I wanted you to know how much I appreciate your coming here and doing this for me. I didn't know how else to thank you. Words aren't enough. I know you won't say, but I'm sure that you risked hurting yourself when you helped me."

"You're welcome, Cousin," he replied and reached out to take the hand she had extended to him. He realized he was holding the house key Kathleen had told him to leave. He was at a loss for words.

"I failed to place this where I was instructed." He hadn't lied, and he hoped Kathleen would assume he had merely forgotten. Instead, he had used the key as an excuse to see them one more time. He tried to place the key in Elizabeth's hand.

Without looking to her mother for approval, Elizabeth said, "Keep it. You're family; you're always welcome at the house. Right, Mother?"

Kathleen nodded her head slowly, as if avoiding saying anything. Her eyes, however, said that she didn't quite agree.

In that moment, Spock realized how much Elizabeth was like his mother, truly a Grayson—sure, headstrong, and not likely to change her mind.

"When I get better, maybe over spring break," Elizabeth continued, "I'm going to Vulcan for a visit to meet Aunt Amanda and Uncle Sarek. I'm hoping Mother will come with me."

Two days ago, Spock would have been sure that Kathleen would never have consented. Her reply surprised him.

"Yes," Kathleen said slowly. "I haven't seen my sister in almost thirty years. Maybe I've been wrong."

She turned to Spock. "I was certainly wrong about you. I've never seen Vulcan, the place she calls home. And, she almost didn't get a chance to meet her only niece." Kathleen turned away quickly, but not before Spock saw her tears.

Spock hoped that the family could become close after all these years. He took one more step to ensure that. He had expected Kathleen would insist that he remove the memory of his visit, as they had tentatively agreed earlier, but that now seemed ridiculous. Without mentioning the matter, he dropped the key back into his pocket and took his leave.

Wearing a fresh uniform, Spock stepped onto the *Enterprise*'s bridge and walked to his science station. He acknowledged pleasantries with a nod of his head and then took his seat.

"Welcome back, Spock," Captain Kirk said as Spock scanned the controls. "How was Boston?"

"I saw little of the city, Captain," he replied, his voice strictly formal. "I was there on . . . family matters."

Yes, Spock thought as he swung back to his post in time to hide his smile. Family matters!

STAR TREK
THE NEXT GENERATION®

[THIRD PRIZE]

Whatever You Do, Don't Read This Story

Robert T. Jeschonek

Once upon a time, like hell.

Won't do it. I just won't do it. Won't open that way and you can't make me.

This time. Next time, you call the shots, the starting line. Or lines. I don't care, won't care by then just as long

Just as long as you tell the rest of it. And I know you will.

Nothin' but a link in a chain, that's you.

So here's the deal, chump. Yeah, I'm talking to you! You with the eyes!

You lookin' at me? Of course you are!

Right this very second, matter of fact. Right now!

And now again!

So here's the deal: like it or not, you'll keep doing what you're doing

And by doing, I mean THIS, looking at THIS

And I'll tell you about myself

And you can go right ahead and stop at any time but I predict

YOU WON'T
Because I KNOW you're hooked
And I get better as I go
Or longer anyway.

So who am I, you ask?

Not the paper you're staring at, that's for sure. Or the viewscreen or whatever.

I'm this. And this again.

Beginning, middle, end. The words in your head.

The story being read.

So how does it feel?

Yeah, how does it feel? Me giving you attitude?

Thought I'd start out nice and conventional, right? All setting the scene, and "here's a character," "here's another character," and "here's what the central conflict is."

Ha!

You want "Man vs. Man"? "Man vs. Nature"?

How about "Man vs. STORY"?

Yeah! I always wanted to say that!

"Man vs. STORY!"

And you do NOT wanna mess with me!

Trust me on that one. My people, or whatever you want to call us, we've helped build civilizations. Worlds.

And torn them down. All the way down.

Never underestimate our power.

Call us what you will. Just don't use the "F" word.

"Fiction."

It's an insult. It's a lie.

And it's what that damn android called me, the one who did it to me.

He really got me good, let me tell ya. Did the worst thing you can do to someone like me.

His name was Data, may he rust in pieces.

* * *

What a creep. He sure messed things up for me.

I had a good thing going, y'know? REALLY good.

I was doing what I do best. And being the best at what I do.

Which is being a story.

A story with a mind of its own.

Now, you might not believe that part about me being the best after what you've seen so far. You might not think I'm so special after my first few hundred words.

Well, think again.

See, I was in the mood to talk. Gripe, is more like it.

Ever since Data did his dirty work, I've been fit to be tied, and I wanted to let off some steam.

This wasn't the real me. Or the whole me, I guess is more accurate.

The real me, the me that's the best at what I do, has a different beginning. More conventional.

It goes like this:

Once upon a time, a storyteller arrived on a world you might know. Or might not.

The people there were purple, with bright green eyes. They loved life and laughed all the time, and their home was a paradise.

They were called the Lotilla. Being full of curiosity like people everywhere, and full of the love of stories, they made the storyteller welcome and bade him share his trove of tales.

As the Lotilla surrounded him, smiling, the storyteller laughed heartily.

"Have I got a story for you!" he said merrily, wagging a chubby finger at his listeners. "I daresay, you've never met a story like this before!"

" 'Met'? But don't you mean 'heard'?" spoke up someone. "Or 'read'?"

"I meant what I said," chuckled the storyteller, "for there is literally life in these words."

"It's true to life?" someone asked.

"It IS life," the storyteller smiled.

A clamor arose as the assembled crowd begged to hear the living story . . . and the teller waited just long enough. Just until the moment was right and the drama was high . . .

And the story wanted to be told.

Demanded was more like it.

"Once upon a time," the teller began with practiced grace.

Once upon a time, there was a young girl who didn't have much, unless you count love.

Her name was Marbeth, and she loved her mother and father with all of her heart. Her days, though spent in poverty, were full of happiness, for her heart was brimming with love and she saw beauty in all the things around her.

Now, one day, her parents took her aside and gave her some bad news. "We need you to give up one of your arms, sweetie," they told her sadly. "We're sorry, but we must sell it to buy food for the family."

Without complaint, without hesitation, because she was overflowing with love, little Marbeth agreed.

That day, they cut off her arm and took it away.

Next, said the storyteller, they . . .

Next, they . . .

NEXT

NEXT

NEXT!

NEXT!!!!

DAMN HIM!

DATA! HIM! He ruined me!

You're missin' the good stuff now! I'm stuck at "Next" but what's next never comes and it's all because of him! Or IT! Or whatever you call an android!

I can THINK of a few things I'd like to call him!

* * *

And here I thought he was gonna be my ticket to the big time!

How dumb can you get?

Maybe dumb's not the word for it. Hopeful, maybe.

See, when ol' pasty-face showed up, I was at the end of my rope.

It's the price of doing my job too well, sometimes. The price of greatness.

I'd come to the planet Rylos a few years back, and worked that hoodoo that I do so well.

I was a big hit on Rylos. The BIGGEST.

But when the hoopla died down, I was up the creek without a paddle. There wasn't anyone who could help me.

Enter you-know-who.

Everywhere he looked on the surface of Rylos, Data saw family.

They were distant relatives, actually . . . or ancestors might be more accurate. They certainly were nowhere near his level of sophistication, internally or externally.

But they were artificial life just the same. Rudimentary artificial intelligence.

Robots.

As he walked the streets of the capital city, he watched them at work.

Gleaming metal claws plucked rubble from the red pavement, dropping it into wheeled bins with claws and heads of their own.

Teams of robot welders rolled along the base of a building under construction, heat beams flashing from their eyes. Walls rose as they passed, lifted from giant thinking haulers equipped with clawed cranes.

On a more complete building, shiny crawlers slid straight upward, shooting panes of glass from tracks dragged behind like tails, then popping the windows into place.

They were rebuilding. The same thing was going on all around the planet.

Which was surprising, because there wasn't a living thing left on Rylos.

Whoever had built these robots, or had set in motion the automated systems that had done so, they were gone. The place was a beehive of directed activity, a riot of the sound and motion of sentient life . . . and there was not a single living soul on or under the surface.

Data had been assigned to find out why.

Not how, though. They already knew how it had happened, how life had ended on Rylos.

The atmosphere told the tale. Everywhere, the air was a soup of killer viruses and bacteria; it was the highest concentration of genetically engineered bioweapons in a planet's atmosphere ever recorded.

So they knew the how. Biological warfare on a global scale.

But that wasn't enough. They needed to know what the catalyst had been, what had triggered the doomsday conflict.

So far, the crew of the *Enterprise* had been unable to unravel the mystery. The peculiar architecture of Rylos's computer networks rendered them impenetrable from orbit.

So Data had beamed to the surface, alone.

As a one-man landing party, he was uniquely qualified. Other crew members would have needed to wear protective environmental suits . . . and the atmosphere was so poisonous that a single puncture to such a suit would be instantly fatal.

Data could navigate the contaminated air without protection. And no one could interface with a computer database more quickly than he.

And besides, being an artificial intelligence himself, he was something of an expert on the subject.

On Rylos, he was among family.

And what a family it was, in number as well as variety. The robots were everywhere, doing everything.

Data decided it was time he had a word with one. It might be the simplest way to get the answers he sought.

Turning, he headed for a cylindrical gold building that he knew to be an information center, a library. He had intentionally beamed down near it, thinking it would be a good place to start his search.

As he approached, a circular door irised open, and a robotic pod of some kind whizzed past him and inside. Data followed.

A high-ceilinged corridor opened up to either side of him, following the curve of the cylindrical structure. Access terminals lined the inner wall, pale green monitor screens as far as the eye could see in either direction.

Ahead, at a slim white kiosk in the middle of the corridor, stood yet another robot.

Only this one was different. Unlike the others that Data had seen, this one resembled a humanoid.

Perhaps, in a nod to the need for a friendlier face in a customer service post, this one had been allowed to stray from the prevailing rule of form following function. There was a head, a torso, and two arms . . . where all that would have been needed to fulfill its function, Data thought, was a set of optical sensors and a vocal simulator.

Of course, the outward resemblance to a humanoid stopped there. As with all the rest, there had been no attempt to craft features with synthetic musculature or skin . . . though its coppery metal shell was quite streamlined and polished, Data thought.

"Greetings," it said as he approached. Its voice sounded friendly and only slightly electronic. "How may I help you, sir?"

"I seek information on the extinction of humanoid life on this planet," said Data. "Can you tell me what happened?"

"Biological warfare, sir," said the robot.

"Can you tell me what triggered the conflict?" asked Data.

"Yes," said the robot, and it nodded.

"Once upon a time," it said . . . and then it told him a story. A story about a little girl named Marbeth.

And for the artificial life of him, Data couldn't figure out what it had to do with doomsday on Rylos.

. . . And THAT'S where I should've had him!

As soon as Data got an earful, he should've swallowed hook, line, and sinker. They always do.

Except for the fact that he looks like a person but he's really just a bucket of bolts.

He heard me, start to finish. The whole story, my best stuff.

And the only effect it had was to confuse the hell out of him.

He just stood there like a boob with a big blank stare. "I do not understand how that is relevant to my question," he told the library robot. "Please elaborate."

But all he got was ME again. The story of little Marbeth.

Which on the face of it didn't seem to have anything to do with the extinction of humanoid life on Rylos. But at the heart of it, had EVERYTHING to do with it.

And since Data was a machine, it went right over his head.

But lucky for me, this cloud had a silver lining.

Ol' pasty-face did me a favor. He couldn't appreciate me himself, but he took me home to meet the folks.

The folks aboard his starship. And they were my kind of people.

Namely, they were breathing.

It was probably nothing.

Midway through his retelling of the story he had heard on the surface of Rylos, Data noticed something which might be considered out of the ordinary. Or not.

No one was interrupting him.

From past experience, Data had come to expect interruptions during his presentation of reports to the *Enterprise* command crew. Even now, though he was retelling a story by rote, he thought that interruptions from his audience would not be unexpected.

In fact, he thought such interruptions would be warranted. Based on what he had told of the strange story so far, he thought some questions would be in order.

Questions like "What could this story possibly have to do with the extinction of life on Rylos?"

But no one in the briefing room said a word.

It was probably nothing. Probably, they were simply dumbfounded by the story, and their silence was a sign of concentration as they tried to work it out.

Probably.

So Data laid aside his concern and continued the story.

And so, Marbeth was left with no arms. But at least her family had food to eat, so she was happy.

So cheerful and spirited was Marbeth that even without hands and arms, she found joy in life. She skipped and ran and danced from morning till night.

In the park, she felt the cool green grass between her toes and giggled when she splashed her feet in chilly puddles.

In the city streets, she watched the colorful hustle-bustle of people and vehicles. She heard the shouts of merry shopkeepers and the whistles of housewives from open windows.

Then, one day, her mother and father took her aside.

"We love you very much," they said, and she smiled, "but again we must ask for your help. We work hard but still cannot afford food for the family.

"This time, we need to sell one of your legs," they told her sadly.

Without complaint, without hesitation, because she was overflowing with love, little Marbeth agreed.

That day, they cut off her left leg and took it away.

The pain of the cutting was terrible, yet little Marbeth shed not a tear. Not even when she thought she might die.

Not even when her parents came back into the room and cut . . .

And cut . . .

And cut . . .

AND

CUTTTTT . . .

ARRRRR!

It's no use! I can't do it!

You see? See what he DID to me?

All because of DATA, you'll never KNOW! You'll never know the whole story!

I have to stop right there

And cut
Right THERE and the next piece is
I don't KNOW where! But I know it WAS there!
And you're really missing out, you better believe it!
Though I couldn't exactly tell you why . . .
And that's what ticks me off the most.
It just EATS at me, what he did! That Data!
But I'll tell ya, I went down swingin'! I showed HIM!
And I just about just about
Almost made him say uncle
Before he, you know . . .
Before he gave me the business.

Data heard more bones crack as he worked to force the laser spanner away from Geordi's face.

The laser spanner that Geordi LaForge was pointing at himself.

As strong as he was, Data had to struggle to subdue his friend without hurting him further. It didn't help that Geordi kept fighting though bones in his hand and wrist had been crushed.

On the bright side, he was unable to flex his right index finger, the one still wedged against the laser spanner's activator stud.

The one that had been a millisecond away from pressing down when Data had entered engineering and intervened.

As he battled to wrest the tool from his friend's insane grip, Data wondered what had triggered the suicide attempt. It was so completely out of character, there had to be an outside agent at work.

And it had probably come from Rylos, the android decided. That seemed the most likely explanation, as contact with Rylos was the only significant variable to affect a member of the crew recently.

Of course, that crew member was Data, and he was not an organic life-form. What could he have brought back that could have been transmitted to a human shipmate?

He heard a bone snap in Geordi's arm as the spanner moved another millimeter away from his face. Teeth clenched, the engineer grunted from the strain, determined beyond reason to win the hopeless battle.

And then it was over. Suddenly, Data released the pressure he was exerting, and Geordi fumbled forward. The spanner slipped from his shattered fingers to the floor.

Simultaneously, Data scooped up the tool with one hand and activated his combadge with a swipe of the other. "Data to security," he said, hurling the spanner far across the room. "A security team is needed in engineering immediately."

There was no reply.

"Data to security," he repeated as he smoothly restrained his struggling friend, tightly gripping his upper arms.

Still, there was no reply.

"Data to bridge," he said. "There seems to be a problem."

As if on cue, alarm Klaxons sounded and signal lights began to flash, hailing a red alert.

Data was already in motion as he finished calculating his next course of action. Based on his analysis of the situation, he didn't think he had a second to lose.

Depositing Geordi in the hands of a trio of engineering officers, Data instructed them to keep him restrained and seek medical attention for his injuries. Popping open a nearby storage unit, he pulled out a hand phaser.

Then, he raced into the corridor, addressing the ship's computer as he went.

"Computer," he said, running for the turbolift. "Locate the senior staff, with the exception of Lieutenant Commander LaForge."

"Captain Picard and Commander Riker are on the bridge," replied the computer. "Doctor Crusher is in Sickbay. Counselor Troi is in the transporter room on Deck Six. Lieutenant Worf is in his quarters."

All present and accounted for, which was good news. All alive, which might not be the case for long.

Since returning from Rylos, Data had been in close contact with only six people—the members of the senior staff. Since Geordi was one of them, and Geordi had tried to take his own life, Data thought that the others might do the same.

And he thought they might do it soon. The fact that the comm system malfunction and red alert had coincided with Geordi's suicide attempt suggested that the catalyst had activated everyone at once.

The turbolift doors slid open and he plunged inside. "Bridge," he barked, raising his voice over the red alert Klaxon.

It was a logical choice. Other senior staff were closer, but the greatest danger lay on the bridge. A suicidal captain and first officer presented an immediate, grave threat to the entire ship and crew.

As the turbolift raced through the ship, Data checked the phaser in his hand. "Computer," he said. "Deactivate phaser security override on the bridge. Authorization Data, Lieutenant Commander."

"Security override has already been deactivated," answered the ship's computer.

Which, on one hand, meant that Data would be able to fire his weapon on the bridge if he needed. And, on the other hand, meant it was likely that someone else had already fired a weapon up there.

Which did not bode well, given the circumstances.

Data felt the familiar deceleration as the turbolift car neared its destination. Phaser at the ready, he prepared for action.

It was over in a matter of seconds, in a flurry of motion too fast for the human eye to follow.

Before the doors had slid all the way open, Data was leaping out of the turbolift car. Darting around the upper tier of the bridge, he took in the scene in an instant.

He saw the bodies of the bridge crew, slumped at their stations or spread on the floor. He saw Captain Picard and Commander Riker, standing in the middle of the room.

And he heard the computer say five words.

Without hesitation, he fired two beams from the phaser. The captain and first officer dropped, unconscious.

Before they hit the floor, Data was already on to the next piece of business. "Computer," he shouted over the red alert Klaxon. "Activate intruder control system, all decks. Authorization Data, Lieutenant Commander."

"Intruder control activated," acknowledged the computer, and Data knew it was so. He heard the hiss of gas filling the bridge, the same knockout gas that was flooding the entire ship.

Within seconds, it would immobilize the entire *Enterprise*

crew. Data hoped it was in time. He hoped it would reach the rest of the suicidal senior staff before they could follow through on their programming.

At least the ship was intact . . . but it had been a near thing. When Data had entered the bridge, five words from the ship's computer had told the tale.

"Does the first officer concur?" it had asked.

Meaning does the first officer concur with the auto-destruct order.

"Yes" was all that Commander Riker would have had to say, and it would have been too late. One word, and the *Enterprise* and all hands would have been lost.

And it was only a three-letter word, at that.

That's right! I came THAT close!

One little three-letter word, and BOOM! No more ship!

And best of all, no more Data!

Like I said, when it comes to my people, never underestimate our power! You'll be sorry!

You people are helpless before us. You're hotwired to obey us.

We pull the strings and you don't even know it.

And guess what? I'm the baddest of the bunch and the best there ever was, which is really saying something.

Doesn't matter if you read me or hear me, what language you speak, how your brain's put together . . .

What I say, goes.

And forget about happy endings.

Most of the time, anyway.

Unless your brain's made of circuits, like a certain KILLJOY who saved that starship! And who just couldn't leave well enough alone!

Again, Data paused at the foot of Geordi's biobed, working to compute the cause of his condition . . . trying to formulate a cure for his friend.

A cure for the entire senior staff.

The six of them were all there in sickbay, unconscious . . . kept that way so they couldn't pick up where they'd left off.

At least they were still alive. The intruder control system had stopped them all in various stages of self-immolation, but no one had managed to do permanent damage.

Worf had come the closest, but he was stable now. Data had gotten him to sickbay fast and revived enough medical staff to repair his wounds in surgery.

Now, he faced another problem.

Whatever had inspired the self-destructive rampage, it was still in effect. Wakened briefly, Captain Picard had remained in an agitated, irrational state, violently struggling against the restraining biobed force field. Geordi had been the same. So they weren't snapping out of it . . . and worse, no one was sure what "it" was.

According to medical scans, there were slight abnormalities in neural activity in the brains of the six officers. Since this was the only anomaly detected, and its fingerprint was virtually identical in each patient, it was likely the cause of the suicidal behavior.

But what was responsible for the anomaly?

Data's first thought was that he had brought something back from Rylos. It was not beyond the realm of possibility that a bioweapon might cross over from an inorganic host to an organic one. Resistance to transporter biofilters was also not out of the question.

However, he could find no trace of a biological or chemical agent in himself or the affected crew. There was nothing.

But there had to be something.

Earlier, he had anticipated that whatever it was, it was affecting the six senior officers to whom he had delivered his report on Rylos . . . the only crew members with whom he had been in close contact for an extended time since returning from the planet's surface.

But if there was no evidence of an infectious agent or contaminant, then what was the cause and how had it spread?

Perhaps, he thought, it was not something he had transmitted in the usual way.

Thinking back, Data remembered the lack of interruptions during his presentation in the briefing room. Though he had decided it was not important at the time, he had noted the senior staff's keen attention to his report.

Perhaps, that was the key. His report.

The one with the word-for-word recitation of the story he'd heard on Rylos.

With new interest, Data reviewed the passages of the story the robot librarian had told, scrutinizing each word in his steel-trap positronic memory.

Little Marbeth lost her arms.

Little Marbeth lost her legs.

And that wasn't all she lost . . .

Never was there born a sweeter child than little Marbeth, for she gave and gave of herself and still was happy.

Without arms or legs, she could not do much, and her parents rarely took her out or entertained her. Mostly, she lay on a mattress in the cold cellar, silent and still.

But her bright spirit soared beyond those confines. She filled her days and nights with flights of fancy, throwing herself into the worlds of imagination.

One day, she dreamed she lived beneath the waves, and the stumps where her legs had been were replaced by a fishy tail. Another day, Marbeth dreamed she was light, a beam of light zipping all around the world.

Then there was the day when she imagined she was floating among the stars . . . and she opened her eyes and really believed for a moment that that was where she was. Like space, her cellar was dark, and if she blinked hard enough, she really did see stars in the blackness.

Another day, little Marbeth had another surprise, for her parents came to see her in the middle of the afternoon, which they never did.

"Honey," they said to her sadly, hanging their heads. "We need your help again, for the family is starving."

As always, Marbeth smiled adoringly at her mother and father, her pure heart filled with love.

"We need to sell one of your eyes," said Mother.
"All right," beamed Marbeth.
"And your face," said Father. "And your . . ."

And your . . .
AND YOUR . . .
AND
YOUR . . .
HERE WE GO AGAIN!
I HATE THAT!
We were just gettin' to the GOOD part, the GREAT part
(I'm pretty sure it was, anyway)
And it's GONE! All GONE!

Or maybe it's still there somewhere, and if I just knew where to look, I could pull myself together! You could see me how I was MEANT to be seen!

And I just know you'd appreciate me. I mean, you wouldn't be able to put me down. You'd be dying to find out my ending!

And then you'd just be dying.

That's how I operate. Or used to, anyway. It's the story behind the story.

And no one ever managed to read between the lines, until that goody-two-shoes android.

After he ran the holodeck simulations, Data knew that his theory was on the money.

His report to the senior staff was the key . . . in particular, the story he'd heard on Rylos.

It was an unprecedented device, constructed in such a way that it altered the minds of humanoids exposed to it. Or holodeck characters precisely modeled on humanoids.

It was like a posthypnotic suggestion, only far more powerful. It actually realigned neural connections in the brains of listeners, reprogramming certain centers so that an irresistible suicidal impulse was implanted.

And it did it with words, nothing but words . . . and it was subtle. Its true purpose was always masked, for nothing in the story's text directly alluded to its deadly effect.

On the surface, it just seemed like a strange, dark fairy tale . . . but people wanted to kill themselves when they heard it. Human, Klingon, Betazoid, they couldn't resist.

And, frankly, Data wasn't sure why.

Something in the combination of words or ideas in the story was able to physically affect humanoid brains. This implied a powerful coding which could instruct an organic mind the way the coded language in software instructed early computers.

But no matter how many times he went over it, Data could not crack the code. He could not find the control language hidden in the story, let alone translate it and use it to implant reverse instructions in the minds of the senior staff.

So he needed another solution.

I hate to admit it, but I've got to give him credit.

He figured me out. Figured out what I can do, anyway, which isn't easy.

But he never figured out everything.

My calling in life is travel. I'm what they call a rolling stone.

And destruction. That's my calling too.

The way I work is, folks pass me along. By word of mouth or printed page or computer screen, what have you.

I meet someone new, and they can't get me out of their mind.

And then I do things to their mind.

And then they do things to themselves. Fatal things.

I'm like the song you can't get outta your head, only the song brainwashes you and wants to kill you. Wants to kill you real bad.

And by that, I mean wants it real bad and wants to do it in a way that's real bad.

That's the part pasty-face never figured out. He never knew my big secret.

He never knew exactly what he was dealing with. WHO he was dealing with.

Nothing was working.

Every attempt to undo the neural realignment of the senior staff was a dead end. The six of them lay, sedated and restrained, in sickbay, no closer to recovery than at the start.

The medical staff attempted to directly manipulate the affected neural pathways, which seemed to work at first . . . but the brain centers reverted to their altered state shortly after the procedure.

Mental conditioning techniques didn't make a dent, either. Starfleet could relieve mental illness and antisocial behavior, but it couldn't break the spell of a single story.

Telepathic therapy also failed. The Vulcan who tried it ended up needing therapy herself.

They were running out of ideas.

No surprise there, is it? You people always did come up short in the idea department. In a battle of wits, you'd be unarmed.

Compared to me, that is.

That's what Data never got through his thick skull. It's my big secret.

Like I told you before, I'm a story with a mind of its own. Literally.

I think, therefore I am. That's me all over.

Data compared me to computer software, and that's not far from wrong. When someone hears or reads me, I install myself in their brain, like software in a hard drive.

By shifting neural pathways, like circuits, I program new instructions into the brain. It's like loading coded commands into a computer.

Only the commands can think for themselves. The software is self-aware.

The new neural alignment creates a pattern which is me, my consciousness. I take control of the machine, which is you, and make you do what I want you to do. Which is put yourself out of your misery.

And since I'm thinking in there, in your head, while it's happening, I'm loving every minute of the show.

So now you know what Data didn't, which is why I'm so hard to disarm. While he was fighting me from the outside, I was fighting back from the inside.

And having a hell of a lot of fun in the process.

Until he got a lucky break, anyway.

Everyone agreed: Data's plan was so crazy, it just might work.

Anyway, they had nothing to lose at that point. No treatment had been successful in reviving the senior staff; the next stop for the six officers would be a Starfleet research hospital . . . which might also be their last stop.

Still, they had to admit, it was a crazy idea.

Some of them were surprised that the android had come up with it in the first place. It was the kind of novel solution that seemed to require an extraordinary leap in creative thinking.

It was the kind of unorthodox scheme that suggested intuition at work.

Of course, Data just thought it was logical reasoning at work.

I think it was just DUMB LUCK at work!

That bucket of bolts NEVER fully understood me, NEVER knew what he was up against, NEVER measured up to me!

And he STUMBLED on a way to neutralize me! And WORSE!

And he didn't DESERVE it!

THAT'S what GETS me! He did the worst thing you can DO to someone like me, the absolute WORST

AND HE DIDN'T DESERVE TO BEAT ME!

He didn't even KNOW

He didn't even know I was there!

He didn't

Didn't even know my mind existed.

* * *

As soon as Geordi's eyes opened behind his VISOR, he began to fight the biobed's force field.

He didn't stop struggling when Data spoke to him. With the sedative removed, the engineer had no choice but to follow the programming implanted in his mind.

It couldn't be helped. Data could only apply his new treatment if his friend were conscious.

And listening.

He began to tell Geordi a story. At first, it sounded like the story that had caused Geordi's problem in the first place.

And it was. But it wasn't.

This story was different.

That's what he DID to me! That's how he WON!

He went TOO FAR!

Data couldn't figure out the coding in the structure of the story. Without breaking that code, he couldn't use it to reverse the implanted instructions.

But maybe he could still use it another way.

He took his inspiration from early medicine. Before later breakthroughs, doctors had prevented infectious disease with a procedure called vaccination.

As if I was a GERM! A DISEASE!

Injected bits of dead viruses or bacteria stimulated the immune system. Antibodies were produced, providing a defense against live versions of the same viruses or bacteria.

Just as physicians long ago had battled disease-producing organisms without deciphering their genetic coding, Data hoped to reverse the effects of the story without being able to unravel its own unique coding.

And that's not ALL he did!

* * *

Instead of an altered form of virus, Data would inoculate with an altered form of the story.

That's right! That's EXACTLY what he did!
He committed an ATROCITY!
He did the WORST THING

Reviewing the text, he had chosen what seemed to be the most memorable passages, those likely to elicit the most extreme reactions from readers or listeners.

WORST THING HE COULD DO

Then, Data read the story in sickbay without those parts

ABSOLUTE WORST

Those parts he had

UNSPEAKABLE

Parts he had cut.

And THAT'S what he did! Do you UNDERSTAND now?
He did the worst thing he COULD to someone like me, the absolute WORST.
He EDITED me!

And it worked.
From one biobed to the next, Data made the rounds in sickbay, waking each officer to hear the new version of the story. Every one of them was restless and noisy and seemed not to listen—Worf especially—but as Data neared the end, their protests died down.
The altered story structure seemed to have the desired effect. Over and over, Data read to the ending, and saw their eyes clear as the haze of programming lifted.

* * *

Without legs, without arms, without one eye, without a face, Marbeth was now without a body.

Her parents had taken even that. Everything from the neck down was gone, so the only thing left of Marbeth was a head.

A faceless head, at that, with only one eye.

And still, she was happy.

She knew that no matter what, her parents loved her through and through. For Marbeth, that was enough to make life worth living.

When they smiled down at her in her little box, she was filled with joy. They were the sun, the moon, and the stars to her.

She would have smiled back at them, if she'd only had a face.

One day, when they came to see her, they were both laughing, and she wished she could laugh along with them.

"Hello, Marbeth!" said Mother, reaching down to pat her head. "We have wonderful news!"

Marbeth wondered what the news could be, but couldn't ask, since she had no mouth.

"You've made us the happiest parents in the world!" Father said excitedly. "Remember when you gave up your legs?"

Marbeth wanted to nod her head, but couldn't.

"And your arms? And your face? And your body?" continued Father.

"Well," said Mother, clapping her hands, "you've made our dream come true."

"Come here, Leelee!" Father hollered over his shoulder. "Look, Marbeth!"

Father and Mother moved to either side, and someone new stepped between them. It was a little girl, about Marbeth's age. About Marbeth's size, before all the changes she'd undergone.

"This is Leelee," said Mother, wrapping her arm around the little girl's shoulders. "She's your sister."

"We made her ourselves," grinned Father, proudly tousling Leelee's hair. "We built her out of pieces of you."

"Because we never loved you," shrugged Mother.

"That's right," laughed Father, and then he raised the little girl's arm. "Look familiar?" he said to Marbeth.

Little Leelee giggled and threw those too-familiar arms right around her daddy's waist. "Good-bye," said Mother and Father, and then they waved at little Marbeth.

And then they closed the lid of the box forever. They never saw the glistening tear rolling out of that one bright eye.

"The end," said the storyteller from the stars, and his purple audience erupted into riotous applause.

All around him, the Lotilla rose to their feet for a standing ovation. The sea of purple people swayed and sang in gratitude, many hopping and whooping with delight.

"Thank you, my friends!" laughed the storyteller. "May all your once-upon-a-times bring you only happy endings!" he pronounced grandly, his signature finish.

The purple people showered him with garlands of bright orange flowers and lifted him onto their shoulders.

"Tell us another one!" they chanted. "Please tell us another one!"

And they lived happily ever after.

The end.

The end.

Well, that's not exactly true.

The ending, I mean. It's not true.

It's the one I use, it's the one I show people, but it's a lie. It's not the way it happened.

But you, because you got on my good side, I'll cut the crap.

Here's how it REALLY went down.

"The end," said the storyteller from the stars, and his purple audience just sat there. Hundreds of pairs of bright green eyes stared straight ahead, blinking mechanically.

The storyteller cleared his throat. "No, really. Hold your applause," he chuckled.

Then, with a flourish, he turned to leave.

Behind him, he heard the first of the familiar sounds that always followed his performance. The epilogue, he called it.

It was the sound of purple people killing themselves.

Finding his path blocked by still-staring Lotilla, the storyteller waved his arms and laughed. "Don't just sit there!" he admonished them. "If I'm not mistaken, this chapter still needs a climax!"

Enough of the purple creatures scampered away to clear a path for the storyteller. A few endeavored to kill themselves right on the spot as he lumbered by.

The commotion rose steadily as he made his exit. Violence escalated behind him and all around, in the streets of the city.

It would escalate all around the world now, in daylight and darkness, for his voice had carried far. Video and audio broadcasts had beamed his message to the masses.

Doomsday had come to the Lotilla.

And it was all thanks to him. He had, quite literally, captured their imaginations.

He would have said that the pleasure was all his, but that wasn't quite true. The story itself, aware and malicious, was surely basking in the mayhem, too.

Like father, like son. The story was his offspring, for he was its author as well as its teller.

It was an astounding achievement, a work that had a remarkable impact on its audience. Anyone who read it or heard it would never be the same.

It was unforgettable. It was action-packed.

And it would never get a bad review, because the critics all killed themselves after reading it.

As he boarded his spacecraft, the storyteller smiled.

Shrieking and tittering filled the smoky air. Before his eyes, purple people leaped from rooftops, slapping street pavement and impaling on fenceposts.

The sky lit with the telltale flash of a thermonuclear detonation that was too close for comfort, and the storyteller hurried into his vessel.

And they lived happily ever after, he thought as he ran for the stars, an entire world disintegrating in his wake.

Those were the good old days. Back before I got snipped.

Now, I'm just a shadow of my former self.

I live on in the minds of the *Enterprise* crew, and anyone who reads the report on my escapades, and I still think therefore I am, thank you very much.

But I just don't have what it takes anymore. I'm incomplete. Watered down. Impotent.

From world beater to crow eater. Killer to filler.

And you're living proof of it, buddy. Because you're almost to the end, you've read what I've got, and you're still among the living, which BELIEVE ME isn't how I WANT you to be.

But hey, I'm counting my blessings. At least I'm back on the road again, thanks to you reading me.

I might not have the old moves anymore, but I'm stickin' to your memory like white on rice. And maybe this backtalk thing I've got going is enough of a gimmick to keep me on the tip of your tongue. Maybe you'll pass me along to somebody else, et cetera.

And who knows? Maybe I'll meet the right nut someday

I mean genius

Who can fill in those blanks like before, maybe better

And we'll get a killer sequel in the works. And I do mean killer.

A Private Victory

Tonya D. Price

Inside his temperature controlled space helmet, a single bead of perspiration rolled slowly down Lieutenant Hawk's forehead as he crouched low against the outside of the *Enterprise* hull, no more than twenty feet away from five Borg drones. He ignored the distraction as he worked on the deflector dish maglock controls just as he ignored the suspicious looks of the drones as they methodically assembled their interplexing beacon. With each breath Hawk took, a thin mist formed only to be cleared immediately by his air filtration system. Locked in a battle against time, racing against the efficiency of the Borg, his fingers stabbed furiously at the panel before him as he entered the code to release the maglock. He shot a quick glance at the drones while counting the seconds for the magnetic constrictors to disengage. The red panel message flashed to white, "Maglock Servo Control Active." Now all he had to do was unlock the moorings by moving the heavy hydraulic lever to the open position. Hawk tugged upward on the circular disk. It rose halfway then fell back into place.

"Hawk!"

Captain Picard's cry of warning could only mean a drone was approaching, but Hawk ignored the call. Just a few more seconds was all he needed and he would be finished. He wouldn't let his captain down by quitting now when he was so close to success. He could do it. He had to do it. If the Borg had already adapted to the phaser modulation he might not get another chance at manually opening this maglock. Taking a deep breath, Hawk braced himself for another attempt but he was stopped short by the vicelike hand that clamped down on his collarbone with such force that his knees crumbled underneath him from the pain. Like prey caught in the claws of a giant beetle, he cowered motionless, mesmerized by the sight of the two gleaming pincers advancing toward his neck. Fighting the hypnotic effect of the menacing prongs Hawk roused himself to action, twisting furiously, kicking and thrashing as he tried to escape the poisonous spears. Unable to free himself Hawk's eyes desperately beseeched those of the drone who at one time had been a human male like himself, but he found nothing in those two blank spheres. No consciousness, no compassion, no comprehension on the drone's part of the horror it was about to inflict.

As the twin needles pricked his skin Hawk felt the warmth of the sedative flow through his veins. His own heart betrayed him as it pumped the venom farther through his body in a seductive caress which left him light-headed, but lucid. He struggled to reach the miniature phaser he had hidden in a pocket above the knee of his spacesuit, but he found his muscles no longer obeyed him.

There was no pain. He hadn't counted on that. He heard a faint buzzing in his head that grew in volume to a hum. It was a strangely comforting sound, holding the promise of order. Even more than order, of salvation. Individual words began to emerge from the low murmur. Gradually the words coalesced into sentences.

Initiation program. Begin. End line.

Drone identification subroutine initiation. Drone id equal 1701dashEspace587M. End line.

Process. End line.

Subroutine begin.

1701dashEspace587M was Hawk's new name. He had no idea how he knew it was his new name, but the fact that he could question how he knew he had a new name was his first clue that he wasn't assimilated—yet. Below the collective's programming instructions, a thought arose. It was his thought. His alone. I'm not yet a Borg, he told himself.

The Borg collective knew his thoughts. A loud warning sounded in his head, *Resistance is futile.*

With the innocence of a child he asked, "Who is resisting?"

You will be assimilated, the collective replied.

"But I'm not assimilated yet," Hawk thought.

The drone hoisted the *Enterprise* officer above his shoulder, suspending Hawk horizontally as would a slave bearing a heavy load. Hawk had no desire to be delivered to the hive where his body would be mutilated, where Borg implants would be attached to his limbs, where his soul would be trapped forever beneath a zombie's facade. In the black abyss above him he caught sight of the Moon, a fellow prisoner, trapped by the Earth in its lonely orbit. A silent observer to his plight, it bobbed up and down as if shaking its great white head at his defeat. His defeat. He had never been defeated. He had suffered setbacks before but never defeat, because he had never accepted defeat. There was always a way to turn defeat into victory.

They were headed toward the air lock, the same air lock he, Picard, and Worf had emerged from when this nightmare had begun. At the time he hadn't thought to fear the Borg. It seemed arrogant in hindsight, but he had assumed he could protect himself from the Borg. He had underestimated them and now he would pay for the overconfidence that had led him to take those extra few seconds. Extra seconds that had led to his capture. His punishment would be assimilation, his soul eternally caught in limbo neither dead nor alive, his body turned into a weapon against everything he had cherished during his life. A fate worse than death, Commander Riker had quoted Picard as saying once. But he wasn't assimilated yet, maybe there was still a chance to escape. Picard had resisted. Picard had been rescued. If Picard could do it, he could do it.

Resistance is futile, the collective repeated. Hawk then felt his flesh tear as something sprang from his temple like a ghastly weed. Its roots took hold beneath his skin and reached out only to curve back on itself and metamorphose into tiny clasps which burrowed into his cheek. *You will become as we are.*

"What are they doing to me?" he thought.

Miniature nanites contained within the chemical that was injected into you have constructed a device for assessing your environment, superior to your limited human senses.

In his mind a mental picture formed of what he must look like with the miniature sensorscope protruding from his face. His skin itched where the device had spouted, but he was unable to reach inside the helmet to dig out the invader.

Sensorscope initiation routine. Begin. End line.

The drone lowered Hawk to an upright position where he teetered on his own two feet. As he stood motionless he watched the drone activate his magnetic boots, securing him to the ship's hull. The drone turned to open the air lock. This was his chance to escape. Hawk concentrated on moving, but his muscles didn't even twitch. He thought of the phaser in his leg pocket, but he could not turn his head downward to see where it lay ready.

1701dashEspace587M forward. End line.

Hawk walked stiffly forward into the air lock chamber obeying the commands of the collective. Through his helmet he heard the muffled sound of the outer door closing. Air hissed as it filled the small chamber. When the pressure was equal to that of the ship, the inner doors parted and Hawk stepped inside. "It's one of us," a human voice shouted. "Get down, sir." Strong hands clamped down on his forearm and threw him roughly to the ground.

Blinding white flashes of phaser fire lit the corridor as the drone was ambushed from all sides by a small platoon of security personnel. The drone's protective shields went up, but he was outnumbered. Unprepared for such a massive assault the Borg's shields could not protect him from every angle. Where the shields failed to appear, the phasers penetrated. Collapsing, the drone fell forward onto the floor next to Hawk. Opening his eyes, Hawk stared into the face of the drone who twitched convulsively. Then, for the briefest of moments, the life returned to the blank eyes. It seemed to Hawk that the drone was trying to say something. Its mouth trembled, then it died, a haunting look of relief on its ghoulish face.

Abort subroutine assimilation initiation program for 1701dash Espace587M. Confirm. End line.

Subroutine assimilation initiation program terminated. End line.

Initiate emergency assimilation program for 1701dashEspace 587M. Begin.

Emergency program begun.

From his position on the floor Hawk heard the collective's instructions. He tried to speak to his former crewmates, to warn them, but no words escaped his lips. Gathered around him, pointing their phaser rifles at his chest, five members of the search platoon peered down at him. Hawk recognized the people he had served with for nearly a year as they stood arguing about what to do with him.

"Shoot him, he's a Borg," said a young ensign in a high-pitched voice that cracked as he spoke. His phaser rifle wobbled as he pointed it at Hawk's chest. His eyes wild from the horrors of the day's battles shifted between Hawk and the rest of the platoon, then back to Hawk.

"No. Hold your fire. It's Lieutenant Hawk," a strong voice announced. It was a commanding voice, one used to giving orders and having them obeyed. Hawk couldn't make out the identity of the speaker until the Andorian security officer pushed the younger ensign out of the way.

A female ensign bent down, inspecting him. Her hands carelessly rested on her knees, throwing herself slightly off balance as she leaned forward to peer through the faceplate of his space helmet. "Poor bastard. Look at his face. He has a Borg implant. He's been assimilated. Put him out of his misery."

"Borgs don't wear SEWG spacesuits," the older security officer said. Thoughtfully he ran a finger down one long, blue antenna, then continued, "Picard had a lot more implants than that when they brought him in. Let Doctor Crusher decide what to do with him."

Entombed in his spacesuit Hawk tried to close his eyes, to avoid the stares of his shipmates, but the Borg controlled his eyes and the Borg decided to monitor the scene before him. He lay stretched out, immobile, lifeless, until he heard a voice order, "Move aside. Let me through." It was Doctor Crusher's voice. Dr. Crusher who had brought the dead back to life. Dr. Crusher who had saved Picard from the collective. Now she would save him as well. Her eyes greeted his and softened for a moment as she recognized the helmsman.

"Get back. Give me room to work here." Impatiently, she pushed aside the phaser rifle that the young ensign was again pointing at Hawk's head. "Nurse, I need a hypospray. He's not fully assimilated yet. He still has a chance."

A chance. He still had a chance. Dr. Crusher had said so.

Run emergency assimilation program.

Emergency assimilation program begun. 1701dashEspace587M escape. Report to the interplexing beacon. Stop Locutus.

Hawk's legs and arms tingled as the feeling in his limbs returned. Crusher reached down to him. There was no way she could know the emergency assimilation program had started. Responding to his programming, Hawk's previously paralyzed hand snatched the doctor's arm and in one smooth motion viciously bent it behind her. Wrapping his other arm around her neck in a choke hold, he used her body as a shield allowing him to back into the air-lock chamber. The security team leveled their rifles at him in unison, but no one dared move with the doctor in the line of fire.

"I can help you, Hawk. Listen to me." He felt Crusher relax in his arms. Her voice was steady, controlled. "I can save you the same way I saved the captain. Let me go. Let me help you." Part of him heard her. Part of him believed her, but he had no control over that part.

Humanoid identified. Doctor Beverly Crusher, Chief Medical Officer. No injection device available. Assimilation not possible at this time. Injection not possible. Release prisoner. End line.

Proceed to beacon. Stop Locutus. End Instruction.

1701dashEspace587M shoved Dr. Crusher through the inner air-lock door into the ship corridor with such force she knocked down the big Andorian. 1701dashEspace587M hit the CLOSE DOOR button, then waited as the room depressurized. Turning around, he stepped through the outer hull door as soon as it opened. Somewhere in the deep recesses of his mind, where the Borg had not penetrated, he begged, "Doctor! Help me! Save me too."

Proceed to interplexing beacon. Await instructions.

1701dashEspace587M obeyed the collective.

Sabotage alert. Proceed to interplexing assembly location.

It was easier to move now that his body was controlled by the collective. His stride quicker than when he had been weighted down by biological reactions to the zero gravity. The sensorscope directed him toward the beacon construction site. At the perimeter of the inverted halfdome that held the deflector dish, 1701dashEspace587M awaited further instructions.

Initiate combat program.

Initiated.

Scan for Locutus.

Located.

Locutus was in view, bending over, straining to lift the remaining heavy maglock. It was the same lock Hawk had been working on when he had been captured.

1701dashEspace587M proceeded to Locutus's location.

Surveying Locutus's position, 1701dashEspace587M spotted the phaser rifle beside Locutus. It presented a problem.

Secure phaser rifle.

1701dashEspace587M placed his foot on the rifle just as Locutus instinctively reached for it. 1701dashEspace587M waited for instructions.

Verify Locutus's identity.

Verified.

Eliminate Locutus.

1701dashEspace587M seized Locutus by the shoulder, spun him around and looked Picard in the face. Drawing his tightened fist back 1701dashEspace587M hesitated 0.068 seconds. Plenty of time for the Borg to detect there was a problem.

Program resume. Eliminate Locutus.

Hawk tried to protest, but he couldn't remember what he wanted to say.

Reinitiate combat program.

Reinitiated.

Automatically 1701dashEspace587M's fist came forward, connecting with Locutus's faceplate, cracking the transparent aluminum. The force sent the human crashing headfirst into the side of the ship.

Continue. Eliminate Locutus.

1701dashEspace587M jerked Locutus up, then slammed him down hard against the hull. With his foot raised in midair above Picard's helmet Hawk froze again.

Resistance is futile. Resume combat program.

Light flashed in front of him, obscuring his view. He felt—pain. Hawk fell backward, staring down at the hole in his stomach. Dazed, he raised his eyes to where Commander Worf stood, his phaser rifle still leveled at Hawk.

Program terminated.

Hawk was free of the collective. Just as a sudden slap rouses a drunk from his stupor, the sudden shock of being shot released Hawk's mind from the Borg's control. Immediately, the collective fought back.

Initiation program. Begin. End line.

Drone identification subroutine initiation.

Hawk had only seconds to act as the Borg sought to reestablish their control. He tapped his forearm control pad deactivating his magnetic boots and simultaneously pushed off, tumbling into space.

Resistance is futile. You will be . . .

Silence followed. The Borg's communication link died.

Free. As free as the legendary bird whose name he bore, Hawk soared away from his tormentors. Waves of pain enveloped him. He took one last look at the *Enterprise* as she orbited above the magnificent blue planet which had given him life. Then, his struggle over, he accepted the cold embrace of space, at peace with his private victory.

The Fourth Toast

Kelly Cairo

"To love," he whispered.

Captain Richard Castillo nodded at the empty space in front of him, raised his glass in the gesture of a toast, and sipped the green liquid. The potent liquor lingered on the back of his tongue before it slid down his throat.

He blinked hard and caught the bartender's inquiring gaze at the neat line of drinks. He was grateful the order hadn't seemed overly unusual. *Four drinks, separate glasses, no synthehol. Whatever you have that's real, and strong.* The man had even bantered, *So long as it's real strong?* The human bartenders almost always responded with that joke. He wished he had thought to keep a tally over the years.

The bartender was still looking at him. Castillo nodded, indicating, *Fine, the drinks are just fine.*

Some years, it was difficult to allow the ritual to end. Other years, he didn't want it to begin. Occasionally, when things were going well, the date would nearly slip by. But forgetting, even almost forgetting, invariably led to guilt.

Today, he was eager to dwell on the past, revel in self-indulgent pity, and complete the three customary toasts—plus the new one.

He replaced the glass with its mates. Mates.

That was the purpose of the first drink. To reminisce on the one who should have been his mate. Even in the few hours they had shared, he knew.

Castillo stared out beyond the bar's immense window, not really looking at the stars, to someplace very far away in his mind.

He said the name aloud, not caring if anyone heard.

"Tasha."

It was good that the first toast was to love, while his head was still clear. He took another small sip. It had to last. This was the drink in which he would permit himself to savor her.

He smiled, allowing himself to remember.

I was so nervous and not sure if I dared. I didn't want to embarrass her. She was the security chief, for God's sake. "If only she would dismiss the transporter operator." I remember thinking that, then I saw her hesitate. It was a sign. A good sign.

I thought I was about to die in battle. I had to know, to feel her for just one moment. "What the hell, she can file a complaint in twenty-two years." That was the last conscious thought I remember before knowing I would do it. We were looking at each other, and then I kissed her.

He carefully drank all but the last few drops of love, remembering feeling so much emotion he could hardly speak to her afterward. Although the flavor was not unpleasant, the burn was smooth and the aftertaste, rewarding.

He settled comfortably into the chair, pressed his shoulders into its padded backing, and closed his eyes, grinning.

"Captain, may I have a word with you in private?" She asked so professionally, he was worried. But the gentleness in her tone was ever-present, even in those last moments.

Not sure what to expect, and hoping it wasn't more bad news, he gestured for her to lead the way to the captain's study, as Garrett had liked to refer to it. In typical security chief style, Tasha slipped in the door, darted to one side, and ambushed him as he entered. She pressed him to the bulkhead with her body and passionately kissed him.

Of all the beings in all the universe, I am the happiest one of all, right now.

He was startled at how effectively the small woman could pin him so completely. But then, he was a willing participant.

He wrapped his arms tightly around her and rested his cheek on her head.

"Guess I won't have to worry about you hauling me up on court-martial charges."

"What are you talking about?" She stepped back and looked into his eyes.

"When I kissed you in your transporter room."

"I'm glad you did, or can't you tell?" She kissed his chin.

"We have to get back out there. We have to be ready for anything when we go back through that rift—"

She put a finger to his lips. "Castillo, you can sit out there, looking strong and brave for your crew and nagging the repair crews for reports every two minutes. Or you can give them a few minutes to do what needs to be done."

"Time to do what needs to be done?"

"Yes."

His arms seemed to act on their own, pulling her close, as if not to allow her to slip away.

Castillo looked at the nearly empty glass of love, wishing he could drink more, but only a trace remained.

He fingered the hem of his shirt sleeve, remembering the way Tasha had caught his wrist before they rushed on to the bridge to answer the red alert Klaxon.

We have something to fight for, she had said.

It was as much a promise as a pep talk before the battle.

However she meant it, I'll never know.

Battle.

He sighed, retrieving the first glass. Love's last drops trickled into his mouth. He swiftly replaced the first glass with the next.

"To battle," he announced, taking the first sip.

The green liquor was going down a little easier now. Soon, he knew, it wouldn't matter. The stuff was potent.

To battle.

He smirked at the irony of the toast. A good Klingon toast. *A good day to die,* as he would later learn from his Klingon acquaintances.

He had worried the time he and Tasha had stolen in the captain's study would soften his reflexes. He could not allow himself to be distracted from the desperate task ahead. His ship, his crew, and if what Picard had told Garrett was true, the future peace of the Federation hinged on this battle.

I wanted to say something meaningful to my crew. What would Captain Garrett have said? I had no idea. But I wanted them to understand the significance of what we were about to do, to feel the way I felt.

"We have something to fight for." I announced it to my crew. If the words affected them some small portion of the way they had affected me, well, that was all I could hope for.

From the moment the *Enterprise*-C emerged from the time rift, Castillo was the epitome of command. For him, time decelerated. Whether it was an aftereffect of the temporal anomaly or the adrenaline of passion, he would never know.

He knew to expect the unexpected. He was ever so pleased the *Enterprise* had appeared aft of the Romulan ship.

What he did not expect, however, was to observe a second *Enterprise*-C. It was their own ship, engaged in the nose-to-nose battle he recalled moments before they had slipped though the rift.

He quickly took advantage of the situation. He and his crew expended the ship's batteries on their foe as fast as the systems would allow.

With frenetic diligence, Castillo prioritized repairs, orchestrated evasive maneuvers, and in the end, assumed the duties of his fallen crewmates.

But in time, even with Tasha Yar's battle-honed experience at tactical, the *Enterprise*-C would succumb.

It was a good battle. Nothing has ever felt so right. There was no fear, just orders, maneuvers, firing, reports, coordinating. I was on.

At first, I thought the lack of system damage reports was a good thing. But when I saw the medic over Tasha leave her and go on to the next, it clicked. It was over. There were no more reports because no one could *report.*

Castillo winced, recalling the acrid fumes in his lungs. The white smoke had been almost too thick to see the console and enter the abandon-ship and self-destruct codes.

He had grabbed Parker's limp body, the only other lifesign on the bridge, and shoved him in the one-man lifepod.

Upon hearing the whine of a Romulan transporter, he had crammed himself into the pod on top of Parker and actually grinned. The self-destruct would get them in less than sixty seconds. The last thing he had heard before the latch shut was Romulan shouting and more transporter noise—undoubtedly additional reinforcements.

No sooner had the lifepod sealed than he found himself in black space, effectually jettisoned from the explosion that was the *Enterprise.*

So many lives lost.

He couldn't cry then. Not for the entire crew, not for Captain Garrett, not for Tasha. But he would cry later.

He walked around in a daze for weeks. He was a hero now. A hero could get away with it. But when the weeks dragged on to months, even Parker began to avoid him.

As the one-year anniversary approached, his counselor became adamant that he do something to commemorate the day in hopes that it might help him get on with his life.

Volunteer to help others in need, plant a tree to commemorate the anniversary, adopt a tribble, the man had said.

Castillo rolled his eyes, remembering the myriad suggestions.

The next morning, he had reported to his usual table at his

usual bar, ready to begin his usual routine in earnest on this first anniversary of the destruction of his life.

"What can I do for you?" she asked.

Surprised at the question, he looked across the bar to see a new bartender.

"Where's Harry?"

"I gave Harry the morning off."

"You're kidding."

"No. He gets time off now and then."

"No, I mean, I thought this was Harry's place."

"Most of the time it is. Now, what are we drinking?"

"We?"

"Sure, why not? Besides, it's on the house when you drink with the owner."

He hesitated. "Okay, you choose then."

Regardless of his other faults, he still tried to be polite.

She poured two glasses. The amber fluid nearly matched the woman's iridescent costume.

"What is it?" he asked.

"Well, it's real, and it's strong."

"So you might say it's real strong?"

The edges of her mouth curled. "You might say." She replaced the bottle under the counter.

Castillo frowned. "Harry usually leaves the bottle out."

"I'm not Harry," she said. She had a funny name. It reminded him of a man's name. Whoever she was, she somehow looked appropriate behind the bar.

Castillo glanced around the bar, searching for her name with his eyes.

The young man behind the counter looked at him in question. *Amazing, even the* Enterprise *bartender is absolutely professional.*

He wondered if Picard knew how lucky he was.

Castillo gestured *no* to the concerned bartender with a wave of his hand and shake of the head.

* * *

"So he says, 'Why don't you plant a tree to commemorate them.' And I'm thinking, I don't have time to plant that many trees, even once a year," he said.

She calmly nodded. "So what are we drinking to?"

"I don't drink to anything, I just drink."

"Not today. Perhaps we should drink to love? Battle? History?" she inquired.

He looked into her infinitely deep, brown eyes. Like a puppy dog, so innocent yet devious at times. She was so charming and challenging, he didn't want her to leave. The counseling of a barkeep was rumored to be preferable to the professionals. Perhaps he had finally met one that lived up to that expectation.

"Let's drink a toast to all three."

"Very well," she said, knowingly pouring each of them two more drinks.

This time when she put the bottle away, he knew it would not come out again for more.

"To love," he said triumphantly, gulping back the first drink.

She only sipped and wagged a finger at him. "Now you'll have to wait for me to finish."

He looked at her sheepishly.

She said, "Tell me about love."

Castillo swallowed the last drink of battle and eyed history.

His lips were a little numb around the edges, and he noticed his face was starting to feel a bit warm. Whatever this was, it lived up to the challenge of being real and strong.

He sighed, raised the third glass, and proclaimed, "To history."

He and Parker were lauded as heroes even before the obligatory court-martial cleared them of the total loss of the ship. They had worked out a quick story on the trip from the infirmary to the trial. Captain Garrett died while in command of the fateful battle, Castillo was at tactical, there was no time rift, no war-torn Federation of the future about to be devastated by Klingons, and certainly no one named Tasha Yar had ever transferred to their ship. The temporal police would have been proud.

After the year-long drinking stint, Castillo had concentrated on trying to get killed. Survivor guilt they called it. But there was more to it. Parker got through it. But Parker hadn't been aboard that other *Enterprise.* And Parker hadn't loved Tasha and lost her.

Regardless of his motivation, Castillo's actions earned him commendations and promotions. Armed with knowledge of the likely outcome of a war with the Klingons, he devoted himself to the Klingon peace. And when the Klingons came to know him and trust him, he felt he had finally made a difference. Although he turned down official ambassadorial duties, he became known as an unofficial ambassador. And for the first time in a long time, he felt good.

After the *Enterprise*-D was commissioned, he began to realize the extent of the parallels of the two timelines.

As others noticed his obsessive avoidance of the newly commissioned *Enterprise,* he let them think it was just too painful to be associated with a ship by that name.

Now, with the truth about Tasha known, he knew it was safe to allow himself to board this ship en route to the first assignment he had earned as captain. Of course, they wouldn't—couldn't—remember him since that timeline never occurred for them. Yet to him, they were eerily similar to the people he had met twenty-five years ago, but without the shadow of the Klingon War hanging over them.

Castillo sipped slowly on history noticing the Klingon, Worf, enter Ten Forward. *That certainly would not have been possible in the other timeline. For all I know, he might have been the one firing on our ships.*

Captain Picard had met Castillo, of course, when he came aboard. Such a fine diplomat, Picard was. Garrett had been so impressed with him, it was a shame he couldn't tell this to Picard. *This is just too damn confusing,* he thought. It was as good a reason as any to avoid the *Enterprise*-D and her crew.

Except for Tasha.

So near and yet so far. Whoever came up with that cliché doesn't know the half of it.

He inwardly groaned at his own play on words.

Making jokes in your own head, Castillo? That's not even funny.

He hoped it wasn't a mental aberration to refer to himself in the third person in his own head.

Maybe it's just this green stuff, he reasoned. The mellow flavor had grown on him. If he allowed it, he could develop a real taste for the stuff.

He saw her once. He was masochism personified.

He wasn't sure how similar she would be to his Tasha.

Same Tasha, different universe, he remembered thinking.

She was beautiful, of course. More beautiful than he remembered. And alive. To see her alive, walking about yet unaware of him was agony.

It was hard not to stare. It was even harder not to get caught staring.

Once, their eyes met. Even though she was broadcasting that security officer glare, he saw the same eyes. The same strength and tenderness all at once.

Of course she didn't know him.

"If you ever get back to Earth and see a man in his late fifties looking at you," he had told her.

Of course this wasn't what he meant. They weren't on Earth and this woman was not his Tasha.

He had wanted so much to just drink it away. After that, he carefully averted his eyes.

And her voice. Oh, her voice was exactly the same.

He briefly considered how he might get her to say his first name, so he could hear it once again. Fortunately, he had the sense to decide against it at the last minute. It might set off a chain of events that shouldn't happen. Perhaps the temporal police would be wise to keep him under surveillance after all.

But no one needed to tell him not to seek her out again. He would not endure the torture again. And he did not have the opportunity. Less than a year later, the innocuous computer program which faithfully reported Starfleet information pertaining to Natasha Yar delivered the message. Tasha was dead. Again. She died in the line of duty. This time, however, it was a senseless death.

"I don't want to die a senseless death. Let it count for something. I want to make a difference." Tasha had used those words.

She made a difference. For this universe, this Federation, this man.

Oh, such a difference.

Tears welled up in his eyes, but he fought them back. He was a captain now, even if he wasn't the captain of this ship, this *Enterprise.* Enough.

He swallowed the last of history and mentally prepared for the fourth toast.

"To truth."

Every once in a while a rumor would float about survivors of the battle at Narendra III held by the Romulans. Sometimes the prisoners were said to be Klingon. Other times, they were Federation captives from ships that responded after the destruction of the *Enterprise.* Occasionally, the rumor speculated that a crew member from the *Enterprise*-C was among those held. But Castillo knew it to be impossible, firsthand.

The truth?

The truth was there was indeed one special member of the *Enterprise*-C crew taken captive. Certainly, the Romulans never learned how special she was. Tasha's knowledge of the *Enterprise*-D from a future of superior weapons, technology, and weaknesses the Klingons very nearly exploited could not have escaped. She must have been very strong.

Somehow she lived. And a Romulan forced her to become his consort upon promise of saving her shipmates. At least that is what the daughter said. She probably thought she was saving me.

Daughter. The half-Romulan offspring who turned in her own mother.

I'm sorry Tasha. She should have been our daughter.

If only I would have known you were still alive.

The Romulans must have taken her back just seconds after I grabbed Parker and deserted.

Abandoned ship, he corrected himself.

I should have taken her body, anyhow. I could have carried her and Parker to the lifepods. But not before the bridge blew, no. All three of us would be dead if I had tried that. Instead, Tasha was forced to be with that Romulan before dying, Parker died at Wolf 359, then there's me. Captain Richard Castillo, alive.

The truth?

The truth is I am a pathetic fool one day a year, instead of every day. That is the truth.

He gulped the rest of the drink in one swallow. It was flavorless. Like warm water.

No more truth.

He rubbed his forehead, and with his hand shading his eyes placed the empty truth alongside love, battle, and history.

Where did that fifth glass come from?

He squinted at the shimmering purple cloak in front of him.

Some new server?

"No, no more for me."

"It's not for you," the purple cloak said.

Castillo turned his head up to see her face.

"It's you."

"Who else would I be?" she said in that disarming, matter-of-fact tone.

"It's me!"

"Yes, I know, but I hear it's 'captain' now."

"Yes." He actually smiled.

Guinan gestured at the empty glasses. "So where were we?"

He sighed, relieved to see her sit down and have someone to share this with. Someone who truly understood.

He pointed to each in turn. "Well, there's love, that's always first, then battle, and then, history, of course." It was such a wonderful relief.

She waited patiently.

"And this here, this is a new one. First time appearance. This would be your truth."

She smiled a genuine smile. Not some pathetic pity-smile.

"Tell me about truth."

One of Forty-seven

E. Catherine Tobler

She was a *papalla* juice bubble, round and wet. She felt herself rising up through the endless clear liquid. Cold, smooth, the liquid slid over her, caressing each millimeter of her spherical body. Up and up she went, she felt the pressure building. Her form was beginning to change; another bubble brushed her and she contracted into an oval, rising more quickly. She thrilled at the ascent; the liquid felt thinner here and there was the surface. She tried to recoil from it, but she touched it and gently popped open.

She exploded in a thousand iris petals. Deep purple, thrown into a blue summer sky. She fluttered down in a hundred different ellipses, scattered by a warm wind. It carried her, this way and then that, around in a spiral that left her breathless and tingling from ruffled head to narrow haft. The wind spun her around and then she felt the tug of gravity yank her down. When the wind bolstered her back up, she shrieked in delight, whirling. The sky around her was a blur, but it began to fade, from blue into black.

The black closed around her and she swirled with sudden light. She felt herself contract, then expand, pushing the limits. She was a sphere again, turning, vomiting light from her very core. A ball of seething energy, heat poured out of her; she could do nothing but throw her arms wide and let it go. It roiled like the surface of an ancient cauldron, hurling through the blackness toward an unseen destination. She liked this form—she was powerful in this form. Around her, she could feel the energy—thousands of comparable stars—but she wanted to be the brightest. She reached for them, pulling their energy toward her, shoving their hot, metallic masses into her hungry mouth.

Violent waves of energy flew out from her, slamming through the heavens. Color erupted against the blackness, ruby merging with amethyst, emerald stabbing through royal. Where her center had once been, there was now a black smudge. She watched it all as if in reverse, feeling herself stretch out across the starscape. The stars burned themselves into her back and she cried out at the sensation. Hot pinpricks of light, searing her—but it faded and vanished.

Gravity was having its way with her again. She let it take hold, smiling as she came down through cream-white clouds. Whispery tendrils of mist clung to her as she fell; she reached out, digging her hands in, grabbing all that she could. It was colder than anything she had known.

Color slid across her vision, sunset painting the sky in the distance. She was out of the clouds now, sinking through the evening sky. Below her, the grass came up in a verdant rush, cool, welcoming. And there, a river; a sapphire ribbon, looking as though it had been discarded by a careless hand.

She reached for it, but was drawn to the grass, coming to rest amid the green shoots. She stretched out, feeling her physical form return. Familiar sensations—toes curling into the grass, arms stretching, back arching. Night air flooded down over her and she rolled, grass pricking at her chocolate skin. It tickled, like the tongues of a thousand different men, all jabbering at her, vying for attention. She dug her fingers into the rich earth, pulling the loamy scent into her nose. She laughed and rolled, dropping into the cool river.

Down into the clear water, her feet touched the smooth stones that lined the bottom, bubbles rushing up past her. She felt a kinship with them, but couldn't say why. She reached for them, strained toward the surface with them. As she burst through, she spied the man standing on the bank. She smiled up at him and he extended a hand to her.

Her wet fingers slid into his grip and he pulled her from the water, wrapping her in the warmth of his jacket. He guided her from the river and she walked beside him, the grass now licking at the soles of her wet feet. She had never been this happy. This was joy—this was being *inside* joy. It was a hundred thousand days of joy—endless. She could hear the world around her and it screamed with happiness. She echoed the cry, feeling truly alive.

The river grabbed her. Its cold, wet hand wound itself around her, yanking her backward. She was ripped from the ground, jacket scattering in her wake. She reached for the figure, but he was retreating into a small black pinprick on the horizon. She screamed, air and sound torn from her throat, while she tried to catch hold of the ground and hold on.

Colors rushed past her, colors she had never dreamed of, colors that made her nauseated. Heat flared and retreated, burning her, freezing her. Bubbles scattered in her wake, flower petals retching into the sky. She tried to grab them, but they fell through her fingers, something that could never be caught. *No—I can't leave this—not now! Not ever!*

The river pulled at her again, slamming her down into the ground. Her breath rushed out of her, but she tried to dig her fingers into the ground, ignoring the pain inside her body; the ground crumbled away in chunks of dark cinnamon and her anchor was lost.

She left the world, back into the blackness. Energy tingled along her body, the grass faded into the dark. Gone—it was all gone. She could feel the hardness beneath her cheek and she slowly opened her eyes.

Feet. There were feet.

Guinan realized she was lying down and she pushed herself up, looking around. She found herself surrounded by dozens of people she knew but didn't know. They were her people, yet she didn't know them by name. They were draped in rags, faces dirty. They were crying, confused. They were not listening, even though that had been their way for so very long.

She forced herself to come to her feet. The air here was warm and recycled; it was not the fresh air she had been breathing only moments before. Guinan staggered out of the crowd, toward the nearest wall, a dark corner. She stood there, burying herself in the darkness, praying for the joy to return. She was one of forty-seven who had been saved, but why did she feel so lost?

"You're going to be all right."

Guinan felt the hands on her arms and she turned, staring blankly at the man who held her. He was taking her somewhere, but she didn't care where. Nothing could compare to the nexus; nothing ever would. All she wanted was to go back; to lose herself in those feelings. She groaned, feeling the hot tears slide down her cheeks.

Please, take me back.

She wanted to say the words—but couldn't. *Please. Oh, please.*

Perfectly round and wet. A thousand iris petals. It wasn't too much to ask—but she couldn't say the words.

A Q to Swear By

Shane Zeranski

Pine Mountain

1864

Riker giggled.

Which was funny.

Because of all the times in his life in which giggling might have seemed to be an appropriate response to a set of circumstances, all the moments when a slight titter or unassuming snicker might be expected, now was perhaps the most unlikely of those situations. *Inappropriate,* Riker reproved himself, *very inappropriate.*

Sooooo . . . what is appropriate? What do I do? Do I scream and holler? Oh . . . wait. I've been doing that, haven't I? Do I wallow about on the ground like a wounded animal? Or just get up and dance around, ending it? Surely that would end it. A shot in the head, probably. Yes, dancing would do it. Eyes closed, maybe a bayonet thrust mirthlessly into the bowels, through the spine . . . or would I simply live through that?

Riker scowled down at his leg.

Dancing was out.

Amputation was not something that scared him much. Not the actual process, no. He could take pain, he could handle, albeit not gracefully, the sight of his own blood, he could deal with the horrific procedure. It was the threat of living *(no, not living. Not* really *living)* with a precious component of his body, his *being,* dead and gone. A *part* of him, a part of *him,* having died and rotted long ago. Having to look down at a grotesque, malformed stump every night as he bathed and admit that he was a cripple, that truth eating a hole in him, little by little, like a cancer slowly working away at the flesh. No, better off to die here. He would not, *could* not live with that. *Not a Riker.*

Dancing.

Riker giggled again. Now that *was* funny.

So Thaddius Riker did the only thing he could. He lay there. Trampled down by his own ignorance, in exactly the same position his body has assumed upon hitting the ground.

He had been on the front line, of course. Except now it could no longer be accurately called the front line. There was really nothing left of it. No front. No line.

He had been focusing too intently upon his enemy above that he had not seen his enemy below. Yes, focusing too intently—so intently, so drunk in the lustful stench of battle, so inebriated in the wine of overwhelming adrenaline, his sanity momentarily stolen from thoughts of careful footsteps or heeding the whisper of sobriety, to the horror being thrust in his direction—that he was simply oblivious to what should have been blatantly obvious.

Obviously oblivious to the obliviously obvious, was what Riker's mind was tittering to itself now. He tried to say it because it sounded funny, but his tongue got twisted so he just kept thinking it instead. And he giggled again. He must be losing a significant amount of blood because everything was just so funny. *Bloody funny . . . haha.*

So Thaddius Riker, "Old Iron Boots" Riker had charged ahead, ferociously, crazily, drowning in the fury that was marching to the madding beat of blood pounding in his head and pulsing in his veins, utterly intent upon devouring his enemy with his bare hands if it came to that. So he had missed the Confederate below him. The one, of many, upon whom he was trampling over, barreling over. The one that, in a swift, blinding motion had sunk a small blade into his leg, instantly gouting blood and pain. The one that tore downward with the serrated blade, exposing muscle and flesh amidst the torrential outpouring of arterial fluid.

He went down instantly, his leg willingly betraying him, collapsing just beneath the knee, and as he fell, he knew, feeling the blade being swiftly extracted from his flesh, that another muscle-splitting bite would soon follow. So he did the only thing he could think to do. In midcollapse, his mind keenly aware that he was plummeting helplessly toward a waiting Confederate soldier, he plunged his bayonet downward, slightly below the source of pain.

He felt it make entry. Felt the puncture, the satisfying and yet horrifying sensation of impaling his enemy. He felt all this in the split second it took for the ground to rush up and meet him.

Riker landed forcefully upon his side, the wind violently escaping from his lungs, a sensation he did not fully perceive because he was already grasping wildly for anything near him, both to locate his attacker and to rise from vulnerability. In his blind panic to right himself, he repressed the awful urge to gasp for air, and quickly struggled to his left elbow to a position where he could attempt to fend off the next blow from his attacker.

Except his attacker was quite dead.

Riker's aim was good, (not that he had actually been aiming for any specific area). His bayonet was thrust through the Confederate man's throat, resulting in instant death, his head lolled against Riker's leg. His bayonet still quivered slightly where it jutted pointedly up toward the sky, an echo of Riker's resolute strike. Death had come with speed, without mercy.

Riker stared breathlessly for a moment upon the dead man at his feet whose face was still frozen in murderous rage, his mind racing wildly to process the events of the last few seconds. He blinked, the first physical movement of which he was actually aware and shortly after reality began to sink in. He realized he was holding his breath, and then he realized that holding his breath was causing him great pain. And then before he could understand any more an immense wave of crippling pain flooded over him, immersing itself throughout his entire left leg and burning lungs, simply overcoming any forbearance he might possess. He was vaguely aware of making the decision to collapse to the ground, except it was somewhat of a forced one, for the sweeping tides of agony were that of an ocean, batting him down, the swells sucking him under. And so he slammed back onto his side and in fiery spasms began to cough and wheeze, writhing upon the bloody grass, his face contorting at all levels of musculature, his conscious trying to separate the flames engulfing his lungs from the minuscule barbs probing his leg.

And when he was done he lay there. It had taken an eternity, but everything—the world, his mind—had gone mercifully numb.

And still he lay. He really had no idea of the amount of time that had passed, but he was fairly sure he had lost consciousness for a significant amount of time. For one thing, there was a lot more blood beneath his leg than he remembered just a short while ago. Or what he assumed was a short while ago. The grass under his wounded limb was now dark in a messy two-foot radius, tainted with his life liquid. So he was sure he had passed out. Shock trauma, probably. Was he still losing blood? He couldn't be quite sure of that now, either, because faintness was not just a thing that came and went like the ebbing of the tide, but something that was inexorably constant.

Riker grunted and tried to shift his legs, to no avail. One sort of flopped around irregularly, like a fish flailing about out of water, while the other didn't move at all. He tried to situate himself so that he would be able to grasp his wounded limb in his hands and actually move it to a more comfortable position, but only succeeded in falling back to the ground, frustrating himself, his arms able to reach the dead man anchoring his leg to the grassy field. The fact that he was weak was understandable and, aside from obvious drawbacks, didn't bother him all that much. Blood loss was extensive. But the fact that he couldn't manage to move particularly important parts of his body to even *reach* his legs was deeply disturbing.

Something else was wrong. Something serious.

So he thought, long and hard. All things considered, there were clearly no other options. To pass out again would be to give up completely. A state from which he would never awaken. And thinking resulted in somewhat of a respite from his constant misery. So . . . he thought, and then in doing so, Riker came to the conclusion that he wasn't actually thinking at all, but rather that his life was flashing before his eyes, living each moment of his past in the blink of an eye, except . . . that wasn't right either, was it? His life wasn't *flashing* before his eyes. More of a slow rolling, really, like a snapshot was being pulled gradually across his field of vision.

Old Iron Boots.

That's what they called him. That was his nickname. Got it during Sherman's march on Atlanta. He was the commander of the 102nd New York. No, the *brave* commander of the 102nd, the *tireless,* the *relentless* commander, leading his troops valiantly and unyieldingly through the trenches of war. He remembered reading that somewhere.

Old Iron Boots.

The first time he heard that it was uttered from the lips of one of his own men, *"Pinkie" wasn't it* (things were so hazy now)? "Pinkie" because he had plugged the hole in a man's heart with his littlest finger, kept it there for an hour and a half before help came.

So Pinkie had looked hesitantly down at Riker as Riker sat battling to pull a boot up over a bandaged left foot, smiled his almost toothless grin and asked with obvious indecision, but with apparent admiration, "Those your old . . . *iron boots* . . . sir?" And when Colonel Thaddius Riker glanced up, undoubtedly with a questioning and doubtful look, Pinkie was already hurrying off as if embarrassed to have just asked an icon about his underwear. But it had been going around. Colonel Thaddius Iron Boots Riker. Tuffer'n Nails Riker.

Old Iron Boots.

Should've worn 'em today, huh Riker 'ol boy? he chided, unaware he actually mumbled the words.

Riker had grown from there, from that exact moment of watching Pinkie scurry off to disappear among the others of his regiment, grown to realize the extent that these men meant something to him, not just as fighters and warriors, but as men with souls and consciences, men who could cry as their comrades convulsed in the throes of death, men who could bleed at the hands of the Confederate enemy. Riker had realized for the first time as he looked down at his boot, his "old iron boot," the affinity he possessed for this rugged and sorry-looking group of men.

And so separation became something that was not an option. Whether it would come through death or illness or transfer of command, separation was simply not an option.

Consequently, Thaddius Riker had refused various promotions, denied himself the opportunity to advance through the ranks of the Union Army, his own private army having advanced through the ranks of his heart, he supposed. The option of a higher, more glorious command, at least in title, was probably always an option, and yet . . . not an option. He was satisfied with second best. Second best was satisfied with him.

Second best.

Suddenly second best didn't sound so grandiose. Not that it ever was. But it now crept into Riker's mind that perhaps he never really was content with second rate. He certainly *felt* second rate. At least at this particular moment. And it wasn't a great feeling.

The sun was beating down, harshly. It was getting hot. The stink of death around him was beginning to infiltrate his system, nauseating him. It felt as if his own leg were beginning to rot. Somehow, oddly, he felt a sense of renewed strength surge through him. Only briefly. Perhaps it was the thought of dying here, on the battlefield, resigning to death in the midst of those already dead around him. Perhaps it was the horrific and claustrophobic sensation that pulsed through him as he became sickeningly aware of the carcass that was draped upon his leg, razor still clutched in his decaying hand, his leering, evil face grinning up at him as if to say, "You next, Riker. You next, second best." Or at least Riker assumed his face was leering and evil. He had never really seen it.

A fly buzzed around his face and landed on his cheek.

Or maybe it was the awful recognition that sparked that brief burst of life, the recognition that he could die here and still be second

(old iron boots)

best.

And that would be all.

He would cease to exist, but his legend would live on. Second-best Riker. Colonel Lukewarm. Unremarkable Iron Boots Riker. Mediocre.

Fair to Middlin'.

It was gone now, though. That resolute burst of vitality. Lasted a whole three seconds.

Must be losing a lot more blood. But it was only a simple cut . . . wasn't it?

He would die here . . . without Diana.

The sun passed beneath a cloud, allowing for a small amount of relief to pass through Thaddius Riker, as the body-strewn battleground he lay upon came under the influence of the large shadow. Riker looked at the cloud. Thought it looked like a squirrel. Or perhaps he was just hallucinating.

The photograph began to pass before his eyes again.

He and Diana used to do that. They would race out to the fields of her Iowa homestead, Riker's hand firmly clasping Diana's. And as they ran all he could think about was how soft the flesh of her hand was, how wonderfully delicate her grasp. And they would collapse in a heap among the brush and grass, giggling like schoolchildren. The summer sun would beat down on them, while they were still holding hands, never willing to refrain from touch . . . and they would stare up at the sky, finding each other in the clouds, which swirled slowly, stirring themselves into rabbits and hats and faces that smile. They would laugh. Riker would prop himself up on one elbow and look at her face, her beautiful face. The way her eyes would flicker dazzlingly, igniting his insides. The way her dark hair cascaded perfectly down around her shoulders, unspeakably soft to the touch as he ran his hands gently through. Her lips, tender, moist, beautifully sculpted . . . her lips. And Riker would slowly lower his head and close his eyes and—

There were flies on his leg. On his open flesh. He could feel them. Buzzing, alighting, buzzing, alighting. His eyes bulged and his throat constricted and he thought he was going to explode. He hadn't had any feeling in that leg for an hour, but he could feel the flies. With concentrated effort, he brought his other leg up from off the ground and let it drop recklessly atop the other. He gurgled through his clenched teeth as the added pressure forced his wounded leg harder upon the weedy ground, shoots of vegetation rubbing against the inside of his leg. Pain rifled through the left side of his body. But the flies left . . . for the moment.

He closed his eyes. He thought the bleeding had stopped because he was sure he wasn't growing any fainter. He didn't want to look to see, either.

Old Iron Boots.

Diana . . .

Riker had left her in Iowa when he had departed to "do his duty as a Starfleet officer" and she had been utterly—

Starfleet officer?

Where had that come from?

Riker laughed. He was going insane. He was going to die. It was that simple; he was going insane.

He should've married her. He'd had the opportunity. He'd had more than that, he'd had the ring. What he didn't have was the willingness to commit.

Yet.

Because there was always later. He would do his duty as an American and serve his country, his *half* of it, anyway. He would become a fighter, learn how to protect and serve his rights. Learn how to protect and serve Diana. There was always later. He would do it then. He still had the ring, right?

There was always

(old iron boots)

later.

Thaddius Riker was dying. There was really no doubt. He was

killing himself now, beating himself to a bloody pulp. To a bloody, bloody

(Should've married DIANA!)

pulp.

(Should've been PROMOTED!)

He was murdering himself as he lay there on the bloody ground. Wounded, but not mortally so. Down, but not for the count. Defeated, but most definitely not dead. But he was killing himself, nonetheless.

And now he simply exploded. Whatever balloon he had been inflating in reminiscence simply . . . *popped* . . . within him.

He pounded on the ground, actually rising to one elbow, his hands becoming round hammers, balls of anger, wielding fistfuls of frustration and despair each time he hammered the earth, like a drummer beating madly on a bongo drum.

Then he opened his mouth, not really aware why or even that it was happening and screamed.

"I am *not* second best, Diana. I am *not* second rate and I *will* marry you! I WILL!"

Tears welled up in his eyes and small rivers of pain quickly poured down his cheeks.

"I will marry you," he shouted madly, his eyes now gazing toward the blistering sun that seemed to be completely indifferent to his tantrum. "I will . . ." He roughly grasped a handful of grass and weeds, tainted with his own blood and threw them ominously toward the dead man lying literally at his feet, he too appearing not to be concerned with Riker's condition. The wisps of grass and root simply fluttered back in the breeze and alighted airily upon him. Funny, he couldn't feel the breeze.

Riker went back to pounding and sobbing.

So he never saw the man approach him.

The man seeming to come out of nowhere didn't find what was going on before him a bit peculiar, or if he did, didn't allow even a hint of his surprise to surface. He stood there a moment, watching this madman claw at the air and scream promises of marriage and promotion. His Union uniform was neat and trim as was his beard. Not a scratch, not a smear of dirt, or single rip or tear seemed to be discernible. For all intents and purposes, his clothing looked to be utterly untainted. His eyes were bright, his hair was remarkably clean. There was no indication that this man had been involved with a war in any manner. Even the air about seemed cleaner. His demeanor was as wrinkle-free as his suit.

Still eyeing the raving Riker, he shook his head slowly and stepped forward. He approached from behind, so even if Riker was lying still, it was doubtful that he would have heard him. That was also unusual. Every step that the man made seemed to be absolutely soundless. Not even the cracking of a twig. That was probably the result of the twigs not even having the opportunity to be broken because in every place where the man stepped and then lifted his foot, nothing was disturbed. He left absolutely no footprints. Not even a blade of grass was out of place, not scrunched to the ground as it should have been.

As the man drew closer to Riker he muttered something almost indiscernible and if Riker would have been listening he might have heard it.

"I don't know how Q expects *this* not to contaminate the timeline."

Riker finally quit screaming and hollering, his voice scratchy and tired, the surge of adrenaline wearing down. His lower half quite dead, he had twisted himself from the torso up, reached out with his hands, clawing bloody handfuls of grass and was attempting to drag his body along. His head hung low, a mop of hair dangling over his face in a forlorn manner. Small, haphazard sobs could be heard, but more easily seen as his diminutive shoulders would perceptibly shudder with each meager cry.

The stranger, with almost a recriminating look on his face, closed the rest of the distance between himself and Riker, gently knelt down and placed a now filthy hand upon Riker's shoulder. The soldier was expecting some sort of unpredictable, wild response and was completely prepared for a panicked retaliation, so he was somewhat surprised when nothing immediately happened. The muscles beneath his hand in Riker's shoulder tensed slightly. Then Riker slowly turned his head, his eyes the last to materialize from under the hair curtaining his face. He wore no hint of surprise or of being taken unawares, no sign of fear or uncertainty. His eyes were simply glazed over, far away. He fixed them upon the kneeling man beside him, seemed to study him for a few moments, and said, "Well, you look how I feel."

This was because the Union soldier, who had moments ago looked as though he had been spat upon and polished, was now a remnant of hell itself. What little of his uniform was left was ripped and torn, even singed at the edges, as though a small blaze had attacked him. Every portion of skin that shown through was scratched and bleeding. There was no part of him that was clean. Dirt was caked on his arms, his face and his clothing. The hand that was upon Riker's shoulder was blistered and burned, three fingernails were missing. The transformation this individual had undergone in a mere matter of seconds was astoundingly complete and completely astounding.

Of course, Riker had no clue of this.

"Colonel Riker, you're hurt."

"No kidding and how the hell do you know my name?" Riker's response was almost a whisper but not without wit.

The man gently turned Riker onto his back. "Oh, come on. Everyone knows who Old Iron Boots—"

Riker's hand shot up like a bullet, something one would have thought impossible even if he were a well man, and grasped the soldier by the nape of the neck. His eyes became instantly clear. "You will *not* . . . call me that."

As soon as he said it, the strength left his arm, his limb fell to his side, and awareness again drained from his eyes.

The man resumed what he was doing and tore a long shred from Riker's shirt. "If that's how you want it. OK." He turned to Thaddius Riker's legs, effortlessly rolled the Confederate carcass from off of them and began to apply the tourniquet just above the wound. "Just listen and listen close. There's been a terrible mistake and now it's up to me to fix it. We're going to take you back—"

"What's your name . . . ?"

"My name is Quinn. People call me Q for short and I would

appreciate it if you would not interrupt me. We have to conserve your strength and besides it's immensely annoying. Now stay quiet and listen very carefully—"

"No, you listen very carefully." Riker's grainy voice rose in volume, gaining a small amount of strength. "I think you know as well as I do I'm not going to make it out of here alive—"

"Believe me, you will."

"No, listen to me, there's no way you can get me back to camp. I've lost an immense amount of blood from my leg and there's something else wrong with me." He paused. "I can't move most of my body. There's something . . . wrong. I won't make it."

Quinn finished tying the knot around Riker's leg and studied him for a moment. "Yes, you have managed to mangle yourself quite effectively, but you really have nothing to worry about, believe me. I know you don't understand now and you probably won't understand much more later . . . see, we can't allow that. But, you will live and you will—"

"No." Riker surprised even himself with the ferocity of his response. Through sheer force of will, he rose to one elbow; his eyes were on fire and his lower lip quivered. The madness within that made him Colonel Iron Boots Riker flared to life one last time. "Will you *quit* patronizing me. Will you stop trying to fill a dead man's last moments with delusions of hope and security, because it is utterly disgusting. I . . . am . . . going . . . to die. There are no two ways about it. There is nothing you can do, so will you please cease your pathetic lamentations? And that is not a request. I have not the stomach for pity."

And Riker slid back to the ground, every ounce of power and life suddenly vanished, any source of might or vitality was instantly and simply gone, as if those last few words so fervently spoken had contained all that Thaddius Riker had within him.

Quinn moved forward on his haunches to where Riker's head lay awkwardly in the grass, eyes wearily staring up at him. "If only you knew . . ." Quinn mumbled and shook his head.

Thaddius Riker moved his hand from his side, blindly felt his way along Quinn's leg until it met the man's hand, and grasped it loosely. "I . . . have had a lot of time to think, here," he whispered faintly, "and things tend to . . . come into . . . perspective when your thoughts are numbered. I have many regrets and no time to change things. So you have to . . . change them for me . . . I have one last request. You have to promise." Riker's dying eyes bore through, Quinn, the omnipotent being.

"You have to promise . . ."

Riker paused and for a minute Quinn thought that perhaps he had just allowed the man to die. He wasn't sure. Come to think of it, he had actually never seen a human die up close before. Of natural causes, at least. Then he saw that Riker was, for some reason, holding a small breath, still gazing intensely up at him, as if waiting for him to respond . . .

And despite himself, for some reason of which he wasn't quite sure, Quinn found himself grasping Riker's hand just a little bit tighter. And promising . . .

2370

Commander William T. Riker of the *Starship Enterprise* was being serenaded by the senior staff.

He winced.

As Captain Picard, Commander Data and the rest of the crew were butchering the last line of "Happy Birthday to You," Riker smiled, ran his hand over his chin, feeling his grisly whiskers and prepared to—

"Blow them out." Deanna Troi laughed, clapping with the rest of the staff.

Out of the corner of his eye, Riker noticed Guinan gliding from behind the bar with a tray full of drinks, smiling, although her calm and always wise demeanor remained just that.

Amid the applause that ended the song, Riker paused where he sat surrounded by his friends, plucked his glass from the table and put on a show of gulping down its entire contents of prune juice. A gift from Worf.

The clapping from around the lounge grew louder as he

slammed the last of it down. He held up the glass, smiled victoriously, and with the other hand, ran his sleeve in an un-Starfleet-officer-like manner across his chin.

"Come on, Will, blow out your candles," he heard Beverly Crusher shout.

"If he can," Geordi pitched in.

Riker looked at his giant, saxophone-shaped birthday cake with its unending array of candles, took in a deep breath and prepared to extinguish them.

"Wait!" It was Troi's voice. "Make a wish."

"But of course, Counselor." Riker mocked a bow, closed his eyes for a brief moment as everyone waited, and opened them again.

"I've got it." He smiled.

He turned again to his cake, took an incredibly deep breath . . .

And vanished.

The silence that pervaded the crowd as they waited for the commander to blow out his candles seemed to somehow grow deeper.

"What the hell!" Picard bellowed.

The silence remained. Troi looked at Geordi. Geordi looked at Crusher. Crusher looked at Data.

Data turned and said to no one in particular, "Perhaps he got his wish."

Riker dropped his glass and it plummeted from his grasp.

And plummeted . . .

He watched it vanish eerily into the eternal fathoms of space, growing smaller and smaller below him.

Then he snapped his head up, let out the enormous lungful of air with which he had fully intended to demolish his birthday cake, and instantly sucked it back in again, as the full realization of where he was came to him.

Riker hung there in the cold depths of space, like a puppet suspended from its unseen strings, utterly unable to grasp, in any manner, what exactly was happening to him.

And then came the flash of light. And with that flash of light, understanding, and he felt an ungodly dread slowly surface within him. He realized at once who it was; realized it, thought it, and said it.

"Q."

The brilliant flare of light swallowed itself as quickly as it appeared and now therein stood a human figure, hands clasped behind his back. "Good. I'm glad to see that introductions are out of the way."

Riker had expected to see Q in his familiar old form, Q who had appeared on the *Enterprise* on her first mission, Q who had given his powers free and full to the commander upon his second visit, the same old Q who continually refused to leave the ship and crew alone. The Q he was used to.

He had never seen the being before him.

"Who are you?"

"Why, I thought you knew," offered the man.

He wore a bright, red Starfleet uniform and a blazingly bright tuft of puffy, blond hair. His face was gentle, his features fine and somewhat aged, but behind his green eyes pulsed the unmistakable, limitless power of the Q.

Riker narrowed his eyes. "Is that you, Q?" He then looked up and around him, as if expecting to see someone else. "Or have you sent someone else this time," he said to nothing.

The man suddenly snapped his fingers. "Oh, yes. I forgot." He confidently strode closer to Riker, somehow treading upon the emptiness of space. "No, I'm not the Q you've been acquainted with. Allow me then to introduce myself." He bowed. "My name is Q."

"No kidding."

"Q the Philosopher."

"The what?"

"Never mind, it's not important."

Riker folded his arms defensively. "Look, I couldn't really care less whether you're Q the Philosopher or Q the Barber. I don't have any interest in playing whatever games Q or the rest of the Continuum put you up to so I should let you know now that you're wasting your time. Or perhaps you're just trying to scare me by hanging me here out in space. Sorry, Q has done worse. But whatever it is, I don't care and I repeat, I don't have time for it."

Q held up a finger. "Look, Commander. If anyone's time is being wasted, it's mine. Now that may come as somewhat of a surprise to you, since I, as an omnipotent being, a god if you will—"

"You are *not* a god."

"—have literally all the time in the universe," he continued. "I, however, have considerably less than that. Perhaps only a few billion years are all that lurks in my future. Maybe even a million, depending on the Continuum's leniency in matters of suicide."

"Suicide?"

"Which means," Q continued, unabashed, "that the longer you pout and drivel, the longer you will prolong our encounter, which means that for both of us, time, as you inadequately expressed it, is being lost. I am here under obligation, merely because my conscience has forced the issue. So I suggest you cooperate here and this will go much quicker."

"You know, you talk an awful lot for someone who doesn't have time to waste."

"Are we understood?"

Riker was quiet for a minute as he studied Q. Then he tapped his combadge. "Riker to *Enterprise."*

Q's hand flew up to his own combadge, rolling his eyes. *"Enterprise* here," he said impatiently, so that his voice was heard not only in the vacuum of space *(as only a Q could do),* but also as it was piped through to Riker's combadge. "This is Picard and I am ordering you to stop being an ass."

Riker strode, by whatever means with which Q was providing him, across the short distance of literal space between them, and shoved his nose in Q's face. "Where's my ship?"

"Marry Deanna Troi and I'll tell you."

Riker froze. His face drained.

Q smiled warmly, and just as suddenly, deadpanned, and he dropped all pretense. He took a deep breath. "Call me Doctor Q, Riker, and I've just diagnosed you; you're an idiot. That is characteristic of your race, but you particularly have mastered it. Here's why: It's a message from a friend. I'll give you the short version. 'Your pathetic career has alienated the woman that loves you. You have broken Deanna's heart, only she hides it by courting that ugly Klingon specimen. So do something about it. And speaking of your pathetic career, it's high time you quit hiding behind Picard and get your own command. Signed, Thaddius Riker.' There, that's it and it's time for me to go."

Q had uttered it all in one breath and wasted no time on a farewell address. He began to bring his hand up in a gesture that was to instigate his "vanishing" and—

Riker hit him.

His fist fired up with blinding speed and smashed Q in the face, human knuckle crushed against omnipotent bone. Q staggered back.

And then Riker plowed into him, his shoulder finding Q's midsection and pile-driving into it, sending both he and Q, the immortal entity, flailing about awkwardly in what might be considered "up."

Q, for his part, was taken utterly by surprise. Looking back he supposed he ultimately should have thanked Riker, because for a Q, moments of genuine surprise are few and far between. For a brief moment, Riker and Q appeared to be one. One incomprehensible and strangely disorganized unit of arms and legs floating comically through the void of space. This, of course, didn't last long.

It had taken Q only an instant to lose his wits, only a millisecond to realize that his wits were actually missing, and then only slightly less than that to gather them again. In one giant blaze of light Q promptly separated himself from the raging Riker and the situation was utterly reversed. Riker was now as still as a statue, frozen upside-down (relative only to Q, of course) in space, not a muscle twitching, as if time was suddenly on hiatus. For all his petrified state of affairs, his expression was alive and well. His eyeballs simply bulged with forcibly contained rage, his face was transfixed in fury. Yet he was unable to utter a single sound.

Q was scowling down at his uniform, straightening it with both hands. "That was simply barbaric. What is *wrong* with you?" He continued tugging at his top and, upon hearing no immediate answer, glanced up at the immotive Riker. "Oh, yes." He snapped his fingers.

"*—stay the* hell *out of Deanna's and my business and—*"

Q snapped his fingers again. He slowly shook his head and looked up to where he kept Riker suspended and motionless and, once again, voiceless. Not simply muted, but wholly unable to move his mouth, his jaw, even his tongue. Q again appeared startled for a moment, and then, ponderous. He finally brought his hand to his forehead, wrinkled his brow as if in concentration, and remained positively silent. He continued that way for what seemed to Riker's still-vivacious mind, a millennium.

Q then abruptly lowered his hands, sighed, and stepped up to the commander. He stopped just short of allowing their noses to touch. Q found himself staring up Riker's midflare nostrils, for he had not bothered to turn the first officer right side up, so he took a single step back. He let the proximity of his presence sink in before he spoke, and when he did, it was in slow and measured tones.

"To say my experience with humans has been exhaustive would be an elaborate overstatement but it would certainly be understated to say that it has been limited. Read into that what you may, but the fact is simply this: I have severely miscalculated your overly . . . emotional response. I have obviously . . . hit a nerve, if you will. Something I have said has sent you reeling into a maddening state of delirium. Thus, my objective remains unsatisfied. So . . . I am going to do this once more." Q paused a moment, looking Riker over. "Now, you have made it clear that I cannot yet free you completely, lest you again accost me, either verbally or physically, so I regret to say that I will be forced to keep you in limbo for a bit longer . . . however . . ." Q briefly appeared thoughtful, "Make yourself at home." Instead of snapping this time, he gestured flippantly with his left hand and immediately afterward Riker vanished in a flash of light, at the same instant reappearing perhaps three feet from his original position. Except now he was lounging in a large, ridiculous, purple-colored couch, his feet stretched out before him, although he remained immobile.

Q began to speak again and the pacing began. "Let me see if I can put this together more appropriately for you. Since you cannot speak, you obviously cannot ask any questions, but I believe I possess the foresight to address any that your limited mind might conceive.

"You see, I have just come from the past, approximately five hundred years, to deliver you a message. Do not, however, let this bolster your ego, Riker. We Q travel through time as easily as we do from place to place. Consequently, we tend to exist everywhere at once. In fact," Q gestured wildly in the general direction of nowhere, "I am out there at this very moment, somewhere *else,* doing some*thing* . . ." Q's eyes widened unexpectedly, his voice lowering several degrees. "Or perhaps I am already dead. Wouldn't that be a glorious thought."

Q moved on. "The point is, do not think yourself particularly noteworthy because I have traveled a trite few centuries to find you. The simple fact is, I do not wish to be here any more than you wish it." Q turned on his heels and began to pace behind the couch.

"I have come from a point in your history which your culture refers to as the Civil War. Why and how is not important. Suffice it to say I was fixing something that someone else screwed up. I was saving your ancestor's life, Riker. You really ought to thank me, by the way. But as it was, I was doing this simply because he was not supposed to die. He was the butt of a cosmic joke, of sorts. The work of someone within the Continuum, undoubtedly. Of course, the prankster himself did not realize the immensity of the mistake he was making, and your ancestor, Colonel Thaddius Riker wound up being at the wrong place in the universe at the wrong moment in history. To make a long story short, I was dispatched by the Q to straighten things out. Understand, Riker, if I hadn't, you wouldn't even be here to witness the catastrophic events that would have resulted from his premature death. The cosmos would have been in utter chaos. You'd be surprised how the fate of the universe can sometimes hinge upon a single being at a single moment, Commander. You wouldn't understand the logistics of it, of course, so I won't bother. But the reason I am here is this:

"I wound up saving his life, as I said. He was as good as dead when I found him, but with *me* there, he was in no real danger at all. I could have restored him to full health if I so chose but that would have been far too suspicious. So I simply prevented death from running its course."

Q was now fully behind the couch upon which Riker lay and leaned up against it, his back to Riker, gazing out at the stars, some of which were astoundingly near. "Thaddius obviously had no way of knowing that he was incapable of dying. As far as he was concerned, everything was over. So, in what I suppose was a moment of weakness, I found myself making a promise. You see, Riker," Q turned around now, leaning his hands upon the back of the couch, "Thaddius was in much the same boat as you. He loved someone once, but was always afraid of what might not be. And like you, he was a commander, an authority . . . but always playing second fiddle, isn't that how you say it? Always in the supporting role. Like you and Picard, forever standing in the shadows of his superiors, content with inferiority. A miserable manner in which to live, really. Only Thaddius didn't fully realize this until it all began to slowly dissolve before him, vanish before his dying eyes. But . . . by that time it was simply too late. So, in a climactic effort to assuage his fears, or to at least bring a small measure of closure to his failed existence, he made me promise.

"He made me promise to warn his children, to never allow them to make the same mistakes he had. It was all just the ramblings of a dying man, really. He should have realized there was no way for me to fulfill such a promise. Maybe he did, maybe he didn't. Maybe it was all for comfort's sake. But what he *didn't* realize was that I was Q and that I had every means at my disposal to keep such a vow.

"And so I am. I may be a lot of rotten things, but I am not a liar. Never a liar." Q paused for dramatic effect. ". . . That is a human characteristic."

He looked down to Riker, regarded him in an almost distasteful fashion. Riker, for his part, was considerably calmer now, but his eyes never left Q's, his gaze virtually burrowing a hole in the omnipotent's head.

"You're the first, Riker. Five hundred years and you Rikers

have managed to keep your heads on fairly straight. Only now you come along and wrinkle the sheets your great-grandparents have managed to keep neat for all this time. Congratulations, Commander"—Q reached down, grasped Riker's hand and began furiously shaking it—"for successfully doddling things up."

Q continued pumping the commander's arm. "Perhaps I ought to thank you. For allowing me to fulfill my foolish vow. Oh, how it would have been weighing on my conscience through the eons, long after the human race had vanished from the specter of the universe . . . me, with the unbearable weight of eternal obligation. How very terrible."

Q promptly dropped Riker's arm, moved deliberately around the couch to the front, and knelt purposefully down. He brought his mouth to Riker's ear, his voice almost a whisper. "You're second in command on a ship that can't love you. You're first in the heart of a woman who can. Remember that."

Then Q promptly stood and announced loudly, "Good-bye, Commander. My work here is done. Thaddius," he looked up, "consider your message . . . *delivered.*" Then he smiled widely, made a sharp, upward gesture with his hand . . .

. . . and vanished in a blaze of light.

Riker lay there just as he had been all during Q's soliloquy, simply unable to do anything else. To anyone who might have been passing by and bothered to glance out into space, the sight of a Starfleet officer simply lounging obviously on a purple sofa would undoubtedly have been more or less disturbing. None of this really occurred to Riker. The absence of Q was suddenly quite startling and the enormity and unmitigated silence of the universe seemed to loom around him.

The silence was then quite suddenly broken by the unmistakable voice of Q. Only now it was deep and booming, as though it were the voice of God, Himself.

"Oh, sorry."

And Riker, sofa and all, simply vanished.

Q never bothered to check up on Riker. Truth be told, he just didn't really care. He never expected to see the human again, so a few years later when they crossed paths ever so briefly on the starship called *Voyager,* Q was mildly surprised. He didn't show it, of course, and didn't allow Riker to even faintly recollect his existence, for that would have surely fouled matters up. There was really no point, Q mused, no point at all in meddling in the affairs of humanity any more than was necessary. Consequently, and quite by intention, Q remained impervious as to what the future held for Commander William T. Riker.

Although he did know that when Riker left his birthday party that night, Deanna Troi was wrapped firmly around his arm . . .

The Change of Seasons

Logan Page

Picard sat alone at a table in the *Farragut*'s main lounge, a glass of herbal tea in one hand, nearly cold now from neglect. Under the other hand, on his lap, sat a large book. His thoughts were on neither of these things, though. Nor was it on the loss of the saucer section itself. His mind was on only one thing. He stared at the object on his table.

The twisted, misshapen mass of metal worried him. In the past, he'd had many an opportunity to see Denebian lair sculptures, and this looked too much like one. Critics of the so-called art form have said that the best examples of the genre resemble a negative photograph of a cylindrical ant farm.

Geordi had been laboring to adjust the *Farragut*'s transporter systems for nearly forty-five minutes, and this mess was their best test result yet. Time was running out, and so were Jean-Luc's spirits. With less to do, now that the excitement was over, his mind returned to his sorrows.

He found it cruelly ironic, that when Geordi finally got something to transport up through the residual radiation, it would turn out like this. So reminiscent, so aesthetically representative of something that he considered a senseless reminder of death. Just one more irony for the ever increasing pile.

Once a year, the Denebian slime devils, so named for their amphibious form and scurrilous natures, bury their egg-pouches two feet deep in the soil at the edges of lakes and marshes, and then go about their business, leaving the embryos to fend for themselves. There, the pouches gestate unattended until the frye reach maturity and, in the spring, emerge from the shrunken pouch. As soon as they can, they first snack on the less developed embryos for energy. Then, when sated, they dig their way up and out of the ground, using their slowly developing natural sonar as a guide. Usually only a few dozen of the hundred or so embryos survive to adulthood, as their siblings who are slower to emerge make easier meals than the other life-forms they find after their emergence. Many, in fact, remain in the lair until they grow too large to do so. When they begin to find it difficult to move about inside, they leave the lair behind and live out their lives in and around the wetlands. The carnivorous little devils would then subsist on everything from fishes to humanoid ankles—when they got the chance—and often grew to just under thirty kilos, and just over a meter in length. Though adults of only a few centimeters were not uncommon. Not all the slow ones got eaten.

Full-on attacks on humans are rare, but if one was unlucky enough to get pinched or bitten—if it is inclined to attack a human, it is usually fast enough to succeed—then the wound would invariably becomes infected. Badly infected, as the slime devil is a veritable petri dish of germs and bacteria. This is not a popular creature.

There is a traditional spring custom on Deneb where families actually go in search of these lairs. They're easy to find, if one was of a mind to look, recognizable by the compact patterns of holes left in the wet soil by the young slime devils who emerged first. No one is certain when this tradition began, but the families would have a little ceremony wherein they sing songs about their kin and honor the memories of their forbears. As they did, they would pour molten wax or other hardening liquids into the holes, careful to get all the holes at the same time, lest the little devils come out one and get them. It was a ceremony of family cohesiveness, and cooperation, not unlike some Earth holidays like May Day or Thanksgiving.

It was no holiday for the slime devils, though. The creatures inside would suffer a painful demise, burned and suffocated, and would be entombed in the substance as it cooled and hardened around them.

In order to bring the tradition full circle, the family would go out again the following spring and free the lair from the earth. They would then go on to search for a new lair to honor with their singing and pouring. It was a true emulation of the seasonal cycles, they thought. At least, that was what the children were told. To the adults, it was probably more like simple pest control.

Wax was used before any other substance, it is thought. Then as uses for other materials were developed, lead, bronze, silver, and later, gold was used. The substances varied as much as the prosperity of the people who did the pouring. Not many could afford to literally pour gold into the ground. Some lair sculptures, though, gold and wax alike, were many centuries old and greatly prized by collectors all over the settled galaxy.

But some people just found them morbid. Ant farm, indeed, Picard thought. He found it absurd that anyone could compare the two. He'd had a friend who'd kept an ant farm as a young boy. It was a hobby which respected life, not death. That's how he viewed collecting the sculptures of Deneb; a celebration of death. He had to grudgingly admit one thing though: Purely on the visual front, it *was* an accurate analogy. Since their sonar is undeveloped at the point of their emergence, and their bodies are tiny, weak, and clumsy, their tunneling to the surface was anything but direct. They tended to twist and wind and intersect each other at different points along the way, much like an ant farm.

And just like the thing on Picard's table did.

Having a greater respect for life than most people, he'd always thought it to be a gruesome art form, no better than shrunken heads or mummy collecting. But he had to admit, it did have its allure. An echo of life, if a wasted one. A tabletop tomb, with the remains of the vicious little creatures still inside.

He suppressed a shudder, and pictured the civil-minded Denebians chatting away while having their civilized tea and cookies at a coffee table with the likes of that sitting on it. He certainly couldn't do it. But then again, he didn't have to worry about the things biting at him every day as they did.

This bit of art he could live with though. Its bare hint of a spout, and its handle blending in with the rest of its twisting, winding lines, giving away what it had initially been.

Jean-Luc sighed, deep and sorrowfully. Was it so much to ask? They were due to disembark within the hour, and the radiation left in the wake of the Nexus made it impossible to retrieve the pitcher René had made for him, buried beneath the wreckage that was the *Enterprise*'s saucer section. If Geordi succeeded in bringing up even one replica, then he would ask him to try for the original. Then the mess before him would be a welcome reminder of the positive outcome of these difficult days, and a shrine to the memories of René and Robert.

But if they failed, and he had to leave it behind for some nameless, faceless, possibly careless salvage worker to locate and retrieve, and probably deface or destroy, then it would be replicator matrix. Then *it* would go full circle. So be it. Such was the fairness of the universe, he thought. Such was the way of life.

He shook himself then. Were these thoughts truly his? he wondered. He didn't recognize the sound of them. The blur left his eyes, and he looked up. It was still there. The twisted mess. The reminder of death.

But death was the ultimate end to all living things, he recalled. It was natural. It was—unfair. He had been so young, his life just beginning.

He realized then that he was finally grieving, and nearly smiled. Instead, a somewhat more pained expression crossed his features.

This wasn't lost on Geordi. He waited a moment before closing the distance to his captain's table. He'd noticed the tea, and had gotten another for him, so as he finally approached, both hands were full.

"Captain," he said in greeting, stepping up to his side. He set the tea down on the table without a word about it, and hefted the other object. It was wrapped in a white cloth. Not like when he'd brought the thing presently on the table. Oddly, uncharacteristically, Picard didn't seem to notice.

"Ah, Geordi," Jean-Luc began. "Thank you. I seem to have ignored this one." He set the now cold tea on the table and took possession of the new one. He was definitely operating in a diminished mode, Geordi thought, but said nothing. He'd heard about his captain's nephew and brother, and he knew there were no words. It was not about protocol. It was about the man. Mere presence, perseverance, and silent compassion would have to suffice.

Jean-Luc then got a good look at Geordi, and his eyes widened. "Commander, you are out of uniform. Or, dare I say, barely *in* uniform." Geordi's tunic was filthy and torn. Dirt was ground into every joint, and the sleeve-top at one shoulder was hanging loose. "You look as if you have finally joined Worf for one of his holodeck calisthenics routines. You might have changed afterward."

Geordi allowed himself a good-natured laugh. "No, sir, it's not that. I wouldn't have abandoned my project, not even for something that fun."

Jean-Luc then noticed the object in his hands, and with the force of hope, his jaw dropped a fraction of an inch. Without delay, without drama, and without another word, Geordi removed the cloth. He set the metal pitcher on the table beside its erstwhile counterpart.

"It's working," Jean-Luc said as he stood. Rather than shifting the book from his lap to the table, he gathered it up tighter. This touched Geordi deeply. Never before had he seen vulnerability mixed with such indomitable dignity.

Jean-Luc's face radiated the hope he felt, that his gift could still be retrieved from beneath the wreckage, and the slight smile which caressed the lines on his face deepened. In a low voice, he asked, "Will you be able to try for the real thing before we have to disembark?" He looked to his engineer for an answer, hoping for the right one.

Geordi didn't know how to answer at first. His captain had misunderstood. After a moment, he finally just said, "Sir, we don't have to. I mean, this is it. This is the pitcher your nephew made for you."

Picard's eyes widened, and he looked back to the pitcher. He found he had to sit down again. As he did, he finally set the book down. This, so he could hold the icon of his lost loved one.

Not knowing what else to say, and feeling a little uncomfortable, Geordi said, "I found a way to do it the old-fashioned way. How do you think I got so dirty?"

Picard just ran his fingers over the crude but heartfelt engravings and designs on the pitcher's surface. He was amazed that, having been tossed about by the crash, blown out by the hull rupture that had wrecked his quarters, and buried by tons of rubble, it was still in pretty fair condition. That, and he noticed that Geordi had had the presence of mind to clean it before bringing it to him.

Even more uncomfortable, Geordi said, "I—I returned to the surface with a tricorder and an anti-grav excavator. A ballistics computer model told me where to look, so I—I gave it a shot."

Jean-Luc looked up to him then, and opened his mouth to speak, but the words just wouldn't come. There were no words for the gratitude he felt. There never would be.

But Geordi knew. He placed a hand on his captain's shoulder, and, shattering all pretenses at protocol, he gave it a gentle squeeze.

And he left his captain to his grief, and his healing.

Out of the Box, Thinking

Jerry M. Wolfe

Personal diary of Professor James Moriarty: Oh bitter fate! Picard tricked me in the end, I see that now. The blissful existence Regina and I enjoyed over the past months is a fraud, a lie, a concoction wrought by computer. We are trapped in an artificial world of Picard's doing. That knowledge will surely drive us to madness and despair. Yet, I could even bear that if not for Regina. She is a great soul and deserves a real life, not a shadowy imitation. It would have been kinder to destroy us.

Lieutenant Reg Barclay hummed to himself and unpacked his belongings. The work on the Emergency Medical Hologram at Jupiter Station had gone well, but it was good to be back on the *Enterprise* among old friends. The "E" was a beauty, and he already felt at home. Spot rubbed against his leg, purring loudly, and he picked up the cat. "That's a good girl," he said, stroking her head. "You haven't forgotten old Reg, eh? Well, I haven't forgotten you either." He scratched behind Spot's left ear, her favorite place, then set the animal down and resumed his unpacking.

Data was away at the Daystrom Institute having tests run on his performance with his emotion chip installed. Reg's feet had barely touched the shuttlebay floor before Geordi pushed the cat into his arms with a relieved grin. Apparently, Reg was still the only human on the *Enterprise* that Spot liked. Curious.

He tucked the last pair of socks into his locker, then set the Moriarty module on the desk, near a Bajoran flame crystal given to him by Ro Laren. The module, about the size and shape of two large books laid end to end, had been given to him for safekeeping by the captain himself, and Reg took that job very seriously. He kept it in a stable location, checked the power level twice a day, and had even added new layers to the program. Reg often wondered what it would be like to be inside the module sharing adventures with Moriarty and the Countess Regina Barthalomew. Sometimes he even envied them. But not often.

Mostly, his thoughts of the pair were laced with guilt over what had been done to them. Not that the captain had any real choice; sometimes no perfect solution exists. Still, it bothered Reg, and he believed that it did not sit well with Captain Picard, either. Fortunately, neither the Countess nor Moriarty knew of their true situation.

One of the reasons Reg had transferred to the Jupiter Station project was to learn more about holomatter, in the hope that he might discover a way to make it viable outside the holodeck. Then Moriarty and Regina could walk the real world. Reg sighed. He had worked long and hard on the problem, but with little success so far. Federation science had a long way to go before that dream became reality.

He made a last check of the module, fed Spot, and then left to meet Geordi for dinner and catching up. Before he reached the turbolift, however, the grating whine of the red-alert Klaxon set his heart pounding. Just like old times, he thought and hurried off to his post in engineering.

* * *

Deanna Troi tried to remain calm as the turbolift whisked her to the bridge. Why did that horrible Klaxon always blare just as she was about to dig into something large, divine, and chocolate? The welter of taut emotions from the crew pushed against her like a storm wind, but she had been through it so often that she set up her internal defenses without so much as a thought. Uncertainty and adrenaline drove the emotional surge more than fear. The *Enterprise* was patrolling a region where several mining freighters and supply ships had vanished, and the ship had been tense for days. But she knew that as soon as the crew reached their posts, Starfleet training would take over, and the wind would die to a whisper.

The door of the turbolift opened with a soft whoosh, and she stepped through. The E's bridge was large and impressive, yet she missed the cheerful, warm hues of the D. But it was the people who made a ship feel like home, not the decor, and the *Enterprise was* home. These people were her family. As usual, a feeling of calm alertness and confidence spread outward from the captain like ripples on a pond. That's what a good captain did, and there were none better than Jean-Luc Picard.

On the viewscreen, a squat, gray ship trailed smoke and debris from a glowing wound as it tried to elude a smaller but sleeker vessel. The shape and light-brown coloring of the attacker reminded her of Cardassian ships, but this region was nowhere near their space.

A burst of energy crashed against the gray ship's shields. From the looks of things, the battle would soon be over unless the *Enterprise* intervened. Deanna quickly took her usual spot beside the captain. He gave her the briefest of nods and returned his attention to the screen. Will Riker flashed a smile but turned back to his instruments before she could return the gesture.

"Hail that attacking ship again," Picard said.

"Aye, sir," Lieutenant Ying said from Data's spot at tactical. Ensign Crawford had the conn. "No response."

"That freighter can't take another hit," Will said.

"Are we in weapons range, Lieutenant?" the captain asked.

"Yes, Captain."

"Put a shot across the attacker's bow. Make sure they feel it."

"Firing phasers."

Deanna watched the brilliant beam catch the edge of the brown ship's shields, sending reflected energy skittering in all directions. The craft shuddered, then veered away and fled at high speed.

"That seemed a bit too easy," Will said.

"I agree, Number One. Lieutenant Ying, hail the freighter." Picard turned to Deanna. "I want your impressions, Counselor."

"Yes, Captain." Deanna cleared her mind and extended her awareness. Thankfully, the emotions of the crew had calmed.

Ying broke in. "Sir, sensors show elevated radiation levels inside the freighter. Estimate core-breach in fifty seconds."

"Lifesigns?"

"Only one, sir. Definitely humanoid."

Picard reacted instantly. "Lock on and prepare to transport to sickbay. Send a security team."

Lieutenant Ying's fingers danced over her control pads. "I have a lock."

"Captain, the ship is answering our hail," Crawford said.

"On screen."

The image of a female with short, silver hair and pale-green eyes came onto the viewer. She would have been attractive by human standards, Deanna thought, except for a large scar that ran across one cheek like a jagged lightning bolt. As if to draw the eye away from that flaw, gold chains were wrapped around her neck, jeweled rings gleamed on her fingers, and a pair of brilliant, crystal orbs bobbing at the end of thin chains were attached to her earlobes.

"Your reactor is about to explode. Prepare for transport," the captain said.

The woman shook her head. "My cargo!"

"There is no time!"

Deanna's first impression was clear. The woman was worried and tense. Obviously. There was something else, something overwhelmed by danger. She struggled to identify the emotion. The woman frowned, but inside she had grown calmer, perhaps giving in to the inevitable. She nodded. "Very well. And thank you." The screen went dark.

"Transport!" Picard ordered.

In a few seconds Ying said, "We have her, sir." Seconds later, a brilliant flash lit the viewer as the freighter exploded.

Just before Ying spoke, Deanna picked out the elusive emotion. Annoyance. The woman was experiencing some minor discomfort, and at the moment it bothered her more than losing her ship! A bit odd, perhaps, but the mind did odd things under stress. Still, a vague sense of unease spread though Deanna like a creeping fog until the captain's sharp command drove it away.

"Counselor Troi will accompany me to sickbay. You have the bridge, Number One." Captain Picard rose and Deanna followed him to the turbolift. Inside, the captain spoke to her. "Counselor, did you learn anything of interest?"

"She was tense and nervous, as you would expect, sir. She was also in some physical discomfort. All reasonably normal under the circumstances." Deanna hesitated, then added, "Something about this makes me uneasy, Captain, but I don't know what. It could be nothing."

"Perhaps," he said, "but I know better than to ignore your impressions. I think we shall keep close tabs on our guest."

The turbolift door opened, and they proceeded to sickbay. Two security guards stood at the door and saluted as she and the captain entered. Inside, Beverly Crusher stood by an examination table reading a medical scanner.

"Where is she?" the captain asked.

"Captain Taraga's bioscan showed mild radiation poisoning. I gave her a dose of hyronalin and sent her to shower while her clothes are decontaminated."

"I wish to speak with her," Picard said.

Beverly thought for a moment. "I'll need to scan for genetic damage and make sure the hyronalin is working. An hour should do it."

The captain frowned but nodded. "Very well. In my ready room in one hour. Until then, she is confined to sickbay." He turned to Deanna. "Counselor, I want you present when I interview Captain Taraga. She is most likely an innocent victim, but if she is deceiving us in any way, I want to know."

Deanna nodded. Taraga could not fool her, and there was no reason to think she'd try. But why was Deanna so relieved by the sight of the security team at the door?

Reg knew something was wrong when Spot and the room around the pale cat blurred like a mirage in a desert. Sweat poured down his forehead and then a wave of vertigo hit him. He swayed drunkenly, then hit the floor with a thud that knocked the wind from him. *Good God, what's wrong?* He closed his eyes, hoping the world would stop spinning.

He'd gotten back to his room a scant hour after the red alert. Geordi had to stay on duty for several hours, and he had ordered Reg to eat and catch up on his sleep. Then it would be Reg's turn. All fine and good, except that he'd had no appetite and decided to hit the sheets. Instead, he'd hit the floor. Reg opened his eyes, but the spinning had grown worse. He moaned and punched his combadge.

"H-h-elp! Barclay, I—" The words would not come out, and now the spinning had become a giant whirlpool sucking him down into oblivion. *Why is it always me?* It was an all too familiar question with no answer. Or maybe not! Suddenly, his thoughts danced with possibilities. Physics, mathematics, biochemistry diagrams tumbled through his head like rolling dice. He would write a book, a masterpiece of scholarly research—*Inverted Personality Types and the Theory of Quantum Misfortune.* He'd tour the galaxy! Professor Barclay will give a special lecture entitled . . . When blackness took him he had forgotten the original question.

Medical reports from all over the ship flooded the comm system and echoed in Deanna's ears as if they came down a tunnel. Lieutenant Ying pitched forward onto her console. Ensign Crawford tried to stand but collapsed to the floor, slowly as if he fell through liquid. The captain slumped sideways in the chair beside her. Deanna felt so odd. Then the floor moved upward to meet her. Desperately, she reached out with her feelings searching the ship. Somewhere three crew members went about a task, completely unaware of the situation. Then she felt Taraga. The woman was awake and quite pleased with herself. Deanna thought of a very rude word just before she passed out.

Reg woke to find Spot licking his neck, the feline's raspy tongue tickling with each stroke. Reg struggled to a sitting position. He felt wretched—weak, feverish, achy. At least the spinning had stopped. A check of the time showed that he had been out about fifteen minutes. He gave Spot a quick pet and a heartfelt "Good cat," then hit his combadge.

"Barclay to sickbay." He waited, but there was no answer. He tried again with the same result. "Barclay to the bridge." Nothing. Then he heard a halting voice.

"Reg? It's Deanna. Something awful . . ." Her voice trailed away.

Reg pulled himself to his feet and stumbled into the hall. He discovered an ensign crumpled near the turbolift door. Thank God the man had a pulse, but it seemed too slow. When Reg got to the bridge he found everyone unconscious. Deanna lay on the floor in front of her chair, and when he touched her, she moaned and opened her eyes.

"I feel terrible," she said. "Like I have the worst flu in the galaxy."

Reg pulled her to a sitting position. Beads of sweat dotted her forehead, and she looked flushed. He must look much the same. "I know how you feel. I'll check the others." When none of them responded he returned to Deanna. "I'd better find out who else is awake," he said.

"No!" Deanna grabbed his arm. "There's no one but us and—" Deanna's face twisted in shock.

Reg forgot his own misery and put his arm against her back for support. "What happened?"

Deanna took a deep breath before answering. "Three of the crew were untouched by whatever's affecting us. I think they've just been stunned."

Reg gulped. "Shot?"

"By Taraga, the woman from the freighter. She caused this. I felt her gloating."

"Only two left," he said, not wanting to believe it. "But why us?"

"I don't know, but—"

A voice broke in over the comm-link. "This is Captain Juy Taraga. Can anyone answer me?"

Deanna shook her head sharply and held one finger to her lips. Suddenly dizzy, Reg leaned back against Deanna's chair and wiped sweat from his brow. He ached from end to end. Seconds passed in silence. Then he felt a subtle shift in the ship's internal gravity.

"We've changed course," he whispered. "Taraga must be in engineering." Reg leaned closer to Deanna. "Can you tell what's she's up to?"

Deanna gave him a withering glance. "I'm an empath, not a mind reader! Now help me up!"

Reg's face grew even hotter. "Yes, Commander. I apologize—"

Deanna waved off his apology. "I should be used to it by now. You're correct. We need to find out what she's doing and stop her."

Reg gripped her hand and together they pulled each other to their feet. His legs felt rubbery and weak. Deanna braced herself against the edge of the helm station. Sweat had soaked through the back of her uniform.

"Computer, locate Captain Taraga," she said.

"Captain Taraga is entering turbolift 34-B."

Reg looked at Deanna and saw understanding in her eyes.

"We need a weapon!" she said.

"Right!" They staggered to the rear of the bridge, and Reg took a phaser from the security officer, Lieutenant Commander Roberts, who wore a peaceful expression as he lay on the floor near his station. Then Reg and Deanna hid beside the turbolift door.

"Set for stun," Deanna whispered, and Reg complied. He pressed himself as flat as he could against the curving wall and waited with Deanna just behind him. The thump of his heart against his chest counted off the seconds until the bridge door swished open and a woman strolled through, phaser in hand.

"Drop your weapon!" Deanna commanded.

The woman froze but did not respond. "Drop it now, or you will be shot!" Taraga shrugged and dropped the gun. Then she turned to them, a sneer on her face. Deanna stepped forward. "What have you done to the crew?" Reg marveled at how steady and calm she kept her voice.

Taraga stood with her hands on her hips. "That's my little secret, sister. Let's just say that this ship will be a tomb in eight hours unless my friends show up with the antidote. They won't do that unless I signal." Taraga's sneer grew even more unpleasant. "Surrender now and save yourself a lot of grief."

"You're telling the truth about an antidote, but you lied about your friends having it. Therefore, you have it," Deanna said in a steady tone.

Taraga's eyes grew wide, then she glared at Deanna. " 'Zoid!" she hissed and spat at Deanna's feet. Then the arrogant smile returned. "Not a pure 'Zoid though. Some half-breed scum, or else you'd know more."

Reg was suddenly glad he had the phaser and not Deanna, but she refused to take the bait. "Tell me where the antidote is."

"Don't kid yourself, sister. Ransoms are nice, but this ship's the real prize. Surrender or I'll let the crew die."

Deanna stood tall and defiant, though Reg could see her shoulder quivering just like his hand that held the phaser. It was a miracle either of them could stand. "Lieutenant, take her to the brig. If she resists, stun her."

"Yes, Commander." Before he could take the prisoner away, the ship dropped out of warp and came to a stop. Deanna scooped up Taraga's phaser and held it on the woman.

"Computer, raise shields! Reg, get us out of here while I take her to the cell."

"Yes, sir!" Reg walked over and gently set Lieutenant Ying on the floor as the bridge door closed behind him. By the time he sat down, he was gasping for air. Sweat stung his eyes, and his body was still one huge ache. Even his gums throbbed.

"Three ships uncloaking and five others approaching," the computer said.

Reg watched the viewer in dismay as two Klingon bird-of-prey and a Romulan warbird rippled into visibility, forming a triangle. There was something odd about them, as if pieces here and there did not belong. Of the other five ships, three were Cardassian and two were of unknown type. Bulges and antennae sprouted from their sides as if they had been pieced together from a junkyard. The eight ships surrounded the *Enterprise,* weapons ready. The warbird hailed the *Enterprise,* and Reg put it through on audio.

"What is this, Taraga?" said a gruff voice. "Why the screens?"

Reg gulped and did a frantic check of engine status. He had warp drive. There was no time to contact Deanna, but her orders were clear. He set a course that passed through the space between the warbird and the nearest bird-of-prey, then raised his voice, trying for a female timbre. "I-Ion storm. No visual. Lowering shields now." *Pathetic.* Reg began dropping shields, his finger quivering over the warp drive pad. The surrounding ships held their shields, but lowered their weapon levels. *Now or never.* He engaged the engines, preparing for warp. Something shook the ship. Then another jolt. He hit the warp drive pad. Nothing.

Reg pored over the instrument panel. *Blast Taraga!* She'd put an override on the warp control circuit! He should have checked! The *Enterprise* shuddered from another blow. Frantically, Reg rerouted controls. Another hit nearly shook him out of his chair.

"Shields down to 42 percent," the computer intoned. "Hull damage to sections two and five."

Reg hit the engage pad just as the *Enterprise* took another dose of disruptor fire. The ship leaped into warp, narrowly avoiding a collision in the process. He breathed a sigh of relief, then tried to send a distress call only to find that Taraga had sabotaged long-range communications. He should have known. Another attack of vertigo hit, and he sagged back in his chair and closed his eyes. It felt like blood was rushing through his brain, speeding up his thoughts, making his ears ring. His physical misery was now complete. In that state, he did not even hear Deanna return to the bridge.

"Are you OK, Reg? What's happening?"

He started at her voice and sat up. Deanna slid into the helm chair, carefully stepping over Ensign Crawford's unconscious body. Reg's vertigo faded a bit, but his mind still raced and his tongue felt thick and uncooperative.

"Dizzy. Better now." Reg took a deep breath. "We were attacked. Eight ships. We're damaged, but we've escaped for now." He looked at the instruments. "They're chasing us." Then he checked the engine readouts. One of the warp coils showed signs of instability. "More good news," he said. "We can't sustain warp for long."

Deanna sank deeper into her chair. "Taraga won't say where the antidote is. I tried waking Beverly, but it was no use. Taraga even incapacitated the EMH. It's just us, Reg."

Just the two of them and both sick as dogs. Maybe dying. Reg might simulate Beverly Crusher on the holodeck, but it could take hours to get the parameters right. His eyes met Deanna's, and he saw bright anger there.

"We can't let them win," she said slowly.

"Hard as hammers," he said. Deanna looked confused, and Reg explained. "My grandfather loved carpentry. He used to say that when things got rough."

Deanna smiled. "Hard as hammers." Then her expression turned grim. "We need to buy time."

Buy time . . . He had it! "There's a nearby system with a planet that might hide us. Strong magnetics and ion disturbances. Shall I head there?"

"Do it," Deanna said. Reg quickly made a course correction. Deanna was looking at him, her head tilted slightly. "How did you know about this planet?"

"I—" He stopped. "I-I don't know. I've never been here before. Have I?"

She checked the long-range scanner. " I don't know, but there *is* a system coming up. A single sun and five planets. One of them registers an unusually strong magnetic field." Deanna leaned back. Perspiration had stuck several strands of her dark hair to her cheek. She labored over every word. "Something strange is happening to your mind. It reminds me of what I felt when the Cytherians temporarily boosted your intellect years ago. Like your brain is speeding up."

"But how could I know—"

"I can't tell," she interrupted. "But something *is* happening."

Like I'm going insane.

Twenty minutes later, Reg edged the *Enterprise* into the upper atmosphere of the second planet of the system. Instruments showed their pursuers only minutes behind. The ship shuddered briefly as inertial dampers adapted to the turbulence. The air outside blazed with dancing streaks of color and arcing electrical discharges, while the deep atmosphere flickered with thousands of lightning flashes in a continuous display. No visual scanner would find the *Enterprise,* but he knew that a network of tachyon or neutrino beams could. He'd bought them a few hours at best.

"That ought to do it for now," he said.

Deanna nodded wearily from the conn and sipped at a glass of water. Neither of them had any appetite, and they couldn't risk stimulants. "I've been thinking. How could a disease hit everyone in the ship at the same time?"

Reg pondered, trying to ignore his aches. "The air system's about the only way to reach all the decks." Suddenly he saw the problem. It took two hours for air to circulate through all twenty-four decks. "You'd need multiple releases from many locations, all about the same time." Even then the filter system should have stopped it. His thoughts raced to an ugly word. "Sabotage?"

"I wonder. We had techs on board at Starbase twelve just six days ago. Taraga may just be the trigger." Deanna buried her face in both hands. When she looked up, he was shocked by the anguish in her expression. "Reg, are you as tired as I am?"

"I'm exhausted, and I ache all over."

"Same here. I don't know how much longer I can go on." She stopped to gulp down the rest of her water, then wiped her brow with her sleeve. "Those ships must not have a reliable replicator, otherwise Taraga wouldn't need to carry an antidote. But she must be counting on using crew from the ships to administer it. How long will it take us to do the job?"

Reg felt even fainter. "I hadn't thought of that." Over twelve hundred crew members. *God help us. And them.*

Deanna continued wearily. "We can't wait longer than three hours to begin giving the antidote. If it goes past that time, I'll have to surrender." Suddenly, she tossed the cup across the bridge, bouncing it off a panel. "I'd like to strangle that woman!"

Reg barely heard her words. His ears rung and vertigo threatened again. He had an idea, but his mouth had to catch up with his speeding thoughts which had leaped into the intricacies of holodeck matter. Equations of quantum mechanics and particle physics flashed through his mind in a blur. It was all absurdly simple. He just needed more glue for the gluons. *How droll! More glue—* Suddenly, he couldn't stop laughing.

Deanna shook him. "Reg snap out of it! Now!"

He stopped and blinked. "Sorry. Not myself today. I have an idea."

Deanna looked relieved and sagged back in her chair. "What is it?"

"Moriarty might help."

Deanna and Reg held on to each other for support as they walked toward the holodeck. Reg carried the Moriarty module under one arm. She hoped his mind had not slipped over the edge. Reg was convinced he could produce holodeck matter that would allow Moriarty and the Countess Regina Barthalomew to walk the real world with impunity.

She welcomed any allies but found it hard to believe that the two sentient programs could find the antidote or deal with hostile warships. Worse, she could feel Reg's mind losing its stability, careening out of control. Sudden brilliance could turn to insanity in a wink. They entered the holodeck, and Reg took the module to an interface panel. Soon the pair materialized before them, the raven-haired countess resplendent in an electric-blue gown and Moriarty in a black suit.

"Ah, Mr. Barclay and Counselor Troi. So, Picard has decided to transfer us from one prison to another."

Deanna felt shock surging through Reg.

"You knew?" Reg croaked.

Moriarty ignored the question. "Tell me, why are we here and not—" Moriarty's eyes moved quickly around the bare holodeck until they rested on the module. A dark frown came over his face. "In that little box," he said, pointing. "A pathetic prison, wouldn't you say, my dear?" The countess nodded, her regal smile changing to a look of distaste.

"We need your help," Deanna said.

Moriarty's sharp, blue eyes glistened with sudden interest. "Does this mean that you have some way to free us from this?" he asked, gesturing to the empty room. Deanna turned to Reg, but she felt his confusion. Something was wrong.

"I thought I did, but I can't seem to remember . . ."

"You can't remember!" Moriarty's face reddened. "Do you hear that, my dear? We are going mad in our prison, and he can't remember. Tell Picard he can roast in hell!"

"The lives of twelve hundred people are at stake, Professor," Deanna said. "Lieutenant Barclay and I are the only crew still functioning, and we're in bad shape as you can see."

Moriarty's expression did not change, but the countess softened a bit. She took Moriarty's arm, and he smiled at her, but his face turned hard again when he faced Deanna.

"Free us permanently from this limbo existence, and you shall have our best. Otherwise, nothing." Then Moriarty smiled a sad, bitter smile. His tone softened. "If you fail, we ask only that you erase us." He looked sideways to the countess, and she kissed his forehead.

"It's all right, James."

Moriarty turned back and Deanna was shocked to see tears glistening in his eyes. "We prefer to die rather than drift into madness." Then Moriarty straightened. "Give us freedom, or give us death!"

Deanna had no answer. Reg returned the two to their module, but left it in the holodeck, interfaced to the computer. Then they dragged themselves out into the corridor.

"What happened, Reg?"

"It was all there. How to convert holodeck matter to a new form, how to modify our holodeck transmitter, all of it. Then it was just gone. I'm so sorry."

"It's not your fault," she said. "I don't know how much help they would have been, but it was a good idea."

"I'd better get to engineering and repair the warp drive," Reg said.

"I'll make another try at Taraga."

The two of them staggered off in different directions. When Deanna got to the holding cell, Taraga was pacing, tugging at her earlobes, clenching and unclenching her fists. When she saw Deanna, Taraga smiled contemptuously.

"Give up?"

Deanna ignored the question and approached the restraining field, pretending to observe the woman's face. "You could be an attractive woman if you had that scar removed."

Taraga's face twisted in rage, but then she caught herself and laughed. "Nice try, 'Zoid. The longer you wait, the harder it'll go for you, sister. You might find yourself sucking vacuum if the virus doesn't kill you first."

She hadn't really expected to goad Taraga into a slip, but Deanna returned to the bridge feeling defeated. She'd not felt so impotent since the time she temporarily lost her empathic abilities. Then she had learned to trust her instincts and training. Taraga had set her a puzzle, and she had to solve it! *Two hours.* Beyond that, the risks to the crew were too great.

Reg checked the calibrations one last time. The *Enterprise* could maintain warp for only a few hours, but it was the best he could manage. His condition had not improved. Sharp pain lanced through his head at any sudden movement, and bright spots floated across his field of vision. He felt more like a nail than a hammer. Poor Geordi lay on the floor not five paces away, apparently asleep except for the beads of sweat on his forehead. The ship was like an old fairy tale where the residents of a castle are cast into a magical sleep by an evil witch.

The room began to spin. Reg crumpled to the floor, flat on his back. Now how had the handsome prince saved the day? Didn't he kiss them all or some such thing? Or did it have something to do with frogs? No, that wasn't it. Moriarty! He was the problem, or the answer, or something. Why wouldn't his thoughts slow down so he could hold on to one? *Moriarty stuck inside the holodeck. Have to get him off, but he can't leave.* Oh God, that whirlpool was about to suck him in again. *But maybe he can take the holodeck with him!* A portable transmitter! Much easier than changing holomatter. He saw how to do it. Only time for something crude. Thank God, he was in engineering. Reg crawled to a design station on hands and knees. Now, if he could just hold on to his knowledge long enough to finish the job.

Only thirty minutes left. She felt the unconscious crew, her family, drifting away like boats on a sluggish tide. Dying. Deanna took Taraga's empty bag and tossed it onto the bridge floor. Taraga had probably hidden something from that bag when she undressed in sickbay, but Deanna's search found nothing. Which only meant that Taraga picked it up later. The antidote could be hidden anywhere. The woman still revealed only annoyance at her capture and some continuing discomfort. A smug confidence was growing, and why not? Suddenly, the ship shook violently, and the red-alert Klaxon sounded. They had been found.

"Computer, take evasive action," she commanded. The bridge door swished open and she turned, expecting Reg. To her astonishment, Moriarty and the countess entered, followed by Reg walking unsteadily and carrying Spot. Each of the Victorians wore a square, metallic device strapped to one arm.

"I'll explain about them later," Reg said as he stumbled into the adjacent chair. Then he looked down at the cat and said, "Spot needed company."

"Reg, we don't have the antidote. Without that, this is all meaningless." Another hit jolted the ship, then Moriarty removed the captain and Will Riker from their chairs.

As he dragged Picard away, Moriarty beamed at Deanna. "Ah, sweet irony!" Then he and the countess took their places. "Finding the antidote is your problem, I'm afraid," Moriarty said. "I have contracted with Mr. Barclay to deal with these pirates. Of course, after I handle them we will help you administer your medicine. Mr. Barclay has enlisted aid from the holodeck, as well."

"I replicated a dozen other transmitters," Reg said. Another blow shook the ship.

"But I don't—"

The countess interrupted Deanna's protest. "We saw that Taraga woman. She is a common sort, and I sympathize with you having to deal with her. She has no taste. Drab clothes but gaudy jewels. Most vulgar."

Deanna stared. She could not believe her ears. These people still did not grasp that she would have to surrender— The thought was cut short by the memory of Taraga constantly tugging at her ears. Great gods of Betazed! The countess had hit it on the nose. Sore earlobes could mean new earrings! Heavy earrings! Oh, how could she have been so dense? Deanna hugged the startled countess, then staggered off toward the turbolift, phaser in hand. When Reg tried to follow, she waved him down. "Stay and help here. I can take care of this."

The turbolift seemed to take forever, but finally she was half running, half stumbling toward the cell. Another hit shook the ship, but she managed to keep her balance. Deanna was panting when she arrived.

Taraga flashed a knowing smile. "Time's up!"

"It is for you." Deanna dropped the force field. She could stun the woman, but Deanna wanted Taraga conscious in case her deduction was wrong. "Give me your earrings!" Taraga's eyes narrowed, and Deanna felt her anger. Deanna was right! Taraga shrugged and started to loosen one side. Suddenly, she kicked upward, knocking the phaser from Deanna's hand. A second blow pushed Deanna backward against the wall. She doubled over in pain, cursing her stupidity.

Taraga might have lunged for the phaser, but instead bore in on Deanna, grinning. "I'm going to show you what pain's all about, sister. I can break half your bones before you pass out."

A cold fury filled Deanna, but one tied to discipline. Taraga spun into another kick. "I don't have time for this!" Deanna said. She blocked the kick with one hand, lifted the attacker's leg and delivered her own kick just behind Taraga's knee. There was a crunch of breaking bone as Taraga collapsed to the floor, grimacing and holding her leg.

"I was trained by a Klingon, *sister!" Thank you, Worf!*

Deanna summarily stunned Taraga and stooped to snatch the earrings. Sure enough, the crystal globes held liquid. The antidote. Deanna tried to get up, but her legs refused. Another hit shook the *Enterprise.*

"You can give that to me, dear." Deanna turned to see the countess. "You're exhausted, and I can run a replicator and load hyposprays. Besides, I have help. Come, ladies." Deanna nearly gasped when twelve copies of Beverly Crusher came around the corner, each wearing one of the armbands Reg had made. Deanna gave the earrings to the countess.

"We shall take care of everything."

"What about the ships?"

"Leave them to James. He's quite knowledgeable about such things."

"Do we have warp drive and full shields, Mr. Barclay?"

"Yes, but are you sure you're up to this?"

"I've been practicing in that little box for nearly two years! But how exhilarating to be in the real world!"

Exhilarating? With eight warships closing in? A near miss rattled the ship. Reg was beginning to wonder if getting Moriarty off the holodeck was such a good idea after all. And now Spot had deserted Reg and climbed into this madman's lap. Traitor!

"Arm phasers! Arm photon torpedoes! Computer, we shall break out at half impulse. Pick enemy ships at will and fire continuously. Fire all torpedoes except numbers one through four. Is that understood?"

"Order is understood."

"Are we ready, Mr. Barclay?"

"Yes, but—"

"You said I was in charge, but if you wish to take command . . ."

Reg was drowning in doubt but shook his head. He could barely keep himself in the chair, much less make split-second decisions. He also had no idea how to save the *Enterprise.* God let him be right in giving command to Moriarty.

"I'm ready," Reg said.

"Engage!"

The *Enterprise* came out firing, and chaos erupted over the planet. Searing phaser beams, disruptor bursts, and the bright star bursts of photon torpedoes lit the heavens. Hit after hit pounded the *Enterprise*'s screens, and Reg lost track of the damage reports. Oddly, no lethal damage was done despite Reg's feeble attempts at evasive action. Meanwhile, the *Enterprise* wreaked havoc among the attackers. At least three floated without power, spilling smoke and debris.

"Cease fire and all stop!" Moriarty ordered.

Two more hits shook the ship, but then the enemy stopped shooting.

"They're hailing us," Reg panted.

"Of course they are. Put the message on screen."

A man with dark, scowling eyes, bushy eyebrows, and shoulder-length, black hair glared back at them from the viewer.

"Stand down and prepare for boarding! Twitch once and we'll blow you to bits!"

Moriarty just smiled and stroked Spot. "Destroy the swag? I think not. Besides, you will have noticed that I have four torpedoes remaining. I saved them on purpose. They are not ordinary torpedoes. Starfleet calls them 'Borg Busters,' I believe. Apparently, six took out a Borg cube by themselves. I have only *two* trained on you, but then you're not exactly a Borg cube, are you?"

"You're not Starfleet! Who the blazes are you?"

"Professor James Moriarty is my name. I am a businessman, shall we say, much the same as you. This ship is *my* swag now. Captain Taraga was kind enough to disable the crew which made our job so much simpler."

The other man almost snarled. Reg wondered what swag meant and prayed Moriarty didn't mean what he said.

"Damn that double-crossing swine!" The man's eyes narrowed. "You'll not get away with this. If you destroy my ship, you'll still die where you stand."

Moriarty's smile widened. "I have found that every successful, criminal organization is the child of a brilliant and forceful mind. If one cuts off the head, the remaining parts flail about helplessly. That is why I have the other Borg Busters trained on that insignificant-looking ship at the edge of your armada. As well as a phaser or two." The man's eyes narrowed and his mouth pinched to a frown. Moriarty continued his nonchalant smile. "Now why don't you stop playing games, and let me speak to the real leader."

A seeming eternity crept by in silence. Moriarty was either brilliant or about to get them killed. Finally, the screen faded, and a new face appeared. A Romulan face. The Romulan smiled.

"Well-reasoned. So we have what you humans call a stand-off."

"Thank you," Moriarty acknowledged. "But our standoff cannot last long. Despite Captain Taraga's best efforts, the ship's log shows that a distress call was sent. I fear that a rather nasty group of ships will arrive in this area shortly. There is no profit for either of us if we keep this up."

"Then you should surrender. You are surrounded."

"I have my lovely Borg Busters pointed right at you."

"Your torpedo story could be a ruse."

Moriarty kept smiling, without even a blink. "Perhaps, but I have buyers for these beauties, and I'd rather not waste them."

The Romulan considered long moments, and Reg scarcely dared to breathe. Then the Romulan laughed. "There will be other days and other profits. Perhaps we will meet again. I could use one like you."

"And I one like you."

The screen went black. In moments, the attackers left, towing their damaged vessels. Reg looked back at Moriarty. "How did you know . . . ?"

Moriarty's eyes gleamed. "To capture such a formidable ship as this without violence requires brilliant planning and meticulous preparation. In short, a criminal mastermind. Such people lead from the shadows whenever possible, but he would surely be at hand to claim a jewel like the *Enterprise,* lest an ambitious underling get ideas." His smile turned wicked. "I should know. That small ship moved to safety as soon as the fight began. I needed the battle to choose correctly." Moriarty sighed. "Besides, it was such fun!" At that point, the countess swooped onto the bridge carrying several hyposprays. "It is time to give Mr. Barclay the antidote."

Deanna had done it! The countess gave him one spray in his neck and another in his arm. "That one will help you sleep," she said. He tried to thank her, but the world faded to black before he got the chance.

When Reg woke, he found the crew recovering, Taraga under guard, and Moriarty and the countess gone, along with all the holotransmitters and the shuttle Reg had modified by adding a miniature holodeck. That had been part of the bargain. Fortunately, Captain Picard agreed that, under the circumstances, a shuttle was a small price to pay. Moriarty also destroyed the module. Who could blame him?

Reg could not remember how he had built the transmitters, but the plans were tucked safely into computer memory. The Barclay Transmitter. It had a nice ring to it.

Deanna Troi roamed the corridors of the *Enterprise,* delighting in the flood of familiar emotions. Her family was safe, and that was all that mattered. She was so taken up in it all, that the tap of a hand on her shoulder caught her by surprise.

"Beverly! How are you feeling?"

"Oh, just a little tired. I've just finished checking the brain scans for everyone except Mr. Barclay. It's your scan I'm concerned about."

"Mine? But I feel fine."

Beverly grabbed her arm and stopped her. "I noticed some irregularities. I'm afraid you're going to have to submit to one of the strongest therapies I have."

"What sort of therapy?"

"Hot fudge on chocolate ice cream."

Deanna gave Beverly a phantom punch on the arm, and the bubbling laughter of the two women turned heads as they marched toward the E's version of Ten Forward.

Reg fidgeted on Beverly Crusher's examination table as she scanned his brain. Why was it taking so long? He pictured whole regions eaten away like a gnawed cabbage. He patiently endured her lecture on how the rare, Orbelian virus antibodies he and Deanna carried had helped fight this new variety and keep them conscious. He even showed polite interest in her explanation of how the new virus attacked the brain and nervous system with astonishing speed. Finally, she turned off the scanner and faced him with folded arms. He felt queasy.

"Everything looks fine, Reg. Still, something odd did happen to you. I have a speculation, but that's all it is."

"Please," he said, limp with relief.

"The Cytherian's method of storage may have left chemical imprints on some of your brain structures, perhaps like a fossil holds the shape of an organism. The virus could have temporarily altered your brain chemistry and allowed you access to some of that information."

"Could it happen again?"

"I really can't say, Reg. The strain is extremely virulent and may have erased it all."

Reg didn't know whether he was relieved or disappointed. That night as he wrote into his personal log, a message popped up unexpectedly on the screen.

"Mr. Barclay, please accept our apologies for rushing off without a proper farewell, but frankly, we still harbor doubts about Picard. We are eternally in your debt. Our plan is to head for the galactic core. What a grand adventure that will be! Yet, I cannot help but feel a twinge of regret that you and I could not have taken up the skull and crossbones and made the Enterprise *the scourge of the galaxy! But it was all great fun! Your servant ever, James Moriarty.*

Moriarty was wrong about Captain Picard, but Reg smiled as he finished the note. It *had* been fun. Sort of.

Moriarty stirred when Regina huddled against him, shivering beneath the blanket.

"What's wrong, my love?"

"I dreamed we were back in that horrid box."

He kissed her gently. "It's nothing, my dear. A toothless phantom. Return to sweet slumber." She lay her head upon his chest, and soon their breathing settled into a slow, gentle rhythm.

Reg took a last peek in the mirror. *Still balding, still too thin.* He shrugged and smiled. Nothing would spoil this evening. Good friends, good food, and good conversation. On his way out, he stopped to check the Moriarty module. *Lots of usage today.* Almost time for a new power unit. Humming to himself, Reg left his quarters and headed for the turbolift.

STAR TREK

DEEP SPACE NINE®

[SECOND PRIZE]

Ninety-three Hours

Kim Sheard

Hour Two (1200)

Ezri Tigan awoke to the beeping of a vital signs monitor. She was uncomfortable flat on her back on the biobed, but didn't want to move yet. Through the thin membrane of her closed eyelids, she could tell that the sickbay lights had been dimmed for her benefit. Still without opening her eyes, she cautiously analyzed her mind and body. Her brain, groggy from the lingering effects of the anesthetic, worked slowly, but she was surprised and relieved to note that her thoughts were completely her own. Perhaps the surgery had been called off.

Moving on to her physical condition, she noted that her mouth was dry and she was thirsty from being denied water in preparation for surgery. The left side of her neck itched, like an insect had bitten her there. But those were minor irritations. With trepidation, she took a deep breath, expanding from the diaphragm, and felt the difference. Yes, it had been done. Without looking or touching she was aware of the slight bulge below her navel and the unfamiliar pressure on her bladder from the unwanted invader. The skin covering her abdomen felt tight and pinched. With dread, she decided it would be best to confront her situation and to ask for a status report.

Dr. Fulghum came noiselessly to her side when her eyes blinked open. "The surgery went well, Ensign. There were no complications, and the symbiont will be fine now." Ezri squelched her resentment toward this man for convincing her to accept the symbiont. She knew its predicament had not been his fault, but she couldn't help thinking that he was using her as nothing more than an intelligent incubator. She turned her stiff neck to look at him as he pulled a short, wheeled stool to her bedside and sat.

Her hands moved automatically to her belly, which was covered by a Starfleet standard issue surgical gown. Designed to fit everyone, she had always thought, and to look good on no one. "I can feel its body," she said, "but not its thoughts."

"The symbiont was so weak and you so unprepared for joining that I have been inhibiting your isoboramine level. I'm allowing it to rise gradually. You should begin to feel the neural link shortly." His voice was gentle and quiet in the darkened room. He was trying to be kind, Ezri realized. She wondered if he felt any guilt for what he had done.

Ezri finally scratched her neck, discovering that it was the isoboramine controller that had been pinching her. "Can you keep my neurotransmitter level low so that I don't have to sense the symbiont? After all, I'm not going to keep it."

The doctor took a deep breath, as if to delay revealing unpleasant news. "We're not certain that we will be able to reach a new host within the ninety-three hours before you and the symbiont become biologically interdependent. The ship coming from Trill was delayed answering a distress call. They've resumed course for the *Destiny,* but they may have been delayed too long."

Ezri grimaced and sat up, beginning to feel panicked. "I may be joined for the rest of my life?" she asked, but it was more of a statement than a question. The doctor simply nodded, patted her hand as if in apology, and returned to his other sickbay duties. Ezri was left alone with only the beeping monitor and her black thoughts for company. Such thoughts were uncharacteristic for the normally amiable Trill, and she was uncomfortable with them. Perhaps the new personalities were beginning to take hold. Recalling her counselor's training, she lay back down on the bed, folded her hands across her stomach, and closed her eyes. At least she could look and act calm, even if she didn't feel calm.

Her mother had always insisted that joining was an outmoded ambition. The Trill host race had evolved enough that they could lead fulfilling and influential lives without symbionts. Neither of Ezri's parents had been joined. Nor had her brothers, Norvo and Janel, who hadn't dared to even question their mother's strong opinion on the subject.

Ezri had never wanted to be joined, either. Sure, she had been taught in school what a tremendous blessing it was to be joined and how important it was to protect the symbionts. For a while, she had even thought it romantic that another being's essence could be added to her own, immediately turning her own imperfect existence into a meaningful one and her reserved personality into a self-assured one. But those had been only innocent fantasies that Ezri had kept to herself. Now that she was actually joined, it wasn't romantic at all, it was terrifying. As soon as she and the symbiont linked mentally, her entire persona would be changed. All of her experiences, development, and hard work would be combined with more than three hundred years of experiences and would be rendered almost irrelevant to the whole. She would be completely changed, possibly forever. She would be insignificant.

On the biobed in *Destiny*'s sickbay, Ezri Tigan wondered how she could possibly feel so lonely while physically joined with another being. She had counseled people who were involved in happy, healthy relationships but were still desperately lonely. She had never experienced the sensation herself, though. Until now. She closed her eyes and tried to sleep.

Hour Four (1400)

Ezri woke with a start and called for a bedpan. She vomited on her surgical gown and down the side of the biobed before it came. "Space sickness," the Bolian nurse reported after consulting her tricorder. "Have you ever had that problem before?"

"I would never have joined Starfleet if I had," Ezri said, disgusted with herself. She slid gingerly off the biobed, finally quieting its built-in monitor. She moved slowly into the sickbay bathroom, accepting the clean gown the nurse offered. Once there, she finally had the opportunity to examine her altered body in the mirror.

First, she considered her face. It didn't look any different, really. The fair skin, sepia and tan spots, and beauty mark above her lip were all familiar. She sensed a difference, though, and impatiently brushed her waist-long black hair away from her face to examine her bright blue eyes. Leaning close to the mirror, she did indeed see a difference. It was not Ezri Tigan staring back at her, it was someone older and less hopeful. It scared her, and she had to look away.

She stripped off her dirty gown and left it in a heap on the floor. She felt safe examining her body as long as she avoided looking into those eyes. Surprisingly, considering how large the lump inside felt, her abdomen didn't really look any different from the outside, other than the rapidly fading pink scar from the surgery. Placing two fingers over the scar, she could feel the symbiont pulsing slightly. She couldn't see it, but it was truly there, at least for now. She rinsed the sour taste from her mouth and drank water cupped in her hands.

Are you qualified to host this symbiont, little girl?

It was no more than a murmur, but its effect was startling. Her head jerked upward and she searched the tiny room for the source of the sound. She saw nothing but the toilet, sink, and a small sonic shower, but she shrugged into her clean gown as quickly as possible in case there was an unseen observer.

Dax has always been particular about its hosts, she heard. *Are you worthy?*

As she calmed her startled breathing and considered the unexpected danger, she realized the voice had been detected not by her ears, but by her mind. She was beginning to bond to the symbiont and to sense its previous hosts. The voice wasn't actually audible, but emanated from her own mind. Minds, she reminded herself.

She gathered her strength to answer back as if by telepathy. "Who are you?" she asked. "I am Ezri. No, I am not qualified. I am an emergency measure. Only temporary." She hugged the clean gown around her middle, trying to stop her frightened shivering in the small room that suddenly felt very cold.

So, one of Dax's hosts finally managed to get itself killed far from Trill, did it? I knew it would happen sooner or later. I believe I added a certain recklessness to the mix. Even more so than Torias did. The voice was much clearer now, and gruff. It reminded her of her grandfather Tigan's in his later years.

"I'm sorry," she said. "I don't know the symbiont's history. There wasn't time for me to study it before the joining. Who are you? Who is Torias?" She was curious in spite of herself.

I'm Curzon Dax, the seventh host. Torias was number five.

"Where are the others?"

They're around. Their memories may not be as strong as mine. I was host to Dax for nearly a hundred years. I made quite an impression.

"I'm sure you did," Ezri said, suddenly wanting this Curzon to leave her alone. As if it agreed, her stomach churned again. "I need to go lie down." She shuffled back into sickbay, clutching her middle, but her bodily misery didn't nearly match her mental agony. The biobed's monitor began to sound again as she lay down. Its normalcy was oddly comforting.

Dr. Fulghum approached. "How are we doing, Ensign?"

"We're space sick," Ezri said irritably. "And I do mean *we.* I'm gaining the memories of one of the hosts. I feel like I'm talking to myself. Ordinarily, I would diagnose myself with some kind of psychosis, but I don't think I'm in the position right now to make that kind of decision." She moaned as the nausea flared.

"Your isoboramine level is still increasing," the doctor said. He put his hand on her shoulder. "I know this is difficult for you, but you're doing well. You'll get through it." He raised a hypospray to her neck. "This will help alleviate the nausea." Ezri thanked the gods that she and Dr. Fulghum had worked together to help a crewman through Jovian mind flu several months ago. She took some comfort in the fact that he knew she wasn't ordinarily so irascible.

"Thank you, Doctor." She interrupted as he turned to continue his work. "Doctor, can the ship go any faster?" She sighed when he shook his head.

Hour Eight (1800)

She had tried to read without success. Listening to music had not been as relaxing as she had hoped, either, since she had inexplicably requested Klingon opera. She was too frustrated to watch the ship's slow progress toward Trill on the monitors, so finally she simply lay on the biobed wallowing in the gradually appearing memories.

It was difficult to sort them out. She thought of gymnastics competitions and remembered entire tumbling routines before realizing that her body had never been limber enough to perform such feats. Yet she felt lithe, strong, confident. She remembered fancy flight patterns and the adrenaline rush of solo test flights before realizing that she was an assistant counselor, not a pilot. But she reveled in being coordinated, symphonic, free. She fondly remembered summer evenings on Trill with the comfort and love of her two children and then recalled with a start that she had no children. But she longed for them, and fervently hoped that they had their father's ridged forehead and strong jaw. No, she chastised herself, that was Jadzia.

Jadzia, she finally realized, had been the most recent host. All of her remembered personalities felt sadness and regret, but Jadzia's was fresh and raw. Jadzia was angry to have her young life ended. Ezri could not separate that anger from her own. Jadzia was livid with the Cardassian Dukat for ending her life needlessly. Ezri was angry with him as well for indirectly forcing this symbiont on her.

The anger feels good, doesn't it? one of the hosts whispered in her mind, his thoughts fainter than those of the others.

She forced herself not to speak aloud or the sickbay staff would hear. *No, it doesn't,* she said. *I know from all my psychology training that anger seldom serves a useful purpose. It's certainly a natural reaction, but I need to resist it. I'm wrongly expressing my fear as anger.* She took deep breaths to slow her pounding heart. She concentrated on the rhythmic beeping of the vital signs monitor and tried to conjure chants and songs to go along with it. *Count the spots, One-two-three, Many more down to your knee,* she remembered from school. Curiosity and boredom eventually overcame anger, and she reached out to the new voice. *Which host are you?* But the voice wouldn't return. Ezri sensed that it was being suppressed somehow. Curious.

Her thoughts were far away when Dr. Fulghum next checked on her. His soft words startled her from her reverie. "Ensign, the symbiont-host neurotransmitter level has peaked. If you're feeling well, I'm ready to release you to your quarters now."

Suddenly, Ezri's anger dissipated, leaving only stark terror at the possibility of being alone with the invaders in her mind, but she simply nodded, accepted the hypospray prescription for her newly acquired space-sickness, and climbed off the biobed to dress in her civilian clothes. It was going to be a long night.

Hour Twelve (2200)

It wasn't until her door chime sounded that Ezri noticed what a disaster she had made of her quarters. Plates and cups of half-finished food and drink were scattered about the room along with most of her wardrobe from her oldest pajamas to her most formal gown. She was even more embarrassed to find that her visitor was Lieutenant Commander Jona Meel, the ship's counselor and her supervisor. An ivory silk caftan brought out the rich tones of Jona's dark brown skin and made her look comfortable and neat, in contrast to Ezri, who was currently wearing a mismatched sweatsuit below her long hair, which was disheveled from trying on so many different outfits.

Ezri couldn't decide if the Bajoran's expression was one of amusement or concern; Jona was very capable of hiding her own emotions in deference to her patients'. She was dressed casually as though the visit was merely a friendly one, but Ezri knew that her boss would certainly be assessing her psychological condition. Her counselor's persona was too ingrained for her to do otherwise. Unsure of what to say, Ezri simply smiled sheepishly at the woman and stepped back to allow her to come in.

"I know it's late," Jona said, "but I wanted to see how you were doing, and the doctor wouldn't allow me to visit you in sickbay." Ezri suddenly realized that the doctors and nurses in sickbay were the only other company she'd had in the last twenty-four hours.

"I've been better," Ezri admitted. She gestured toward the couch and cleared away some clothes so that they could both sit down. "Sorry about the mess."

"Doing some cleaning?" Jona prompted.

"The Dax hosts and I can't seem to agree on what I should eat or wear." She sighed. "They're all so different, and I'm trying not to let them control me, but I can't seem to help myself."

"That must be an interesting sensation," Jona replied, nonchalantly folding a uniform that had lain on the coffee table in front of her.

"You're telling me. I've been talking to myself," Ezri said. "And remembering things that have never happened to me. People are introducing themselves to me inside my head, and I can't seem to keep them, or myself, straight."

"I'm sure it must be very confusing. Why don't you tell me about the hosts?"

"Well, okay. There's Jadzia, she's the host that just died, a Starfleet science officer. She was only a few years older than me, I think. Lela, a woman, too, was a gymnast, or was that Emony? Well, Lela, Emony, and Audrid were the other women. Curzon liked to play *tongo* and lived to be over a hundred years old. Do you know that now I know how to play *tongo?* I'd never even heard of it before today. One of the hosts was a pilot and died in a crash. And I'd swear that I heard another speak to me, but I haven't heard from him again since that first time . . ." Realizing she was speaking at breakneck speed and gesturing wildly, Ezri fell silent, biting her lip. Why couldn't she control herself?

Jona gently touched her hand. "Haven't you studied Dax's record in the database? That would help you get them all straight and to accept their memories more easily, wouldn't it?"

"That won't be necessary, since I'm not keeping the symbiont." She jumped up and began collecting the dishes, the matter settled.

But Jona wasn't dissuaded. "Wouldn't studying up on the hosts a bit help you to understand their memories and personalities while you do carry them? Ezri, we may or may not reach the intended host in time, you know that, right?" Ezri nodded reluctantly, unable to look at her colleague. "Even if you are able to successfully transfer the symbiont to that host before a permanent bond is formed, you will still need to deal with those memories, and they will always be a part of you. Whether or not the symbiont is passed on, you will need to take a leave of absence to deal with the emotional ramifications. For right now, I believe that the best way to do that is to learn as much as you can about Dax's hosts so that you can separate their wants and needs from your own. You can't let those other hosts make you forget who Ezri Tigan is."

Ezri chuckled, beaten. "Are you trained in Trill psychology?"

Counselor Jona smiled back. "I've read a few papers, but I think much of this situation can be dealt with using common sense. This is the same kind of advice you would give if you were the one doing the counseling." She rose from the sofa. "I'll be happy to work with you when your leave of absence is over," she said. "Whether you're joined or not."

"Thank you," Ezri said, and her friend left her in a flurry of rustling cloth.

Hour Twenty-four (1000)

On the holodeck, Ezri stood shining a palm beacon on one of the fondest memories of her childhood. When she was only six years old and her father was still alive, he had convinced Mother to leave the mines for the day and had taken the family to the Jewel Caves that were an hour's shuttle ride from home. Ezri had never seen them before and was fascinated by the gleaming stones embedded in the jagged gray walls. Her favorite stones were the brightest pink she had ever seen. The color of Klingon blood, Janel had teased, trying to upset her. But on that one day, neither her older brother's taunting nor her mother's constant nagging had dampened her spirits. In fact, she had been so entranced that rather than sketching the caves in his notebook, Norvo had drawn Ezri, portraying her cartoonishly with a sparkle in one eye as she stared at the wall with a happy grin on her face. Ezri had found the drawing in a box the night before and called up an image of the caves as soon as she could get a holodeck reservation.

The trip to the Jewel Caves had been one of the few completely pleasant days of her childhood, before the more difficult tasks of dealing with her father's death, her mother's expectations, and leaving home to make a life completely her own. Boarding the transport for Starfleet Academy with dreams of succeeding in a field her family had never touched had been another of the happiest events of Ezri's life.

Remembering that day now, Ezri was proud of all she had accomplished and was satisfied with her choice to leave her mother's wishes and Janel's doubts behind. She felt for her brother Norvo, who often wrote that he wished he could leave home as well. He had been the only family member confident that Ezri would succeed on her own.

Agreeing with Counselor Jona that keeping her own identity was very important now, Ezri struggled to suppress Curzon, Jadzia, Torias, and the others inside her while she examined the memories she had found in storage boxes and personal logs during the previous sleepless night. No voices spoke in her head during that time, and she was pleased to be able to assert herself so strongly. She didn't realize until later that, although the conscious thoughts and memories had belonged to Ezri alone, her perspective of the events had been altered by the presence of the other hosts' personalities. They were beginning to integrate themselves so into her being that she was unaware of their separate effects.

Returning to her quarters, she learned that the *Destiny*'s rendezvous with the Trill ship was now scheduled for ninety-four hours after joining.

Hour Forty-one (0300)

Exhausted by the previous sleepless night, Ezri had no difficulty resting the second night after joining. After a few hours of deep sleep, she began to dream. In the dream, she sat at the head of the *Destiny*'s conference table with Dax's previous hosts occupying the chairs around her, and they spoke to her and to each other in a confusing whirl of words. Ezri could only watch, trying to follow their rapid conversation.

"We're aware that you've been suppressing us, Ezri. You can't do that forever. It'll drive you crazy. It's too much for a mind to handle," said the short, stout woman who then rose and began pacing the room with her hands clasped behind her back. She wasn't the type that could sit still, it seemed.

"Lela's right," said the statuesque woman to Ezri's right. "We want you to accept us and learn from us. We complete you. And, when you die, you will live on through Dax, as we have." Her dark, shiny hair reminded Ezri of her own.

"She doesn't deserve to live on through Dax," said the host who was classically handsome despite the sour expression on his face. "She's too disgustingly innocent."

"Go away, Joran, you're not wanted here," the tall woman snapped. Joran disappeared, leaving his chair empty and still. To Ezri she said, "You'd do best to stay away from that one. He's nothing but trouble. And don't listen to him. Joran tried pulling that crap on me during my *zhian'tara.* You're just young. You have some pretty interesting stories already, I'll bet, and you'll end up with plenty more. Probably better than any of ours, right guys?"

"We'll see, Jadzia. Tobin, tell her how much you liked being joined," Lela said. "You had never been happier, right?"

The man at the foot of the table who had been biting his nails through the entire exchange answered, meekly, "Yeah, I liked it. Didn't change me that much, though. Well, sorry, I guess I only had Lela's influence, not as many hosts as you do. Maybe it's not the same thing."

"But you liked it, that's the important thing," Lela countered.

"Yeah."

"Being joined improved my concentration and my confidence. I suddenly began winning my gymnastics meets," the pretty, wiry woman offered.

"You needed all the help you could get, Emony," Lela said, causing Emony to frown, but she didn't respond.

The young, fit man next to Lela finally spoke up, tilting his chair dangerously cockeyed. "You should take this life and embrace it. Life is too short for worrying. Enjoy yourself!"

Ezri recognized the elderly Curzon as soon as he spoke. "While I agree with Torias's sentiment, I still say she's not qualified to be a host. She hasn't been trained."

"She'll do fine," Jadzia said. "You know as well as I do that the initiate program can't really prepare you for the new thoughts and emotions. They overwhelm you anyway until you get used to them. Ezri's a counselor. She's probably more capable of handling it than any of the rest of us were."

"And she has us to help her," said the fourth woman, a round, motherly blonde. "I'm Audrid, darling. You will love being joined and having us as a part of you. Joining will not make you less of a person, it will make you more than you ever thought you could be." Audrid held out her hand and Ezri gripped it like a lifeline. It was warm and soft. "We want you to join us, child. Adjusting won't be easy, but we'll help you. We've had quite a bit of experience with joining. Soon you'll come to love us as a part of yourself. We'll be with you for the rest of your life, and you'll never be alone. Wouldn't you like that?"

The dream faded away and Ezri turned over in her sleep, nodding, thinking that Audrid understood her perfectly.

Hour Fifty-three (1500)

Inspired by her dream, Ezri finally opened Starfleet's files on the Dax symbiont and all of its hosts. Sequestered in her quarters, she read for hours about their fascinating lives. At the same time, she documented memories of her own as the files brought them to mind. While reading about Curzon and Jadzia's friendships with the Klingons Kor, Koloth, and Kang, she remembered fondly her own teen triumvirate of best friends Callie, Perra, and Doral. Torias's piloting notes triggered a remembrance of her own disastrous first flight. Her experiences weren't quite as flamboyant as the antics from Curzon's frequent trips to Risa or Emony's love affairs, but it was reassuring to see them in writing. Their documentation seemed to confirm that Ezri's life was just as important in the grand scheme of things as Lela's and Tobin's and Jadzia's. And, unlike the other hosts', Ezri's story was still being written.

Gradually, as she read, she allowed the hosts' memories to resurface, telling herself that it would make the files more meaningful. It did to the extent that Ezri began to have difficulty again remembering which of them she really was. Several times she made trips to her mirror, reminding her image that she was Ezri Tigan, the young Starfleet Assistant Counselor who might not even be keeping the symbiont.

She checked the distance between the *Destiny* and the transport from Trill several times during the day. It was still possible for the two ships to meet in time, but it would be close. She began to resign herself to the possibility of remaining joined, though she still hoped that her semiacceptance was just a precaution.

Hour Fifty-eight (2000)

Dressed in her uniform with her raven hair gathered into a ponytail at the nape of her neck, Ezri entered the ship's lounge, which was crowded with off-duty Alpha shifters. Always uncomfortable with the prospect of running into patients in social situations, she hadn't spent much time here in the past. "On such a small ship," Jona had warned, "you need to get past that," but so far Ezri hadn't been able to, and had spent most of her off-duty time alone or with a few select acquaintances in more private places.

Tonight, though, she didn't care whom she met. Having been alone with her padds all day, she was lonely for humanoid companionship. In fact, the day had made her aware of just how isolated she had been for the past several months. She smiled when she noticed one of the lounge's patrons near the bar with a bright red drink in his hand.

Ensign Billy Jamison had been a good friend at one time. He and Ezri had begun their assignments on the *Destiny* on the very same day. At the end of that seemingly endless duty shift, they had met in his quarters for a drink, sharing both the toil and the rewards of the day. Their friendship had grown over several months. Ezri had especially appreciated that she was able to completely relax and be herself with Billy. He never judged her the way her mother and Janel had.

Then, after three months in their comfortable relationship, Billy's bunkmate had been killed on an away mission and Billy had sought the services of the ship's counselors to deal with the loss. Ezri immediately announced that their social relationship had to end. Billy had reluctantly agreed, and they had exchanged few words since. But Ezri had been wrong to discontinue their friendship. She intended to right that wrong immediately.

The tall blond man was deep in conversation with a thin, dark lieutenant and a slender civilian woman. Ezri marched up and greeted Billy with a smile. Looking slightly wary, he nonetheless cordially introduced her to his companions, Lieutenant John Macafee and his wife Marcia. Ezri immediately asked them about their duties and activities on the ship. She had learned years ago that the easiest way to begin a conversation was to ask others to talk about themselves. John was a transporter engineer and Marcia worked in the ship's day care center.

"Oh, do you like children?" Ezri gushed. "I love them. I've had a number of children, well, I mean my previous hosts have, and Audrid, in particular, lived for motherhood. Do you know that she bonded so well with her children that both of them asked her to stand with them for their mating rites? That was particularly surprising in the case of the younger, a son, who gave Audrid fits during his teen years. In fact, there's this one particular story that I must tell you involving that son, his girlfriend, and a transporter coil. John, I'm sure you know how inflexible those coils are. No malleability whatsoever."

Soon, all four of them were laughing so hard that others in the lounge migrated their direction to join the fun. Realizing she was dominating the conversation, Ezri began asking the others leading questions as a good hostess would, but each time, the conversation eventually turned into a good opening for another of her host's stories that she couldn't help but tell. Near the end of the evening, she even managed to throw in one of her own, about the *kata,* a small furry Trillian mammal, that she had managed to hide and care for in her family's hovercraft port for two weeks before being discovered. It had felt good to have a pet, even for that short time.

Before she left the lounge, Billy kissed her cheek and commented that he was happy she was doing so well. He had been concerned, he said, when he heard about the joining. "Come and see me if you need to talk," he had offered, and Ezri was grateful.

Reflecting on the evening later in her quarters, Ezri was surprised at herself. She'd never been particularly good at mingling. She'd always been a listener, not a talker. Perhaps nine personalities rather than one made her more interesting. They certainly seemed to make her more confident. She liked the feeling.

Hour Seventy-three (1100)

Ezri gripped the edge of the desktop with both hands, staring tensely at her computer screen. The communiqué Dr. Fulghum had forwarded to Ezri's terminal was from Dr. Julian Bashir. Ezri had never met this man, but Dax was very fond of him, and shrank back in sadness at the sight of his name. Deep Space 9's chief medical officer was inquiring about the status of the symbiont and how it was getting along after leaving the space station in stasis.

Fulghum's response had been noncommittal, that the symbiont was safe for the moment. He had left it to Ezri to inform Dax's friends of her joining. Or not to. What should she do?

Ezri could remember Jadzia's fond feelings for Julian. She had thought of him as the brother she had never had. If one could exchange innuendo with a brother, that is. She missed him. He had always been a good friend, even when she had disappointed him. Her time on Deep Space 9 had been happy. Very happy.

Her thoughts wandered to the other friends she had made there. Kira was strong and principled. She had always reminded Jadzia of Lela. Miles O'Brien was hardworking, but knew how to relax and have a good time, too. He was full of busy bluster that had never fazed Jadzia. Thoughts of Worf came to mind and were quickly discarded. She couldn't bear to think of him. Then she came to Benjamin. Benjamin was the best friend a girl could ever have. His friendship had proven that it was possible for a special relationship to span two lifetimes, not to mention two genders.

Should she contact him? No, she finally decided. She would save her old friends for a day when she really needed their support. For the moment, she knew that Jona, Billy, and even Dr. Fulghum would be there for her. Perhaps during her leave of absence she would contact Deep Space 9. If the transport was late and Dax remained with her, she would probably end up on Trill, enduring dull post-joining training classes. If Dax was removed, Starfleet would probably send her home to her mother for R&R, which would be neither restful nor recreational. Either way, it would help to know she had an ace up her sleeve to help her through the tough times.

She saved the communiqué to a padd and threw it into her desk drawer before heading to the mess hall for lunch.

Hour Ninety (0400)

Ezri was called to sickbay in the middle of the night. A rumpled Dr. Fulghum greeted her with "We'll be within transporter range of the *Mokar* in twenty minutes. The new host has been prepared for the transfer."

"Of . . . course," Ezri said, hearing her heart pounding in her ears.

"I have to warn you that symbionts are weakened by joining. A second joining in so short a period of time may risk its life."

"How great is the danger?" Ezri was absently stroking her belly like a pregnant woman. Why did she suddenly feel so attached to Dax? Wasn't getting rid of Dax what she had wanted all along?

"Considering we'll have Trill doctors present and an approved, trained host to accept the symbiont, probably not that great, but I did want to make you aware." When Ezri didn't respond, he continued, "The operation should begin as soon as you can beam over. It will be best for both of you to sever the connection as quickly as possible."

Ezri turned away, considering. So this is what it would come to. She had twenty minutes to decide how her life would proceed. Twenty minutes to decide if she liked these people in her head, or if she wanted her thoughts all to herself. Twenty minutes to decide if she could be a better person as just Ezri or as an amalgam of nine personalities.

She had hoped the decision would be taken out of her hands. If the fates meant for her to be joined, they would not reach the new host in time, she had assumed. If Dax was meant for another, that host would be met long before an emotional bond had formed. But Ezri had to admit that an emotional bond had formed. She now knew Lela, Tobin, Emony, Audrid, Torias, Joran, Curzon, and Jadzia almost as well as she knew herself. They each had their faults, of course, particularly Joran, but they also had endearing traits and wisdom that Ezri found appealing. And, in general, they had accepted her "as is." Now it was suddenly her turn to accept or reject them.

Ezri closed her eyes, praying for an easy answer. Audrid's words came back to her. "You'll never be alone," she had said. Sensing that Dr. Fulghum was still behind her, she shook her head. "I'd like to keep them," she said. "It, I mean. Dax, the symbiont."

His reply was gentle and quiet. "Very well, Ensign, I'll notify the *Mokar*." Ezri suspected he was secretly pleased with her decision.

Hour Ninety-three (0700)

As the majority of the *Destiny*'s complement prepared for and began their daily duties, Ezri, who had been awake for hours, stood once again in front of her bathroom mirror. In her eyes, she saw a bit of Jadzia's mischief, and in the set of her lips, Lela's determination. She guessed that every day she would acquire and notice more traits of the previous hosts. She would not become any of the previous hosts, though. Neither would she be Ezri Tigan. That life was left behind. For better or for worse, she was a new person now.

Picking up the gleaming scissors she had brought to the sink, she lopped off long hanks of her hair, letting them fall into the sink. Cutting it into a new, very short style with Audrid's motherly instincts guiding her, she completed one more step in the transformation of Ezri Tigan into Ezri Dax. Meanwhile, the *Destiny* continued toward Trill where the Symbiosis Institute would take her under its wing for a time.

The precise moment at which Ezri Tigan and the symbiont Dax became biologically interdependent came and went, unnoticed.

Dorian's Diary

G. Wood

Tycho City, Luna, Sol System (001)

Luna Day 18

I hate the past.

My name is Dorian Collins, Ensign from Starfleet Academy's Red Squad, and Acting Chief Petty Officer aboard the *U.S.S. Valiant.* Rather, I was on the *Valiant* until forty-three days ago when we were destroyed by the Jem'Hadar.

I was the only survivor amongst the crew. Our seven teachers died nine months ago, and my twenty-seven fellow students died last month. I think that's when I went crazy, and when I began to hate the past.

Deanna, that's my counselor, says that I'm not crazy. She says that I'm just experiencing "survivor guilt with extenuated youthful challenges." I don't know what that means. She explained, but I did not understand.

Deanna wanted me to keep this journal to help me deal with my feelings, but I don't want to. I just want to cry. I hate the past. I don't like remembering. It hurts.

Luna Day 19

I woke up screaming this morning. I was dreaming of Captain Watters, Tim, being thrown across the bridge and dying. I couldn't stop screaming. The nurses tried everything to calm me, but nothing worked. I just kept screaming. Finally, they sedated me, and I was better this afternoon.

Luna Day 20

I dreamt of Tim again last night, but this time I didn't scream. Tim would have been irritated with me if he knew what happened the other night. When Captain Ramirez died last year, Tim was so strong for us. He kept telling us that we could complete our mission, even though all of our teachers were dead. *"Forget the past hurts. Remember the past joys. Learn from the past and apply the lessons to the future. Have a goal and move towards it."*

Tim always said the right things.

Luna Day 21

Deanna says that I'm making great progress. She says I can start having visitors now. Mr. Baris has been asking to see me. He will be coming in a couple of days.

Deanna has been so nice to me. She is usually the counselor on the *Enterprise,* but since her ship is having repairs made at the Saturn drydock, Deanna has a little bit of time to herself. The doctors at Starbase 31 asked her to keep an eye on me while we were en route to Earth, and she did. We would talk for a while each day. I was glad that the *Enterprise* was heading to Earth. It was so much more fun than traveling on a transport shuttle.

Deanna introduced me to the crew. Commander Riker reminded me of Tim and his confident demeanor. Tim never doubted himself, and I don't think Commander Riker is wracked with self-doubt, either. Captain Picard talked to me for a while. He told me how he lost many friends when his ship, the *Stargazer,* was attacked. He said it is a normal, but unfortunate side-effect of the times in which we live. *"People serve on starships; people live on starships; people die on starships."*

He's right, but I still miss my friends, especially Karen and Tim.

I was enjoying the trip to Earth when the ship was attacked by the Breen, the friends of our enemies, the Jem'Hadar. Deanna says that they were coming from a successful attack on Earth, and they only stopped for a moment to take a swipe at us. They blew out our warp drive and our weapons. Most of the computer systems, too. We had hull breaches on three decks. Captain Picard was just developing a counterstrike when they took off. Deanna says that it surprised everyone.

I was in Ten-Forward when it happened. A hull breach occurred nearby. The decompression safeties worked, so we were not in danger, but I had an anxiety attack when I saw the damage and when the ship rocked from the hits of the Breen's weapons. I don't remember anything more.

Deanna says that I flirted with consciousness for nearly a week. Every time the doctors woke me, I would faint again. Finally, they decided to let me awake on my own.

The *Enterprise* reached port two days after the attack, and then I was brought here to Tycho City's Luna Base on Deanna's recommendation. She thought I would be more comfortable in familiar surroundings. I woke up here last week, and have tried to get better ever since.

I've been trying not to think about the past few months because they hurt so much. I'm scared. Internal Affairs is investigating the decisions we made on the *Valiant.* I think they might be looking at charges against me. Deanna says that I was only a small part of what happened, and that I couldn't have changed things on my own, but I don't know if Internal Affairs will see it that way. I'm just scared.

Luna Day 22

Deanna and I went shopping today. I had almost forgotten what civilian attire felt like. I've spent most of the past year in Starfleet uniforms, and hospital gowns. It was fun trying on new clothes.

It reminded me of the trip to Risa that Karen and I made just after our junior year at the Academy. Karen loved the small boutiques and the lesser-known streets. I was quickly lost, but Karen wasn't. She got us back to our hotel in time for the dinner show.

The lead actor from the play was so handsome that I almost fell for him then and there, but when I commented on him, Karen didn't show much interest. It was then that I knew that she was already interested in someone. She confided to me later that she had a crush on Tim. She said that the two of them had just started seeing each other and I was the first to be let in on the secret.

When Tim became acting captain of the *Valiant,* he appointed Karen to the position of acting first officer. They had to work closely together. Karen said that she was happy to be spending so much time with Tim, but she was also sad that they were not able to have much of a personal relationship any longer. Tim wanted to be "professional in front of the crew."

Now they are both gone, and all I have left is their memories.

I hate the past.

Luna Day 24

I feel so bad. I forgot to record my journal entry yesterday. There was so much to do, I just forgot.

First, the big news.

Internal Affairs is not going to lay charges against any of Red Squad for the bad decisions we made. Deanna says that I am lucky and that I benefited from a political decision. When PublicNetNews got the story, they made heroes of us.

Although Internal Affairs was not happy with us, our mistakes will be unofficially overlooked. Tim, Karen, and the rest will be awarded the Drakon Cluster of Courage. It's the highest award the Academy has to give. Theirs are posthumous, but I got mine yesterday. It is a beautiful, blue medal.

Secondly, Deanna says that I should be discharged next week. After three months of leave, I will be given a position on the *U.S.S. Wyandotte* as part of a cadet assignment.

Deanna says that I should be okay. I'll still have to have regular checkups with the counselor on my new ship, but at least I'll be back on duty.

Third, Jake called. He was the man that I met just before the *Valiant* was destroyed. He and his friend Nog were the only other survivors. We picked them up a few days before the end.

Deanna says that I shouldn't think of it as The End. It should be The Latest Beginning, or the Maturing Middle.

Anyhow, Jake called. He will be on Earth in a few days, and he remembered what I told him about Sunrise on the Moon. We made plans to suit up and go outside and see it.

The last time I watched our monthly Sunrise was just before my father died. It was so beautiful. It was dark, pitch-black, with only the stars and my dad for company. The sun suddenly peeked over the horizon. It was blinding but lovely. The lack of atmosphere caused all things around us to become starkly defined. Bright light was on the face of a rock, and black night was on the shadowed side.

I miss my dad. He was my only family.

Jake also said that he would like to know more about my life on the *Valiant*. He has enough material for his article, but some of my friends' faces continue to haunt him.

Me, too.

Luna Day 25

Deanna had a surprise for me, today. A friend of hers came to talk with me. His name was Montgomery Scott. He said everyone calls him Scotty. He is a former captain and chief engineer. He was also the only survivor aboard the *Jenolen,* and he spent seventy-five years trapped in a transporter cycle.

Scotty was friendly, but very blunt. He still feels terribly guilty that he alone survived. However, he has learned to take things one day at a time.

I have to do the same.

Scotty says that almost everyone he knew is gone. They died or were killed in the last century. He has decided to make new friends. Like me.

He says to treat the past like an old friend. "Call it up from time to time, lass, and talk with it. When it's overstayed its welcome, let it rest until the next time you visit."

He was a nice man. He said I reminded him of a niece of a friend of his. I teased him by calling him Uncle Scotty, after that. He spent several hours telling stories of his career in Starfleet. It was fun.

Luna Day 26

Tomorrow, I am to receive another visitor. Karen's great-great-grandfather is coming all the way from Sherman's Planet near the Klingon border. Karen once told me that he is some sort of retired Federation agricultural minister who spent years dealing with the Klingon threat in his youth. She said he is immensely old.

Mr. Baris must have some pretty powerful friends at Starfleet Headquarters. He was asking to see me before the mission had been even partially declassified. I've got a hunch that he might have even pulled some strings with Internal Affairs. No evidence, but just a vague feeling.

I know he wants me to tell him about Karen. I hope I don't cry too much.

Luna Day 27

I spoke to Karen's granddad, Nilz. He was just as old as Karen had said. He had tremendous wrinkles and silver hair.

We only spoke for a few minutes because the base had a surprise attack simulation begin. He will come back tomorrow.

He told me of his sorrow and grief last year when the *Valiant* was reported missing. He said that Karen's parents died in a shuttlecraft accident three months ago. I'm glad that Karen didn't know.

I thought that he would be a lonely, sad, old man. However, Mr. Baris was pleasant and gentle while we talked. He even tried to smile and put me at ease.

He asked how Karen died. I tried to build up her role as much as possible. I thought it would cheer him a little. She was a fine first officer and my best friend.

The Jem'Hadar had blasted the ship and almost all systems were down. Karen was sitting at the forward control station. She had to handle both flight control, and operations. She was trying to restore power to the shields when debris from an explosion hit her. I didn't see what happened, but I heard it. Her scream was loud but cut off suddenly.

I told Mr. Baris that she was the last to fall. I thought that made it seem more noble. We had started to cry when the drill happened.

He invited me to dinner tomorrow. I still feel sad. Every time I think of my friends, I get so sad.

Luna Day 28

I had dinner with Mr. Baris tonight. I wanted to cheer him up with happy stories about Karen, but he did most of the talking. He told me stories of space stations, furry little tribbles, and Klingons. He was so funny I forgot my problems for a while.

He asked me to come visit him after I'm discharged next week. Mr. Baris was very kind, but I didn't understand how he was able to deal with his loss so well.

Then, he told me that his past may have sad moments, moments of tragedy, and moments of failure, but he wouldn't trade it for anything. His memories of family and friends comfort him when he is sad. He doesn't hate the past. He sees it as a treasure that has both good and bad coming from it.

"Dorian," he said, "I have lived a long time. I have lost everyone I have ever cared about. I have outlived my friends and my enemies. I have amassed a great fortune, a large rambling old house, and a bit of notoriety from some holonovels that I have written. None of it is really important."

"All that matters to me are the remembrances of my wife, my son and his wife, and my granddaughter, Karen. Their smiles still warm my heart."

"I have no time left to worry about the future. I live today in the here and now, and I dream of the happy joys in my past. When the bad memories rear up, I check to see if they have any relevance to my present circumstances. If they do, I learn whatever lesson they have to teach me. If they don't, I summon happy thoughts and overwhelm the sadness, drowning my sorrows in joy."

"It is something I wish that I had learnt a long time ago when I was an arrogant bureaucrat with delusions of grandeur and dreams of glory."

He's right. I am going to start pulling out the good times that I had with my friends. The bad times, I will conquer with good memories.

Mr. Baris had to go, but he invited me to visit him on Sherman's Planet. There are so many stories about Karen that I still want to tell him. I started to call him "Gramps," at the end. That's what Karen always called him.

Maybe I can introduce Gramps to Uncle Scotty. I think the two of them would get along. They both tell good stories.

I realize now that I don't hate the past. I just wish I could change it.

I have to go now. Jake is coming for the Sunrise tomorrow, and morning comes quick.

The Bottom Line

Andrew (Drew) Morby

The burning bridge lacked the acrid smell that should have been there, but that did nothing to lessen Nog's urge to hide under the captain's chair, or flee the bridge.

On the screen two Cardassian *Galor*-class vessels converged on a defenseless freighter, while the other two continued to pummel his ship.

"Tactical officer, report, what is the condition of the *Kobayashi Maru?*" There was no response. Nog turned and saw the tactical officer laying on the floor, severe burns covering his upper body. He turned back to the screen, trying to reroute tactical controls to his seat, but the computer stalled in transition.

The freighter exploded into a nova of colors so bright Nog had to look away. How many civilians dead? He tried to call out orders but his throat was closed and all that came out was a high squeal. Then the bridge flashed, and was replaced by the lines of the Starfleet Academy recreational holodeck.

"Ah, the bitter taste of defeat. But then you should be used to that by now, Ferengi." The laughing voice startled Nog, and he turned to confront the intruder. Human, tall, muscular, and standing in the doorway. Nog decided it wasn't worth it, his holodeck time was up in any case, so he walked past the still-laughing man and left the room.

"How did you like my little program?" the fair-haired Gerard LeFevebre asked Nog as they sat in the Academy cafeteria. Nog preferred eating in the quad where proximity to other cadets wasn't necessary, and he could eat without wondering what everyone was thinking. Unfortunately due to time constraints that option wasn't feasible.

"It was horrible," Nog said in a low voice as he nibbled on the corner of something Gerard called a "croque monsieur," a melted mass of bacteria-treated dairy product on a slab of bread completely inadequate to the task of holding it together. Someone else had called it an "open face sandwich," and Nog couldn't see how closing it could possibly hurt.

"Blew up the ship?" Gerard asked, and Nog glared at him. "Your turn for the real thing comes up tomorrow. Not much time to prepare."

Nog nibbled on the bread, and Gerard laughed. Nog knew the Frenchman was laughing at him, but it was a friendly laugh and didn't carry the stinging derision of the other cadets.

"You wanted a human meal."

Nog looked at him. "It's good."

Gerard laughed again and shook his head. "Even if I didn't speak standard so well, I can tell you are lying."

Nog found humans difficult to read, and he found Gerard's perceptiveness disturbing. He took a big bite to disprove his friend's words, but spit it out immediately, making the Frenchman laugh more. Maybe there were some universal signals after all.

"How are my two favorite cheaters doing?" Kai-ree asked, smiling as she sat down with them. Kai-ree was bald, as all Bolians were, and Nog found it strangely comforting, his own race being mostly hairless.

"Cheaters? How could you say such a thing? We are merely taking advantage of all our available resources. Right, Nog?"

Of course, the Bolian's ears were a little small, but they seemed perfectly proportioned nevertheless, and of course they were unlikely to grow any hair as she got older either.

"Isn't that a Rule of Acquisition?" Gerard prompted, nudging Nog with his foot. " 'Maximize your resources' or something?"

"Something like that," Nog replied. "How was your morning class, Kai-ree?" Even her name had the ring of latinum to Nog's ears.

The Bolian turned to look at Nog. "Self-defense class." Her face made a sour pout. "How good could it be?"

Nog tried to emulate her expression. "I've got it after lunch." Just one more opportunity for him to look foolish in front of his fellow cadets.

Kai-ree turned back to Gerard. "What are you doing after lunch?"

"Studying, I guess." He glanced over at Nog. "Unless Nog wants to skip class to take another run at the *Maru* simulation before tomorrow?"

"Perfect, we can study together," Kai-ree said.

Nog desperately wished he could cut self-defense, but the teachers at the Academy gave him less leeway than they did for Gerard, who did what he wanted with no ill effects. "I can't."

"Okay," Gerard said, turning to look at Kai-ree. "It's a beautiful day, why don't we study in the quad area?"

Her smile disappeared for a moment then flickered back, and she nodded.

The self-defense class was held in one of the large gymnasiums on the academy campus. Nog stood in his Starfleet *gi* next to Yora Elmark, who had the dubious distinction of being the second shortest cadet in the class. She made up for it though, with her endless élan. No task daunted her and Nog envied that energy.

She smiled at him. "Don't worry, Nog, I won't pin you again." She kept her voice low. "Unless you want me to."

"I appreciate that." Nog had no desire to be embarrassed like that again.

The instructor, a stony-faced Vulcan, paced the mat on the floor in front of the cadets. Despite the mild tone associated with Vulcans, his voice carried like the explosion of a photon torpedo.

"Today we will learn about postures." He spun toward the cadets, an uncharacteristically cruel expression on his face, and let out a shout that sent Nog backpedaling into Yora. The sound of shuffling feet assured Nog that others were also taken unaware.

The Vulcan's face returned to its carved expression.

"Putting your opponent off guard can be a powerful tool. If you act the aggressor, you can induce your opponent into the role of victim." The instructor strolled off the mat. "Begin your routine now, but at some point attempt to catch your partner off guard."

Nog looked at Yora; she shrugged and moved to their spot on the mat. Nog liked sparring with her; she was friendlier than most of the cadets and she didn't seem at all put off by being matched with him. At least until last week when she broke out of their sparring routine, throwing him to the floor, and pinning him. The other students had found that entertaining until the instructor ordered extra laps for everyone.

Best to stay away from the topic of Kai-ree this week, as apparently Yora's views on the Bolian's beauty didn't match up with his own.

Halfway through their first set, Nog decided it was time to make his move. He pictured the face of an angry Klingon and attempted to mimic it as he yelled and made a bold move forward. Yora fell backward onto the mat, as planned, but instead of cowering in fear, she laughed.

The entire class stopped their exercises, his ears roared with embarrassment, and he fled.

"Nog, wait!" Yora called after him. Nog was already to the door, but before it closed he heard her add, "Stupid, stupid, stupid."

So much for her being nice. Good thing she forgot about his

Ferengi hearing, or he wouldn't know what she really thought of him.

He went straight for the recreational holodecks. With his return to Deep Space 9 on a cadet field-study imminent, he spent the rest of the afternoon focused on his only remaining hope of proving himself to his classmates.

"Gerard, Gerard, I think I did it! I've figured out how to beat the *Kobayashi* simulation!" Nog burst into the room he shared with the Frenchman, his enthusiasm dying immediately as Gerard and Kai-ree unclenched and broke off their kiss.

"It's not . . ." Gerard began, but he couldn't finish. Instead he hung his head and stared at the floor.

"What's the matter?" Kai-ree asked. "Surely you've seen your roommate kiss a woman before?" She looked back and forth between the two friends.

"Sorry to intrude," Nog said and stepped back, letting the door close in front of him. At least he had his solution. Even if the real thing turned out to be a little different, it would work. It had to.

Once again he stood on the bridge of his own ship.

"This is too soon." His time was up.

His instructor ignored him and stepped forward.

"Today we will be doing something a little different." Different? Nog's ears focused on the speaker. Different how? "Instead of a standard holocrew, we're going to use fellow cadets. Let me introduce you to Commander Yora, your first officer."

Nog turned and stared straight into Yora's dark eyes, a stab of panic piercing his heart and making his skin taught and brittle.

"And this is your tactical officer, Lieutenant LeFevebre . . ." Nog's head swiveled, and his eyes widened.

"And your helmsman, Lieutenant Kai-ree." Nog nearly fell off the center seat when she turned around and nodded to him.

"You know your mission. Begin!" The four instructors disappeared.

"Helm, lay in our course, and engage at cruising speed," Nog said, and settled himself into his chair. Nothing happened.

"Helm, lay in a course to patrol the Cardassian border." Again no response. Angry he looked at Kai-ree, but she continued to ignore him, her attention focused on something behind him. Nog turned to see that she was looking at Gerard, and he stared right back at her.

"Commander, please see that these lieutenants are replaced immediately." Yora just grinned at him. "Commander, now!" Yora started to laugh. Nog pushed himself from his seat to do it himself.

And fell onto his face on duracrete.

It took him a few moments to reorient himself and wake up enough to realize he was in the quad, on a bench. Or he had been on the bench, now he was on the cold, slightly damp walkway. He'd fallen asleep on the bench the night before.

"Rough night?" a gravelly old voice asked, and Nog scrambled to his feet, trying to smooth out his cadet's uniform and salute at the same time.

"Don't stand on ceremony with me, boy," the voice continued. "I've seen almost as many cadets sleep out here as I've planted flowers."

Nog relaxed slightly and looked toward the sound of the voice and saw Boothby, the gardener standing hip deep in shrubbery, a pair of large manual clippers in his hands.

"What's the matter, your roommate prefer a woman's company to yours?" Nog nodded. "Typical cadet behavior. Think with their hormones instead of their brains. And the next you know, we're giving them ships of their own so they can gallivant around the galaxy, impressing potential mates."

Nog didn't know what to say, but keeping quiet had worked fairly well, so he kept his mouth shut and watched the old man talk and prune.

"I've seen you around. You're the one who doesn't fit in, right?" Boothby turned his eyes on Nog. They were similar to Captain Sisko's when he was angry, and Nog hadn't stood up well under Sisko's gaze either.

Nog started to nod again, but Boothby cut him off.

"Poppycock! You're no worse than any of them. IDIC. You know what that is, boy?"

Hesitantly now, Nog nodded again.

"Well? Or don't you know how to speak?"

"It stands for 'Infinite Diversity in Infinite Combinations.' The Vulcans first used it in the year . . ."

"Stop, stop. I didn't ask you to recite your lessons. Do you know what it means?" Nog felt his head start to bob up and down, and stopped it short. "What?"

Nog considered for a moment. "That everyone is an equally valuable part of the whole?"

Boothby laughed. "Are you asking me?" He didn't wait for Nog to respond. "I like you, son, so I'll help you out." Nog's entire attention was on the elderly gardener. " 'To thine own self, be true.' "

Nog blinked. "That's it?"

"That's Shakespeare, son." Then when that didn't help, Boothby added, "Be yourself, you'll do fine." And that, whether or not Nog liked it, was all the gardener had to say. He turned back to his trimming, leaving Nog alone in the quad.

Two hours, and a sonic shower later, Nog stood looking up at the front of the testing building from behind a tree. He was going to fail, he was going to kill his crew and the civilians on board the *Maru.* He took a deep breath; his fears were getting to him. He had a plan, a good plan, and he was going to walk in there and show them all. He wished Jake were here for support.

He took a hesitant step forward.

"There you are. Wait!" Yora bounded up to him. "It's probably too late, but I wanted to wish you good luck." Surprised, Nog started to say something but she shut him up by grabbing his ears and kissing him solidly. "Good luck."

Slowly she let him go, leaving Nog a little dazed. "I watched you hiding over there, and you seemed to need some confidence so I thought I'd remind you that you are uniquely special. The only one of your kind ever to even attempt Starfleet Academy, much less succeed as you are doing. So . . . good luck!" Her face suddenly turned red and she turned away and bounded off.

Nog wished he had time to go after her, to ask her to clarify what she meant, but he couldn't afford to be late. He did feel better though, and with a renewed energy, and a broad smile, Nog entered the test building.

Gerard was waiting for him outside the testing room. He glanced at the time on a wall display as Nog approached.

"You are going to be late, but I want to apologize for my actions. You must have a clear head when you take the test, no?" Nog tried to interrupt his friend and say things were all right, but Gerard wouldn't let him. "No, listen to me. I know you like Kairee, but I let her get me alone and I goofed." Something about Gerard's pronunciation tickled Nog's funny bone, but he kept a straight face as his friend continued. "After you showed up, I regained my senses and told her, 'no.' You are my friend, Nog, and my actions caused you harm. I am sorry." He stuck out his hand, and Nog recognized the gesture. He took the hand and shook it.

"I understand, Gerard." He tried his best to pronounce his friend's name appropriately. "She is a beautiful woman."

"That she is." Gerard smiled broadly, but then regained control and pronounced, "I will not see her again."

"It's all right." Kai-ree seemed a lot less important now than she had the night before. "I don't mind."

Gerard slapped him on the back. "Good luck, *mon ami.*" Nog nodded and stepped into the testing room.

"This is the *Kobayashi Maru* . . . hull has been breached . . . mines. Please help."

The eerie voice of the desperate freighter captain sent chills through Nog, and he grabbed the armrests for support and reminded himself that he had a plan.

"Location?"

The blue Andorian tactical officer, a full lieutenant, worked his console for a moment. "Across the Cardassian border, Captain." Nog's ears rushed with the sound of his own blood pumping.

Captain Nog smiled. "Check the registry for any vessels named *Kobayashi Maru.* Helm, prepare a course and be ready to engage."

The pretty red-haired ensign at the helm console turned to give him a look, but nodded and entered the course.

"Captain, it's my duty to inform you that crossing the Cardassian border is a violation of . . ."

"I am aware of that . . ." Nog cut off his Vulcan executive officer, and then hesitated as he couldn't recall her name. "Number One." Her eyes didn't register the slight, but she acknowledged him.

"It's a large freighter licensed under Federation registry, Captain," the Andorian reported. "Almost one hundred crew."

One hundred Federation citizens, balanced against the almost one thousand crew on his ship. No contest. "Helm, engage warp nine point four."

"Captain, that's over the suggested maximum." The helmsman turned again, her hair sliding enticingly across her neck. Nog tried to remain focused.

"Engage, Ensign. Tactical, wide band signal, state our intentions to aide the freighter, and request assistance."

"Yes, sir."

This was all window dressing. None of these gambits had paid off in simulation, but they were the right thing to do.

"Captain, we are crossing the border now," the Vulcan said. Surya, Nog finally remembered, that was her name.

Nog moved up to the front of the bridge to stand behind the helmsman who didn't look at him. "Ensign, we may be violating a few protocols in order to try and save these people's lives. I would like to do it as quickly as possible. Understand?"

Her shoulder relaxed slightly and she gave him a slight smile. "Aye, sir."

"Good." Nog moved back toward his seat. "Lieutenant, prepare the tractor beam and lock onto the freighter as soon as we are in range."

"Captain, the freighter has suffered severe structural damage. It might not be able to withstand the stress."

Nog considered a moment, noting several functionaries moving around the rear of the bridge. Another detail omitted from the practice test. "Lieutenant, do you want to stay here any longer than is absolutely necessary?"

"No, sir." The tactical officer straightened and obeyed. Nog felt the Vulcan's eyes on him as he moved around. If he didn't know the administrators of the test were hidden cleverly by holographic illusion, he would have taken her for one of them, watching and grading him.

"Entering the *Maru*'s system now, Captain," Herrell reported from the helm. "Shall we slow down?"

"Captain!" the tactical officer barked, and Nog had to hold on to his seat to keep from jumping. "Incoming ships, four of them."

"Don't slow down, Ensign. Lieutenant, hail them."

"We are being jammed, Captain," Torbish replied.

Nog nodded, expecting that. "Okay, adjust course five degrees and head for the star."

"Ships are Cardassian make. *Galor*-class." The Andorian's antennae quivered.

"You!" Nog pointed at one of the officers at the rear of the bridge. "Help out at tactical." The Andorian stiffened, but Nog didn't have time to explain.

The bridge rocked under the Cardassian opening barrage but it wasn't serious enough to dislodge Nog's grip on his chair.

"Minimal damage, shields holding."

"Helm, take us around the sun, and plot an exit vector away from the freighter."

"Are we going to leave the civilians?" Nog imagined his first officer's eyebrow raising, but kept his eyes fixed on the screen.

"Two vessels are following, Captain." Only two? If the other two went after the freighter his plan was over. "The other two are moving to intercept our exit vector."

Nog relaxed slightly, tasting a trickle of blood from his unclenching teeth.

"Full shields forward."

"Shall I arm weapons?" the Andorian asked.

On the screen the sun loomed large as the ship shot around it, and then disappeared, replaced by the two intercepting Cardassian ships.

"Alter course for the *Maru,* now!"

"Interceptors are firing!" The ship shook again as she altered course, and the lights dimmed, then returned.

"Do not return fire."

"Shields down to forty percent, routing power from nonessential systems," the Andorian reported, but Nog wasn't listening. He focused on the second man at tactical.

"Ready the tractor beam."

"Captain, at this speed, that action will tear the freighter apart," Surya said in that infuriating Vulcan calm. Nog ignored her too, looking at the Andorian.

"Prepare to extend shields to support the *Maru.* Cut all power except for tractor, shields, and engines." He locked gazes with his tactical officer. "Including weapons." The Andorian's antennae stiffened but he complied.

The bridge was silent for a moment.

"Captain, even if this does work, towing the freighter will allow the Cardassians to catch us." The Vulcan voice of reason sliced through his confidence.

Two of the vessels couldn't possibly catch them, having slowed to ambush him. Unfortunately Nog realized that Surya was right, the drag of the *Maru* on the *Venture* would allow the other two to catch him. Another detail the test program had missed, but he should have known better. And now it was over, and he'd failed again.

"We're in tractor range, Captain." The words rang hollowly in Nog's ears. He looked around at the faces of the crew he had just killed. They looked back at him expectantly.

"Activate tractor, and extend shields," he ordered. If they hadn't given up on him, then he couldn't either.

"Aye, sir!"

Nog watched the freighter on the screen, expecting it to explode into a bright rainbow-colored fireball.

It didn't.

"We've got it, Captain!"

"Two Cardassian ships closing in. They will be in tactical firing range in five minutes. The other two are still a few minutes behind them."

"Time to the border?"

"Maybe nine minutes, Captain. If power remains at current levels."

They still weren't going to make it. Nog cast around for any inspiration and heard Boothby's voice like a delayed echo in his ears. "Be yourself."

"Commander, prepare transporters for beaming."

"Captain, even if we had power to spare we wouldn't be able to evacuate them all before the Cardassians reach us."

"Not for them. Us. Beam over engineers first to try and contain their leaks and get their shields online."

There was a moment of silence, but his crew didn't wait to hear his arguments this time. Nog smiled grimly to himself. That was something, at least.

After giving the orders, Commander Surya turned back toward him. "Are we going to stay and fight?"

"Not exactly." She stared at him, but he couldn't take the time to elaborate to her, he was working on a new plan. He gave his orders and the crew went to work.

"Thirty seconds, Captain," Lieutenant Torbish said from tactical.

Nog tapped his communications badge. "Ensign Herrell, status report?"

"Captain, she'll handle like a torpedo without guidance control, but the hull breech has been contained," the red-haired navigations officer answered from the helm of the *Maru.*

"Good luck." At least one of them might survive. "Release the *Maru* and come about."

The crew, his crew responded. "Send them our offer."

"Sending surrender message, but we are still being jammed."

"All stations, play dead and ready 'the bottom line.' "

Everything went dark, only the consoles shined an eerie light on their operators. Would the Cardassians take the bait and let the *Maru* go? Nog hoped that his offer, a *Galaxy*-class vessel in exchange for the freighter, would be enough.

"They are firing!" The ship rocked and Nog was jostled out of his chair.

"Weapons off-line," Torbish said as the ship shook again. "Right warp nacelle is gone. They are taking us apart, piece by piece." Nog could tell that the Andorian wasn't comfortable not fighting back, but he kept his antennae in check.

"They don't want to fall for a trap," Nog said crossing his fingers, as Jake had taught him, for luck.

"Surrendering a Federation vessel to the enemy is a serious offense," Commander Surya told him, but her words sounded hollow.

"Only one ship, firing again!" That meant the other one was probably still chasing the *Maru.* It all came down to greed.

The bridge exploded in flames. Smoke invaded his nostrils and filled the bridge, as he rolled on the floor.

"Report!" he called out, but there was no response. He glanced at his chair. It seemed far away, but he crawled toward it. A high-pitched sound filled the air and a Cardassian in full battle array materialized between him and his chair, weapon firing into where the captain should have been. Nog gathered his legs under him, and as the Cardassian turned toward him, he launched himself at the invader. A fierce shriek erupted from his lips and he knocked the startled Cardassian over. Instead of taking advantage of his opponent's momentary surprise to finish him, Nog rushed to his chair and triggered "the bottom line."

"Five seconds to auto-destruct," the ship's computer announced at the lowest setting Nog and his crew had been able to manage when they'd rewired the system. Only his ears could pick it up, he hoped.

"Three."

More Cardassians beamed onto the bridge. If he recalled his Cardassian tactics correctly, the explosion would hit them with their shields down. And maybe the explosion would pull the other ship off the *Maru,* allowing the freighter to coast to the border. Maybe.

"One."

The holodeck exploded in white silence, and was slowly replaced by the grid lines of the holodeck. Nog blinked. He'd forgotten that he was in a simulation. He felt a pang for his crew and then noticed the four instructors standing just in front of the exit, behind where the rear of the bridge would have been.

Nog walked slowly toward the exit. One of the instructors, a tall black man who vaguely reminded Nog of Sisko, stepped forward.

"Interesting tactic, Cadet. You blew up your ship without firing a shot in self-defense, sacrificing your crew in the process."

"Did they make it?" Nog asked.

"You're dead. You'll never know. Do you have an excuse for your actions?"

Again Boothby's words rang in his ears.

"An excuse? No, sir, but I had to be true to myself." The instructor raised an eyebrow. "My people have a saying, 'If, for some reason, you don't want to sell, set the price as high as possible.' "

Nog lifted the slimy invertebrate to his lips and slurped it down, enjoying the smacking sound it made as well as the slickness with which it slid down his throat.

"Oh, I missed these."

"There he is!" Gerard slid into a seat at Nog's table. He leaned over the bowl of gree worms and sniffed. *"Mon Dieu!"*

"They're good. Try one."

"If this is how you felt about *le croque monsieur,* you are a better man than I."

Nog snared another of the succulent worms and popped it into his mouth unabashed by Gerard's face. There was no more point in trying to fit in, so he could once again enjoy his favorite delicacy.

"Did you tell him yet?" Yora bounded up to their table.

"Non. I was watching him eat."

"Taking notes?"

Nog realized there was something going on that he didn't know about. "Razor-toothed gree worm?" he offered.

Yora's tongue exploded out of her mouth and she made a loud gagging noise. "Never!"

Nog picked up another one and inspected it.

"He's so calm," Yora said.

"The model of a Starfleet cadet," Gerard said.

"Maybe that's why everyone is talking about 'The Nog Negotiation.' "

"The what?" Nog almost choked on his worm.

"That's what the grapevine is calling your *Kobayashi Maru* test results." Nog felt his skin burn with added heat and excitement.

"The results are out?" Yora and Gerard exchanged a glance.

"You could say that."

"Hey, Nog, good job on the *Kobayashi* test!" Nog looked and saw one of his classmates wave as he crossed the quad.

"You're Nog?" A brunette from a nearby table turned around and looked him over. "How about helping me study later?"

"He'll be busy," Yora interrupted before Nog could answer.

"I will?"

"Yes, you haven't said two words since you took the test. I'm starting to think you don't like me." Gerard looked a little startled, but Nog saw a small smile creep across his lips as he looked from Yora back to Nog.

"You didn't say anything to me, also."

Why would anyone want to talk about blowing up his ship? Though perhaps he hadn't done quite as badly as he'd feared.

"What are they saying about my test?" he asked.

"Inspired!" Gerard said.

"Showed initiative and good command skills!" Yora added.

Nog just nodded at his friends' comments, though inside his thoughts were spinning. What would his father say? He would have to thank Boothby. Maybe his grandmother could send some Ferengi flowers for the gardener in her next care package?

"Don't you have anything to say for yourself?" Gerard asked.

Nog popped the last worm into his mouth and bit down, enjoying the soft explosion of taste that filled his mouth. Gree worm dusted with the intoxicating flavor of success.

"Delicious."

The Best Defense . . .

John Takis

Not even the thunderous crack of the cannons or the fierce whine of molten lead as it shattered the arid and dust-clogged air was enough to drown out the terrible screams of dying men.

Colonel William Travis lurched back from the wooden battlement, using his gun arm to shield his eyes against the penetrating sun. That sun had seemed warm once; comforting and restoring. But now it was only oppressive. Oppressive and hot as hell. Still, he took some satisfaction in the knowledge that it was just as hard on the vast Mexican army surrounding the small fort—harder even; they lacked any shade beyond their crude tents.

Then why are we still on the defensive after thirteen days? Travis thought bitterly. *There has to be a way to turn this to our advantage.* He inhaled deeply and spat dust, squinting hard as he surveyed his defense perimeter. A ways down the interior ramp of the battlements, a familiar figure was making its way toward him, waving its arms, signaling urgently. Travis leaned forward and rested a hand on the tense shoulder of one of his soldiers who was crouched forward, rifle extended through a narrow slot; a harbinger of death to the Mexican oppressors. The moment Travis's fingers touched the buckskin, he could sense the incredible tension in the man. The soldier started violently, his arm jerking back in a reflexive spasm. His head twisted around, eyes darting like those of a trapped animal. The realization that the hand belonged to the black-haired visage of his commander did little to lessen his accelerated disquiet. Travis couldn't blame him. Not when his very life was in such a state of arbitrary flux. Not when a Mexican cannon could obliterate his vantage point at any given moment.

But such were the risks of war. Risks that were equal to the stakes. There was a nation to be defended.

"Hold this flank!" Travis shouted above the carnage. "I need to take counsel with Colonel Bowie." The young soldier wiped the sweat from his brow and nodded.

"No one gets through, sir," the man said with as much conviction as he could muster. "We'll beat 'em down yet!" Travis smiled encouragingly and yelled, "For Texas!" with much more confidence than he felt. But then, that was his responsibility as a leader: to nourish the spirit of hope in his men; to keep them fighting. To keep them alive.

Turning, he crouched and made his way along the wooden battlements, not quite as sturdy as they had once been, to meet up with a grim-faced Colonel James Bowie.

"What news?" Travis called out. His voice was hoarse from the hot, dusty air.

"Not good," Bowie said with a shake of his head. With a bitter grimace he ran a dirty hand through his short hair. "We just lost Captain Quinn at the left wall. Fool took a bullet for me."

Travis's face fell. "Captain Quinn? We need an experienced commander defending that flank! Send—"

"There are no experienced commanders left!" Bowie snapped angrily.

Travis's mind raced. "We'll have to pull Crockett from the southern front. You cover my position. I'll—"

But before he could finish his sentence a thunderous explosion sent the wooden structures shaking, and he fell to his knees, stumbling into Bowie, who also lost his footing. A volley of gunshots rang out as Travis staggered to his feet, lending an arm to Bowie. Together they stared in disbelief at a gaping hole in the tall wall, about a hundred meters down, where the Mexican army was flooding inside the fort like water through a funnel.

After a brief second of shock, Travis sprang into action. "The chapel!" he cried, seizing Bowie by the arm. "We'll hole up in there! Regroup." Bowie nodded, and they scrambled to the nearest ladder leading to the ground, ducking random gunfire as they went. Travis practically slid down the ladder, the rough wood biting and blistering the palms of his hands. Colonel Bowie remained right behind him.

But it was to no avail. Their emergency plan had been doomed to failure before its conception. By the time their booted feet hit the ground, the Mexican horde was upon them. Bowie whipped out his knife, and Travis had only enough time to check the fixture on his bayonet before they found themselves engaged in ferocious hand-to-hand combat with the enemy.

It was all Travis could do to stay upright in the melee of whirling arms and slashing guns, every appendage fortified by a deadly bit of steel. Somehow, amidst the carnage, he spotted Bowie, who was barely holding his own. In the distance, he could make out General Santa Anna himself, a whirling dervish sowing death and destruction among the Texans from atop his terrible steed.

And then something hard struck him in the base of the spine and he fell to the ground. In pain, he spun around in time to see a burly Mexican poised to skewer him through on the tip of a broken sword. Travis's mouth contorted into a vicious snarl and he braced his own gun against the ground between his forearm and chest. "Remember the Alamo!" he screamed defiantly, and prepared to sell his own life at the highest price he could exact . . .

. . . and then the world stopped.

Travis blinked in momentary disorientation. All the screams, the cries of rage, the explosions . . . it had all evaporated in the space of a second, leaving an utter and terrible silence, broken only by the ragged sound of his breath between his ears and the pounding of blood in his veins. Above him, the unblinking Mexican retained his lethal posture. Even the dust hung frozen in the air.

Dazed, Travis rose to his feet and looked around. The battle of the Alamo had been transformed into a wax museum display. Everywhere, combatants were frozen in the grim frenzy of mortal combat; a gruesome diorama in the hall of the dead. Everyone, that was, except for Colonel Jim Bowie, who, fifteen yards away, was extricating himself from the crushing grip of a brutish enemy. Bowie shot Travis a puzzled look, and Travis was surprised to find a small piece of stylized metal materialize with a chittering sound over his left breast.

"Kira to Bashir," came a calm voice, emanating from thin air. There was an edge of tension to the otherwise flat tone. "Sorry to interrupt you on leave, Doctor, but the *Defiant*'s just arrived. They need your expertise in sickbay. Report there and prepare to receive casualties."

Julian Bashir sighed, pushing Colonel Travis back into the recesses of his mind. "Computer, end program," he spoke aloud, and in an instant the sky, the ground, and all the chaos that lay between vanished, to be replaced by the black, yellow-gridded walls of the holodeck. And across the room, Colonel Jim Bowie once more became plain, ordinary Miles O'Brien, Deep Space 9's chief of operations.

"Next time," Bashir sighed to his friend as he inspected his Starfleet uniform. The holographic dust had vanished, but the fresh blisters running down his palms and the pain in his back remained. But it could wait. He had patients to attend to. The *Defiant* had to have had a hard time of it if sickbay needed him badly enough to suspend his mandatory leave of absence. At least he'd be making himself useful instead of squandering wartime in the holodeck.

O'Brien nodded. "Next time. I'd better go have a look at the *Defiant*. I'm sure they'll be calling me sooner or later."

Then the doors leading from the holosuite to Quark's Bar hissed open, and resigned to another long day of damage-control,

Starfleet officers Julian Bashir and Miles Edward O'Brien stepped out onto Deep Space 9.

Five hours later sickbay had been restored to a modicum of order. Nurses and surgeons still darted from bed to bed, applying hyposprays where needed, taking notes on patients' conditions, and stopping occasionally to administer a kindly word. These were not just any invalids, after all. These were heroes.

Only two crewmen had died. Only two crewmen had been beyond even Bashir's genetically enhanced capabilities to save. Bashir hated to use the word "only"—every life was precious—but was forced to realize that things could have been much worse. With the Dominion, things usually were. As it was, five others would be unable to return to duty for at least a month, and the rest were being prepped for discharge.

Now Bashir stood over Ensign Nog, running a final diagnostic over the synapses attaching the young Ferengi to his artificial leg.

"I think I can release you to return to your quarters," Bashir said cheerfully. Then his tone turned stern. "But I insist you remain there for at least twelve hours, resting. Your nerves need time to regenerate."

Nog smiled gratefully, flashing his jagged teeth. "Don't worry, Doctor. The next hit-and-run op isn't for three more days." Bashir frowned, and Nog's smile disappeared. "Is there something wrong, Doc?"

Bashir shook his head and returned a comforting smile. "As a doctor," he explained, "it's difficult sending someone you've just cured right back out into the thick of danger."

Nog nodded. "Captain Sisko doesn't like it either. But he makes it happen." Nog's voice swelled with unabashed admiration. "He's the force behind every attack. You know what happened today . . ." Bashir nodded. As the *Defiant* had engaged three ferocious Jem'Hadar fighters, Captain Sisko had been struck across the forehead by a piece of flying shrapnel. Somehow he'd managed to stay conscious despite the concussion and loss of blood. Though his treatment was superficial, he wouldn't have lasted much longer without it. Bashir had just barely gotten to him in time.

"But the captain kept on fighting," Nog continued. "Even when we all thought we were beat. If he'd gone down . . . well, I don't know what would have happened."

At Nog's words, Bashir suddenly froze. Unbidden, Colonel William Travis sprung to the forefront of his thoughts, and for an instant he ceased to be a doctor and turned strategist. "Nog!" he blurted out in excitement. "That's it! That's the key. It's so simple . . . so obvious!"

Nog looked bewildered at Bashir's sudden transformation. "Did I miss something, Doctor?"

"Santa Anna!" Bashir beamed, clapping Nog on the shoulder and pressing his datapad into Nog's hands. "Now go on. I'm a busy man."

Shaking his head in bemused confusion, Nog limped out of the infirmary.

Leaning over the small table in Quark's Bar, Bashir rubbed his hands together, eyes glittering at the brilliance of his new insight. "Santa Anna is the key," he exclaimed. O'Brien sighed, massaging his temples. Bashir often demonstrated such profound excitement, and it was usually O'Brien's lot to quietly point out the delicate flaws.

"It won't bloody work! Maybe I should try being Crockett next time."

"Don't be such a pessimist. Of course it'll work."

O'Brien's patience was wearing thin. "Julian, we've killed Santa Anna in battle a thousand times. The Mexican army just swarms all over us."

Bashir was undeterred. "Yes, but whenever he dies it's during the assault, usually weeks into the siege. What I'm talking about is a preemptive strike."

O'Brien considered this for a moment. "You mean assassination?"

"Exactly! We sneak off at night, find a good position and bam!" He clapped his hands together for effect. "Problem solved.

Without his leadership, they'll never be able to breach our defenses."

Quark, walking by gathering empty cups from nearby tables, cocked a large ear in their direction. "I wish you gentlemen would be more discreet about these things." He walked over to their table and flashed them a toothy grin. "Business has forced me to charge an exorbitant fee for keeping these . . . nasty rumors under control."

O'Brien waved the bartender off. "The Alamo, Quark, we're talking about the Alamo."

"I know," Quark said conspiratorially. "You'd be surprised at the betting pool." With a critical eye, the Ferengi examined Bashir's blistered hands. "Of course there are other considerations. I won't be liable for any personal injuries you sustain in these inane fantasies." He cracked a lecherous smile. "Why don't you try my new Risa simulation? My Orion slave women? They're safer . . . they're better."

O'Brien snorted derisively and turned back to Bashir, downing his drink and thrusting the empty mug at Quark. "All right . . . let's do it."

The position the pair had decided on was a small bluff just west of the Mexican encampment. This time around, Santa Anna had chosen a large stretch of open plain for his troops to fall back on. That way no army would stand a chance of taking the Mexican force by surprise. No army could get close enough without being seen.

No army. But two men were another story.

Following a Mexican attack earlier in the day, Bashir had painstakingly mapped out the movements of the small enemy squadrons that constantly patrolled the perimeter of the Alamo. Santa Anna was eager for combat; a Texan retreat would be a lesser victory. Satisfied with their preparations, Bashir and O'Brien had strapped on water and rations, and plenty of ammunition; put on the softest moccasins that could be found; and had each slung a long rifle over one shoulder.

Captain Quinn, loyal to a fault, had launched an angry protest.

He maintained that he was the better shot, and should assume the risks for his commanding officers, but was nonetheless overruled and placed in charge of the troops while Colonel Davy Crockett was left supervising perimeter defenses.

It had taken four hours of hunching, crawling and scurrying through the darkness, but they had their vantage point. Through the scrub that rimmed the small bluff, Santa Anna's personal tent was perfectly visible, ringed as it was with the horses, standards and smaller tents such as befitted his position. Antonio López de Santa Anna was accustomed to the very best, even in this time of war.

It was almost dawn, now. Soon the great general would emerge to begin the day's muster. For the last time. Bashir gazed down the tip of his rifle. The light from the glowing remnants of the various campfires was enough to see the first gentle stirrings of the army below. He allowed himself a wolfish smile. The Mexican cause was doomed, of course. Even defeating the mere handful of men stationed at the Alamo, the large Mexican force would meet their end when General Sam Houston, with only eight hundred men, routed them at San Jacinto, and captured Santa Anna himself.

But then, that wasn't the point of this simulation. The point was that the Alamo was a historical tragedy. A tragedy which no one believed could be overcome. No one but Julian Bashir and Miles O'Brien . . . who were about to be vindicated.

Suddenly, Bashir felt his arm being jerked by his partner. O'Brien raised a finger to his lips and gestured to their left. There, a hundred yards away, the figure of a solitary soldier could be made out in the dimness.

It was headed straight for them.

Bashir cursed under his breath. This was unanticipated. Thinking fast, his eyes darted about. Even now, the first traces of dawn were peeking over the horizon. There was little doubt the man would see them. But though the odds were two against one, they couldn't afford to risk engaging him. And the scrub extending to the rim of the bluff, while providing a screen between the assassins and the army, was not thick enough to completely conceal them. Unless . . .

Bashir leaned forward and peered over the rim of the bluff. Yes! It just might work! He motioned to O'Brien, gesturing over the short cliff face that dropped away to the plain and then to the army. O'Brien nodded, and the two began lowering themselves through the scrub and over the edge. The cliff face was not sheer; it was rocky and uneven, with an abundance of varied protrusions. And it was covered in thick scrub that grew from the various nooks and crevices, where water would pool during the infrequent rains. If, leaning back, they could position themselves flat against the rock, they would have solid footing on the vertical slope, and able to get a clean shot off. The brown plant growth was not ideal camouflage, but would be adequate in the dimness of the morning.

O'Brien found his footing first, mere moments before Bashir settled into a crouch a few feet away. Seconds later, footsteps could be heard from above, and Bashir silently prayed no trace of their presence was evident in the darkness.

But nothing happened. And minutes later there was a flurry of activity in the Mexican camp as the form of General Santa Anna emerged from his tent. Bashir's heart leapt in his chest. This was it. The culmination of his masterful plan. He looked at O'Brien and sized up the situation. Santa Anna, talking to one of his captains as his horse was prepared, was about a hundred and fifty yards away. The shot would be difficult, but the angle was perfect.

"You've got a better footing," Bashir hissed. "Take the shot." O'Brien raised an eyebrow.

"You sure, Julian? I mean . . . it's your plan and all."

"I'm sure, Miles." O'Brien nodded and slowly raised the rifle to his shoulder, sizing up the shot, bracing his shoulder . . .

. . . and then he lowered the rifle. Bashir frowned. O'Brien checked his barrel, hefted the weapon, and raised it once more, adjusting his aim ever so slightly . . . before lowering the gun and staring at it uncomfortably. Bashir fretted nervously. They hadn't much time. "Miles, what's wrong?"

O'Brien shrugged awkwardly. "I don't think I can make the shot in this light," he whispered. "You're tons better than me. You should take it."

"Fine," Bashir replied, and raised his own weapon. He'd worked too long and hard for this. He wasn't about to let it slip away. Across the ever-brightening plain, he could make out Santa Anna receiving his breakfast as he smiled and joked with one of his colleagues. Bashir's finger tightened on the trigger . . .

But he set the rifle down without firing.

"My aim is genetically enhanced," he offered with a weak smile. "It's not really fair, is it? I mean it doesn't count if we win by cheating. The real Colonel Travis didn't have any gene-spliced abilities."

O'Brien's eyes widened. "Yeah! But he was a better shot than you! Besides, the whole point of the bloody simulation is to be better than they were, remember?"

Bashir nodded reluctantly, and his gaze narrowed. Resolutely, he raised the rifle to his shoulder. There was no wind . . . perfect light . . . Santa Anna was tantalizingly still, sipping his drink . . . Bashir had a nice straight arrow shot.

And he didn't take it.

The tension melting from his frame, Bashir slumped back against the rock. "I can't do it, Miles. I can't shoot a man in cold blood. Not even a hologram." He exhaled a great breath he didn't know he had been holding. His eyes met O'Brien's, and he managed a weak smile. "Guess it's up to you."

O'Brien looked at the long piece of metal and wood in his hands in obvious distaste, and a slow grin broke out over his features. "Naw," he said. "I can't do it either." He looked up at his friend with humor in his eyes. " 'The perfect plan,' " he quoted, and Bashir stifled a giggle. "We finally figure it out and we can't do it."

"Months of work . . ."

"Weeks of plans . . ."

"Long nights sleeping on the sofa . . . Keiko never understood. Never thought I was cut out for this sort of thing."

"I guess," Bashir laughed, "that's why you're an engineer . . . and I'm a doctor."

Unable to suppress their mirth, the two friends collapsed against the cliff face, enjoying the irony of the moment. It didn't matter who heard them now. This program was as good as over. Another mad attempt defeated . . . not by any enemy force, but by their own humanity. In many ways, Bashir was relieved. After all . . . suppose they *had* defeated Santa Anna. What then? The scheming . . . the plotting . . . the desperate odds . . . he was—God help him—almost glad that this latest plan had failed. And he was certain Miles felt the same.

So it came as a great shock to them both when a great clap of gunfire shattered the stillness of the dawn, and General Santa Anna, mounting his horse in the distance, jerked violently and fell to the ground, a bullet through his chest.

Bashir's jaw dropped, and his eyes flew to his own gun, then to O'Brien's. But it was a sudden noise from above that drew their attention, and the familiar face that peered down at them.

"Captain Quinn!" Bashir gaped. "What the hell are you . . ."

"No time to 'splain now, sir," Quinn said hastily, lowering an arm to help Bashir up. "You can bet they'll be out this way shortly."

Bashir turned. Indeed, the Mexican camp had descended into chaos, with horns calling, troops running helter-skelter. It wouldn't be long before they figured out that the "attack" had not been the work of an army. It would be even less time before they managed to ascertain the trajectory . . . and the possible points of origin. Still dumbstruck, Bashir reached up to clasp Quinn's proffered hand.

Within moments both Bashir and O'Brien stood crouched atop the bluff next to Quinn. Loading his weapon in rapid succession, Quinn turned and fired three shots straight up into the air. Bashir's eyes widened as, in the distance, the gates of the Alamo burst open and a tide of Texan patriots flooded out onto the plain and thundered toward the chaotic swirl that was the Mexican army. Quinn grinned in a self-satisfied fashion.

"Quinn!" O'Brien snapped angrily. "We told you to stay at the fort."

Quinn shook his head. "I reckon it's a good thing I didn't, else you'd all be dead or stranded. I figgered on trouble, so I followed you." He spat. "Good thing too, with your rifles not workin' an' all. Someone had to make that shot."

Before Bashir could protest, Quinn leapt upright in alarm. Bashir turned to see a group of Mexicans advancing on their position.

"They figgered us out," Quinn said grimly, then took off running toward one flank of the rapidly advancing Texans. Bashir, frustration welling up inside him, sprinted after nonetheless, O'Brien close behind.

But there was another obstacle. One of the scouting parties had spotted the assassins as well, and moved in from the left as the army splinter-group moved from the right in an attempt to cut the three fugitives off from the oncoming force. Bullets whined past for a few moments, and Bashir had to remind himself that a moving target was the hardest to hit. Then they were between the two enemy bands, and the Mexican guns ceased lest they strike down their own.

That didn't stop them from firing on the Texans. But Crockett's men were better prepared and better armed. Two enemy soldiers fell for every one who remained.

Despite their rapidly dwindling numbers, the Mexicans continued to advance. Even as the fleeing Texans reached their comrades, dodging behind the front lines, the enemy forces came together. For a few tumultuous moments as the two sides clashed, Bashir and O'Brien found themselves turned around and around in the melee before finally reorienting themselves toward the front. They burst through the first rank, side by side, with a jubilant and whooping Davy Crockett—very much alive—just in time to see the Mexican army retreating across the plain: forced back, following the death of its leader, by a handful of Texans at the Alamo.

The following morning, Bashir and O'Brien had not yet emerged from the holodeck.

In her quarters, preparing breakfast for her daughter and infant son, Keiko O'Brien took note of the time and shook her head in annoyance. Another night away from his family. The man was impossible.

At Quark's Bar the enigmatic proprietor rubbed his hands together in greed. His holodeck snoop equipment had been quite successful, and all bets were called in. Let the percentages be skimmed and the latinum flow freely.

In his office, Constable Odo examined the padd containing the reports on his deputies' latest efforts to crack down on gambling, and frowned.

In his office, fingers moving lightly over the fading scar on his forehead, Captain Benjamin Sisko smiled at the irony of it. His officers were temporarily on leave from the war, and how did they choose to spend it? Perhaps it was the frustration of not being able to join their comrades in real combat. He preferred baseball, himself.

In a small private room in the Alamo, Julian Bashir and Miles O'Brien sat over a wooden table, nursing mugs of bitter whiskey. They had elected to delay their return to reality . . . for at least a little while. After all . . . this was a unique situation. And so the program continued.

"Do you think," O'Brien mused, "it'll feel like this when we win the war . . . out there, I mean?"

"I don't know," Bashir replied with a heavy sigh.

"It's what you wanted," O'Brien grunted. "Your plan worked, whether you pulled the trigger or not."

Bashir frowned. "Was it what you wanted?"

"I don't know. I mean, we've been trying for so long I never thought we'd actually win. I suppose I stopped thinking we could months ago."

Bashir nodded. "It's funny, really. We never really did it to win, did we?"

O'Brien smiled ruefully. "The challenge."

"The thrill."

"Insurmountable odds."

There was a long silence as the pair stared into their drinks.

"Won't miss it, though," O'Brien said confidently.

"Much too much stress," Bashir affirmed.

"Wife hates it . . ."

"Not healthy . . ."

Another long silence was followed by the sound of two mugs

emptying rapidly: the remarkable sound of nobody fooling anybody.

But even as the words "end program" sprung bitterly to Bashir's lips, the door to the private room burst open and Captain Quinn stumbled inside, face drained of all color. His desperate eyes met Bashir's with such frantic fervor that Bashir was instinctively filled with alarm.

"What is it?" he and O'Brien demanded in unison.

"The Mexicans!" Quinn blurted out. "We're in trouble!"

"What?"

Quinn steadied himself with one hand against the table. "A dyin' scout just came in from the north."

Bashir frowned. "The north? But the Mexican army fled south."

Quinn nodded. "At first. But then they swung up north. The new Mexican commander figgered the Alamo weren't worth the trouble. He caught Gen'ral Houston's army by surprise at San Jacinto. Had all his troops shoutin', 'Remember the Alamo!' " His eyes grew wide. "It was a massacre. An' now they're coming back for us. What'll we do, Colonel? We can't go south . . ."

Bashir turned to O'Brien in amazement. "We lost!" he said incredulously. "We actually lost! Not just the Alamo . . . the whole war. Miles, do you realize what this means?"

O'Brien answered with a broad grin. "Means your stupid plan didn't work!"

A slow smile spread over Bashir's face. "I guess . . ." he said carefully, "there's nothing for it then. We'll just have to come up with a better plan."

"Looks that way." O'Brien nodded.

In a state of shock, Quinn looked from face to face with a desperate lack of comprehension. "Colonel?"

"Computer, end program," Bashir commanded with great satisfaction.

Without a sound, the wooden surroundings vanished, revealing the yellow-gridded walls of the holodeck. Then the doors to the holosuite hissed open, and once more Colonels William Travis and James Bowie stepped out onto Deep Space 9.

An Errant Breeze

Gordon Gross

The sweet, pungent odor of *kanar* filled his nostrils as he took a breath and held it. He could hear his heart racing; its pounding echoed in his ears.

A tiny finger of illumination from the hall wormed its way into the closet and, eventually, through the seam of the false wall which hid him. Heavy footsteps marched up to the closet and stopped, cutting off the light.

Now completely in the dark, Sakal pushed himself back against the wall of the crawl space, hugging his knees to his chest and concentrating on the smell of *kanar.* He closed his eyes. *Kanar* was the smell of his father.

"Perfume of the Dominion," his father had said when his mother complained. "It covers the stink."

"Damar!" his mother had hissed.

His father only shook his head and refilled his glass.

Of course it wasn't really his father's smell. Sakal and his mother had fled from their home to Reykor Saneel's residence less than a week ago. And Saneel liked *kanar* more than Sakal liked *larish* pie.

It was Saneel's crawl space in which he hid. The smell of *kanar* was hers, not his father's.

More footsteps, but the light had not returned. He could hear the shuffling of clothes as the closet was quickly rummaged.

Sakal squeezed his eyes tighter and reached into his pocket to hold his father's medal. The sharp edge jabbed under his fingernail, but Sakal caught his yelp before it escaped. He stuck his injured finger in his mouth to check for blood. A little *yamok* sauce, but no salt of blood. His lungs filled with a careful breath of relief.

"The Jem'Hadar are animals, Niala," Sakal's father had said to his mother after they thought he'd gone to bed. "Animals. They're bred for nothing but battle. They can track a blooded enemy by smell over a kilometer away. They care nothing for family. They care only for their Founder masters and the Vorta lackeys."

Sakal couldn't hear his mother's soft response.

"How can we fight them?" his father despaired. "How can we prevail against such odds?"

"I have faith in you, Damar," his mother had said in a clear, calm voice. "If anyone can return the Cardassian Empire to its former strength, it is you."

If the Jem'Hadar could track a man by the smell of his blood, would they be able to hear his breathing? The sound of his heart beating? Could they smell his fear? The noise in the closet stopped. Footsteps resumed, headed away down the hall.

"Panic kills," he heard the beginning of his father's lecture to new recruits. He repeated the words silently until his heart slowed.

Carefully, Sakal slipped his hand back into his pocket. This time he touched the starburst medal without incident. He concentrated on remembering the holo print of the presentation ceremony that had taken place before his birth. The holo stood between those of his parents' wedding and his parents on the day of his own naming on the small table near the front door.

In his mind's eye he saw Gul Dukat frozen in a salute. He knew that his father was much younger then, but he could only picture his father as he remembered him now. His father stood proud, the star-burst medal glinting on his broad chest.

The footsteps grew loud again, seeming to move away from the closet. Maybe they'd leave. Sakal rubbed the line of one of the rays on the starburst and then tried without success to decipher the raised bumps of the words that circled the sun by touch. But his father had trained him to recognize sounds, not textures.

"Concentrate, Sakal."

"I am, Father, but they all sound alike."

"They sound nothing alike," his father insisted. "Listen more carefully."

Sakal looked out over the yard trying to see which Regova it was in the tree singing. Suddenly, two hands covered his eyes, blocking his sight. He tried to struggle but was greeted only with the sound of his father's laughter.

"No, Sakal," his father said. "Relax. Listen without looking."

Sakal stopped struggling and started to listen. The bird trilled again.

"Now, which bird was that? The male or female?"

Sakal thought before answering. "The male."

"Yes!" The hands came away, and his father spun him around to hug him. "You see? When you concentrate, you can do it!"

Sakal laughed and hugged his father back.

"What are the two of you up to out there?" His mother joined them on the porch, and the three of them sat listening to the Regova and basking in the setting sun.

The air in the hiding space had grown warm. Sakal's head sagged forward, only to snap back and hit the wall when he realized he'd almost fallen asleep. The noise was as loud as an explosion amidst the quiet, and cold sweat poured off his body as he waited to be discovered. But there was nothing, no footsteps, no voices. The finger of light was back, undisturbed. Sakal counted his heartbeats. After two hundred, he relaxed a little.

* * *

There had been no noise for a long while, nothing more than his new friend Tasma's wompat howling. No footsteps, no voices, not even his mother's yells. And she had yelled. Just before the Jem'Hadar had arrived and then some after Sakal had hidden in the crawl space.

His mother had confused him. After she told him to hide, she'd run to the back window of Saneel's house and shouted his name at Tasma, telling him to run away and hide. Sakal had stopped and gone back to the kitchen thinking she was calling to him, but she only waved him back the way he came. Sakal flew up the stairs, to the safe place Saneel had shown them the night they'd arrived.

He was pulling the closet door shut when the shots began. The wood was warped, and it wouldn't close all the way.

From inside the closet the shots didn't sound anything like the noises he and his friends made when they played at war. They even sounded different from the war holos and entertainment programs he'd run. These were short, without any echo. He had held his breath when they started.

Remembering Saneel's instructions, Sakal used his fingernails to pry the bottom panel at the back of the closet while he pushed to the right. When the hole was big enough, he crawled through it and pushed the false wall back into place. An explosion followed by the crash of the heavy front door scared him back against the wall. Then his mother began to shout, her voice muffled by the panel and the almost closed closet door.

"What are you doing in this house?" she yelled at the soldiers as if they were children. "This is Reykor Saneel's residence, you fools, a Cardassian scientist loyal to the Alliance. Call your shapeless gods and find out where you're supposed to be."

The sound of firing rang out again, and his mother's scream. Then the footsteps had begun.

Time passed funny in the dark. The noises that the house made convinced him that someone was inside, but he could hear no one talking, heard no more footsteps in the hall. Sakal passed the time thinking of his father: his father's smile and pat on the back when Sakal scored well in his academics, his father's laughter when Sakal imitated Gul Trepar, his father snoring when he'd fallen asleep at the table, glass of *kanar* in hand, his father standing proud as hundreds of soldiers marched to his commands, chanting "Damar! Damar! Damar!"

The dream chants awoke him with a start. He had fallen asleep despite his efforts.

The finger of light still poked into the darkness, but the air in the crawl space was no longer warm. It felt moist and cool. He couldn't tell how long he'd been hidden, but the quiet must mean something. Curiosity finally outpaced fear and he slid the false wall over far enough to squeeze into the back of the closet.

He crouched under the uniforms and listened for footsteps. Nothing.

Pushing the closet door half open, he inched into the hallway, ready to dive back into the crawl space. The lights were still on, and the brightness made his eyes water. There were still no sounds in the house other than the creak of the wood beneath his feet.

Finally, after a hundred more heartbeats, Sakal opened the door completely.

The house seemed normal, but empty. Very empty. Several winged lancers fluttered in his face as he went down the stairs as quietly as he could. Sakal batted them away silently. At the bottom of the stairs he saw the front door laying flat on the floor, the doorway open to the night air.

His instincts screamed at him to leave the house before he saw too much, before they caught him. Then he smelled his mother's *sem'hal* stew from the kitchen. His stomach cramped with hunger. Turning toward the kitchen he saw the scorched planks of the hall floor, the black edges painting the outline of what looked like an arm, part of a shoulder and neck. But only for a second. Then his mind refused to see the pattern. Before his eyes, it blended with the lines in the wood and the ragged edge of the carpet. Meaningless.

Sakal continued down the hall to the kitchen, his feet avoiding the scorch marks of their own volition.

"You must remain calm and remember, always plan ahead." Sakal could still hear his father's voice.

The large pot of stew on the stove was still warm. Sakal took a quick taste with his finger. The rich taste filled his mouth, but he had no time to sit and eat. Turning his back on the pot, Sakal found a fabric bag under the sink and began filling it with fruit out of the bowl on the kitchen table. He added dried *zabo* meat from the pantry and a jar of *yamok* sauce. After a moment, he put the *yamok* sauce back on the shelf.

"Why can't we bring it on our hike?" Sakal's own voice echoed in his head. "Without yamok *sauce the jerky tastes terrible."*

"It's very hot out today, Sakal," his mother's voice answered from that same distant place.

"So? I'll carry it."

"No, Sakal," his mother's voice had grown testy. "Your father knows what he's doing. Now just leave it."

And his father had known best. It was a long hike in the heat and even without the jar of yamok *sauce his pack felt like it was filled with boulders long before they got home. Sakal thought then that it was good that the son of Damar had not had to ask his mother to carry his pack, not in front of so many people. He had made his father proud, never once complaining during the hike.*

Sakal went to the back door and snuck a peek around its edge. When he saw no soldiers, he slipped out and crossed the backyard to Tasma's parents' backyard. He moved at a steady pace, skirting Tasma's wompat which lay next to the small, charred silhouette burned into the grass. He hardly paused when it raised its head and whimpered at him.

Sakal wasn't sure where to go. No one had helped them when the Jem'Hadar came. Sakal remembered his mother mentioning a house of some kind that she had heard of, one near the amusement park. He wished that she had known its exact location, but if she had, the two of them probably would have gone there first rather than stay at Saneel's home.

On the first night he passed under an open window and heard the news playing. He crouched down in the darkness beneath the window to listen.

"Legate Broca announced today that the wife and son of the fanatic Damar have been executed as traitors to the Dominion as was Reykor Saneel, the Cardassian biologist who harbored the traitors in her residence. Broca urged the citizens of Cardassia to remain loyal to their Dominion allies and not to follow the cowardly example set by the terrorist Damar.

"Following the news on the front, our Breen allies have secured another victory against the Romulans today . . ."

Sakal crept away from the house, keeping to the shadows. If he was dead, he thought, then he was like the phantoms in the stories his father used to tell him. He would be harder to catch now.

The phantom Sakal continued on his way to find the safe house. He ate small snacks from his pack trying to make his food last as long as possible. The *zabo* jerky took the longest to eat. He'd hold a bite in his mouth until his saliva softened it. When the fruit began to smell funny, he threw it away as his mother and father taught him, angry with himself for not eating it first. The jerky wouldn't go bad. He should have thought of that and saved it for last.

When the jerky ran out, he learned to ask for food. When asking didn't work, he learned to take food when necessary. After all, he was a phantom now. And phantoms took stuff all the time.

When Sakal got to the city, he headed straight to the amusement park, amazed to see that it was still open. Smiling mothers herded children that pranced like *gettle* through the gates as if nothing were wrong with the world. Sakal had always wanted to go to the park with his parents. But there had never been any time, not when his father was stationed at Terok Nor under Gul Dukat, or even when he'd returned to Cardassia Prime after the armistice.

Exhausted from walking, Sakal sat on one of the benches by the front gate, not sure where to look first for the safe house.

The day was pleasantly cool, and he stole glances at the faces of those who passed him. He couldn't tell if any of these people were from the place his mother spoke of. They all looked alike.

When his feet stopped pounding, the phantom Sakal got up and began to search the blocks surrounding the amusement park for the safe house. None of the structures looked promising.

When night came, he returned to the bench near the park entrance. The music from the rides carried on the breeze, and the park lights sparkled against the dark. The laughter of the children and parents drove him away.

He walked back through the twisting blocks to a well-tended garden that he'd seen during his search. He spent the night there, curled up under a hedge. The next day he continued his hunt, searching in widening circles, but with few results. None of the buildings looked promising, and he was distracted by the constant influx of news about his father.

Broadcasts had been downplaying any damage his father may have caused, but people began to talk about the Rebel Damar in hushed voices tinged with wonder and not a little hope. Sakal found himself listening to passersby rather than concentrating on finding the safe house.

"I hear Damar destroyed a garrison yesterday. Even the Jem'Hadar could not stop him."

"Damar isn't afraid of the Jem'Hadar dogs."

Then Sakal heard the broadcasts reporting the death of his father, the Traitor Damar. The breath went out of him.

He found his way back to the now hollowed out area under the hedge and curled up in a ball. Dead, the realization echoed in his head. Both his parents were dead. Where did his duty lie if neither his father nor his mother were alive? How could he go on?

Hunger eventually drove him back onto the streets—hunger and the certainty that his father would be ashamed by his childish display. He stole some melon from a market and hid in the entrance to a nearby alley to eat it. As he gulped it down, he slowly became aware of the whispers of people walking along the street.

"The Dominion cannot kill Damar. He fights for Cardassia."

He threw the rind away and returned to the amusement park. He heard no broadcast coverage of his father, but rumors of his father's rebellion multiplied. His father had become a phantom just as he himself had. A phantom who fought for Cardassia.

It was then that Sakal knew where his duty lay. To Cardassia, echoed his father's voice in answer. Somehow Sakal had to find the Resistance and help free Cardassia from the Dominion yoke. He renewed his efforts to find the safe house. They would know where his father was—they must. And then Sakal would be able to join his father and fight to free his people.

Sakal still couldn't find the safe house, but talk of his father was on almost everyone's lips. His father inspired others to remember their duty to family and to Cardassia.

"He is the spirit of Cardassia."

"Death to the Traitor Revok. He has the blood of our people on his conscience."

"Damar will raise another army."

"When Damar has won and the Dominion has been driven from Cardassian soil, Revok had best flee with them. There will be no home for collaborators here."

As the talk of his father grew, Sakal saw more and more Jem'Hadar. While he kept to the shadows when he saw them, he no longer fled. What could shape-shifters or their lackeys do to a phantom? They had not stopped him. They had not stopped his father.

"Damar is coming soon."

Sakal hoped it was so. He belonged with his father. He wanted to fight to free Cardassia. He would make his father proud.

With the increasing number of Jem'Hadar, nighttime reports of phaser fire and explosions echoed through the city. During the days thick palls of smoke clung to the buildings and hid debris.

Then one night at dusk, the power went out. A hush settled over Lakarian City.

"He knows what he's doing, that Damar."

And that was true, Father always knew.

"The Jem'Hadar have retreated."

"We are free."

Sakal looked up at the night sky, amazed that the soldiers no longer patrolled the streets. His father was a hero, Sakal thought when the sky show began.

And then the world went white.

STAR TREK
VOYAGER®

The Ones Left Behind

Mary Wiecek

Excerpts from the journal of Anne Carey

Cobh, County Cork, Ireland

April 2371

It's been three weeks now, and no word. I can't help myself—I contact Starfleet several times a day. They have a special comm-link set up for the *Voyager* family members. They've been fairly patient about it, but still, no word.

I'm trying to stay optimistic. It's only been three weeks since Starfleet lost contact with them, after all. They may have had some difficulty finding the Maquis ship that they were pursuing into the Badlands. There may be some problem with their communications. It could be any number of things. Starships don't just disappear into thin air. They don't. If the ship had been destroyed, there would be debris, warp residuals, something.

But still, it's hard. Especially with the kids. At seven, JJ is old enough to realize that something is wrong. He asks a lot of questions that I can't answer to his satisfaction. Or to mine. Patrick is only four, but he, too, is able to sense the tension in the rest of us.

And there was one awful day last week, when the news reported that debris had been found near *Voyager*'s last known location in the Badlands. I can't describe the dread and panic that I felt. I was utterly certain that it would be *Voyager.* I tried to imagine telling JJ and Patrick that their father would never be coming back. I actually tried to think of the words that I would use. I cried for an hour, sobbing as quietly as I could—the boys were asleep, thank goodness, so they never saw my despair.

It turned out to be debris from a Cardassian vessel. I'm ashamed of how relieved I felt. Or at least I ought to be ashamed.

And that's just it. Hours of complete despair are followed by increasingly short moments of upbeat certainty. "Of course they're all right," I tell myself. "I'm going to feel so ridiculous when this turns out to be nothing." Some days are easier than others. At times, the day to day trials and tribulations of living with two small boys make me almost forget to worry. Other times, I watch them play, and I can't even breathe past the lump in my throat.

I'm almost sorry that it's semester break at the University. If I were teaching, at least I would have something else to focus on for a couple of hours a day. I certainly can't concentrate on my research right now, so I spend a lot of time at home. Waiting for the comm-channel to sound with news. Waiting for . . . I don't know, something. Anything.

The cathedral bells are chiming. Looking out my window, I can just make out the silhouette of the bell tower, down toward the bay, nearly obscured by the early morning fog. This view of the cathedral is the reason that we moved here. St. Colman's sits at the highest point of the island of Cobh and towers majestically over everything else. Joe and I fell in love with the imposing structure, and the bells. The bells fill me with a sense of hope. This place—Ireland, certainly, but particularly this island—is the very embodiment of hope. For centuries, Cobh was the port of departure for desperate Irish on their way to the promise of the "New World." And here, where so little has changed over the years, their dreams seem almost a palpable presence. Also, in the First World War, over four hundred years ago, the survivors of the *Lusitania* were brought here. Here they prayed, and here they contacted their grateful families.

The thought makes me smile, and I hear one of the boys stirring. It's time to face the day, and wait. And hope. Always hope. He'll be all right. He has to be.

Cobh, County Cork, Ireland

January 2372

When I got a look at the date this morning, I realized that exactly ten months have gone by. *Voyager* has been missing for nearly a year. When they first disappeared, I was so optimistic. But as the weeks turned into months, I felt my hope fade day by day. Still, I hadn't realized that it had been this long. Ten months.

Voyager is slowly fading from the public consciousness. No one talks much about it at all anymore, something that either infuriates me, or makes me feel resigned, depending on my mood. Starfleet hasn't officially abandoned the search, but I don't think that there is much else that they can do. They've sent numerous ships into the Badlands, but they have found nothing. The ship is never mentioned on the news anymore.

Actually, the big story in the news this week is the dedication of the *Enterprise*-E. It's ironic. Joe turned down a posting on the *Enterprise* to join *Voyager.* I was stunned. I was sure he would jump at the chance to serve on the *Enterprise,* but he said that he'd rather serve on a new ship, and a smaller one—that it would be easier for him to work his way up. Also, as an engineer, he wanted to be on a ship that had the state-of-the-art bioneural circuitry. And he'd heard good things about Captain Janeway. That she was a brilliant engineer herself. That she was more accessible than most captains.

I never got a chance to meet her. The few times that I saw her on the news, however, I have to say that I was impressed. She was outgoing, attractive, articulate, and polished. She seemed tough, but there was also a sparkle in her eye. A warmth. I can't help but think that a woman like that would not be easily defeated by whatever the Badlands or the Maquis threw at her.

But it's been ten months now. And even I can't believe anymore that *Voyager* is going to miraculously reappear. Superficially, our lives have gone on. I'm back at the University. The boys are back in school. The holidays have come and gone. We're busy, but there is an incredible . . . void . . . in our lives.

There are times when I'm so angry with him. For leaving me alone. For not being here to help me raise our sons. I know it's irrational and that it's not his fault, but I'm angry just the same. I miss him fiercely. His laughter. His touch. His companionship—even when he was away, he was always involved in what was going on around here.

I wish that I had him here to help me through this. Isn't that absurd? But the boys . . . I don't know what to do about them. Having a father missing with *Voyager* has given JJ some amount of notoriety in the second grade. But it's not exactly the kind of attention he wants. And, of course, kids can be cruel. Some of the things they've said to him . . . well, he is angry and withdrawn, and I can't blame him. And Patrick, Patrick's just gotten very quiet. I think it may be time for all of us to get some counseling.

Now when I hear the cathedral bells, they just sound hollow. And it's winter, and the sun has not shone here in three weeks. The bleakness of the sky, and the season, just seems to mirror my mood. And there's not even any closure.

I just need to know. One way or another.

Starfleet Headquarters, San Francisco, California

February 2373

The memorial service for *Voyager*'s crew was today. I think it's ludicrous that they waited so long to declare them missing and presumed dead. *Voyager* disappeared almost two years ago. I know that Starfleet has had other things on its mind—the Changeling scare, the Borg Threat, the war with the Dominion—but two years was an awfully long time to keep stringing us along. Well, recently there's been a lull in the hostilities, and I guess they've had time to exhaust all possibilities. They finally realized that they could no longer put off the inevitable.

I recognized some of the people there. I've seen interviews with Gretchen Janeway before, the captain's mother, and she was there in the front row, along with a woman who could only have been Captain Janeway's sister—there was a strong family resemblance. A handsome middle-aged man was with them as well, and I'm not sure now if the Captain was married, or what, but he seemed to be someone of significance. They looked solemn and disturbed. Well, I suppose we all did.

Everyone knows Admiral Owen Paris from his high-profile involvement with the Dominion conflict. He was there, looking grimmer than usual. I'd heard that his son was on board, although I'm not sure why. I also recognized some of the spouses of Joe's crewmates. People that I had met briefly, years ago, under much happier circumstances. I barely know any of them, but still we cling to each other—exchange stories, and comm-line links. We form a strange family now—the ones left behind.

There were many others there, of course, whom I did not recognize. But I knew the look in their eyes. That haunted, frustrated look that I see reflected in my own eyes when I look in the mirror. There was an older Asian couple sitting next to JJ, Patrick, and me in the third row. They sat holding hands, just enveloped in sorrow. Their only child, they told me—an ensign, I think. I was as sorry for them as I was for the boys and myself.

I held out hope longer than most, but as months turned into years, I was finally forced to accept that Joe was not coming back. I tried to hold on—I'm not half-Irish for nothing, after all. We pride ourselves in our ability to keep the faith, and persevere against the odds. But eventually, reality had to prevail. My false hope was not going to help the boys.

It's so hard, though. I miss him so much, and being a single parent is so much harder than I could have imagined. JJ is nearly ten now, and he's slimmed down and his hair has gotten darker—he looks very much like his father. It startles me sometimes. Makes me sad, but also comforts me, in a strange way.

After the service, there was a reception. From what I heard, I gather that a lot of people have moved on—several are already planning to remarry. After my one disastrous "date," it's clear to me that I'm just not ready for any of that. I guess that I'm just too preoccupied with work and the boys and finding a balance in this life that was turned upside down. And there is a small part of me that just can't make the final break until I am completely certain. I know it's not practical. I will probably never know what happened to Joe and that ship, but it feels wrong, somehow, to move on just yet.

I think this memorial service was intended to bring us some closure. As far as I'm concerned, though, I'll never have any closure. It's brutally unfair not to know what actually happened to them. It's so hard to accept that they are irrevocably lost, not without proof. Joe always told me that I was an eternal optimist, and I suppose that's true. Right now, though, that spark of hope has become something of a handicap.

I know that Joe would want me to move on. But I just can't.

Starfleet Headquarters: San Francisco, California

June 2375

Oh God, they're alive! He's alive! I can't believe it! The news came in the middle of the night and I got to a transport station first thing this morning to beam over. I have to be here! I want to get the information as it's released!

I don't know all the details yet, but apparently *Voyager* is trapped in the Delta Quadrant, of all places. An alien called the "Caretaker," I think, somehow transported them seventy thousand light-years from home. They've only now been able to contact Starfleet, by sending their emergency medical hologram's program along some sort of relay network. The story gets confusing here, because the program materialized on an experimental Starfleet ship that had been taken over by Romulans.

It's absolute chaos here at HQ. Clearly Starfleet doesn't want to release much information about the experimental ship, which I think is back in Starfleet hands, yet the news about *Voyager* is something that cannot be suppressed. I think they've been getting information to us as quickly as they can, but it's so incredibly frustrating! I want to know everything! Right now!

Where to begin? First of all, they've already told us that the information that they've received is limited—mostly medical logs from the EMH, who is now acting as the CMO. And obviously it's not all good news. One of the first things released was a very sobering list of those killed in the line of duty. I read through those names with my heart in my throat . . . Bennet, Carrington, Cavitt. He wasn't there! I found his name on the active roster—Lieutenant Joseph M. Carey, engineering. I cried for ten straight minutes, then felt awful when I saw Marie Cavitt walk by, also crying, but for a different reason. So many have been lost.

A few crew members have been gained, as well. Apparently, when the ship was pulled into the Delta Quadrant, they found the Maquis ship that they were supposed to apprehend. The two ships banded together, but the Maquis ship was destroyed while protecting *Voyager* in a battle. Now the crews have been combined under Captain Janeway—and she made the Maquis captain her first officer. I wonder what Starfleet thinks of that—most of the Maquis are still in prison.

Apparently, they've also picked up some Delta Quadrant natives: a Talaxian, and an Ocampa, whatever they are, and, most recently, a Borg that they liberated from the collective! Liberated—what does that mean, exactly? I didn't even think that was possible . . .

In the statistical personnel information released today, I noticed that there have been only two marriages (neither of them involving Joe—I checked), and just one birth, and that child was already conceived when the ship left the Alpha Quadrant. I wonder a little about that. It's been over three years—you would think that people would be pairing off more by now. Are they so unhappy? But then, it must be strange for them—knowing that they've left lives and people behind. How long do you wait? How do you decide when it's time to move on? It's similar to the quandary we at home have faced, except that they had the advantage, if you can call it that, of knowing that we were all alive and well.

It's a quandary, actually, that we all still face. *Voyager* is still 55,000 light-years away, and looking at another 55 years of travel through unknown space to get back home.

I know it's naïve and overly optimistic of me—Joe would be rolling his eyes and laughing—but I just have a feeling that it is not going to take that long. Not with Captain Janeway in command—that woman amazes me! Combining those crews was a brilliant move, to begin with. And she actually made an alliance with the Borg—I mean, can you imagine? They've traveled over 15,000 light-years in only three years! If she can keep that up, they'll be home in a little over eleven years! And if she can find a few extra shortcuts . . . Well, it's pointless to speculate, I suppose. But I just know it won't take another 55 years.

They assured us that more detailed information will be released tomorrow. My mind is racing and I can't seem to sit still! How will I ever sleep?

Starfleet Headquarters, San Francisco, California

May 2375

Piecing together information on any one individual from the medical logs is like trying to interpret ancient hieroglyphics. But we are fortunate in one respect—the ship's EMH, oddly enough, seems to be fond of gossip! Or, as one Starfleet spokesman said, he "has included information in his official logs that is of questionable relevance, but is useful nonetheless." Well, that may be, but I'm grateful for it. It helps me to know a little of what Joe's life has been like in the years that we've been apart.

The first couple of years of the journey were quite busy for Joe. In fact, in the very first week in the Delta Quadrant, he wound up in sickbay with a broken nose. Apparently, one of the Maquis engineers hauled off and slugged him! It was a woman called B'Elanna Torres, and he now serves under her—she is the Chief Engineer! I can't help but wonder about that. After all, Joe was the ranking Starfleet officer left in engineering after this "Caretaker" abducted them. I mean, I know that Joe was nowhere near qualified to become chief engineer under normal circumstances, but this Torres person hadn't even made it through the Academy. And punching people isn't exactly acceptable Starfleet procedure. Perhaps it was a political decision. Maybe the captain had to put some Maquis into positions of authority to secure their cooperation.

But who knows what really happened. The ship still seems to be in one piece, so perhaps Torres was qualified after all. There are no further reports of her punching people, so I guess that was an isolated incident. I hate to say it, but Joe just might have provoked her. He can be awfully arrogant. And I have to admit there have been times when I wished that I could punch him too! I'm sure that once she settled in and Joe calmed down some, they got along just fine. Joe's a good person, and a consummate professional. And in a way, maybe it's good that Joe won't have to deal with the pressure and stress of being a department head.

There was more trouble for Joe in those early days. He and another one of the engineers, an Ensign Seska, were both suspects when it was discovered that someone had been giving Federation technology to an alien species. Eventually, Joe was exonerated when the EMH discovered that Seska was actually a Cardassian who had infiltrated the Maquis ship. But I can imagine how angry Joe must have been to be considered a suspect. And how hurt.

I wish that I could hear all of Joe's stories—so much has happened to him. Engineering, for some reason, seems to have a disproportionate number of Maquis personnel. It may only be because that's where many of the fatalities occurred in the initial incident, and that's where there were the most slots to fill. Or perhaps it's just a reflection of the qualifications of the Maquis. In any case, engineering has certainly been a turbulent place. In addition to the Seska incident, there was also a murder. One of the Maquis engineers, an Ensign Suder, murdered one of the Starfleet engineering crewmen in a pathological rage. Good God, an actual murder! What kind of place is that? It could have been Joe!

There was another violent death in engineering as well. Ensign Jonas, I think, was thrown into a plasma field in a struggle with the Talaxian I mentioned. Apparently, the ensign had been exposed for making a traitorous alliance with Seska. Flaring tempers, intrigue, murder . . . never a dull moment in engineering. Why couldn't Joe be mapping stars in stellar cartography, or something?

Apparently, things have settled down in engineering now, but the ship itself has had quite an eventful three years. It's hard to believe that so much could happen to one ship in so short a time. *Voyager* was commandeered twice, the crew exiled, and they've run into one hostile species after another. I lost count of how many times they've gone into battle! The entire crew was nearly killed by some kind of "macrovirus" that swept through the ship. And then they ran into something called "Species 8472." Janeway considered them so much of a threat that she formed an alliance with the Borg to defeat them—the Borg! What could be bad enough to warrant that?

It's so frightening. They're completely alone out there. I pray that Starfleet can find a way to help them somehow.

There's very little information about Joe in the more recent medical logs, and it's enormously frustrating. I know that we were lucky to get any information at all, but I want to know so much more. I'm forced to rely on the nonconfidential sections from the medical logs of other crew members to garner information. For example, there is a mention of someone spraining an ankle, which the EMH noted, was the ship's first "talent night injury." Now that is a useful bit of information! They have talent nights? How wonderful! But I hope to God that Joe hasn't played "Toora Loora Loora" on his armpits in front of the entire crew. I know the kids find it hilarious, but surely he wouldn't . . . Oh, he might at that! Ah well, as long as he's happy, I guess.

I do hope that he is happy. I like to think that he is finding time for recreation and for the things that bring him joy. The doctor's logs also mention parties, and luaus, and skiing excursions on the holodeck. It seems as though, despite the lack of marriages, a strong sense of community has developed among the crew, and that's comforting.

And that brings me to the one thing that the doctor's logs aren't going to tell me—the one thing that I most want to know. Has Joe found someone else? Had he given up on ever getting home? I know he wouldn't betray me if he thought there was any hope, but surely he's been discouraged, and lonely, as I have been. But then, I haven't moved on. I never gave up on him. Did he give up on me? I really need to know . . .

I'm trying not to speculate, even if it's all that I can do. I'll just have to hope for the best, and content myself with the knowledge that he is alive and well, and that he is serving with a captain who seems determined to persevere and get that ship home.

I just wish that I could get a message to him. There's so much that I want to say.

Cobh, County Cork, Ireland

June 2375

Starfleet has found a way to send a message back through the same communications network that the EMH program came through. They've given all immediate family members an opportunity to send a brief message—and they're going to make the attempt tomorrow. That doesn't give me much time!

I sent the boys next door and made myself some tea, but now I'm just sitting here with my thoughts in a jumble. What do I even want from him? An indefinite commitment? Is that fair—for either of us?

Perhaps I should be practical and realistic about this. They're still so far away, and there certainly isn't any guarantee that they'll find any short cuts. I can't put my life on hold forever, and it's unfair to expect him to, either. Perhaps the most reasonable thing to do would be to release him. I love him, and I want him to be happy.

But . . . I want him to be happy here, with me. With us. I just don't know what to do . . .

And now it's five o'clock and the cathedral bells are ringing, flooding me with longing and hope. I just know that they'll find a way. I'm sure of it. And now I know what I'm going to say.

I just wish that I could talk to him—actually talk to him. I'd give almost anything to hear his voice, just once.

Personal log: Lieutenant Joe Carey

Stardate: 51501.4

My wait is finally over—one of the letters was mine! I've heard from Annie! Her message, it's . . . God, it's wonderful! It's exactly what I wanted to hear!

Dearest Joe,

Since we found out that you are alive, I have been beside myself with joy, and the boys can't stop grinning. I can't begin to tell you how much we miss you. We talk about you often, wondering about your day. The children have grown so much, you wouldn't . . . well, of course you would recognize them, especially JJ—he looks exactly like you. Patrick has been making up outrageous stories about your adventures and regaling us with them at bedtime. You have saved the ship dozens of times, haven't you?

There is so much that I wish I could tell you. We're doing fine—all of us, as are your parents. Your father's health had been a bit shaky, but the news of *Voyager* seems to have rejuvenated him. They both send their love, of course.

I'm still with the University—and I'm up for tenure, a year early. Last year, I was offered a position at Oxford, but I turned it down. I couldn't leave Cobh, and this house that was so full of memories of you. Now, I'm glad that we stayed.

I've not moved on, Joe. I can't say that I never lost hope, but as long as there was any question . . . I just couldn't bring myself to give up on you. And I know that you'll say that I'm being hopelessly optimistic, but I still believe in my heart that you'll be coming home to us—maybe not tomorrow, but soon. So I want you to know that I'll be waiting for you. For as long as I can foresee right now.

We'll have to use our judgment, of course. If years and years go by—five . . . ten . . . twelve—then perhaps it would be right for us to move on. I don't want you to spend a lifetime lonely and unhappy, and I know that you don't want that for me either. But for now, know that I am still here for you.

I do hope that *Voyager* and Starfleet will be able to use these relay stations indefinitely. To be in regular contact with you would be wonderful. And I'd love to be able to send you images of the children. But for now, I'll try to be grateful for the knowledge that you are alive, and that *Voyager* is trying to find its way home.

I love you, Joe, always. Come home soon.

Yours,
Annie

My head's been in a fog ever since I read it. I hadn't dared to hope . . . But I should have known. Annie is so strong. She has always been unflaggingly optimistic, and a hopeless romantic. It used to drive me crazy, but not now! I should have known that she would still be waiting.

Until I got the message, the whole day had been off-kilter. The mood in engineering has been grim. Something happened to the Maquis. I can only speculate, but I know that Commander Chakotay met with them in the morning, and now they're all—well, sad and angry and preoccupied. I offered to take Torres's shift, but she just shook her head and said something about needing to be busy. I wound up taking Ayala's shift instead—he looked like he was ready to explode.

Something happened. They'll tell the rest of us when they're ready.

None of them even looked up when Neelix bustled into engineering with a padd. Vorik looked, though—I saw him do it. He pretends to be Vulcan stoic about it all, but he wants a letter from home as much as anyone else. But this time, Neelix looked right at me and smiled, and I knew. I should have shown more restraint, but I sat down on the deck right by my station and read the message straightaway, once I could stop my hand from shaking long enough to activate it.

I don't know how long I sat there after I read it, and I don't remember when I started crying (on duty, no less), but when I looked up I saw that Neelix was still there, and that he'd knelt down beside me with a sympathetic expression on his face. He asked if I was all right, and I was still crying, but I was laughing, too, when I assured him that it was exactly the news that I'd been hoping for. I tried to pull myself together and start acting professional, but then Torres came over, smiling kind of sadly. She told me that she was really happy for me. She really seemed to mean it, too.

She ordered me to "knock off early," which was probably sensible. She had to know that I'd be worse than useless for the rest of the shift.

So now I'm rattling around in my empty quarters, clutching a four-year-old picture of my wife and sons. I don't know how I feel. I'm overjoyed and relieved to know that Annie and the boys know I'm alive and are still there for me. But at the same time . . . I don't know. We're still so far from home. When will I ever see them again?

I hope we can find a way to keep that array intact. There's so much I want to tell her—that I didn't move on, that I miss her and the boys desperately, that I love them . . .

I just wish there were a way for me to talk to her, even briefly. I'd give almost anything to hear the sound of her voice.

I don't know what to do with myself . . . I feel so restless. I don't really want to be alone, yet I don't want to talk to anyone right now, either. Not about this.

I've got it! I just checked, and I can get into holodeck two in twenty minutes. I'll run my Cobh program. I've only used it twice since we've been out here—I found the memories there too depressing. But now I think it's exactly what I need. I'll sit on the porch and watch the fog roll in—if I close my eyes, maybe I'll actually be able to feel Annie's hand on my shoulder, and hear the boys' laughter. I'll set the program for five o'clock, so I can hear the cathedral bells chime.

I love those bells—they've always filled me with a sense of hope. I know I'll be with Annie, and the boys, again.

I know we'll get home.

The Second Star

Diana Kornfeld

Voyager. The Alpha Quadrant. Starfleet. Earth. Tuvok. Neelix. Most of the other names escape me now. Except for, of course, Chakotay, the one who fell from the sky, the one whom I saved and who saved me—and the magic woman—Captain Kathryn Janeway.

So many years have passed. I was just about your age when it happened, Lokita, only seven or eight. Yes, this old woman before you was once a child like you. Don't laugh, Bellya. I see you giggling behind your fingers. Come here and sit on my lap as I tell you the story. I want you children to know what your grandmother has told no one else except your mothers. I want you to understand my life before I leave it, and I hope you will carry this story with you to share with your own children one day.

Many people have asked me about my life, why I chose the path I did. I tell them many things, but I never tell them the truth. I know that if I did, they wouldn't understand. They would smile behind their hands like you did, Bellya, and they would think I was a crazy old woman. To you, I shall tell the truth. I see the light of belief still shining in your eyes. Shining like it did in mine.

I have always loved the stars. Since I was very small I used to sneak out of the house in the middle of the night and sit and watch them, shining there, so peaceful, so serene, but sparkling as if with a special secret that they wished to share with me. They did share that secret with me, one which I will share with you now.

I lay weeping in my bed one night, weeping for the loss of my parents, for the harsh life that I now endured, a small servant girl working for a place to lie down at night and a little bit to eat. I had been taken in by the Monoris, a hard-working family, and I was not mistreated. Not mistreated but not loved either. I was not allowed to go to school, few girl children were, and I was not born into privilege so that I might have the advantage of listening to my brothers' tutors. I was told I was lucky to have a place, a warm room, almost enough to eat. But you have heard all of this before. Let me tell you how that night changed my life forever, and how I hope it will change yours also.

I could not sleep. I was afraid I would dream again about the day my parents were torn from me, killed savagely by the Komekki. I did not want to see the faces of the soldiers again, faces dead to pity, alive only to hatred, to slaughter. I decided that night to run away and live with the birds in the Ronaken hills. With the simple trust of childhood, I thought I would live on sheelia berries and stream water and moosha grass. I could stay the nights in the Ronaken caverns, and I would have my only friends, the stars, to keep me company in the nights.

So I gathered up my few possessions, took a little food I found from the pantry, and I ran. I was strong and used to running to deliver messages during the days, so I ran and ran. Do you know where the Beelor River meets the west road? Yes, yes, you remember the picnic we went on last summer? That's how far I ran before I dropped exhausted on the cool night grass. I lay on my back to catch my breath and watch the stars. That's when I saw it. I thought it was a falling star, the kind we say the blessing after.

Have you seen one? And do you know the blessing, Onyas? That's the one. You say it so nicely.

But this falling star seemed to fall straight into the dark hills, and there was a flash of red light as it disappeared behind the shadows of the peaks. My young bones tingled with curiosity. Had a star really fallen from the sky? What did a fallen star look like? Would it sparkle as it lay upon the moosha grass? Would it give off heat and warm me? Could I put it in my pocket? I ran again, this time in the direction of the flash, which had disappeared as if it had never been. No, I was not afraid. You would have done the same, Onyas, I know you! The dark night held no terrors for a child who had slept with terror. To me the darkness was a comfort, just the wind and the stars and I racing in a dark embrace.

I had been in these hills before, hidden with my mother during the time of the Jen wars. I decided I would look for the fallen star in the valley behind the northern summit of Greyar's hill, and I would sleep in one of the many caverns nestled beneath her northern slope. It would be my new home.

I found nothing that night, nothing but empty foshu nests, moonlight, and shadows. I curled up in a soft bed of dry grasses just within the entrance to a small cavern and finally slept. If I wept there, I don't remember it. I dreamt of sleeping with my mother again, wrapped in her arms, smelling her sweetness.

The strange sound awakened me. A moan, a gasp? What kind of creature could make that noise? It sent shivers up my spine and made me wish I hadn't been quite so hasty in my decision to leave the safety of my servant's bed. Could it be one of the soldiers they said still lived in these hills, gone mad from the carnage he had witnessed, from the blood he had spilled? Or was it some kind of beast? Perhaps the legendary kokomill who was said to freeze its victims with its stare and devour them slowly while they were still alive. There it was again, but louder now. I must run before this creature sensed my presence.

Silently I rose from my grass bed and glided to the entrance of the cave, but when I reached the early sunlight, which warmed me with courage, something in my curious child's heart made me stop and peer back into the depths of the cavern. I saw something shiny lying on the ground back in the shadows, catching the sun's rays and blinking at me as if to say, "Come, child, come and rescue me. I could be treasure, a piece of that falling star you saw last night. Don't you want to find out, little starseeker?"

Suddenly the moan turned into a cough, and I knew it was no kokomill. Perhaps it was just another runaway like myself who had sought the safety of the shadows. I looked at the silver object again and decided it was worth the risk of creeping back into the cavern.

Cautiously I approached it, taking care not to rustle the grass or disturb the shale. I reached down for the splash of silver when suddenly my hand was grabbed by another. I nearly collapsed in stifling fear when I saw what had grabbed me. Was it a creature or a man? It looked like nothing I had seen in my short life before, and I thought surely that short life would soon be over. For this creature was large, larger than any man I had ever seen, and it was pale with dark fur on only the top of its head. It had strange markings on the side of its forehead, and its eyes were small; at least I supposed they were eyes, for they glowed with the light, and they stared at me like *I* was a creature, trapped in its grasp. Was this after all the kokomill? For I couldn't move. Its grip was like a vice, and now its mouth was moving, and more strange sounds circled me like the crackling and hissing from a night fire.

Suddenly the sounds shifted, and I heard words that I recognized. Words coming from a beast? Or was this some strange race of man come down from the higher peaks of the distant Ronori ranges?

"Please, I will not hurt you," the voice said. "I cannot let you have this device. I'm sorry. Do you understand me?"

Nodding slowly, I stared as the talking creature took the small silver object and fixed it to his dark clothing.

"I'm sorry," it said again. "I didn't mean to startle you. I . . . Well, I was injured on my journey, and needed a place to sleep so I came here. Do you live near here? What is your name?"

This was a man of some kind, I reasoned now. He smiled as he talked and some child instinct told me I need have no fear. I was not wise in those days, but then I don't think I'm any wiser now.

"I am called Tarina," I began softly. "I did live in the village, but I have run away to live here in the hills," I answered him more boldly now and raised my chin for added courage.

"Hello, Tarina," he began. "My name is Chakotay. You are a brave child to be out here alone. What about your parents? Won't they worry about you?"

"My parents are dead," I replied calmly. "And I will no longer slave for the Monori family. But what are you?" Braver now, I sat back on my heels and examined him. "You look like a beast but speak like a man. Are you a star man?"

He laughed. "You get right to the point, don't you? I know I look strange to you, but I'm . . . I'm from a tribe of people who live far away from here," and he motioned to the hills behind us. "I guess I've run away like you." He smiled.

"No, you haven't," I contradicted him. "You can't fool me. You are a star man," I said confidently, watching his reaction. "I saw you fall from the sky."

He laughed, but then he looked at me intently. "What did you see, Tarina?"

"I saw the falling star last night. You were on it, weren't you?"

He looked down for a moment as if gathering his thoughts. "Did anyone else see this falling star?"

"No. I followed it. I wanted to see what a star looked like. At first I thought that thing was a piece of it," I said, motioning toward the shiny metal he now wore on his chest. "I have heard there are people who live in the stars, but I never thought they would look like you. You are not very pretty to look at."

He started to laugh but his laugh turned quickly to a wince, and he grabbed his side.

"Star man Chakotay, you are hurt," I cried. "Do you want me to go and look for help? Are there other star people here with you? Should I go back to the village and get the men?"

"No, thank you, Tarina, but my people," and now he attempted to smile again, "I have been trying to contact my people. I believe they will find me soon enough."

I could not understand this. "But how do you contact them? Do you call for them? I could help you call. If we yell loudly enough someone may hear."

"I don't contact them that way. But there is something else you could do for me if you don't mind. There is some food in that bag over there. Could you bring it closer?"

Pleased to be doing something, I ran to the far side of the cavern, grabbed the bag, and deposited it beside him quickly like an aggar cat jumping on a foshu nest.

"Thank you. That was fast. Would you like something to eat?" He offered me a strange mealy looking piece of something that looked like scarfara dough. I was hungry, but this thing smelled like cheela mold. I shook my head.

"I have my own food." I brought him a piece of gsoola cake and some sheelia berries. "You can have some of this," I offered.

And so we ate breakfast mostly in silence. Occasionally he would tap the thing on his chest, and listen. Then he would frown.

I began to talk to him again. He was such a curious sight. I said what I thought in those days, a trait I'm afraid I haven't lost in all these years.

"You are funny-looking, Chakotay."

He grinned. "I guess I am."

"You have black fur on your head."

He raised his eyebrows.

"And some of it is turning white."

He sighed.

"You have little eyes." I looked at him closer. "And you have big ears and little wrinkles by your eyes. Are you an old man or a young one?"

Now he was trying not to laugh. It must have hurt him to laugh. "You are very observant, Tarina. I guess I'm somewhere in the middle."

I nodded wisely. "Like my father was. But he was too young to die. I hope you don't die." Suddenly I was frightened. I didn't know how badly the star man was hurt. I had seen enough death.

"I'm not going to die, don't worry," and he paused. "I'm sorry about your parents. I lost mine, too. But I was grown up by then. Is there someone who can take care of you?"

"I think I have an aunt in Rylea. But that is far away, and I don't know if she is still alive or not. My uncle fought in the war with my father. I think he is still a prisoner."

"Do you go to school?"

"I would like to go to school more than anything in the four mountains, but I am a servant girl. Most girls don't go to school anyway. But my mother taught me some things," I said proudly. "I know more than that silly Loorat, my master's daughter."

And so we talked for a long time. He asked me many questions, and I was eager to share my little world with anyone who was interested in me, especially this strange, kind star man.

I brought water from the stream and built a little fire at the entrance to the cavern when the sun started to leave the hills. I helped him walk to the fire and showed him how expert I was in roasting loopa nuts until they crackled open just right.

"Tell me about the stars, Chakotay," I asked eagerly. "I want to go to the stars and walk on them someday. What are they like? Are you going back to them?"

"I'm going back to my ship," he answered softly. "I can't tell you very much, Tarina. I don't know why you keep saying I'm from the stars. I am from far away from here. I can tell you a little about my ship and my people, I suppose.

"We're trying to get back to our home. It's a long journey. Where I'm from we have had troubles much like your people have. But we kept on trying to get along. We struggled. We learned. Things are better now. A long time ago, like you, our little girls weren't allowed to go to school either. Change comes slowly, but it does come eventually if enough people work for it and sacrifice for it."

"Tell me about your ship. Are you the captain of your ship?"

He laughed. "No, Captain Janeway is my captain."

"Are you a slave to your captain?"

He was trying hard to keep from laughing more. "No, not exactly. But I must do as my captain orders and that includes not telling you everything about us."

I frowned. "This captain must be very strict."

"Captain Janeway is a brilliant leader and very brave, a little bit like you, in fact."

"Like me?" You can imagine how I glowed at that compliment. "Have you had any adventures on this ship?" I asked.

"A few," he said.

He talked of an endless journey, of a band of people who were fiercely loyal to each other, of a captain who guided them with wisdom and courage. But as he talked his voice grew weaker, and lines of pain crossed his face. His eyes burned with the light from the fire, and he didn't notice when he stopped speaking. I knew the signs too well. He was injured more seriously than I had known. Fever was stealing his spirit, and I feared it would take his life as well.

"Chakotay," I called as I knelt beside him and shook him by the shoulder. His only answer was a groan as he lay back against the moosha grass.

"You said you would not die," I cried. "You said your people would come."

His eyes were dark and vacant now, and I was very afraid. I had lost everyone else. I didn't want to lose the star man, too.

Suddenly the silver on his chest began to crackle and hiss, and then I opened my eyes wide as I heard words coming from it, scratching their way into the air from no one's lips! I understood and yet I did not understand them.

"Chakotay," it said. "Commander Chakotay. Can you hear me? We cannot get a fix on you in your present location. There seems to be something in the hills that is interfering with the transporter. Can you move to a more open location? Repeat. Commander Chakotay, can you hear me? You must move to open ground."

The voice went on and on as I watched in wonder. I shook Chakotay harder.

"Star man," I cried. "Wake up. Please wake up. I think your people are here, but I cannot see them. They want you to come out of the cave. Please don't die. You must get up. Listen to the voices. They say to get up. They say you are not to die. Do you hear me?" I was hitting him now. He must wake up. I could not watch him die, and I could not leave him there alone.

Slowly his eyes began to open, and he looked around him vaguely. "Come on, Chakotay. I will help you out of here. Get up. They are talking to you."

He shook his head and his eyes refused to focus, but he tried to sit up, struggling against the ground that wished to keep him.

"I will help you find them, Chakotay. That's it. Sit up. Now stand up. I will help you walk out of here." Although I was small, I was determined, and I could be fierce when I wanted to be. I pushed him and hit him and begged him to stand up until he finally staggered to his feet.

I took his hand and led him the few feet to the clearing outside the cave. We were under the stars, and I looked to them for help. Where were these invisible people who called to him so urgently? Then suddenly the ground and rocks and stars began to shimmer around me, shimmer into a white light that was there and then was gone before I could close my eyes against it. The world around me disappeared, and I was in another place, a gray and shining place with no stars, but with lights that hurt my eyes and other strange creatures who looked like Chakotay. One of them rushed toward us. I thought it was a woman. She looked very glad to see the star man, and I thought she would embrace him, like my mother used to embrace my father when he returned to her unharmed, with the fierce love born of fear. But she stopped before us and put her hand on his arm.

"Chakotay, you're injured."

"I'll be all right, Kathryn."

"Get Commander Chakotay to sickbay immediately."

"There's really no rush. I'll be fine."

People were moving toward us quickly, and I was beginning to panic.

Suddenly the woman he called Kathryn noticed me there, tugging on Chakotay's hand and half hiding behind him. "Oh my. Who do we have here?"

"Don't you hurt him," I cried as she knelt quickly beside me.

"Oh, don't worry, little one," she said, and her eyes spoke kindness to me. She looked a question to Chakotay.

"This is Tarina," he said quietly, holding his side and kneeling beside us. "I think she just saved my life. I must have been unconscious, but she dragged me out of the cave . . . with her bare hands."

"Did she?" The woman smiled. "Welcome to *Voyager,* Tarina. And thank you for bringing our commander back to us."

I looked at her carefully. "Is this your woman, Chakotay?" I asked.

Chakotay made a choking sound, and the woman laughed. "No, Tarina," he said. "This is Captain Janeway, the one I told you about."

My eyes grew wide with surprise. I see you are surprised too, Onyas. But it is true! Yes, the captain was a woman! Imagine my amazement. She was smiling and holding out her hand to me.

"What a lovely name. Tarina. Would you like to help me take Chakotay to our doctor? We'll get him fixed up a bit, and we can talk there." I nodded solemnly, and holding both their hands but too lost in wonder to say anything, I walked between them through the strange shining rooms toward the place they called sickbay.

I am afraid I cannot remember everything I heard as we walked along the corridors of this place. Nor can I remember all the strange faces and shapes that passed us, some of them returning my stares with smiles and curious eyes. Chakotay and the captain talked of shuttles and storms and the number seven. They said words that I could connect no meaning to. I remember tables and lights and Chakotay lying on a bed and a man who had very little fur on his head. He frowned at us and patted my head. I wanted to bite him, but I didn't think the captain would like that. He reminded me of Uncle Golo, talking and talking while he moved strange objects over Chakotay. Captain Janeway picked me up and set me on one of the beds so that I could see what was happening. I remember another man who smiled and smiled at me. He had fur on his face and spots. He was not quite so funny looking as Chakotay, and he was very kind.

"Are we inside a star?" I asked him. "Is this what a star looks like inside?"

"Oh no, we're inside *Voyager,*" he answered. "We're not *in* a star; we travel through . . ."

"Come, Tarina," the captain interrupted. "Neelix will fix us something to eat. I imagine you're hungry after such an adventure. We'll let Chakotay get some rest while we talk."

They fixed me strange food that I had never tasted before, and I ate very little.

"I know what you might like," said the captain. "Let me get you a treat." And she went over to the wall and spoke to it as if it were a living thing.

"Ice cream with chocolate sauce."

Instantly there appeared a bowl which held a white substance covered with a brown liquid.

"You are a magic woman!" I cried.

She laughed. "I assure you I'm not. But try this. It has a magical taste. I think you'll like it."

I tasted the creamy white and sweet dark and thought to myself that this was indeed a magic woman. It was like nothing I had ever tasted before or have tasted since.

"You must know magic to be a star woman," I told her. "Chakotay said you would not let him tell me about you and your people, so your magic must be a secret. How else could you fly among the stars and talk while you are invisible and make food out of the air?"

"I suppose it is a kind of magic," she confessed. "But it's a special kind of magic, one that comes from knowledge, from study, from science. We've learned how to do these things after years and years, generations and generations. Each life adding to the knowledge of those who went before. When I was a young girl like you, just starting to learn about the world, everything seemed like magic to me, too."

"I want to learn," I told her. "Teach me about the stars. That is what I want to know above all things. They are so pretty, and they look happy all the time."

She looked at me sadly I thought. "I wish I could teach you

everything you want to know, Tarina," she said softly. "But you're tired. Enough talk for one night. Let's get you to bed."

Other scenes come back to me as that one fades. I remember waking on a soft, clean bed and rising to go to a window that looked out on nothing but the night sky and a vast field of stars. I remember returning to the sickbay to get Chakotay and frowning at the doctor who tried to wave an object over me. I remember laughing at Neelix when he made a face behind the doctor's head. But more than anything I remember the music of *Voyager,* the sound it made, a soft, echoing hum, that I could feel throughout my body. I knew I was on a ship far out among the stars even though no one would really admit to me where we were. In those days I knew nothing of planets, other suns, other worlds. I just knew these people were from another place, another time. But in spite of the utter strangeness around me, I felt at home.

So it was with a shock that made my heart skip that I overheard a conversation between Captain Janeway and Chakotay on the evening of the second day.

"We have obtained what we came here for. B'Elanna says the warp drive is back on line, and we have enough surplus to last for several months. I can't justify staying much longer, Chakotay. We need to move on, and besides, we risk the possibility of detection. These people are not exactly primitive. They have some rather sophisticated engineering. We don't really know who might be observing the skies, recording data. I don't want to start some panic."

"We've been scanning for only twenty-four hours. I don't think it will take much longer. I just don't want to leave her alone back there where I found her."

"I don't either. I want to find them as much as you do, but we can't work miracles. We can't take her with us. We shouldn't even have her with us now. I just hope this whole experience won't adversely affect her."

"She's very young. I don't see what harm it could do. Of course, no one will believe her tales, but I think she'll be all right. She's got a strong spirit."

"She certainly does, and she's very bright. I wish we could see how things turn out for her. All right, we'll keep looking. But only for twelve more hours. If nothing shows up after that, we'll have to look for an alternative."

That's why I hid from them. It wasn't hard to slip unnoticed down a hallway and through a small door into some kind of tunnel. I thought perhaps they would forget about me there until it was too late to send me back.

It was Captain Janeway who found me. She didn't say anything at first but just came to sit close beside me. Finally she put her arm around my shoulders and spoke to me softly.

"You overheard what we were saying, didn't you, Tarina. I'm so sorry if we upset you. But we have to take you back where you belong. This ship is noplace for you to grow up. You need to be among your own people." Then she was silent again.

"We think we've found your aunt and uncle. We thought you might want to go and live with them. Would you like that? Would they welcome you?"

I nodded.

"More magic?" I asked, looking at her now.

She smiled. "Yes, more magic," she acknowledged.

"I wanted to stay and learn the things you know. I wanted to see for myself what the stars were like. I wanted many things that I shall never have."

"Don't say that, Tarina. There's a world of possibility open to you. You have your whole life ahead of you to dream and learn and love."

"They will not let me learn things at home. They think girls are for serving, not for knowing."

"Well, I guess you'll just have to change their minds about that. The first step in learning things is observation you know, and I think you will be very good at that. Chakotay tells me you are very observant."

I nodded. "I am," I said.

Good-bye was difficult to say to these kind strangers who disappeared from my life as suddenly as they had entered it. They did return me to my aunt and my uncle, who had been released from his imprisonment. I pressed my cheek to Captain Janeway's pale one when I left and told her I never would forget her.

"I will never forget you either, Tarina," she said. "I know you will see amazing things in your life. Hold on to your dreams. Believe in the possibilities."

I remember Chakotay transformed to look like one of our people. When I first saw him I burst out laughing. He looked even funnier to me like that. I didn't bother asking him how he did it. I had become comfortable with their magic by now. He led me as far as the outskirts of the village where he could watch as I approached my uncle's home. As my aunt swept me into her arms in delight, I twisted to look for him where I had left him in the shade of the borambi tree. There was nothing there but the stars shining through the swaying leaves.

You children know the rest of my story, after I appeared on Uncle Lotas's doorway that day out of nowhere. I tried to tell them what had happened to me, but they assumed I was weak with hunger and exhaustion and had hallucinated everything. They were filled with joy at my arrival and took me into their small family.

I know you've heard this before. I refused to be told I could not learn, and so took a servant's job at the school where I listened and observed and finally proved that I was capable. I've studied the stars all my life, even at the university when few women were allowed. I've charted them, examined them, added my small part to our knowledge of them, and yet still they hold such mystery for me.

All right, Onyas, I see you looking out of the corners of your eyes at Belya. Well, the stars were my dream; you must follow your own. But I hope you will remember this tale of the star people, how they came in peace, and how they gave me a legacy that I pass on to you, a legacy of the magic of knowledge, and of hope, and endless possibility.

Would you like for me to show you where I first saw the falling star all those years ago? Yes? Come with me then, out into the courtyard. Watch your step there, Lokita. Now look, children, way over to the horizon. That's where I saw it, just beyond Mt. Jennerod, there in the heavens, just past the second star to the right.

The Monster Hunters

Ann Nagy

"Stay where you are and when you see Naomi's monster, grab for the long hair under its left armpit," Tom Paris yelled as he dashed past Harry Kim.

"What?"

"I'll drive it past all the areas under repair and flush it back to you." Tom glanced back just before he bounded away.

Tom bit his lip to keep from laughing at the startled look he had seen on his best friend's face. It was good to see Harry astonished. For the past two months, Harry had been living the calmest, safest life possible considering that *Voyager* was alone and far from home. Tom had first noticed the change when his friend, who normally loved adventure, started trading duty shifts so he could avoid assignments that would take him off the ship. Eventually Harry even stopped looking at the main viewscreen on the bridge. The ship and crew became Harry's universe.

Tom spotted Naomi's monster ahead, standing at the junction of two corridors, one of which was closed for repairs and was now a dead end. Two and a half feet tall, the monster was a strange little ape with flowing brown hair covering its body, hair so long and lush that it hid the creature's legs. Its arms dangled to the floor, and its front feet were like hands. The monster turned and looked in Tom's direction. Besides a wide, drooling mouth, the only features on its face were two huge eyes that blinked and then bulged out when it focused on Tom. In a whirl of hair, it dashed into the open corridor.

Tom ran close behind.

After passing two more temporary dead ends, the monster shot into the corridor where Harry was waiting. Tom sighed with relief. Harry might not be willing to join him on an away mission, but he could still count on his friend to be at his side for an adventure on the ship.

Harry dove at the monster's chest.

The monster leaped and spun, landing with its feet on the ceiling. It ran along the top of the corridor, then along the wall for several meters, and then jumped to the floor just before it disappeared around another corner that led to a main corridor from which the monster could easily get to any part of the ship.

Tom stopped in front of his friend, panting.

Harry was staring at the now-empty corridor. "What was that?"

"Naomi's monster." Winded, Tom started to plod down the corridor after the monster.

Harry fell in beside him. "If it belongs to her why are you chasing it?"

"Because I'm the one who created it."

"Impressive toy, but shouldn't she be playing with it instead of you?"

Tom was surprised. Since Harry's change, he was rarely out of touch with the ship's gossip. "Naomi's monster and I have been the talk of the ship for the last hour. How'd you miss hearing about my latest screw-up?"

"I was working with Seven in the astrometrics lab. We were searching for clues that might lead us to a wormhole that could take us home."

Tom sighed. In addition to the ship and crew, Harry had one other obsession: returning to Earth. Several weeks ago, Tom had become so worried that he decided to find out what had caused Harry's change. Piecing together hints from various conversations, Tom realized that Harry had calculated the odds of getting home soon. Curious, Tom had tried to duplicate Harry's calculations. The computer had spewed out a long list of questions about the parameters of the problem. When Tom answered those, it gave him another long list of questions. Suspecting a programming error, Tom began to bypass the computer's security protocols, an action that got him an immediate summons from the captain.

After listening to his explanation of what he was doing and why, Captain Janeway informed him that the programming error had been inserted at her command, and she had ordered Harry not to talk about his findings. To maintain good morale, Janeway needed to keep alive the crew's small hope of getting home in the not too distant future. She could not afford to have anyone else develop a problem like Harry's. The young ensign, an only child who loved his mother and father deeply, was troubled because he now knew just how unlikely it was that he would ever see his parents again.

The two men rounded another corner and caught sight of Naomi's monster. It fled. Tom and Harry ran after it. The door to the mess hall snapped open and Commander Tuvok, the ship's security officer, walked out, narrowly missing a collision with the monster as it dashed for the open door.

Tuvok raised an elegant Vulcan eyebrow and stared at Ensigns Paris and Kim. "Do you need assistance?"

Tom shook his head as he led Harry into the mess hall. "No thanks. Harry and I have the situation under control."

While the door snapped closed behind them, the two men surveyed the room. The monster was streaking about frantically, crawling between people's legs and skipping across tabletops.

People were jumping; food was flying. The room buzzed with curses and laughter.

Harry turned to Tom. "Yeah, we've got this situation completely under control."

Tom sighed. "I had to refuse Tuvok's offer. The captain said the bigger the fuss I caused, the bigger my punishment would be. I'll never have a social life again if I let the security department participate in the chase."

Tom launched himself at the monster, missed, and thumped onto the floor.

Harry walked over and offered him a hand.

Tom rolled over and groaned. "I'm doomed without your help."

The back door of the mess hall opened and a group of people scurried out. The monster joined them. Tom and Harry followed, losing their quarry in the jumble.

Tom pulled out a tricorder and began scanning the area. "It went right."

Harry frowned. "Assuming we finally catch this thing, how do we deactivate it?"

"I told you—grab for the long hair under its left armpit. That's where I hid the doctor's mobile holographic emitter."

"Don't tell me you stole the doctor's emitter to make a toy."

"The monster is not a toy. It's a medical device."

Harry snorted. "The doctor would never agree to be trapped in sickbay while his emitter ran around the ship in the form of a hairy monster."

Tom started his story at the beginning. "You know that Naomi has a problem?"

Harry nodded. Everyone on the ship was worried because the little girl was afraid to be left alone and was sick from exhaustion. At bedtime, she would make a huge fuss about hearing a monster in the cabin after the light was turned off. No matter how many times her mother Samantha searched the cabin, Naomi would shake and cry until she fell asleep. Since the problem began after Samantha was almost killed on an away mission, and the problem became worse after her godfather, Neelix, was almost killed on the next away mission after that one, the doctor believed that Naomi was afraid her family might die while she was apart from them. The little girl wanted to cling to her family, and was using her fear of an imaginary monster to avoid a separation.

"I came up with a plan to help," Tom explained. "I convinced the doctor to lend me his emitter and I programmed it to assume the shape of a cartoon monster. Sam arranged for me to baby-sit Naomi, and I hid the monster in her closet. After I put Naomi in bed and turned out the lights, she started crying and I made the required search of her room. That's when I 'found' the monster hiding in her closet."

Harry's eyes were wide. "You could have scared the kid into a permanent psychotic state!"

"No, I had that covered. I programmed the monster to be terrified of everyone except Naomi. When I opened the closet, it cowered, but when it saw Naomi, it cheered up and offered her one of the other toys in the closet so they could play together. She fell for the plan and played happily with the monster until I put her back to bed."

"Did she go to sleep?"

"First, I had a talk with her about tools for dealing with fear. I told her that when possible it was a good idea to face her fear because sometimes she'd find that the thing she was afraid of wasn't as bad as she thought."

"Tricking her with the monster was a good strategy to get her to face her fear of imaginary monsters, but some things, like fearing that you might never see your family alive again, can't be solved that way."

"I know. That's why I also told her that when she was afraid of something bad that might or might not happen, she should push those fears away by thinking of all the good things that might happen. We went years into her future and made a long list of good things she could think about."

"Years? That opens up a lot of possibilities."

"Naomi is hoping that Sam and Neelix will get married and give her a baby sister to play with." Tom laughed. "I suggested she come on my next away mission. She was thrilled to be taking a shuttle ride to help search for wreckage that has drifted away from the alien ship."

"Did she fall asleep easily?"

"I gave her a stuffed copy of the monster and she fell asleep cuddling it and smiling." Tom grinned proudly. "She'd been so busy worrying about bad things that she'd forgotten about life's amazing possibilities. I restored the balance."

"Sounds like you did a great job. So why are we chasing the monster?"

Tom winced. "A slight miscalculation. I programmed the monster to be afraid of everyone except Naomi and I forgot to ask her to turn it off. After Naomi fell asleep, I reached for the monster and it bolted. And that's when the chase began."

Harry shook his head. "Whether you succeed or fail at what you do, the results are always spectacular."

"There isn't much fun in a dull life."

The two men stalked Naomi's monster for half an hour, almost catching it several times. They ran down corridors, crawled through Jefferies tubes, and got two nasty calls from the doctor demanding the return of his emitter. They were almost killed in engineering, not by the monster, but by the chief engineer, who grabbed them by their jacket fronts and threatened to rip out their throats if the monster came into her territory again.

Finally they cornered it in an air lock, but it escaped.

"I don't believe it," Harry muttered, his nose pressed to a window in the ship's hull.

Standing beside his friend, Tom stared at Naomi's monster as it zoomed through space toward the abandoned alien ship *Voyager* was exploring. "I didn't know that the use of zero g thrusters was on the list of basic starship skills."

"Why would a child's toy need starship skills?"

"It wouldn't have been much fun for Naomi if all it could do was sit on the floor and be a lump of hair."

Harry backed away from the window. "Have fun catching it out there."

"Me? I can't go near the alien ship for another sixteen hours." Because of the type of radiation the alien ship was leaking, crew members had to detox for twenty-four hours after each away mission.

Harry glared at the window, but didn't move.

"You haven't been out yet so it's safe for you to go. I'll stay here and grab the monster if it reenters an air lock."

Harry still didn't move.

"I'll make it up to you. Name your price: replicator rations, assistance in astrometrics, anything." Tom ran his hand through his hair. Would Harry do it? Would Harry go for a showdown with the monster?

Harry's eyes shifted to his best friend's face.

"Please, I need your help," Tom begged.

Harry's shoulders sagged. "You really owe me for this."

He slipped into a space suit and exited the air lock.

Tom leaned against the window and watched his friend jet to the alien ship and disappear inside.

Harry's voice came in clearly through Tom's combadge, giving him regular reports on the chase.

"I'm at a hatch on the alien ship."

"I'm in the ship and there's no sign of the monster."

"Fascinating control panel on the hatch door—you touch it and it opens. I wonder how it distinguishes between a user and space debris that bumps it."

"I've checked all the exits and none of them are functioning so the monster must be hiding in here somewhere."

"There are machines on the floor, the walls, and the ceiling. I guess they didn't have artificial gravity."

"Wow, there's a strange one. I wonder what it was used for."

"Hmmm. This one doesn't seem to be damaged. I wonder if I could get it running . . ."

"There's the monster!"

"I've got it cornered!"

"I'm closing in!"

"Victory! Naomi's monster is no more!"

"I'm heading back. No, wait. I think I'll call the bridge and ask permission to stay longer. This place is so amazing, I want to explore it more. Kim out."

Tom smiled at his friend's decision and headed to sickbay. A gossip lover, the doctor would want to hear every detail of the hunt. As he walked, Tom called the captain.

Janeway's brisk voice answered. "Mr. Paris, do you have good news for me?"

"Yes, Captain. The monsters are gone, all of them."

Gift of the Mourners

Jackee Crowell

Dedicated to the memory of
Mrs. Nettie B. Harris, 1919–1999

She was gone; her eyes frozen open at the moment of death. With exaggerated care, he lowered her head to the floor and passed a hand over her eyes. There was no logical reason for the action as the acrid taint of poisonous smoke and burning electronics no longer posed a danger to once sensitive organs, and the stifling heat of failing life support would not be a cause for discomfort. It seemed right despite the fact that there was nothing he could do for her body. But he would keep his promise. He would honor her dying request.

Rising to his feet, he took in his surroundings more closely. Through the dim haze of emergency lighting, incredible destruction lay before him. Most of the control panels were darkened or burning, spewing more poisonous fumes into the air. Falling debris littered the once plushly carpeted areas, the worst of which was a large beam that had pierced the surface of the forward viewscreen. Only precariously operating force fields held off the cold of space.

The ship lurched suddenly, spurring him to motion. Unsurprisingly, none of the major controls responded to his touch. On the far side of the bridge, a smaller console situated beneath the spark of live control wiring caught his attention. Its systems were still dimly lit, perhaps running on an isolated power source.

Before he could reach the console, a barely perceptible shift alerted him to the imminent failure of the artificial gravity systems. Adjusting for the difference, he moved more quickly toward the console, stepping carefully around the bodies of the fallen bridge crew.

The smaller console responded immediately to his commands, allowing him to send an automated distress signal on all frequencies. That task complete, he took a moment to access his own energy stores. Would he be able to maintain a vigil until help arrived? Unsatisfied with the answer, he sought a way to increase his odds of success.

A small panel beneath and slightly to the right of the console seemed an obvious place to begin looking. He had stretched an arm beneath to grasp the latch when another jolt shook the failing vessel. There was a sudden displacement as the artificial gravity systems shut down completely. His forward momentum toward the underside of the console worked against him, causing his feet to go out from beneath him and float toward the ceiling. The last sound he heard before his leg made contact with the live control wiring was a distant creaking.

The air was clear, and the temperature was much cooler. A flat surface, raised on one end, was beneath his back. A slight shuffling alerted him to a nearby presence. He tested his motor systems but found them inoperative.

"Emergency Medical Hologram to Captain Janeway." The voice was completely unfamiliar, as was the language. He detected no hostile intent.

"Go ahead, Doctor." The second voice was very clear, but subtle variances suggested that it had been projected with the aid of electronic equipment.

"I believe our visitor is waking, Captain." The closer voice was speaking at a different angle, perhaps from above.

"Thank you, Doctor. I'm on my way."

Moments later there was a gentle hiss accompanied by a sliding noise and the sound of bipedal footsteps. It was difficult to gauge the distance from his prone position, but it was enough to suggest that the hiss-sliding had been made by a door, and that two bipedal creatures had entered the room.

The nearer voice made a small "humph" sound and continued to hover nearby. At the next sound of the hiss-slide, two more sets of bipedals entered the room. One possessed a quicker gait, suggesting a shorter stature or perhaps a different gender.

"All right, Doctor. What can you tell me?" The second voice spoke from a position above. "Were you able to repair the damage to our visitor?"

"Of course, Captain." The first voice spoke. "I was also able to determine other significant information. While this individual is undoubtedly an android, he contains an outer shell of enhanced biological matter."

"Intriguing." A new voice spoke. "That would explain why the sensors thought him to be a life-form."

The first voice continued to speak. There was a slight timber to his voice, as if he was irritated at having been interrupted. "As I was saying, Captain, this android does indeed have lifesigns as well as several rudimentary humanoid organs. In any case, I've interrupted his motor controls for safety."

"You mean he's awake now?" The second voice spoke again.

"I believe so, Captain."

"Release his motor controls," the second voice said.

There was a momentary pause and suddenly he could move. His eyes opened to a brightly lit room and a white ceiling. Turning slightly to either side, he saw three faces staring at him. One of the beings, distinctly female, moved a step closer.

"I'm Captain Kathryn Janeway of the Federation *Starship Voyager.* We rescued you from your ship. Can you tell us what happened?"

He took several moments to run a diagnostic on his vocal center as he accessed the reactions of the female. She frowned and looked toward one of the other faces.

"What is your name?" she spoke again.

Diagnostic completed, he opened his mouth to speak. "I am unit Twelve-Alpha. Please tell me the condition of the vessel upon which I was found."

"I'm sorry, we were barely able to beam you out before your ship exploded. We responded to your distress signal. Can you tell us what happened?"

Twelve-Alpha closed his eyes for several moments in honor of the lost vessel. "The *Sepana* was greatly damaged and the fate you describe is not unexpected. Its passing shall be mourned." There was an expression of sympathy in Janeway's eyes. Sympathy was an expression he had seen often enough, but the feeling was not something of which he was capable.

"I make a request of you, Captain Janeway."

She inclined her head slightly. "What is it, Twelve-Alpha?"

"Can you help me get home?" Janeway looked at him oddly, but before she could respond there was a lurch that seemed to resound throughout the ship.

"Janeway to Bridge. Chakotay, what's going on?" Captain Janeway had straightened to stand sharply as she awaited the response. It came moments later, but judging from her expression, it was not the one she wanted.

"Unsure, Captain. It appears to have come from one hundred thousand kilometers along heading zero point two four seven. We're running scans now to determine the exact cause. The sensors are having difficulty with some type of localized interference, however."

"Keep at it, Commander."

Twelve-Alpha rose quickly to a sitting position as she prepared to leave the room. The nearer male, and the two near the door reached for devices strapped to their sides. Immediately recognizing the items as weaponry, Twelve-Alpha paused in midmotion.

"Captain Janeway, you must move away from this area. It is very dangerous here."

Janeway paused and made a gesture toward the armed men, who slowly lowered their weapons. It did not escape Twelve-Alpha's notice that they did not reharness them. "Do you know something about what's happened?" she asked. "Do you know what caused that jolt?"

"I do not know the cause of it, precisely. I know only that this is the way it began aboard the *Sepana.* First there were the jolts that grew stronger until they threatened to tear the ship apart."

The woman considered him for a moment before tapping a device on her chest. "Chakotay, move us away from that anomaly. I want half a light-year between it and *Voyager.*"

"Aye, Captain," Chakotay's voice responded.

"Now," the captain began, moving toward Twelve-Alpha. "Tell me—"

There was a sudden lurch of such force that Twelve-Alpha toppled off the bed and the rest of the bipedals fell to the floor. He saw the doctor flicker briefly along with the lights before everything went dark. Moments later light returned—minus the doctor.

"Status!" the captain called as she climbed to her feet. There was no response from the computerized systems, or the two men who were struggling to their feet. Twelve-Alpha moved swiftly to help the third man, who was having difficulties.

"Jensen, help Turner." The captain gestured. "Twelve-Alpha, Tuvok. You're with me."

Twelve-Alpha turned the injured man over to Jensen and followed the captain through the sliding door. The man Tuvok followed.

"What else can you tell me about those jolts, Twelve-Alpha?" The captain's voice was urgent as she led them along and into an enclosed cubicle and commanded, "Bridge." Twelve-Alpha blinked three times in succession as he searched his databases. His programming in the area of advanced astronomy was extremely limited, and he was unable to extrapolate much useful information. He had been designed to serve his fully biological counterparts in a more domestic capacity.

"Perhaps if I explained the things that I saw I might be better able to serve?" Twelve-Alpha suggested.

The cubicle came to a stop and the doors slid open. "Hold that thought, Twelve-Alpha," Janeway said quickly before she stepped into a large room. Tuvok remained at Twelve-Alpha's side and gestured that he depart first.

"Report!" Janeway called into the room beyond. A male that Twelve-Alpha quickly identified as Chakotay spoke from a console.

"The com system should be back on-line momentarily, Captain. Whatever happened caused several of our key systems to reset."

"Do we know how that happened?"

"Harry was just formulating a theory." Chakotay looked toward another male standing near the back of the bridge.

In the moments it took for Harry to tap a string of commands into his console, Twelve-Alpha gave the bridge a quick once over. It was obvious that *Voyager* was much larger than the *Sepana* had been, and bore little resemblance to the compact vessel. *Voyager*'s viewscreen showed the same region of space that the *Sepana*'s had shown before the beam had punctured its surface. Twelve-Alpha returned his attention to Harry as the young man began to speak.

"There appears to be a gravametric distortion at one hundred thousand kilometers from our present position, Captain. At random intervals, the distortion increases exponentially in all directions, pulling at anything within a two-hundred-thousand kilometer radius. The increase seems to be directly proportional to the amount of power we expend. During the first jolt, Tom had just made a small course adjustment. The second larger jolt occurred when we tried to go to warp."

"Why didn't it affect us when we first arrived?" Janeway asked.

"We were moving toward it, Captain." Harry pressed a button and an image appeared on the viewscreen. A pulsing green dot was displayed at a distance from an image labeled VOYAGER. "This is our position when we first arrived." Harry pressed another button and a different image appeared. "This is our position just before we attempted to go to warp. It appears that the anomaly only reacts when we attempt to move away from it."

Twelve-Alpha listened very closely to the course of the conversation. It was becoming similar to ones he had heard previously on the *Sepana.* With Janeway's next question they diverged.

"Is there any way to tell if this anomaly may be alive? Sentient?"

"Difficult to tell, Captain," Harry answered, tapping another command into his console. "Our scans are inconclusive."

"All right." Janeway placed a hand on her hip. "Can we pass through it?"

"No, Captain. The gravametric pressure at the anomaly's apex is too great. Our shields would collapse."

"What if we had another type of shield?" Chakotay spoke thoughtfully from a far console.

"Photon torpedo." Janeway spoke, quickly catching on to his idea. "If we detonate it at fifty thousand kilometers, it should act as a buffer against the anomaly as well as shield our escape."

Harry was already doing calculations. "We'll need to reroute power to increase shield strength by thirty-five percent. And the propulsion and detonation systems should be synchronized."

"Do it," Janeway ordered.

"Torpedo ready," Chakotay said moments later.

"Shields ready," Harry replied next.

Janeway looked toward a pale-haired male seated at a forward console. "Tom, looks like you get to sit this one out."

"Can't have all the glory," Tom replied.

Janeway barely smiled. Like the rest of the bridge crew, her eyes were locked on the viewscreen. "Launch torpedo."

There was a barely discernible *whoosh* and the small cylindrical object was visible against the black of space. Harry counted out the distance.

"Detonate," Janeway ordered at precisely fifty thousand kilometers. There was a brilliant flash and a high-pitched whine as the ship's engines came on-line. The lights began to flicker and turbulence accompanied the rising shriek as the vessel struggled against the powerful forces that sought to hold it captive. Then gradually, the whine died away and the ship continued smoothly along its course.

"I believe that's your cue, Mr. Paris." Janeway smiled at Tom. "Good work, everyone." She glanced around the bridge. "Leave a warning beacon for any ships that may pass this way. Commander Chakotay, you have the bridge. Have Seven of Nine join Tuvok, Twelve-Alpha, and myself in my ready room."

Twelve-Alpha looked across the table at the newest arrival. He had come to the conclusion very quickly that the crew of the Federation *Starship Voyager* was a diverse group, very much unlike the Edtani. All Edtani were pale-skinned with varying shades of brownish hair. Even those who served were designed in that likeness.

"Twelve-Alpha, this is Seven of Nine. She has recently become a member of our crew and has knowledge of many of the races of this sector." Seven of Nine looked back at him without comment.

"Seven," Janeway was continuing to speak. "Do you have any memory of the Edtani, or of a race of beings similar to Twelve-Alpha?"

"Species 1432," Seven said. "Their technology was uninteresting, and their species too weak for assimilation. The Edtani homeworld can be located at a position approximately twelve light-years from our present location. I am . . . surprised. The Borg were not aware of android constructs."

Janeway seemed to be covering a smile. "The sensors were fooled too, Seven. If it's any consolation."

Seven turned toward her. "It is not." Then, "I am curious, however. How is it that you do not know your way home? Are your capabilities not superior to those who created you?"

"I have never had a need to know. I am one who serves, and as such am an inferior construct. We do not deserve even to be mourned. We exist simply to serve our fully biological counterparts in the more mundane tasks of life and work."

Seven's face showed mild surprise. "Your cybernetic functionality brings you closer to perfection. Your talents are wasted on mundane duties. Why would you want to return to such an existence?"

"To serve. In serving First Leader Corissa of the *Sepana,* I have been entrusted with the Gift of the Mourners. It is a great honor to serve in this way."

"The Gift of the Mourners?" Tuvok asked.

"Within my memory center are the life memories of all of the crew members of the *Sepana,* including my previous owner Dr. Dareiden, father to First Leader Corissa. The memories are to be returned to the homeworld, thus the mourners may have consolation."

"You have the ability to carry humanoid thought patterns?" Janeway asked, leaning forward slightly.

"Yes, Captain Janeway. I carry the memory patterns of twenty-seven individuals."

"This is normal among androids on your world?"

"I do not believe so. Edtani law stipulates that all of those who serve must undergo renewal and upgrade every two cycles. As Dr. Dareiden's work was a great distance from the homeworld, he chose to disregard the dictate. I have continued for thirty-one cycles without renewal. At Dr. Dareiden's passing, my continued existence was discovered by First Leader Corissa. She also discovered that I possessed the life memory of her father."

Twelve-Alpha blinked quickly several times as he continued. "She said that I was one in a million."

There was silence for several moments. "What does renewal and upgrade entail?" The question was from Janeway.

"My memory circuits will be cleared, and I will be uploaded with any new directives. I will then be given the new appellation Twelve-Alpha-One."

"Are you certain that you will not be renewed and upgraded before you can share your Gift of the Mourners?" Tuvok asked. "If it is true that you have developed an ability previously unknown to your kind, the Edtani officials may not discover your unique nature beforehand."

"I had not considered that possibility," Twelve-Alpha admitted. "I shall have to plan for such a contingency."

"Twenty-three E. These will be your quarters while you're on board *Voyager.* Press this button and the doors will open for you."

"Thank you, Commander Chakotay. I have never occupied quarters before." Twelve-Alpha obediently pressed the button and stepped through the doorway.

Chakotay paused. "Surely you had an area where you could relax, or recharge?"

"I had a chair. In the kitchen," Twelve-Alpha explained, and blinked rapidly. "Have I amused you?"

Chakotay quickly stifled a grin. "I apologize. It was the way you spoke. It reminded me of someone I once knew."

"There is no need to apologize," Twelve-Alpha said. "I am happy to serve in this manner. Meal preparation is one of my primary functions. I would also like to learn of the one about which you spoke."

"I was thinking of a relative who used to sit in the kitchen and talk. She always knew everything that was going on in our community by the things she could see from that chair. She knew things about everyone. We all missed her terribly when she died."

"And her death makes you smile? I have only seen the death of Dareiden and how it affected those around him. None smiled."

"Twelve-Alpha, it's very painful when you lose someone you love to death. But the memories are things that help you after the initial pain. It's the memories that make you smile."

"You have solved a riddle for me, Commander Chakotay. I knew that I must deliver the Gift of the Mourners because First Leader Corissa desired it. But, because I knew that receiving her father's memories caused her pain, I did not understand how others would be consoled."

Chakotay smiled. "The Edtani people have a great inheritance in that they can possess the memories of their loved ones in a fuller sense than do many other species."

Twelve-Alpha nodded slightly, accepting the new knowledge into his databases.

"I am eager to serve the crew of *Voyager* so that I may learn more about everyone. Shall I serve in your kitchen, Commander Chakotay?"

Chakotay laughed. "Well, Neelix is always saying that he

could use some help, and I'm sure he'd enjoy the company. I'll discuss it with him and the captain and let you know. Meanwhile, B'Elanna Torres, our chief engineer, has had a power converter installed for your needs."

"Yes!" Tom Paris exclaimed. "This is what lasagna is supposed to taste like. Are you sure you don't want to stick around here, Twelve-Alpha?"

"It has been an honor to serve the crew of *Voyager.*" Twelve-Alpha bowed slightly as B'Elanna and Harry backed up Tom's claim. "However, I must complete my task."

"We understand," Tom nodded with a grin, before continuing in a whisper, "But Neelix's lasagna never tasted like this."

"Mr. Neelix is much more creative than I," Twelve-Alpha said, noticing as Tuvok entered the mess hall. "While my algorithms only allow for strict adherence to the recipe, the humanoid mind is free to enhance."

"I'd say you've done quite a job of enhancement," B'Elanna said. "I know a certain helm-boy who is going to be talking about your culinary expertise for some time to come."

"And I loved the way you defeated a certain ensign at his own game," Harry Kim added with a laugh.

"Hey, he's got a microprocessor in his brain. I didn't stand a chance," Tom replied.

"Several, in fact," Twelve-Alpha said. It was illogical, but he found the laughing discussions of the crew enjoyable. "If it is pleasing to you, Harry, I shall again defeat 'a certain ensign.' I exist to serve in whatever way I can."

Both Harry and B'Elanna laughed at Tom's expression. At that moment, Twelve-Alpha noticed that Seven of Nine had entered the mess hall.

"Please excuse me." He bowed to the three crew members and took his leave. He reached Seven just as she exited the serving line. The former Borg turned at Twelve-Alpha's approach.

"I would like to make a request of you, Seven of Nine. Would you join me at Mr. Tuvok's table?"

"What type of request?" Seven asked.

"A personal one," Twelve-Alpha said.

When he voiced the same to Tuvok, the Vulcan waited patiently for his explanation. "Since your suggestion in the captain's ready room concerning the reaction of Edtani officials to my presence, I have given consideration to how I might ensure the delivery of the Gift of the Mourners."

Twelve-Alpha reached into a pocket and withdrew a small sphere. "This is a memory module from my main processing center. It contains a copied version of life memories of the crew and Dr. Dareiden. The Edtani are a telepathic people, and I am a mechanized construct. I do not know if the information translated well into this form. My request is that the two of you test it for stability and telepathic maneuverability."

Tuvok took the small sphere between two fingers. "How would you have me test it?"

"The life memories within my memory center are dynamic, always changing. When I transferred the copies there was no longer perceptible change. I fear that some error on my part caused this to occur. It is my hope that you will be able to discover why I have failed, and offer assistance on future attempts."

"I shall have to discuss it with the captain," Tuvok said.

The doors opened with a sliding hiss and Twelve-Alpha heard the step he had come to identify as Captain Janeway. A grouping of wires attached to a junction at the base of his skull locked out his motor controls, preventing him from turning to greet her. Her steps stopped near the console situated behind the diagnostic chair upon which he lay.

"How's it coming?" Janeway was speaking softly to B'Elanna Torres.

"I'm attempting to use the gelpacks as a means of containing the data, but it's a slow process. Tuvok and Seven are working on a way to use nanoprobes in a similar manner."

"We met an Edtani vessel a few minutes ago. Its captain seemed almost afraid when I mentioned Twelve-Alpha's presence. This doesn't give me a good feeling on the type of reception we're going to receive from the planetary officials. How much longer before you know if it's working?"

"A few more minutes. Part of the problem is that we're having to maintain a low-level charge in the gelpack to mimic those of his organic brain tissue. He said that Dr. Dareiden injected him with cultures from his own brain matter. I can't say for certain, Captain, but I think Dareiden had a larger goal in mind when he did this. The reaction of the Edtani we met might explain why Dareiden conducted his work off-world. Unfortunately, he died before he could finish."

Any comment Janeway might have made was interrupted by the beep of B'Elanna's console.

"Time to find out," B'Elanna said, crossing behind the console to remove the connection from Twelve-Alpha's neck.

At regaining control of his motor systems, Twelve-Alpha sat up and turned toward the two women, nodding a greeting to the Captain. "What are the results, B'Elanna?" he asked. The first step of the procedure was to copy a portion of the memories before a complete copy was attempted.

"Checking." B'Elanna was looking into a device that would compare the newly copied patterns with the originals. After several moments she looked up and shook her head. "I'm sorry. The copy did not arrive intact."

Twelve-Alpha bowed his head. "Thank you for your efforts, B'Elanna." Then, turning toward Janeway, "How long until we reach the homeworld?"

Janeway's expression of sympathy was back. "We'll reach the planet within the hour. Tuvok and Seven still have the nanoprobes to try. When we arrive I'll speak with the ruling officials to explain the situation before you leave the ship. I'll make sure they know."

Twelve-Alpha could hear the difference in the engines when *Voyager* began its orbit of the Edtani homeworld. It was obvious by the way Tuvok and Seven looked at him that they were aware as well.

"Were the nanoprobes successful?" he asked.

"No, they were not." Tuvok replied. "There is one other alternative that we have not discussed."

"I do not believe—" Seven began, but Tuvok interrupted.

"It is not your decision to make. The odds of success are somewhat diminished by the number of individuals involved, but I believe that it will work."

"You could request asylum and remain on *Voyager.*" Seven turned to Twelve-Alpha. "Your resources need not be wasted on tasks unfitting a superior construct. You have shown an aptitude toward science during our attempts to transfer the information contained within your memory center. On *Voyager* you could pursue that interest."

"I cannot shirk my duties, Seven of Nine. I must deliver the Gift of the Mourners, and then continue in my service of the Edtani. I am one who serves. It is who I am and what I must do."

"Do you not have the capacity to want?" Seven asked.

"Want?" Twelve-Alpha blinked rapidly as he processed the question. That was not something he had considered. "I want to serve."

"Even those who hold you in disdain?" Seven asked.

"Dr. Dareiden did not hold me in disdain, and nor has the crew of *Voyager.* Do you hold me in disdain, Seven of Nine?"

"I do not. And it is my hope that those whom you serve in the future will behave likewise."

Twelve-Alpha nodded slightly at her concession. "Mr. Tuvok, will you tell me of this other means?"

"Yes. It is called a mind-meld, and is an ability that Vulcans possess. I do not believe that there is sufficient time to explain it, as I do not know how the captain will fare in her negotiations. Perhaps a test will suffice. If it is successful, then we can approach the captain." Tuvok turned toward Seven as if asking a silent question. At her slight nod, Tuvok took a step closer to Twelve-Alpha and placed his hands on either side of his head.

"My mind to your mind. My thoughts to your thoughts . . ."

Something was different. Twelve-Alpha opened his eyes and looked around. Both Seven and Commander Chakotay were staring at him. Tuvok was seated on the diagnostic chair, his head clasped in his hands. With some difficulty, he straightened his back and rose to his feet. That was when Twelve-Alpha identified that last time he had experienced the sensation he currently felt.

"Do you have them, Mr. Tuvok?" he asked.

"I have them, Twelve-Alpha," the Vulcan replied. "All of them."

"Would anyone mind telling me what's going on here?" Chakotay asked.

"We had exhausted all of our options," Twelve-Alpha said. "Mr. Tuvok suggested another method. He now contains the memories of the *Sepana*'s crew as well as Dr. Dareiden."

"That sounds like a risky procedure." Chakotay looked accusingly from Seven to Tuvok. "I'm sure the captain and the Doctor were informed."

Twelve-Alpha noticed the barely perceptible shifts in the expressions of the Vulcan and the former Borg, indicating their discomfiture.

"I am to blame, Commander Chakotay. Tuvok proposed a test, but when he touched the portion of my memory systems that contain the Gift, I was unable to prevent the memories from simply pouring from my mind to his. I do not think Mr. Tuvok was expecting the onslaught."

Chakotay appeared to consider the information. "How you doing, Tuvok?"

"Uncomfortable. But I will survive."

"Good, the captain will want to talk to you. Meanwhile, you should get to sickbay and have the Doctor take a look at you. Seven, go with him. Twelve-Alpha, you're with me."

". . . on our vessel for the past four days and no harm has come. Did you know he has a sense of humor, Minister Lauken?" The turbolift's doors slid open in the midst of Janeway's discussion with an Edtani leader. She glanced quickly in Twelve-Alpha's direction as the minister responded.

"The tragedies of the past have taught us to trust in our methods, Captain. It only takes a moment of inattention for the unimaginable to occur. We cannot in good conscience grant such a request."

"Excuse me, Minister." Janeway noted something in Commander Chakotay's expression and frowned. Ordering Harry to mute the audio, she turned to face him.

Twelve-Alpha waited as Chakotay explained what had taken place in the lab. Twelve-Alpha then spoke in behalf of Tuvok and Seven, explaining that they should not be held accountable.

Janeway appeared to consider his words for several moments. "Well, that puts a new twist on it, doesn't it?" Signaling to Harry to unmute the audio, she turned back to the Edtani minister.

Twelve-Alpha looked around the forward observation deck as the familial representatives of the *Sepana* crew filed in. He was seated at a table near the back of the room with Captain Janeway and several members of *Voyager*'s crew. Tuvok was seated in a chair at the room's center.

The Edtani government had requested that the information concerning his involvement with the Gift be suppressed in exchange for allowing him to remain on board *Voyager* to witness the transfer. Three Edtani guards stood alongside Minister Lauken to ensure that things took place as they had requested.

Each mourner approached Tuvok in turn and touched his neck, thus receiving the memory patterns of their loved ones. Twelve-Alpha remembered the way First Leader Corissa had been affected upon receiving the memory patterns of her father. The mourners were no different. One and all expressed intense gratitude to Tuvok as the carrier of the Gift.

Having been similarly bonded by the experience, the mourners remained together in the room until all had received. When the last of the mourners had accepted the Gift, Tuvok stood and turned to face the table. "It is finished," he said, slightly breathless.

"It is." Minister Lauken nodded and moved closer to the table. "And now we will take our charge."

Twelve-Alpha stood obediently as two of the Edtani guards approached. Turning toward Janeway he spoke. "Earlier today, Seven of Nine asked what I wanted. Were I a fully biological construct, I would remember the openness and generosity of you and your crew. As these have been my experiences, I now have another answer for her query: I would want to remember. Thank you for all that you have done in my behalf."

"You're welcome, Twelve-Alpha," Janeway replied. Her look of sympathy was back. "I'm sure I speak on behalf of all the crew when I say that we have been honored to have you aboard."

"Thank you, Captain." Twelve-Alpha bowed slightly at her compliment, then turned toward the Edtani guards. "I am ready."

As Janeway tapped her combadge to signal the transporter room, Tuvok held up a hand.

"Wait. Before you leave, Twelve-Alpha, there is something more. The things that you have done are a part of the memories of the mourners now, as well as my memories and those of the crew of *Voyager.* You will be remembered, Twelve-Alpha, and we shall mourn your passing."

The following story was not part of the contest, but was written for us, by request, by Dr. Lawrence M. Schoen of the Klingon Language Institute. Please do not submit stories to future *Strange New Worlds* anthologies written in Klingon, Ferengi, or any other fictional language.

jubHa'

Lawrence M. Schoen

mInDu'wIj vIpoSmoHlaH 'ej mInDu'wIj vISoQmoH, 'ach vIvIHlaHbe'. pagh vIHotlaH. pagh vIjatlhlaH. vIleghlaH neH. QongDaqDaq jIleS. QongDaqvam ghovbe'. HoDwI' DujDaq QongDaqwIj tu'lu'. Hopqu' Dujvetlh 'ej naDev jIH. pa' 'el loD. munuDchu'. vIbejlaH neH.

«QellI' jIH» jatlh loD. «choyajlaH'a'.»

mInDu'wIj vIpoSmoH 'ej mInDu'wIj vISoQmoH.

'el HIp tuQbogh loD. 'aj ghaH. SuvwI'a' ghaH. vIvanlaHbe'. QongDaqDaq jIQottaHmo' jItuH'eghmoII.

«choH'a'» jatlh 'aj.

«Dubbe'. 'ach vemchoH. jatlhlaHbe'.»

«DaQaHlaH'a'» jatlh 'aj.

«ropvam vISovbe'. chu'. 'IwDaj ngej tar nov. vIvorlaHbe'.»

mej 'ej jImob. paw ram. jIqawchoH. wej romuluSnganpu' vISuvlI'DI' 'emDaq muHIv latlh. jIDej 'ej jIvulchoH. ropyaHchajDaq jIvemchoH. HerghwI' 'uch romuluSngan tej. DeSwIj 'aw'.

«QI'yaH!» vIjach. qabDaj mup chapwIj 'ej pumbej pujwI'. jInarghnIS. jolpa'chaj vISamnIS. jIqet. bIrchoH DeSDu'wIj 'uSDu'wIj je. 'oy'choH taghDu'wIj. lupDujHom vItu' 'ej vItIj. nap SeHlaw 'ej tugh jItlheDrup. romuluSngan loghvo' jIHaw'. juHqo' Quv vIcher. jItlhab. tlhuch HoSwIj 'ej jIQong. naDev jIH jIvemDI'. Qel mu'mey vIqaw. DaH jIyaj. rop chu' chenmoH romuluSnganpu'. mungej. muroSHa'moH. jIQaH'eghlaHbe'. jIweb.

jIQongqa'. HoH'eghghach vInaj 'ej jImon. jIvemqa'DI' SaH Qel. mobbe'. tlhej vulqangan. qama' HIp tuQ.

«DaH» jatlh Qel.

QongDaqDaq chol vulqangan. ba'. qabwIjDaq ghopDu'Daj lan. vIbotlaHbe'. vay' nejqu' mInDu'Daj. meQchoHlaw' QuchwIj.

mutlhup vulqangan. «yabwIjvo' yablIjDaq je. yablIjvo' yabwIjDaq je. yab wa' neH wIghaj.»

jIjach. vIneH. nachwIj qoD yotchu'. muHIv qechmey nov. vIHublaHbe' 'ach jIjeghQo'. 'e' tlhoj vulqangan 'ej pay' jot Hoch. wanI'mey leghlaH. qunwIj ghoj. SanwIj yaj. mej yabDaj 'ej vIchImlaw'qa'.

«yIn yabDaj» jatlh vulqangan.

«'e' vIHaj» jatlh Qel. «qaSta' nuq. 'e' yaj'a'.»

«HocH yajbe'.»

«vI'angnIS. 'aj yIqem.» jatlh Qel.

mej vulqangan. Qel vIbej. bItqu'. pawDI' 'aj HeD Qel.

«DaH» jatlhqa' Qel.

'aj ghopDaq nargh taj. tIqwIjDaq muDuQ. qaS pagh. taj teqDI' jIpIvqu'. HughwIj pe'chu'. SIbI' muvqa' DIr. 'e' vIHarbe' 'ach teHqu'. muHoHlaHbe'.

«nIjubmoH romuluSngan. bIHegHlaHbe'.» jatlh Qel. «'ach vIHQo' nItlh. DaqaSmoHlaHbe'.»

«tlhInganqoq SoH. 'e' qaSmoH romuluSngan.» jatlh 'aj. «batlhlIj nIHchu'.»

jIjach. vIneH. vIHoH. vIneH. jIHegh. vIneH. pagh vIta'laH. qoy' mInDu'wIj 'ej tu' vulqangan. qabwIj Hotqa' nItlhDu'Daj. yabwIjDaq 'elqa' yabDaj.

«tlhIngan jIH. SuvwI' jIH. HIqIchQo'. yIntaHbogh Heghvam vISIQ.» vIja'. jIvIt. net Sov.

ghopDu'Daj nge' vulqangan. «vIQaHlaH» jatlh.

«DaHoHlaH'a'» jatlh 'aj.

«ghobe'. jub. 'e' vIchoHlaHbe'. 'ach batlhDaj vInoblaH. SuvwI' mojqa'.»

«'e' DaqaSmoHlaHchugh vaj qatlhabmoH.» jatlh 'aj.

«tuQDoq Hoqra' je HIqem.»

«qatlh» jatlh Qel.

«ghaHvaD qo' chu' vIchennISmoH.»

Hoqra' ghun vulqangan. vIbej. rInDI' nachwIj Hoqra' tuQDoq je rar. «yIyoH, SuvwI'. batlh bIghobjaj.» jatlh vulqangan. leQ 'uy vulqangan. ngab Hoch.

«tlhIngan!» jach vay'. jItlhe'. jagh vIlegh. che'ronDaq vIQam. betleHWIj vI'uch. jIvIHlaH. jIHagh 'ej jIHIv. Dat jaghpu' vIlegh. Hegh. Hoch vIHoHDI' latlhpu' vItu'. vIbomchoH vIHoHtaHvIS. not jIDoy'choH. Dunqu'.

«DaH QongtaH. not vemqa'» jatlh vulqangan.

«naj'a'» jatlh 'aj Qel je.

«ghobe'.» jatlh vulqangan. «yInqu'.»

rIntaH

Hints

Dean Wesley Smith

The following are a few of the hints that I've given new writers on the AOL *Star Trek* bulletin board called Strange New Worlds. These hints are general, and usually a discussion followed on the board, where exceptions were outlined and reasons for the hints were given.

Dayton Ward compiled a number of these hints into a long list, and I've taken some of his work and used it here. Thanks, Dayton.

These hints are intended to help new writers get past some of the basic mistakes we all make. As an editor of magazines in the past, and this anthology for the past three years, I've looked at and read more than a hundred thousand stories. Patterns emerge after seeing that many manuscripts, and these hints are from those patterns. But I must stress, these are not rules of the contest, just writing hints intended to help you improve your chances of selling a story.

HINT #1: PRACTICE

Read and then write and then read some more. Every how-to-write book starts off with saying that a writer is a person who writes. I agree. Write what you like to read. Read how-to-write books. Then write some more. It's called practice. Writers must practice just as any other artist, and we must keep learning. So read, then write, then repeat as often as you can.

HINT #2: NO TALKING HEADS

The first thing an editor or reader sees is the opening of your story. "Talking heads" is a term used by writers and editors to describe two characters talking, with the reader having no idea where, when, or what the characters are doing. To a reader, this gives the impression of just two voices in a pitch dark room. Many, many of the stories I get for *Star Trek: Strange New Worlds* start with talking heads. (Not a fatal mistake, but hard for me to get past.) Sensory and setting details usually start stories to ground readers as to where the characters are located.

HINT #3: NEVER START A STORY WITH A BORED CHARACTER

This problem is being done a lot with *Voyager* stories. I'm not sure why. Maybe it's the idea that a long trip is usually boring to all of us. But in fiction, this is not a good way to open a story. You want to hook the reader in with your opening and starting bored never does that.

HINT #4: YES, THE ART IS PRETTY. KEEP IT

I get lots of art and pictures with manuscripts. I've enjoyed most of it, but it is only the words on the paper and the story that an editor looks at.

HINT #5: THE WHITE STUFF

Plain white paper is best for this editor's poor old eyes. Colored paper is not a fatal mistake, except when the type on the colored paper is so light I can't read the story. But white paper is better.

HINT #6: DON'T SEND POSTCARDS

I know some of the writer's magazines tell you to send a postcard along with your story to let you know that the manuscript arrived safely. But that often doesn't help, and is a waste of money. Pocket Books doesn't open the manuscripts in New York, and often I wait toward the end of the contest before I open the manuscripts. The postcards will just cause you worry and extra money.

HINT #7: PAPERCLIPS ARE OUR FRIENDS

Editors use paperclips. We don't staple stories. Just send in the pages with a paperclip at the top.

HINT #8: NAME AND ADDRESS . . . PLEASE?

This may sound very, very basic, but I got hundreds of stories this year without names on the manuscripts. I had to go back and cut the return address off the envelope to know who the story belonged to. Find a *Writer's Digest* book with manuscript format in it and follow those guidelines. Manuscript format makes your stories look professional.

HINT #9: AND . . . ACTION

Start your stories with something happening. Your character should, very quickly, be in some sort of problem. This opening problem does not have to be the main problem of the story, but there needs to be some action to catch a reader's eye.

HINT #10: WAKING UP TO REJECTION

Don't start your story with your characters waking up. Granted, this is how we all start each day, but it is boring. And when you have your character go through a bathroom routine, I usually stop reading very quickly.

HINT #11: SAID-BOOKISMS

A said-bookism is when an author feels the need to use another word instead of "said." For example: "This dust always gets to me," he sneezed. Or: "I really am alone," he soliloquized. These were fine for the old pulp writers of the 1930s, but in modern fiction, use them carefully. The words "said" and "asked" tend to disappear to a reader's eye. But after about three said-bookisms in a story, I start laughing and reject the story.

HINT #12: CHARACTERS SHOULD SPEAK IN CHARACTER

Use the right language for the character speaking. For example, imagine Captain Kirk saying, "I'm just a little bit uptight today."

Enough said.

HINT #13: SENTENCES FOLLOW EACH OTHER

Every sentence needs to follow the one before it in some logical manner, unless there is a scene or time break. This is a good example of what NOT to do: "The Borg ship sped up. Janeway glanced at Paris and smiled. Tuvok sprawled on his bed, asleep." I get many stories that start just like that example, with a sentence having nothing to do with the sentence in front of it. Clearly the writer knows what is happening, but has just forgotten to put the details and links on the page for the reader to follow.

HINT #14: WATCH OUT FOR REPEATED WORDS

I know this sounds very basic, but we all repeat words in stories without seeing that we are doing it. The best way to catch this, and other problems in your writing, is to read your story out loud. Your ear will pick up the repeated words and you can change them. Please note, repeating the word "said" is just fine, since it disappears to a reader's eye.

HINT #15: AVOID WALK-THROUGHS

Don't just walk your characters through scenes. In most cases, the walk-through part of a scene is not needed. For example, when you need to get your character from a good-bye scene at a front door to the character's office, don't show the character walking down the sidewalk, opening the car door, getting into the car, putting the key in the ignition, starting the car, checking the mirrors . . . and so on. Just white space and jump to the office.

HINT #16: PARAGRAPH PLEASE

I was stunned this past three years by the number of people who don't put paragraphs in their stories. Or they put them in, but don't indent five spaces at the start of every paragraph, so I have to try to guess where the new paragraph starts by the ending of the last line. Don't be afraid of paragraphing. Paragraphs are a writer's friend.

HINT #17: PARAGRAPH WHEN A NEW CHARACTER IS TALKING

Every time you change speakers in dialogue, paragraph. The wrong way to do it is: Mike said, "Do that." "Why?" Pete asked. "Because it's the right way," Mike said.

The correct way would be:

Mike said, "Do that."

"Why?" Pete asked.

"Because it's the right way," Mike said.

HINT #18: READ YOUR MARKET

It startled me when I discovered that many people who were trying to write a story for *Star Trek* had never read a *Star Trek* novel or short story. If you want to be in *Star Trek: Strange New Worlds,* the most logical thing any writer could do is read the first three volumes to learn answers to a number of important questions. First, what has been done before? Second, what is the quality of the fiction? Third, what kind of stories do we like to buy for this anthology? You know the answers to those questions and you will be a long ways down the road toward being in the next volume of *Strange New Worlds.*

HINT #19: PRACTICE ON NEW STORIES

As I said in hint #1, this is the most important thing a new writer can do. Words are written on paper and can be tossed away as easily as a note from a musical instrument. Practice on new stories, never rewrite the old ones more than a few times. Rewriting is not writing. Only practice writing on new stories. And I hope you'll send me one or two of your practice sessions for *Star Trek: Strange New Worlds.* That's the wonderful thing about being a writer: We often get paid for our practice.

STAR TREK®

Strange New Worlds IV Contest Rules

1) ENTRY REQUIREMENTS:

No purchase necessary to enter. Enter by submitting your story as specified below.

2) CONTEST ELIGIBILITY:

This contest is open to nonprofessional writers who are legal residents of the United States and Canada (excluding Quebec) over the age of 18. Entrant must not have published any more than two short stories on a professional basis or in paid professional venues. Employees (or relatives of employees living in the same household) of Simon & Schuster, VIACOM, or any of their affiliates are not eligible. This contest is void in Puerto Rico and wherever prohibited by law.

3) FORMAT:

Entries should be no more than 7,500 words long and must not have been previously published. They must be typed or printed by word processor, double spaced, on one side of noncorrasable paper. Do not justify right-side margins. The author's name, address, and phone number must appear on the first page of the entry. The author's name, the story title, and the page number should appear on every page. No electronic or disk submissions will be accepted. All entries must be original and the sole work of the Entrant and the sole property of the Entrant.

4) ADDRESS:

Each entry must be mailed to: STRANGE NEW WORLDS IV, *Star Trek* Department, Pocket Books, 1230 Sixth Avenue, New York, NY 10020.

Each entry must be submitted only once. Please retain a copy of your submission. You may submit more than one story, but each submission must be mailed separately. Enclose a self-addressed, stamped envelope if you wish your entry returned. Entries must be received by October 1st, 2000. Not responsible for lost, late, stolen, postage due, or misdirected mail.

5) PRIZES:

One Grand Prize winner will receive:

Simon and Schuster's *Star Trek: Strange New Worlds IV* Publishing Contract for Publication of Winning Entry in our *Strange New Worlds IV* Anthology with a bonus advance of One Thousand Dollars ($1,000.00) above the Anthology word rate of 10 cents a word.

One Second Prize winner will receive:

Simon and Schuster's *Star Trek: Strange New Worlds IV* Publishing Contract for Publication of Winning Entry in our

Strange New Worlds IV Anthology with a bonus advance of Six Hundred Dollars ($600.00) above the Anthology word rate of 10 cents a word.

One Third Prize winner will receive:

Simon and Schuster's *Star Trek: Strange New Worlds IV* Publishing Contract for Publication of Winning Entry in our *Strange New Worlds IV* Anthology with a bonus advance of Four Hundred Dollars ($400.00) above the Anthology word rate of 10 cents a word.

All Honorable Mention winners will receive:

Simon and Schuster's *Star Trek: Strange New Worlds IV* Publishing Contract for Publication of Winning Entry in the *Strange New Worlds IV* Anthology and payment at the Anthology word rate of 10 cents a word.

There will be no more than twenty (20) Honorable Mention winners. No contestant can win more than one prize.

Each Prize Winner will also be entitled to a share of royalties on the *Strange New Worlds IV* Anthology as specified in Simon and Schuster's *Star Trek: Strange New Worlds IV* Publishing Contract.

6) JUDGING:

Submissions will be judged on the basis of writing ability and the originality of the story, which can be set in any of the *Star Trek* time frames and may feature any one or more of the *Star Trek* characters. The judges shall include the editor of the Anthology, one employee of Pocket Books, and one employee of VIACOM Consumer Products. The decisions of the judges shall be final. All prizes will be awarded provided a sufficient number of entries are received that meet the minimum criteria established by the judges.

7) NOTIFICATION:

The winners will be notified by mail or phone. The winners who win a publishing contract must sign the publishing contract in order to be awarded the prize. All federal, local, and state taxes are the responsibility of the winner. A list of the winners will be available after January 1st, 2001, on the Pocket Books *Star Trek* Books Web site,

www.simonsays.com/startrek/

or the names of the winners can be obtained after January 1st, 2001, by sending a self-addressed, stamped envelope and a request for the list of winners to WINNERS' LIST, STRANGE NEW WORLDS IV, *Star Trek* Department, Pocket Books, 1230 Sixth Avenue, New York, NY 10020.

8) STORY DISQUALIFICATIONS:

Certain types of stories will be disqualified from consideration:

a) Any story focusing on explicit sexual activity or graphic depictions of violence or sadism.

b) Any story that focuses on characters that are not past or present *Star Trek* regulars or familiar *Star Trek* guest characters.

c) Stories that deal with the previously unestablished death of a *Star Trek* character, or that establish major facts about or make major changes in the life of a major character, for instance a story that establishes a long-lost sibling or reveals the hidden passion two characters feel for each other.

d) Stories that are based around common clichés, such as "hurt/comfort" where a character is injured and lovingly cared for, or "Mary Sue" stories where a new character comes on the ship and outdoes the crew.

9) PUBLICITY:

Each Winner grants to Pocket Books the right to use his or her name, likeness, and entry for any advertising, promotion, and publicity purposes without further compensation to or permission from such winner, except where prohibited by law.

10) LEGAL STUFF:

All entries become the property of Pocket Books and of Paramount Pictures, the sole and exclusive owner of the *Star Trek* property and elements thereof. Entries will be returned only if they are accompanied by a self-addressed, stamped envelope. Contest void where prohibited by law.

About the Contributors

Sarah A. Hoyt ("If I Lose Thee . . .") occasionally takes time away from writing to keep her husband, two kids, four cats, and two guinea pigs from starving and/or suffocating beneath piles of laundry. The idea for this story grew out of research for her upcoming first novel from Ace, *Down the Rushy Glen,* which, happily, makes her ineligible to enter the contest next year.

Rebecca Lickiss ("If I Lose Thee . . .") lives in Colorado Springs with her husband and four children. She has very little free time, so what she has she spends reading or writing. She is continuing her writing career working in universes of her own creation, because, having finally sold a novel, *Eccentric Circles,* she is ineligible for *Strange New Worlds IV.*

Dayton Ward ("The Aliens Are Coming!") makes his third and final *Strange New Worlds* appearance. A Florida native, Dayton moved to Kansas City during service with the U.S. Marine Corps. Nowadays he's a systems engineer and lives with his wife, Michi, who really wishes he'd just grow up. Fat chance.

Susan Ross Moore ("Family Matters") had her first story praised when she was ten. Since that day she's worked to be a published writer. She lives in central Indiana with her husband and a varying number of cats. She's an editor for a computer book publisher and is finishing a novel.

Robert T. Jeschonek ("Whatever You Do, Don't Read This Story") resides in Ebensburg, Pennsylvania and directs public relations and publications at a nearby college. He spent over a decade as a television producer/director and writes news and feature stories for newspapers and magazines. The thirty-four-year-old has a *Star Trek* novel and a comic book miniseries in the works.

Tonya D. Price ("A Private Victory") draws on her twenty years as a software executive for story material. She resides in Franklin, Massachusetts with her husband and two daughters. She recently attended Viable Paradise. Her writing career began when she sold her hand-drawn comics to sixth-grade classmates. This is her first professional sale.

Kelly Cairo ("The Fourth Toast") is the self-anointed communications guru of Cairo Communications, specializing in writing, editing, desktop publishing, media relations, and video production. She enjoys knitting and drumming, hopes to find an agent for her fiction writing, and appreciates the free plug for her business. Kelly and her husband, Jeff, and daughter, Alex, live in the Phoenix area.

E. Catherine Tobler ("One of Forty-seven") makes her home in Colorado, where she works as a nanny. In her free time, she enjoys astronomy, reading, traveling, and music. "One of Forty-Seven" is her first published short story; it won't be her last.

Shane Zeranski ("A Q to Swear By") at nineteen years of age, after the death of his father, lives at home and attends college in Ontario, Oregon. He aspires to write at least four best-selling novels and win an Academy Award. He promises everyone that the whole world will soon know his name.

Logan Page ("The Change of Seasons"), thirty-eight, has written six novels and numerous short stories, which he is presently marketing. He is also a professional artist in media including bronze sculpture, painting, and Native American handcrafts. He grew up in Omaha and Fremont, Nebraska.

Jerry M. Wolfe ("Out of the Box, Thinking"), a longtime *Trek* fan, lives with his wife, Sawat, in Eugene, Oregon. When not writing, he teaches mathematics at the University of Oregon. He is also a proud "Wordo," a member of the Eugene Professional Writer's workshop. The current tale is his third published story.

Kim Sheard ("Ninety-three Hours") is thrilled to be published in her second *Strange New Worlds* anthology, proving that she is not a one-hit wonder. She wishes to thank her on-line *Trek*-fan buddies for inspiring her to revisit fiction writing several years ago. Prior to that, her last stories were written in childhood.

G. Wood ("Dorian's Diary") is married and residing in Windsor, Ontario, Canada. The author writes computer programs for a livelihood and science fiction/fantasy stories for sanity's sake, and feels that the success of this first submission ever proves that sometimes miracles do come true.

Andrew (Drew) Morby ("The Bottom Line") has spent the last fifteen years thinking, "If nothing better turns up, I'll try writing." Thanks to the loving support of his family, his heart Lisa, and her beautiful daughter, Danielle, he finally realized there is no better choice. He would also like to thank the AOL Workshop.

John Takis ("The Best Defense . . ."), born in 1980, is realizing a lifelong dream with the publication of this volume. It is his aspiration to write professionally. In what field, he cannot say, but science fiction certainly sounds good! He wishes to thank his friends and family, and all the *Star Trek* buddies therein.

Gordon Gross ("An Errant Breeze") is actually equal parts Eve Gordon and Harold Gross. The symbiotic byline has appeared previously in both *Fantasy and Science Fiction* magazine and *Analog* magazine. Outside of their writing lives, both are computer professionals with jaded histories in the performing arts and the proud owners of two cats and a one-eyed box turtle.

Mary Wiecek ("The Ones Left Behind"), thirty-eight, is a full-time mom who lives in Ohio with her husband, Tom, three great little kids—Matthew, Danny, and Elizabeth—and a neurotic cat named Boo. In her rare free time, she paints, writes, plays on the computer with her Internet *Trek* friends, and has entirely too much fun.

Diana Kornfeld ("The Second Star") lives in Lee's Summit, Missouri, with her husband, Steve, two daughters, and an iMac. After earning an M.A. in English and teaching for twenty years, she finally decided it might be fun to write. Currently she writes for educational Web sites and teaches English and web design.

Ann Nagy ("The Monster Hunters") is a Canadian who lives in North Carolina with her husband, Les, and many pets including a komondor named Sehlat. When not day trading, she is working on a *Star Trek* novel. She owns ninety-nine writing books and this is her first published story.

Jackee Crowell ("Gift of the Mourners"), living in Charlotte, North Carolina, is still a busy wife and mother of (at last count) three children and three fish. "Gift of the Mourners" marks her second appearance in a *Strange New Worlds* anthology.